Storm Dreams

Jeb R. Sherrill

Acknowledgments

A special thanks to everyone who helped this book come together.
My cover illustrator: Dave Groshelle
My editors: Carol Woods and Sumittra Wongsaprome
My English teachers: Ila Zbaraschuk and Keith Lindsey
My writing teachers: Don Whittington, Jon McCord and Jack Ballas
My first editor: Don Muchow
The Lesser North Texas Writers club and the DFW Writers
Workshop
And of course the many beta readers who gave amazing feedback on
what I know was a challenging book to read: Bill Ryce, Bill Francis,
Shawn Scarber, Kristie McKay, Marc Morris, Krista Wolcott,
Gerardo Delgadillo, Carl Droste, David Pflugrad, Ken Snow, Ed
Sherrill, Janet Sherrill, Stan Sherrill, Connie Snow, Carmen Vargas,
and probably a few I've forgotten to name. Thank you all.

Don't you think a dream would be shy if it were seen walking about
in the waking world?
-Psyche, *Till We Have Faces* by C.S. Lewis

Chapter 1

Cassidy rolled from the burning carcass of his downed fighter. The crumpled bi-wing lay in ruins, its propeller impaled in the burnt soil. He stumbled to his feet, gripping his chest. A rib or two must have shattered on impact, but he couldn't remember the crash. He couldn't remember much about the battle at all, just a rage of gunfire followed by an uncontrolled plummet to earth.

A clap of thunder brought his gaze skywards where a grey Zeppelin broke through the billowing clouds of smoke. Crackling green energy forked around the airship, cutting the sky like an alien storm. That ship doesn't belong, he thought. The craft was from outside, but outside *what* he couldn't say.

Glancing around, men slumped in the twisted wrecks of burning fighters. More blazing hulks plummeted from the sky. Brits. Krauts. Frenchies. Dead and dying. Pilots on fire. Cassidy stood in the middle of a war to end all wars examining his clothes for the first time. Flight cap. Goggles. A long, thick leather jacket. He jerked back the lapel to expose his shirt and the wings above his breast pocket. Eagle wings. American. He was an American pilot.

American? He knew the word, but not the meaning. It was a country of some kind. Perhaps a kingdom.

He looked up again as the Zeppelin sliced through the fire and turmoil, parting the atmosphere as if pushing reality itself aside. It stood out against the rolling clouds even though its colour looked as grey as its surroundings. Cassidy's mind fogged with wisps of memory. Planes. Gunfire. Nothing before the battle.

But, my God, what a craft, he thought, as the gigantic dirigible plummeted towards him, a wingless bird diving for prey. It levelled out twenty feet above the ground and headed for him. How could such a craft fly so low and fast?

A lone figure climbed down an extending rope ladder, his slender body silhouetted against the fire and smoke. Cassidy stood transfixed as his world erupted. Cannon fire tore gashes in the soft landscape. The crashing hulks of biplanes and Eindeckers filled his ears with the crunching of metal and the whip of canvas, but he couldn't see the planes anymore.

He snapped his mind around as if he were seeing reality for the first time. The muted colours. The constant screams, gunfire and explosions even at moments nothing seemed to be causing the sounds. It felt fake. *He* felt fake.

Cassidy looked at his own aviator fatigues. Was he a downed pilot? He'd known a moment before, but the information had slipped away. American. Something about being American.

The mass of the grey airship looked *very real* above as it flew towards him, its rounded bulk skimming the ground like a low-flying storm cloud. The gondola, with windows reflecting the fire and storm, rode just above the burning grass now. The ship's nose passed over him, dizzying his senses as it blotted out the sky, turning the scene above into a rushing moving swath of grey tarp and shadowy ribs.

Clipped images of airships flashed through his fractured memory, but nothing ever this close. How could anything be so huge? It was a flying building. A nudge down and the craft would crush him like a sparrow.

He fell to his knees, shielding his head with both arms against the monstrous Zeppelin. Glancing beneath his arm, the dangling figure came into focus. It was definitely a man, an officer in flight uniform. The uniform looked American like his own, but Cassidy still couldn't picture what that meant. The officer's leather coat flapped wildly in the gusting wind. The twin straps of his unbuckled aviator cap whipping the sides of his chin. Goggles gave him huge frog eyes, and his grey scarf tore at the air, switching directions like a weathervane oracling the wind's destination.

"Hurry, man," the officer yelled. "Jump on, damn you."

Cassidy stumbled to his feet. The rope ladder neared. The man's arm stretched out like the snatch hook of a mail train.

"Grab tight, or die," the officer hollered. "He's waking up."

Who's waking up? Cassidy shouted in his mind, or to the wind. Who could tell the difference?

The world erupted as he ran. Fire. Rifles. Cannon. Shreds of dead soldiers and shards of mangled planes. The silhouette of a dark castle rose in the distance. The structure felt like a distant memory, something altogether separate from the rest of the world.

Beneath his feet the ground shimmered and hazed like ice about to break. He raced hard to catch the airship. Staggered as he neared the rope ladder. Regained his balance and sprinted hard.

The ladder swung past and Cassidy leapt. His hand slipped, but the extended arm caught his wrist in a steel grip and hauled him to the rungs. He wrapped one foot around the backside of the ladder, holding tight with the boot heel as his other foot caught the front side. Instinct told him how to balance.

The officer grinned, his pencil-thin moustache forming a straight line. He saluted and began to climb. Cassidy followed as the ground beneath became translucent and the sounds of war stuttered.

The Zeppelin nosed upwards as a mechanism cranked the ladder into the gondola. The officer already stood aboard as the blasting air whipped Cassidy like the tail of a kite. "Haul him in, boys," the officer hollered. "Heave it."

Two men wound the crank as Cassidy passed into the square opening of the gondola. Two others grabbed his arms and lifted him aboard. Outside the huge windows the world shuddered and vanished. For a moment the Zeppelin appeared to be flying through open space.

Giant bulb-like pods floated past. They looked like tiny worlds bobbing in space.

"They'll be on us, boys," the officer shouted. "Man the guns." He snapped another salute, turned and ran through the door.

The men who'd pulled Cassidy in clapped him on the back. "I'm Jayce," said a young-looking pilot in a breathless tone. "This is Karl," he said pointing to an older man. "That's Ned and Franz on the crank."

The two men waved as they dropped the handles and followed their captain out the door.

"Franz? German?" Cassidy asked.

"We're all friends here," Jayce said as Karl followed the other two. "Captain's name is Banner. He saved your ass. You owe him."

Cassidy nodded and tried to keep up as Jayce made for the door as well. "Yes," Cassidy said, "but saved me from what?"

"Your dreamer was waking up," Jayce said as they made their way between cabins and past the galley. "Once your dream is gone the Armada finds us fast."

Dreamer? His dream? Cassidy struggled to remember where he'd just come from. "What's the Armada? Is that bad?"

"Better believe it," Jayce said as they reached the bridge where Banner stood spinning a large spoked wheel like the helm of a Spanish galleon.

"Can you pilot a Fokker?" Banner asked over his shoulder.

"I don't know. Can I?"

"You're a pilot, aren't you? Doubt they're much different from the Sopwith you were flying," Banner said, spinning the wheel sharply to the left as the outside scene shifted to pink and yellow clouds.

Cassidy shrugged. "I don't know. Fokkers are Fritzie planes."

"It vill keep you in ze sky," Franz said with a mock salute and exaggerated German accent.

Jayce tugged Cassidy's arm. "Come on."

Cassidy stalled. "Look, I'm grateful. I *guess* I'm grateful, but what am I supposed to do?"

4

Banner turned from the wheel. "You'll earn your keep like every other man. Now get out there and shoot planes down."

Cassidy let himself be dragged down the corridor, trying to force his fragmented memory to catch up. Nothing processed fast enough. What had the captain's name been again? This was a sea vessel. No, an airship. He was being pulled along past a series of cabins. Yes, it was some kind of airship. Why was it so hard to keep hold of information?

A staircase in the rear of the gondola led them up to more cabins extending along the belly of the main cell. "What am I?" Cassidy asked, as they rushed down the narrow hallway, his mind only catching bits and pieces of information.

Jayce shrugged. "You're a pilot."

Cassidy tried hard to get his bearings, and even harder to keep them. "Am I?"

Jayce laughed as they approached a hatch in the deck. "I guess we're gonna find out. Time to do your thing," he said, pulling up the hatch and exposing a cloud-coloured Fokker dangling beneath the Zeppelin's belly from a steel U-shaped arm.

"How?" Cassidy hollered over the roar of wind that rushed up through the open hatch.

"It's just a one-seater," Jayce yelled, trying to overcome the roar as well. "You won't have a gunner. The good news is she's fast and you have two Spandaus made to fire between the props, so don't worry about shooting yourself down. Latest stuff."

Turbulence jostled the little craft. It looked like the arm could snap any moment. "You can't start a plane like this."

"Just wind the booster magneto. Can't miss it. If it won't start, armstrong's the only way to go. You'll have to reach over the guns and spin the prop yourself."

"Don't I get a chute?"

Jayce shook his head. "No point. If you go down, you're lost. It'll be impossible to pick you up in a fight." He shrugged. "Besides, the ground won't last. We've flown into another dream bubble, but it won't be long."

The ground won't last? Dream bubble? Cassidy tried to slow his racing heart. "I can't do this."

"You will or we're all going to die." Jayce handed him a flight-cap and a pair of goggles. Cassidy stretched the cap over his head, buckled the straps beneath his chin and pulled the goggles over his eyes. He hardly noticed what he was doing as he flexed his fingers into leather gloves, tied his scarf and tucked it into the front of his jacket. He somehow knew he'd done these things a thousand times, but couldn't remember a single instance.

The savage wind rushing up through the hole excited him, even through the terror. "Why can't I remember anything?"

Jayce shook his head. "You'll have to come up with some of it yourself. We're not supposed to exist like this."

Cassidy's chest tightened. "What do you mean I'm not supposed to exist like this? I exist because I say I exist."

"That's the spirit. Just remember to stay close to the ship. If we gate between dreams or anywhere else you'll be lost if you don't stay in our slipstream."

"How will I know?"

"You'll know."

Wind whipped around Cassidy's legs as he dangled over the edge, and Jayce steadied him as he climbed into the cockpit. The rushing air felt so good. It reminded him of—

"What's your name?" Jayce shouted as Cassidy stood on the seat, bridging the gap between the plane and gondola with his body.

"Cassidy." He knew that.

Jayce nodded. "Don't get shot down, Cassidy. This is our only fighter."

The hatch closed and latched with a harsh clack, shutting Cassidy out. He was alone again, with nothing but the sound of wind gusting in his ears. The controls looked familiar. Stick. Pedals. Magneto and dials.

Everything in German, but he could read it perfectly. He must have flown one of these before. Had he been a spy?

The drone of multiple propellers buzzed in from his six and Cassidy twisted to see three bi-wings broaching the rear horizon. *Jagdstaffel...* Where had he heard that word? Damn, he thought, realizing how much time he'd wasted thinking. The distant flashes of mounted guns already tore at the Zeppelin's tail rudder as the fighters tried to cripple the airship. They looked like old German Albatrosses, the ones that resembled birds spewing hellfire from their beaks. But no one used those anymore. They were outdated craft.

Bullets tore past, fracturing the sound barrier. Cassidy pumped pressure into the tank, revved the magneto for a few seconds and hit the switch. The engine started, turned the prop a few times and choked out. He tried again as bullets skimmed his top wing, but the engine only clicked. He glanced back. One of the fighters had closed in, intent on taking Cassidy's Fokker out before he could catch air. A large purple shape loomed in the distance behind the Albatross. Another airship? No. It looked more like a separate sky.

The Albatross opened fire again. "Oh hell," Cassidy shouted as he gripped the latch to his Fokker's support ring and pulled hard. For a moment nothing happened, then the steel arm clicked in two places and the Zeppelin shrank above him. His fighter dropped like a lead weight. The Fokker's wings tried to grab air, but without the aid of the engine's pull it plummeted into a nose dive.

Flashes of dogfights erupted in his head. For a moment the sky was filled with fighters. Fifty perhaps. Sixty. He hated the enemy. The Germans. Hated them so much. Needed to blast them all out of the sky.

Cassidy pulled himself back from his memories as the ground rose to meet him. The landscape looked misshapen, as if a child sank his fingers into a lump of clay and twisted it. He revved the magneto again. The engine choked out a second time. The warped ground grew closer.

"Damn," he shouted into the wind and climbed out over the guns, pinning his body between the wing and fuselage. The air rushed so fast it was hard to breathe as he reached out and grabbed for the slow spinning prop. It spun into his hand. He gripped a strut to steady himself and gave the prop a hard snap. The blade whirled inches from his face, engaging the engine. The Fokker caught air.

Cassidy edged back into his seat and pulled back on the stick, careful not to pull too hard and tear the wings off. As the Fokker levelled out, he gunned the throttle and rose to meet the fighters above. Pure instinct, like another presence, took over his hands and feet as the Zeppelin came into view, its guns blazing away at the Albatrosses.

The fighters looked like pieces on a board in his head. He sized up their piloting as they made their way around the airship. They were good. Each seemed to know what the others were thinking. He could tell by the way they synchronized their attacks.

As he neared the rear of the Zeppelin, Cassidy noticed the damaged elevator fin. Smoke billowed from one of the main engines. The three fighters moved into formation above him, probably trying to combine their firepower on the airship's internal gas cells. They flew close to each other in a perfect triangle. Only inches between their wings. Perfect. Too perfect. He would use that against them.

Cassidy aimed his nose at the centre of the formation and rolled, twisting up between the three, forcing them to scatter. One flew into a burst from one of the Zeppelin's Lewis guns. It shredded the Albatross's right wing, spiralling it into the twisted landscape.

Adrenaline surged. The other two fighters had rallied, but Cassidy rolled right and dove behind the Zeppelin before they had a chance to come round. Instead of continuing down the side of the airship, he pulled up and rolled his fighter back over the top, flying inverted to the canvas hull. The two Albatrosses had moved to meet him on the bottom side and he caught them from behind as he dove. They flew in perfect formation again, only inches apart.

Cassidy pinned the control stick between his legs and pulled both levers on the Spandau guns. Bullets ripped loose, shuddering the Fokker as they spewed between the blades with an odd rhythm. An internal mechanism was keeping the rounds from firing as the props passed by. He knew that rhythm like he knew his own heartbeat, but he'd never flown with guns like these. Had he?

His blast caught one of the fighters near the left wing strut and spun the Albatross sideways into its partner. The fighters collided, splintering into a cascade of wood and shredded canvas. Cassidy watched them fall. Snippets of other downed fighters flashed in his head. The image of himself falling from the sky. Standing among the wreckage of twenty or thirty planes. Fire. Smoke.

Wiry pink clouds untwisted beyond the Zeppelin's tail, revealing the vague shape of the bulbous purple mass he'd seen before. It throbbed. Undulated. Pulled at him with an invisible force. The tug felt almost like words, but broader and more distant than words. More like solid tugging emotions.

Cassidy's chest felt heavy. He needed the purple shape, whatever it was. Or, *it* needed *him*. It was hard to separate the concepts. He longed to be part of it as the throbbing pulse reached out like a mother trying to cuddle her child.

A crack of electricity sounded behind him. He twisted to see the Zeppelin vanishing into a wall of green light. The sky crackled with unknown energies. Banner was leaving him.

Chapter 2

Cassidy's heart thundered into his ears. His mind tore free of the purple shape and he pulled the fighter around. The adrenaline of combat shifted to fear as the great ship's gondola and mid-section vanished, leaving only the tail of the Zeppelin sticking out of the green gate.

The shape beyond the clouds wanted him back. Banner wanted him aboard the ship. The purple mass was a complete mystery, and the captain of the airship was only slightly less of one. He came about and throttled towards the Zeppelin. At least this captain wore an American uniform and spoke like a Yankee.

Slipstream. What had Jayce said? Cassidy urged the Fokker towards the vanishing rudder on the Zeppelin's tail. Why did this German plane feel so natural instead of the—what had it been? Soap with caramel? Camel? What had Banner called that fighter?

Cassidy tried to think of concrete memories as he accelerated. Flashes of being aboard the giant vessel. An airman named Jayce. Banner's outstretched arm. The bitter dogfight before... Before what?

Concepts.

Pictures.

War.

Fighters like a flock of distant ravens in the sky.

The Zeppelin's tail slid into the gate. Cassidy pushed the Fokker to full throttle. The wall of green faded as the nose of his fighter touched it. Sparks of electricity illuminated the instruments with arcs and waves of light. The world shifted from pink and yellow clouds to one of intense cobalt.

The colours seemed off, as if the spectrum had moved several notches towards red, but snagged on blue. Cassidy sniffed the hard odour of ozone. There were no clouds and, as he dipped his wing, he saw nothing but empty blue below. No earth. No ocean. Dear Lord, he thought as the airship continued to pull away at full speed into the strange new world.

The Fokker's engine sputtered. It wasn't getting enough gas. He pumped more pressure into the tank and tapped the temperature gauge with his gloved finger. There had to be a leak somewhere. He'd pushed the fighter hard, flying at full speed for too long, exhausting most of the fuel, but there should have been more. Perhaps he'd taken a bullet to his tank. Pumping up the pressure helped, but he had to keep pumping. Cassidy couldn't slow or he'd risk losing the Zeppelin.

Pushing forwards on the control stick he dipped the Fokker and made his way beneath the body of the grey behemoth. Cassidy spotted a massive hook on a line dangling from the Zeppelin's body. Standing in the cockpit, he braced his left hand on one of the Spandau guns, caught the hook and slipped it into a metal ring bolted to the main struts. Jayce waved from the open hatch as Cassidy matched speed to the slowing ship. Two more lines came down, which he attached as well. He cut the engine and let the wires carry him into position where the steel U-shaped hitch locked into place on either side of the cockpit.

Cassidy shook as he tried to reach the open hatch. Jayce lowered a short rope ladder. Cassidy grasped the rungs, but his arms and legs trembled harder as he put weight on them. His foot slipped.

"Grab my hand," Jayce shouted.

Cassidy grabbed. Leather gripped leather as their gloves met and held tight. Jayce hauled him aboard.

As the hatch closed, cutting off the howl of rushing wind, Cassidy lay against the cabin door and breathed in the silence.

"The captain'll want to see you," Jayce said with a grimace as Cassidy glanced up through half-closed eyes.

Cassidy exhaled half a laugh and closed his eyes. "Why am I so weak?"

"Your body's just getting used to being solid for this long," Jayce said, pulling him to his feet.

Solid? "What was that purple shape in the air?" Cassidy asked.

Jayce stopped. "What purple shape?"

"You must have seen it. It was huge, up in the air."

"That's just the sky," Jayce said, heading in the direction of the bridge.

Like hell, the sky, Cassidy thought and limped down the corridor. "Magneto on the Fokker is shot. I almost died."

Jayce nodded. "We need a new plane."

Ned looked up from the navigation console as they entered the helm. Banner flipped a switch and turned from the wheel to face them. "My god, where the hell did you learn to start a fighter in mid-air like that?"

Cassidy leaned against an aluminium support beam. He hadn't learned it. But someone he couldn't remember had once told him about trying it as a stunt.

Banner gripped him by both shoulders and shook him hard. "That's the best damn flying I've ever seen. And let me tell you, not a man under me isn't a full ace, including Karl, and he's the engineer."

Cassidy narrowed his eyes. "I thought I was the only—"

Banner laughed and gave him a soft slap to the side of the face. "I needed to know what you could do. No doughboys on my ship. You did good."

Heat flushed Cassidy's cheeks. "You put *me* in that death-trap of a plane, and anyone else could have flown it? I could have been killed."

"Hah," Banner said, returning to the wheel and flipping the switch again. "Wouldn't really be death, now would it? Besides, I already knew how good you were."

Cassidy started to ask what the captain meant about death, but instead propped himself against one of the aluminium supports and took a deep breath. "How could you know what I can do? *I* don't know what I can do. Or what the hell I am."

Banner stiffened. As if on some unseen cue the men filed out of the bridge, leaving them alone. Jayce avoided Cassidy's gaze as he exited behind the others. The captain's hand still held a single spoke of the helm to keep the ship steady. He sighed. "I rescued you from slavery."

"That purple shape in the sky?"

"That purple shape...I suppose it looks like that through the atmosphere." Banner took a deep breath. "I need men. Fly for me and I'll take care of you."

"Why?"

"To be free," the captain said, turning to the helm, eyes gazing out the window at the deep cobalt beyond. "I need pilots like God needs angels."

Cassidy's stomach churned. "Am I really a man? There's something wrong. I don't feel..." He wanted to say he didn't feel *real*, but that wasn't enough. He felt like a fish that woke up at the top of a tree picking apples.

Banner didn't turn around. "We'll have to dock for repairs with our tail shot up like that." He spun the helm starboard and the Zeppelin drifted right. "First day with us and already a shore leave. Your lucky day. Jayce will find you a cabin and some gear."

The conversation was over. Cassidy could tell by the set of the captain's shoulders. Fire rose in his chest, but he pushed himself away from the girder and shoved the door open.

Jayce stood outside. "Ready for your new quarters?" the young man asked.

Cassidy glared. He felt empty as he pushed past. His mind still ran with fog as he marched down the corridor, trying to focus on his surroundings. The wood floors, doors and cabins were trimmed with a great deal of brass. Glass sconces adorned the walls. This battle-ready airship looked like the inside of a luxury liner. What kind of a war machine was this? Why did it feel so solid? So real?

"It was an experiment," Jayce said, as he helped Cassidy into one of the cabins and let him flop onto the fold-down bed.

Cassidy felt dizzy as he rolled so he could still see the young man, though he had to fight to keep his eyes open. "An experiment?" Cassidy mumbled, as he drifted to sleep.

The world was crisp. It shuddered and righted itself like a bad signal coming back to full strength. Cassidy flew a Sopwith between the spires of an ancient castle. Its bricks looked like the scales of a dragon as the colours shifted in the sunlight. The turrets were too big and too high, but oddly natural in context. *He* felt natural too, as if he'd just woken up to blasting wind stinging his cheeks.

A dot appeared in the sky at least a mile away.

"Cassidy. Cassidy. Wake up, Old Boy."

Cassidy awoke to the Englishman shaking his right shoulder. Brewster, Banner had called him, sat down on a stool a few feet from the bed. He appeared to be in his late thirties, a veteran age for any airman. "What the hell?" Cassidy asked, trying to force himself awake. He sat up and rolled the cramped muscles in his shoulders.

"You overslept."

Cassidy tried to remember what he was doing in bed. "Do dreams have dreams?" he asked, uncertain why he was asking.

"Just one," Brewster said, leaning forward. "The one you escape."

Cassidy stretched and leaned forwards as well. His foggy mind registered his surroundings in blurry frames: wood panelling, a desk, a hat rack. Another rack for clothing. "Then I *am* a dream?"

"Nicer than barracks," Brewster said, ignoring the question. "Germans paid a pretty pfennig for a ride in cabins like this."

Brewster seemed as English as anyone could be. More so. He felt like the old cadet buddy every airman had. The kind one knew for years even though Cassidy was sure he'd never met the man. "Is all this…?" Cassidy asked gesturing around.

"*Real?*" Brewster shrugged. His handlebar moustache drooped as he grimaced. "The ship's *real* as anything, I suppose. It's from the *real* world, if that's what you mean."

"Jayce said something about an experiment?"

Brewster's forehead furrowed, then he nodded and pulled out a pipe and tobacco. "He meant the airship itself. It was a luxury Zeppelin before the war. German government took it over and souped it up for recon work. That and some other kind of mission we don't know about. There's some equipment up in the main cell even Karl can't identify and he's seen everything. No telling what the bloody thing does."

"Why can't I remember anything solid?"

Brewster shrugged. "Captain likes to give you a few days to settle in. Take a breather before you get to that sort of thing."

Cassidy gritted his teeth. "Why the hell don't I feel *real?*"

Brewster drew in a deep breath. "Bottom line," he said, lighting his pipe and taking several puffs, "because, yes, you're a dream, and dreams are never fully formed. You're a caricature." He pulled out a crumpled pack of cigarettes and passed one to Cassidy.

"You only smoke pipes?" Cassidy asked.

"Can't smoke fags. I've tried. My body doesn't know how. Only carry them around because I hate smoking alone. See, we're just exaggerations. Very few details. Most of us only exist for a few minutes, perhaps a few hours before we melt back into the Everdream. If Banner hadn't picked us up, it would have been back to the soup." He took another puff. "If we'd rescued you a few days ago, you might have been a child. A dog. A tree. An old love letter. None of us know how it works, but for now you're whatever someone created you to be in whatever dream you were in." He gave Cassidy a sardonic nod. "You're more solid than most I've seen. That means something, I'm sure. Banner jabbers a lot about your dreamer's identity being latent in your subconscious. Damned if I know what that means."

A cold heat settled in Cassidy's stomach. He took the cigarette and let Brewster light him up. "My head keeps shifting around. I feel like everything's missing."

"It's like that," Brewster said. "Your missing memory is just the first thing you notice. Me, I don't have a navel. Some of us don't have all our toes. *Franzie* doesn't have a gun, if you catch my meaning. Bit of a problem when it comes to the ladies and taking a piss. Oddly, he doesn't have to. All depends on how much detail we were given in the dream."

"But Banner?"

"He's different," Brewster said nodding. "None of us know why. He's crisper. More solid." The Englishman sent a cloud of smoke into the air.

"Don't you worry about smoking in a Zeppelin?"

Brewster shook his head. "Nah. We're cut off from the air-bladders. Besides, Karl hates hydrogen. We switched to helium a couple years ago."

"Where did he get helium?"

"You'll find out," Brewster said, standing up and opening the door. "You were supposed to gear up."

Cassidy grimaced and stood with him. He hadn't even bothered to remove his boots before nodding off. "I don't like having Germans on board."

Brewster scoffed. "You mean Karl and Franzie? They're not German."

Cassidy narrowed his eyes.

"I'm not Limey. You're no Yank. I told you, we aren't *real* people. For all you know, some French kid dreamed you just to fill a spot in a dream he was having about his dad. You're as likely to be a plane as a pilot from dream to dream."

"But I know I hate Germans."

Brewster's faced shifted. He took Cassidy by the shoulders and locked him with his gaze. "That's just dream memory. We're all friends here. That's what's important."

16

"What if I want to go back? I mean, to the Everdream?"

"Don't talk like that," Brewster said with a scowl. "Don't ever talk like that."

Cassidy followed Brewster down the hallway to the cabin marked Waffenkammer in gold letters. "We don't expect any trouble, but just in case." He opened the door to a room full of rifles, side-arms and ammunition. "Take your pick."

Cassidy reached out and grabbed a large wooden holster with a cleaning rod and kit strapped to its face. The pistol butt stuck out the side, almost at a right angle. He flipped the lid and withdrew the bizarre sidearm. It felt familiar in his grip, like the Fokker had. He *must* have been a spy.

"Mauser C-96," Brewster said as Cassidy examined the piece. "Most people call them—"

"Broomhandles," Cassidy finished. "I know." He pulled back the slide over the breech and checked the chamber before slipping the bottom end of the wooden holster into a slot on the Mauser's handle. The holster created a rifle-butt for the pistol. He sighted down the seven-inch barrel.

"Kicks like a mule," Brewster said, grabbing a couple boxes of .307 rounds from a shelf and another box of metal slides to hold the bullets.

C-96's didn't have external clips like the Lugers. Cassidy knew this, but nothing about who had told him. The knowledge was a random fact that popped up when he first saw the weapon.

"Do you know how to load it?" Brewster asked.

"I have a feeling I do," Cassidy said, filling one of the slides with shells and pushing them past the chamber into the internal magazine. "But I don't know why. I'm not Jerry, am I?"

Brewster laughed and clapped him on the back. "Lot of countries use Broomhandles," he said. "I like my Webley. Of course, I'm dreamed to be a Brit. Banner prefers German Lugers. Go figure."

Cassidy felt distant as he turned the weapon over in his hands, chambered a round and slid the Mauser back into the holster.

"You okay?" Brewster asked.

"I don't like not knowing where I am."

Brewster smiled. "Not that it will give you any idea of location, but we've been flying through various dreams ever since picking you up and we'll be leaving soon. The Armada is pretty thick here, so we only risk entering the Everdream to rescue pilots."

"Everdream? The Armada? You keep saying that."

"Everdream's a long story. The Armada is made up of dreams, kind of like us. Police," Brewster said, pocketing a handful of shells for himself. "Those of us who escape aren't well liked by the powers that be in the Everdream. Don't worry," he said, noticing Cassidy's worried look. "They can only do so much where we're going."

When they entered the control room Franz and Jayce stood staring out the bow windows. Cassidy took in the room better now that he was well-slept and relaxed. Aluminium girders ran downward from the airship's belly, past the floor and continued, he assumed, until they met somewhere below his feet. Brass pipes wove between girders in all directions, making the ceiling look like a mass of metallic vines.

The helm itself was a large wheel, almost three feet in diameter, which stood in the centre of the bridge. It looked as if it had actually been taken from some Spanish galleon, its surface decorated with gold trim, its wood stained and polished. Below the helm lay two foot pedals. Jayce explained that Karl had installed them to eliminate the need for a second helm to steer the elevator flap. Banner hadn't liked the idea of needing a second pilot in the rear of the control room—as most Zeppelins had—preferring to steer port and starboard with the wheel and pitch the ship up and down with the pedals.

Cassidy had never seen anything like it, though fragmented memories of Zeppelins lodged in the recesses of his mind. Remembering things made him feel more there and he found himself taking every opportunity to drag things out into his consciousness. There had to be more. Dream or no dream, he had to have a past.

The sky turned a desperate shade of blue and then purple as Banner nosed the craft down out of the clouds. Thick cumulous mounds tore as the ship ripped through them. "The Twilight," Banner said over his shoulder. "Beautiful, isn't it?"

"This isn't a dream?" Cassidy asked Brewster as the ship levelled out.

"No," Brewster said, leaning in as if confiding a secret. "This is between the Everdream and the *real* world."

An odd shape, like an upside-down floating mountain, broke out of the distance, half obscured by a patch of thick clouds. "Arcadia," Banner announced as he throttled the ship forwards. "It's a good place for repairs." He glanced over at the German. "Franz, tell Karl I want some kind of gun platform up top. I'm tired of us getting caught with our pants down." He glanced back. "Cassidy, you stink. Get a shower and have Brewster find you something nice to wear. You can't get laid like that."

Chapter 3

Cassidy wanted to stay at the windows, but Brewster took him astern to the head to freshen up. Cassidy shaved, splashed on cologne and donned the clothes set out for him: khaki breeches, a white shirt, an airman's coat and a new white scarf. All this he did as fast as possible, retrieving the Mauser from his room and hooking the wooden holster to his belt as he ran for the control room. He wanted to go anywhere but this ship which had begun to feel like a cage.

Arcadia turned out to be exactly what it looked like at a distance: a floating island nestled deep within a mass of thick nebulous clouds. Closer up, however, he could see that the upside-down mountain was topped with smaller snow-capped mountains and a city that looked like a cross between a mythic metropolis of the future and a turn of the century shipping port.

At least forty airships drifted around the island; some docked, some coming into port and others leaving. Some were no more than dirigible balloons with large propellers attached to their wooden baskets, while others looked like galleons dangling beneath a mass of balloons. "They're beautiful," Cassidy said, as one of the ships passed off the starboard bow.

"Yes, but none of them are like this lady," Banner said, cutting the throttle to mooring speed and made his way towards a dock in one of the bright towers. "They're mostly Twilight crafts. They'd break apart trying to enter the *real* world. This girl is solid everywhere she goes. Her name is *Nubigena*," he said, steering the nose of the airship into the mooring dock. "There isn't a pirate here that wouldn't give both his ears and probably his John Thomas to have her."

"Hence, we always go in armed," said Brewster. "Chester and Karl will stay here and man the Lewis guns, just in case."

Cassidy adjusted the Mauser on his left hip, butt pointed towards his navel in cross-draw fashion. He didn't know where he'd picked up the habit, but it seemed logical for a pilot. Nothing more difficult than drawing a weapon from his shooting side while seated.

Banner brought him out of his memories by slapping a wad of cash in his hand. "My tab is good in the main establishments, but if you want to pick something up along the way, you'll need this." He strode past Cassidy and out of the control room. The others followed.

What if I don't want your damn money? I'm not a mercenary, he thought, as he examined the paper. It looked like bank notes, rectangular thin sheets printed with a dull blue ink, but of some currency he'd never seen before. He followed the others down to the dock. Over his shoulder he watched the Zeppelin float out from its mooring. He still couldn't believe how huge the vessel was. It appeared at least eight hundred feet long and a hundred feet or more in diameter. Angled black script spelled *Nubigena* across the starboard bow. My God, what a ship. It still felt as if the craft could crush him at its whim. Why had Banner picked *him* to crew on such a vessel?

Dock riggers, passing travellers and shipmen stared and pointed at the airship. They craned their necks as they walked. Many stopped and gawked as it drifted in the wind like a stallion flexing his muscles at the hitching post.

"They know it's different," Brewster said, nudging him in the ribs. "Most people here are native to the Twilight, though there're a few escaped dreams like us that hide out in the lower areas. They serve on the local airships," he said, and prodded Cassidy towards a bizarre building that appeared to be made of folded paper. It rose above them twenty stories and seemed to grow straight out of the ground. "There're even a few people that find their way here from the *real* world. Pilots, mostly. Slip in through open gates in the air. There's only a few on the ground anywhere."

Cassidy marvelled, watching the colours and angles shift as the diffused light cascaded over the surface of the building. He couldn't see a door, only a huge aperture which opened into a main lounge from the street outside. The light dimmed when they passed the threshold as if an invisible barrier cut down on the outside light.

Another airman came towards them on his way out. "He's *real*," Brewster whispered. "Found his way here about a year ago." The airman looked German, in full flight uniform with an iron cross at his throat. He possessed the tell-tale arrogant poise, rigid chin and nose aimed slightly above everyone's head.

Cassidy flipped the lid on the holster beneath his jacket, but Brewster put a hand on his arm. "That's—" Cassidy began.

"Manfred von Richthofen. We're not at war here, and you and I aren't involved in the Great War anyway," Brewster said, as Banner stopped several feet from the handsome German.

"Pilot of the Storm," Richthofen said in a grim tone, his German accent thick and sharp.

"The Bloody Baron," Banner said with a laugh. "How's the war?"

"Ridiculous as usual," Richthofen said, "but *I'm* still winning." He greeted Franz in German and Cassidy understood them perfectly. Could he read *and* speak that damned language?

The Baron looked over Franz's shoulder at Cassidy and lost his smile.

"This is our new man," Banner said, regarding Cassidy with a nod. "Picked him up in a dream last night. Hell of a pilot, but won't stop frowning."

A strange glance passed between Banner and the Baron, who forced a smile. "It is good to meet a fellow pilot," Richthofen said, and offered Cassidy his hand.

Cassidy didn't move. He hated the man, but not just because he was German. A violent seething rose up from his stomach making him want to pound the man's face into the ground.

"Perhaps next time," Richthofen said, withdrawing his hand. Well, *auf wiedersehen*." The German airman gave the group a stiff bow. "We will meet again."

Banner and the others gave brief salutes and the Red Baron exited the hotel.

Brewster dragged Cassidy to the bar and ordered two mugs of beer. "That man has shot down—" Cassidy began.

"I know," Brewster said, stopping him with the flat of his hand. "None of the *real world* affairs are any concern of ours. The only loyalty you have is to Banner and that ship outside," he said jutting his thumb towards the docks. "Now sit back and enjoy the shore leave."

Cassidy grimaced and sipped at his beer. There was blood between him and that man, even if he didn't know why. "What if I don't want to be part of this crew?"

Brewster sighed. "The captain saved your life."

"Seems more like I was shanghaied," Cassidy spat.

"Can I get you guys another beer?" the female bartender asked, before Cassidy got another sentence out. Full lips, short dark hair and shining eyes gave her an ethereal look. Her skin glowed with a soft inner light, her features elven, ears slightly pointed. Native, Cassidy thought. What were these Twilight people?

A woman with similar elven features wearing a silver outfit that showed off her ample bosom approached Brewster from behind. She slid her hand across his chest and played with the collar of his jacket. "Can't believe you stayed away this long," she said, toying beneath his shirt with her other hand. "It's been months."

Brewster laughed and grinned at Cassidy. "Sorry, Old Boy. Got to go."

Cassidy watched as the woman led Brewster up the steep stairs to whatever rooms lay above. He tried to get another beer, but found he could only order whisky on the rocks. When he tried to explain the problem to the barkeep, his mind cut to other thoughts and questions. He gave up and nursed the whisky for several more minutes while the rest of Banner's Boys left one by one with equally exotic natives.

Banner no doubt was consorting with Germans or other unsavoury characters in port.

A silky voice slithered into his ear from behind. "You're on your captain's tab."

A woman with thin features and bright green eyes inclined her head as Cassidy turned. Her short red hair blazed, even in the dim light. The markings of green leaves on her skin poked out of her gown, inching up her throat as if trying to take over her head. Tattoos or make-up? He couldn't think straight as she took his hand and led him to the staircase. The steps were glass and didn't appear connected to either wall. Nor did the gilded handrail. It took several furtive steps to trust the glass, but they felt solid as rock.

The room she took him to was a suite with a decadent sitting area and an oval bed. Silk drapes hung on all sides from the thirty-foot ceiling, enclosing the purple satin sheets. Shining crystals adorned the walls, giving the room a soft pulsing light that ebbed and flowed every ten seconds or so.

"My name is Shea," she said. "Or whatever ever name you prefer. You're a dream, right?"

"I don't know for sure."

Shea let out a loud, almost manly laugh. "You *are* new," she said and spread out on the bed. The release of a single button at her cleavage exposed large round breasts. Her hips formed just the perfect bulges beneath the silken fabric, and her legs extended over the edge of the mattress towards him, slim and smooth, and spread just enough to suggest easy entrance. The green leaves he'd seen inching up her neck, branched out to make their way down her arms, between her breasts and vanished again beneath the gown. They appeared again where the fabric draped over her outer thighs and continued down her legs all th way to her feet.

Cassidy stood speechless. He couldn't remember the last time he'd seen a woman naked, but assumed he'd never seen a body like this. She was reading him somehow. Exposing parts of her body as he thought about them, but just enough to make him *need* to see more. He wanted her in ways he couldn't admit, even to himself. The bulge in his pants hurt. Like an animal, he wanted to ravage her into the bed. He wanted to grip her, devour her, inhale her. The knowledge that he *could*, the fact that she was lying there on the bed with her only intent being just to indulge him, sent his mind over the edge.

"I'm sorry," he said, turning away.

He heard her sit up. "What?"

Cassidy took a deep breath and tried to think of anything but the way her chest rose and fell with shallow breaths. "There's a lot missing. I can't remember much, but there's a blurry...something in the back of my head. She-" He cut off, uncertain what he even meant.

But Shea seemed to know. She blinked as he turned to look at her. "You're a dream," she said. "Even if you did have someone where you came from, she's gone."

Cassidy shook his head. "I have this feeling, like a dull ache in my chest. Perhaps she's back in the dream right now, waiting for me. Perhaps it was a woman who dreamed me and she can't find me right now, because I'm gone."

Shea stood and re-buttoned her gown. "You're a strange man, Mr. Cassidy. Banner paid extra for this. *Real* men, dreams and Twilights would—"

"Kill for you. Die for you, I'm sure," Cassidy said. "But I don't want it like this."

Shea took a deep breath and exhaled. "You could be killed tomorrow on that insane airship of his."

"I don't even know who I am."

She sighed deeply. "Sleep well, Mr. Cassidy. I *will* be the girl of your dreams, and you'll never get a second chance." She exited with an exaggerated swing of her hips.

Cassidy lay alone in the bed made for five as the pale diffused light outside slipped away and a purplish night took its place. There didn't seem to be either a bright day or a dark night in this place. Endless dawn and dusk that shifted close to one or the other, but perhaps never got all the way to either one.

The bed's silk drapes danced and murmured above him in the gentle breeze that drifted in through the open terrace door. He tried to remember his dream again. Tried to remember anything of his life before Banner whisked him out of whatever reality had been his own.

Cassidy stood and let the breeze play over his skin, naked except for a pair of breeches that hung just past his knees. The room's private terrace opened out over a sea of open sky.

The *Nubigena* fought its mooring, listing starboard and port against the purple backgdrop. The other ships, balloons and various dirigible airships stood out against the sky as well. All dreaming to themselves as their crew and captains spent their time with ladies of the night. All except the *Nubigena*, which still looked restless, pulling at her tethers and moorings. And of course him, someone with nothing better to do on a night such as this than stare out at a sky without stars. Had he ever seen stars, or were they just myth memories?

A lone figure waved to him from several terraces over. It was Banner. He motioned back inside the hotel and made a sign like taking a drink, then vanished into his room.

Cassidy sighed. There was nothing *else* to do. He pulled his clothes on, squared the officer's hat Brewster had given him and headed for the lounge. The wall sconces gave off only dim light now, just enough to walk by, though it brightened up a little as he reached the all but empty lounge.

Banner sat at the bar already, nursing some type of dark bourbon. "Shea too much for you?" he asked as Cassidy took the stool beside him.

"Whisky on the rocks," Cassidy said without thinking to the bartender. He drank about half in a single draught and braced himself against the burn. Wished he could change his order, but couldn't make his mouth work.

Banner smiled and took another small sip. "Never saw Shea have *that* effect."

"I wasn't in the mood." Cassidy stared at himself in the bar mirror over bottles of red, green and blue liquid. He didn't recognize himself.

The image only *looked* familiar, like a man he'd once known, but lost touch with. The reflection of Banner nudged him with the finger of his drinking hand. It took Cassidy a moment to recognise the tapping on his arm as being related to the movement in the mirror.

"You're your own man now," the image of Banner said beside him. "You'll find yourself."

Cassidy shook his head and surveyed Banner's grey eyes and confident grin. "How do I know my dreamer doesn't miss me?" He downed the rest of his whisky. "How do I know I'm not some recurring part of his dream that he, or she, misses. Do I have a family there? Does anyone love me?"

Banner narrowed his eyes and polished off his drink with a gulp. He motioned the bartender to refill them both. "I don't think—" he began, but stopped as another man sat down next to Cassidy and ordered cognac.

"Only peaceful men sleep," Manfred Richthofen said, as the bartender placed a small stemmed glass in front of him and filled it half way. "I thought you were a peaceful man, Captain Banner." He gave a dark grimace.

In the mirror, Cassidy watched Banner return the look. "Not tonight."

Richthofen lit a cigarette and blew a plume of smoke in the air. "I guess I should thank you."

Banner only grunted.

"You don't like to drink with Germans, Mr. Cassidy," Richthofen said.

Cassidy sighed. He poked at his glass and watched the ice dislodge and clink to the bottom. "I wouldn't think you'd want to drink with Americans."

The Baron sniffed and took another drag. "It's just a war. A year ago..." He shrugged. "Well, times change."

Chapter 4

Cassidy took his drink to a booth in the far corner where a tiny table light beckoned him. Banner and Richthofen didn't turn to watch him go. Neither did they move closer together, though they did exchange more words before Richthofen finished off his cognac and left. Banner glanced back at Cassidy, polished off his own drink and returned to the stairway, leaving the lounge in silence. Cassidy tried to imagine what dark secrets the two men must share. Was Banner a traitor? Was he even American? Why did he, himself, hate Richthofen? If there's no war for me, I'm not really an Allied pilot. If there's no war, what am I good for?

The Mauser poked his ribs beneath his jacket. He *was* a pilot of some kind. A soldier. That much he couldn't forget or deny. Perhaps serving with this *Captain Banner* was the only war he could fight. The Everdream. Could he just go back?

A cocktail waitress approached his table. She was young and almost *too* pretty, her features elegant with eyes that shone with a hazy glow in the dim light of the lounge. "Another drink, Mr. Cassidy?"

Cassidy nodded. She took his empty glass and left a folded piece of paper. He waited until she'd left to open it.

Zeppelin. 6:00. Bring your gun. Banner.

Cassidy crumpled the note and touched it to the candle's flame. He dropped it in the ashtray and it crinkled in on itself until it became a fine ash he flattened with his index finger. War already?

"How long have you worked here?" he asked the waitress when she returned with his drink.

She placed the glass of whisky with three cubes of ice in front of him and gave a shy smile. "Forever," she said. "I've always worked here." She walked away.

He reached for the glass, but thought about the note. His watch—assuming he could trust it—said six o'clock was only two hours away. The drink had muddled his thinking, though not nearly as much as he would have thought considering the amount he'd drunk already. He took a deep sigh and pushed the half-full glass away.

"Shame to waste good scotch."

Cassidy looked up to see a man standing at the edge of his table. He wore a dark, pin-striped banker's suit and a white snap-brim Fedora. "What business is it of yours?" Cassidy asked as the man sucked in on a long thin cigar and let a thick cloud of white smoke billow out.

"It's not *real* scotch anyway. *Real* scotch has taste," he said sitting down across from Cassidy. "It drinks *you* just as much as *you* drink *it*. It's smooth. It's liquid light."

The man didn't look Twilight. His skin and clothes had too much detail. A *real* person perhaps, like Richthofen, but something in his feral features chilled Cassidy's blood. It wasn't anger, as it had been with Richthofen. This was different. "What do you want?" he asked, straightening.

"I'm looking to hire a pilot," the man said ashing his cigar on the table.

Cassidy knocked back the rest of his drink and stood to go. "Thanks, but my life is complicated enough."

The man grinned widely. "Perhaps I'll see you again when you get tired of ordering the same drink."

A cold lump welled in Cassidy's stomach. He slammed the empty glass down and made for the stairway. His heart thundered in his chest as he tried not to look back at the man, whoever he'd been. Whatever he'd been. Did everyone here understand these things except him?

Cassidy returned to his room and stripped down to his breeches again. The night had grown colder, but he enjoyed the sensation of goose pimples. It made him feel attached and the world felt so distant, as if he weren't natural to it. As if he were a *real* man traipsing through someone else's dream. A *real* man, he thought. What's that?

Cassidy walked out to the terrace where the light breeze had become a gusting wind, chilling him deeply. Reality felt crisper as his body reacted to the change in temperature.

The tethered airships pitched against the darkening purple. Still not a true night. Strange that there was night at all in a place called *Twilight*, but something inside ached for the real thing. Whatever the case, this place seemed to have its own sense of time and reality.

The *Nubigena* listed, even more restless than before. Cassidy wondered how long he had been standing there. A glance at his watch said it was 5:30. The darkness turned a lighter purple as he watched the sky, though no actual sun crested the edge of the island. Dawn, or what passed for it here, would probably break around 6:00.

Cassidy returned to his room and dressed. He pulled the Mauser from its wooden holster, field stripped it and gave the barrel and inner workings a good cleaning. Why was this all so automatic? Why had he chosen this of all weapons? He reloaded, slipped it back into its holster and clipped it to his belt.

Whatever he would one day prove to be, this morning he was a soldier. One of Banner's men. And he'd play the part for the moment. By the look of the strange shadow down by the dock, cast by the flickering fire of lantern light, this might prove a very short assignment.

He made his way out of the lounge and into the silent lobby, the other pilots still asleep. He imagined them cuddled up to women whose names they probably couldn't remember, dreaming of other women they wished were there. How much did the other crew remember of their own lives?

Shea. It would be impossible to forget the woman he *hadn't* slept with. He concentrated hard, trying to bring up images of women he'd known before. Nothing but blurry figures appeared. He looked at his watch. Ten minutes to go.

Cassidy stuck to the dark areas in the lee of the buildings that staggered towards the wharf where light wouldn't touch for hours. He kept his hand beneath his coat, glancing about for whoever had cast the shadows he'd seen from the terrace.

The air felt different. It held moisture now, making the breeze cold against his cheeks and hands. The airships, both soft bodied and galleon style, tugged against their moorings as if trying to wake. The sound of canvas sails whipped in the higher winds.

A glint of dull silver flashed from the corner of a storage shed. Cassidy flattened against the wall, Mauser in hand. He aimed at the spot where he'd seen what looked like a Luger.

Banner stepped out from the shadows, pistol pointed at the ground. He nodded, glanced back around the corner and edged along the side of the building.

Cassidy lowered his Mauser and followed on silent feet. He glanced behind every few seconds, trying to classify the shapes of various clusters of darkness. The *Nubigena* drifted overhead. The ramp had been pulled away, leaving the Zeppelin attached to the island only by a row of tether lines and its nose mooring.

A movement to his right caught Cassidy's eye and he swung his weapon to bear. A loose corner of tarp flapped against a pile of cargo. He turned back to the sound of Banner thumbing the safety off his Luger.

A man crouched behind a crate with his back to them, but stood up as Banner touched the muzzle to his left ear. "You the look-out?" Banner asked.

The man nodded, eyes wide as he turned to look at them. Cassidy only glanced at the man. Kept his eyes trained on the shadows to their flank.

"How many more?" Banner asked.

The man whimpered as Cassidy took another glance. The man didn't have the elven features of the Twilights and his skin was dull and thick, like cured animal hide. No distinctive details to the man's face. "T-two," he said.

The double-click of another pistol came from a deep patch of darkness near one of the buildings. Cassidy dropped to his knee, levelled the Mauser and cracked off two shots; one high, one low. A pistol clattered to the ground. Three more beats and a body tumbled after it.

"How many now?" Banner asked the man on the ground. His voice still sounded smooth and even, like he was asking the time of day.

"Two," the man replied again.

"Two more in ambush or two more up in my ship?"

"T-two."

Banner grimaced and shot the man in the chest. The man clutched at his blossoming shirt and collapsed.

"How would anyone have gotten onto the ship already?" Cassidy asked, as he probed the darkness again.

Banner nodded. "Good question. I don't know why they haven't at least extended the ramp," he said, crouching to examine the body.

Cassidy stepped back so he could speak with Banner *and* keep his eye on their blind spots. "You did kill him in cold blood."

Banner grimaced. "He's only a dream."

"*I'm* only a dream."

Banner grimaced. "He's not like you. Not nearly as solid. Looks like an Armada bounty hunter. They're not after the *Nubigena* itself."

"I didn't think they had much jurisdiction here."

"We don't need much," another man said, stepping around the side of the building. "Jurisdiction is for the Law." Unlike the one Banner had just downed, this man was dressed in a light tan suit, sported a matching Fedora and carried no weapon. Two others who looked like dock workers joined him, levelling bolt-action rifles.

Banner grinned. "Cassidy," he said glancing over, then gestured to the man in the suit, "what do you think the chances are this guy is bluffing?"

Cassidy highly doubted it, but didn't reply, choosing instead to keep his Mauser trained on the leader's forehead.

"Dead or living," the man in the suit said, his face drawing in with impatience.

"Cassidy," Banner asked, as if the man hadn't said anything, "what do you think the chances are that *I'm* bluffing?"

Cassidy had no idea of that either, but kept his gun trained as Banner slipped his Luger back into its holster.

"They said you were mad," the well-dressed man said, shaking his head.

"Really?" Banner's grin widened. "Who sold us out?"

The man's face broke into a matching smile. "Someone from the *real* world. A man named Richthofen."

Cassidy's stomach turned. Goddamned German piece of shit.

"Yes, that's what I thought." Banner gave a slight nod and two shots rang out in quick succession. The two riflemen's heads exploded out the front. Their ruined faces held no expression as rifles clattered to the ground and the bodies thudded down beside the weapons.

As the second body dropped, it revealed the cold expression of Manfred Richthofen who holstered his smoking Luger. "They pay well, but don't know who to trust."

The man in the suit inhaled sharply and set his jaw, trying to hide the fear now visible behind his eyes. "Shall I give the Armada a message from you?"

"Sure," Banner said, giving Cassidy a quick nod. Cassidy squeezed off a single round, but kept his weapon out even as the body crumpled to a heap.

"A good message," the Baron said.

"Thanks for the tip," Banner said, and elbowed Cassidy.

Cassidy grimaced, but returned the pistol to its holster.

Richthofen gave them both a quick salute and faded back into the shadows.

"I still don't trust him," Cassidy growled.

"You don't have to trust him." Banner started back. "Just trust me."

"Give me a good reason," Cassidy snapped. "I just killed for you."

"Killed a dream," Banner said turning to face him.

"You're a dream too."

"Yes and no."

Banner returned to the hotel, but Cassidy remained behind. Six shots had been fired and no one came running. Six shots, five bodies. The dead men blurred on the ground, their colours shifted to black and white and their shapes dissolved into nothing.

There'd been an edge to Banner's voice. Something about the way he said, "only dreams." The crew might love him, but Captain Banner was something different. He didn't consider them equal. If it came down to sacrificing one of them, Cassidy wondered what would happen.

He examined the empty place the bodies had been moments earlier. If *he* died, would he fade like that?

The wind blew cold against his skin and the host of dirigibles drifted above him like ambivalent gods. One war to another, he mused and wondered why the thought tugged his heart towards his stomach. "Am I even *real?*" he asked the *Nubigena*. It hovered above him, nudging the air gently.

He thought about Shea stretched out on his bed. Thought of how his heart yearned for some unknown bond. Why couldn't he remember if he'd ever even been with a woman? What was the emptiness he felt as she had exposed herself to him? He'd been aroused, but cold inside.

Cassidy took a deep breath. Banner was his new captain, but in a war and an army he hadn't signed up for. The Great War, the one that still remained a part of his mind in bits and pieces was simpler. Us. Them. He supposed that this was much the same with Banner, except for the lack of patriotic duty. No love of country to fuel his blood. Just survival. Loyalty to cap and crew. Could he live on that?

Cassidy stared up at the *Nubigena* again. She stared back, her long round body nodding to him in the silent wind. Not the home he would have wanted, but it seemed better than this island. Compared to the hotel with cold women and the distant existence of the *real world*, as Banner called it, the great Zeppelin was loving by comparison.

Do I have a purpose in this world? he thought, then wondered which world he meant.

Chapter 5

Cassidy watched the storm through the porthole of his quarters. After six months, life aboard the *Nubigena* had become something akin to normal. Since he had no memory of what normal really was, he supposed this must be it. Despite a wish to break out and see the world, perhaps find the one who'd dreamt him, Cassidy had decided this was as good a place as any to learn the ropes of this reality. Today he was playing yet another game of stymied chess with Brewster, an exercise which always ended in frustration.

"Just try, Old Boy," Brewster said. "*Pretend* you know how to move."

The Englishman had spent weeks trying to teach him how to move pawns, but he couldn't hold the knowledge long enough to use it. The game simply wouldn't stick. It was as if his mind refused to create certain types of habits.

"It's like riding a horse. One never forgets."

Cassidy sighed without turning around. "How do you know I used to play?"

"Everyone plays chess. Besides, you've told me you see aerial battle like a board game."

"Yes, I see the concept in my mind, but I can't connect it to the pieces." Cassidy watched the Englishman mull over the board. "And explain to me why you can't play both sides yourself. You remember how the pieces move, but you can't play the game without an opponent."

Brewster took a deep breath and rubbed his chin. "I know. That one bothers me too. I play fine with Franz."

"Yes, but he always has to make the first move."

Brewster nodded, still staring at the perfectly set pieces. "I can set them up, though. And I *do* usually win."

Cassidy moved to his bed and began field stripping and cleaning his Mauser. It was one thing he could do without thinking, and the actions made him feel like something made sense. Everyone showed holes in their behaviour; like Ned, who ate all day but never drank anything, or Jayce who no one had ever seen use the head, unlike Franz who everyone knew just couldn't. They were all a patchwork of half memories and quarter lives. Everyone except Banner. "Where's he taking us now?" Cassidy asked.

Brewster pushed the chessboard aside and smoothed the short brown hair beneath his cap. "Well, we've spent as much time in the Twilight as we usually dare. Longer, really. You might get to see the *real* world very soon."

Cassidy finished his gun-cleaning, slid a fresh line of shells into the external clip and chambered a round. He hadn't wanted to admit it, but the thought of visiting the *real* world filled him with more anxiety than joy. His feelings ranged from hope that the elation of being there might make him feel more *real* himself to the intense fear that it might not. He settled on the latter.

"You'll like it." Brewster stood. "It's a good deal more dangerous for us in some ways, but it's a tough journey for the Armada. They've got nothing like this girl," he said, thumping his fist against the *Nubigena's* hull. "Their ships are made of dreamstuff. They steal real fighters, like the ones you shot down, but they, themselves, can't hold their bodies together where we're going."

"Why are you so loyal to him?" Cassidy asked.

Brewster paused. "He rescued me. What else would I do?"

Cassidy shrugged. "Go somewhere. Have a life."

Brewster shook his head. "I wouldn't know how." He glanced at his watch. "Blast. Gun duty. Cheers." He left for his post on the new gun platform Karl had constructed atop the Zeppelin.

Cassidy sat back and eyed the chessboard from his bed. It felt so foreign and yet familiar at the same time, like a country he'd studied in books, but never been to. On the other hand, there was also a déjà vu about it. He felt like he'd all but won tournaments of some kind, but doubted it had ever actually been chess.

Brewster burst back through his door minutes later. "Come on, Old Boy. You've got to see this."

Cassidy leapt to his feet and followed Brewster to the bridge. When he got there, the Englishman nodded to Banner at the helm. "He's never seen one, Captain. Thought he might enjoy."

"Enjoy what?" Cassidy asked, and then he saw it. Miles in the distance a coloured aura floated towards the ship. At a distance it looked like a curtain of rainbow, but, as it neared, it looked more like a cloud of colour.

"Usually, we just see them in the real world, but sometimes they float out beyond it," Banner said, his mouth widened in an excited smile. "Here there's more colour. And they're a lot more solid."

"Northern lights," Brewster said.

"Aurora borealis," Banner said, preferring the more exotic term.

"Is it safe?" Cassidy asked.

Banner nudged the throttle forward. The *Nubigena* sped up and tipped its nose several degrees towards the glowing mass of gasses. In moments colour filled the sky and the ship slipped into it as if it were a solid cloud. The cloud penetrated the gondola, filling the bridge with a rainbow vapour that cast the controls, deck and the airmen themselves in bright shades of shimmering colour. Cassidy looked down at his own hands. They shifted through the spectrum as he wiggled his fingers. "Is it always like this?" he asked.

"This side of reality," Brewster said, his mouth breaking into an even wider grin. "There are entire worlds in some of them."

As he said it, wraiths of men began sliding through the walls from the front of the ship. They didn't float, but stood in mid-air as if the deck were moving beneath them, picking them up from whatever plane they had occupied moments before. The spectres hardly regarded Cassidy or the rest of the crew as they chattered in languages he couldn't understand, but they sounded Slavic of some kind. Their clothing ranged across the sixteenth and seventeenth centuries and most of them appeared to be aristocrats or royalty of one country or the other.

"Prussians," said Brewster.

"And Russians," said Ned.

"Guests!" said Banner with glee in his voice. He cut the engines, checked the buoyancy and belted the helm and pedals, letting the craft drift through the borealis. "To the galley," he said, and led the crew aft.

Cassidy brought up the rear. He paused and watched more spirits speed through the gondola's hull. Banner certainly knew his craft, but letting the Zeppelin drift without a pilot seemed absurd, even for him.

When he arrived in the galley the party was already in full swing. Banner had Ned bring in all the champagne he could find and ordered Karl to make something appropriate for the occasion. The old German, however, had begun preparations at the first sign of colour. He'd been the unofficial ship's cook for years and knew that job almost as well as mechanics.

The guests exchanged jovial banter with their host. Their English was spotty at best, but Banner didn't seem to care. Neither did he mind that none of them could eat or drink anything but their own spectral food and ale. He appeared to have decided to make up for what they could not.

"Cassidy," Banner bellowed over the volleys of foreign tongues, "Eat, drink. Enjoy."

Cassidy sat down as Karl placed a meal in front of him and a flute of champagne by his left hand. The shimmering colours ran through the liquid, tinting it into a layered drink of bright hues.

"Is good, no?" a man in a Russian jacket and hat said. He sat down and regaled Cassidy with stories of war, royal pageantry and conquests of the fairer sex. Cassidy nodded as best he could, and made polite exclamations when they appeared necessary. "You're a pilot, no?" the Russian said, after a story of the first time he'd fired a musket. "You fly?"

Cassidy nodded.

"Yes," the Russian said, slapping the table, surprising Cassidy that the man could actually *touch* the surface. "You look like a pilot. I mean, you look like one who would be a pilot." He shook a bony finger. "I've seen you before." He shook his head. "No, I mean, I've seen pilots like you before. You," he said, wagging the finger in Cassidy's face, "not you, but—ah, is good food, no?" The Russian slapped Cassidy on the back. It felt like a soft electric jolt. "Is strange. I am ghost. *You* are ghost too, eh?"

"I'm a dream," Cassidy said. He still hadn't touched his food and the champagne was going flat in his flute.

"Ghost. Dream." The Russian shrugged. "You fly," he said, giving a raucous drunken laugh. "You fly to the stars."

Cassidy poked at the steak with his fork. The Russian got up and joined several others in a conversation in his mother tongue. Cassidy couldn't shake the coldness the phantoms brought with them. Nobles, rogues, gypsies and escaped convicts, riding their own invisible vessel, whatever it was, through the coloured lights. They could be *real*, in a sense, within the floating rainbow. Here they stood talking and drinking aboard a ship just passing through as if it were the most natural thing in the world.

He looked up to see Banner staring at him from across the table. The boisterous captain lifted his flute in cheers. Cassidy lifted his and tried to match Banner's smile. He sipped and let the silver bite of alcohol sting the back of his throat. Just be young, the captain seemed to be saying. Why do I feel so old? But he emptied the flute and dug into the steak. Damn the doubt, he thought and wiped his mouth with a linen napkin. He smiled and laughed a genuine guffaw.

Banner gestured wildly, slapping everyone who came near on the back. He motioned for Karl to bring more champagne. Banner's appetite was as ravenous as his hunger for laughter and conversation. Though he never stopped talking, he still managed to down plate after plate of food. Not even Brewster, who seemed a bottomless pit when it came to pork chops, ate a tenth as much.

The coloured fog finally thinned and the phantom guests began departing. One by one, they bowed their farewells and whisked away through the back of the galley and off towards the tail of the Zeppelin, where they no doubt remained within their floating cloud as the *Nubigena* drifted out of its boundary.

Most of the crew returned to their duties as the crowd thinned, leaving only Cassidy, Banner, the thin haze of the outer Borealis and a lone man at the end of the table. The man stood, leaning on a pair of crutches. His brown jacket cast a sharp contrast to the blurring blues and greens slowly fading from the air. Even now, reds and yellows washed from the surface of the table and chairs.

Banner stood, his face white.

The man in the brown coat wore an expression of indignation and pain, but as he opened his mouth, it turned to one of pleading. "Why did you leave me?" he asked. "Why?"

The skin at the edge of Banner's eyes tightened and quivered. It was as if only the two of them existed now. Cassidy felt like a mere observer floating in the air. "I did what I had to do," the captain said, but it came out as a whisper Cassidy could barely hear. "You gave me no choice."

There was something familiar about the man Cassidy couldn't put his finger on. Something in the eyes, perhaps, or just the general visage. The man clenched his fists against the crutch's handles and wept as the colours faded completely, and the borealis yanked him away with the rest of its ghostly prisoners.

Banner slumped to his chair, letting his elbows dangle over the arms. He looked up at Cassidy with desperate eyes that reminded him of the man's eyes. "I'd no choice," Banner repeated.

Cassidy nodded. "An old crew member?" he asked, trying to keep the bitterness from his voice. But it was probably true. Some dream that had been sacrificed for whatever was necessary at the time. He met Banner's eyes though, and gazed into them, unblinking. For a moment he saw Banner for who and what he was. A wave of sadness ran through Cassidy and tears rolled down his cheeks. "I'm sorry," he said, but didn't know why.

Banner gave a deep sigh and forced a thin smile. "I think it's time you saw the *real* world."

Chapter 6

Cassidy stood by the girders, out of everyone's way, or, at times, beside the helm where Banner pointed things out as they slipped between various layers of the Twilight. It was a region more vast then Cassidy had imagined at first.

Banner always wanted Cassidy on the bridge now, though he hadn't been assigned any specific duties. Upside down worlds, crystal caverns and regions of pure light passed by as the ship moved from gate to gate. Thousands of floating islands like Arcadia dotted the landscape, but so did floating trees, giant boulders and buildings with no ground on which to stand. Other islands looked man made, dangling from a series of giant gas bladders that made them look beautiful but fragile, the taught lines all but invisible at a distance.

"We're having to go a back way," Banner explained, as the sky shifted hues and the crackles of the last portal faded. "Better for our situation."

Something about the colours told Cassidy they'd gated into a dream. How these strange paths through the Twilight and the Everdream worked was still beyond him. "The Armada?" he asked.

"What else?" Franz said from one of the consoles.

Cassidy looked up to see if Banner had anything to say on the matter, but the steely eyes remained fixed on the horizon, his jaw set. He wasn't smiling.

"At least it's a pretty day," Cassidy said sarcastically, trying to break the awkward silence.

"Dammit," Banner shouted.

Cassidy thought he was being reprimanded, but a moment later the captain spun the wheel hard to starboard and an Armada skyship banked beyond the port windows. Cassidy looked over at Franz as if to say, 'how did he know?' Franz shot back a look that seemed to reply, 'he just does.'

"Shall I take out the Fokker?" Cassidy asked.

Banner shook his head. "Too late. This is an ambush."

Cassidy glanced wildly out the windows as fighters banked and dove. Twenty. Perhaps forty. A fleet. "But how?"

"Someone tipped them off." Banner's tone was flat and even. He took a deep sigh and dipped the *Nubigena's* nose. A fantastic city spread out across the world below. Its black spires and tall pyramids stretched towards the sky.

"How do we fight?" Cassidy asked.

"We don't." Banner gritted his teeth and motioned Franz to push the throttle all the way down. "There's a sleeper dreaming now," he said, and aimed the ship between two of the twisting spires. "One who has the same dream every night."

Cassidy braced as the Zeppelin shuddered and the Armada's guns rattled around the Gondola's hull. "Won't they follow us?"

"Damn right, they'll follow us," Banner said and slammed the right pedal to the floor, jerking the ship upwards again as it reached the two spires. It wasn't enough. The trajectory still appeared to take them into the ground just past the towers. But as they slid between, the sky crackled and the world changed.

Blackness. Only blackness. Not dark. Not a lack of light, but thick tangible black.

Banner opened the flap on the speaking tube and addressed the crew, his voice loud but calm. "Gentlemen," he said, as the Armada ripped its way into the reality around them. The bridge looked hazed, as if seen through a dark lens. "I need you to listen carefully." He glanced at Cassidy. Banner's grey eyes looked like steel, but fear played behind them. He spoke into the tube again. "I need you all to close your eyes, lay flat on the floor and concentrate on anything you can, as hard as you can. Anything as solid and *real* as possible. Don't let your mind become blank." He nodded to Cassidy. Cassidy began lying down. "This will be bad," he said. "I've been here before."

Before Cassidy put his head to the floor, he noticed a man with a thick grey moustache which seemed to cover half his face floating out in the black void. The man floated in the murk naked, his grey skin wrinkled. His arms flailed, features twisted with fear. The expression on his face made Cassidy want to hide. He closed his eyes.

All sound spun through his ears and leaked away as his stomach sank to the bottom of an infinite well. Thinking felt like trying to climb a mountain of mud and every concept he tried to lock onto slipped out of his head. Planes. He thought of planes and sank his nails in. It was as though he were being dragged through the sky by the tail fin, whipped left and right by an agile pilot who rolled and dove as though trying to shake the devil.

The control stick. Cassidy locked onto the control stick. He gripped it with both hands. Dug both feet into the pedals, not caring which way they steered him, only that they were *real* and solid.

Was anything *real* or solid?

The plane vanished, and he spun through space without a body. Fingers gripped for ledges a thousand miles away and feet thrashed empty air for footing, but they were far below, fathoms down in a black sea.

Chess. He was a black knight on a wooden checkerboard. That image vanished as well. He flailed, his hand slipping from the chess piece, back to the control stick of his fighter, the handle of his Mauser. Like the brittle rungs of a ladder collapsing, he fell from one to the next. The *Nubigena* sailed off without him, leaving his consciousness spinning in space. Banner's eyes stared back at him from somewhere in his recent memory. Steel. Grey steel. Something about the man was more real than anything he'd ever seen and the captain's iron hands gripped his shoulders and slammed him downward. Cassidy's feet struck ground. His boots met a solid floor.

He blinked, taking in the world with short shudders of sight from where he lay on the cool aluminium. Banner stood at the helm, fists gripping the wood spokes, knuckles white. His knees had buckled several inches and sweat poured down his face, but his gaze appeared to remain locked on some horizon far beyond the void.

Franz lay on the floor beside Cassidy, eyes closed, body fading to nothing, to solid, to nothing, to solid again. Everyone else on the bridge was gone. The Armada had vanished. The Void became a series of concentric circles that reminded him of rubbing his eyes through his eyelids.

Cassidy gripped the floor as the ship lurched from side to side, jerking at the helm and pedals. Banner yanked the wheel back to level, but he slumped forwards against the wooden spokes, having to use the weight of his whole body to right the floundering vessel.

Cassidy stumbled towards him and caught the wheel with both hands. Banner glanced over, and blinked, his eyes raw and glassy. The eyes returned to the familiar steel grey. He nodded and together they held the helm straight. Cassidy put his weight into the right pedal to keep the nose up as Banner put his on the left to keep it down.

The blackness broke around them, turning the sky crisp as the colours returned more vibrant than Cassidy had ever seen. The atmosphere crackled, and he realized they had just slid through another door and into the centre of a grey electric storm.

Banner collapsed to the floor. Cassidy belted the helm and set the pedals as he'd seen the captain do. He knelt and held Banner by the shoulders.

"Shouldn't have cut through that dream," Banner said. "How many did we lose?"

"I don't know," Cassidy said. "Franz is here." He glanced back to make sure the young German had remained solid. "The Armada's gone."

Banner closed his eyes and opened them again. A tear ran down his cheek. "I'm sorry," he said, and passed out.

"Nietzsche," Brewster said. "German philosopher. Rough life, from what I hear. Deep fears. Probable madness."

Cassidy nodded. "To think he dreams of that every night." Clouds drifted in gentle strips across the sky like pieces of smooth silk rippling around the new gun platform atop the Zeppelin. It was Brewster's turn at watch and Cassidy had come to keep him company.

"Not just that," said Brewster, "he's also dead. His fear, his *dream* was so strong that it burnt itself into the Everdream. The damned thing never went away when he woke up, and so it remained after his death."

"Damn," was all Cassidy could think to say. "But I saw him."

Brewster grunted. "Dream ghost. Strange creatures. Solid as hell, but mostly mad."

The Englishman fidgeted with the pair of Maxims Karl had fixed to the swivelling turret. Thank God the old engineer hadn't been one of the crewmen lost to the void. Chester, Charlie and Jayce hadn't been seen since the journey through Nietzsche's dream. Ned had been presumed lost until they found him huddled beneath a table in the mess, babbling about "the darkness of his soul."

"Are the others dead?" Cassidy asked as his friend searched the skies for any signs of Armada fighters through the narrow windows in the gun turret.

Brewster raised an eyebrow.

"I mean *our* guys," Cassidy said.

"Wish I could say, Old Boy. Still back in the Void, for all I know."

"Can't we rescue them?" Cassidy asked. The thought of the three men drifting forever in someone's nightmare made his stomach queasy. The darkness. The drifting isolation. He didn't want to ever shut his eyes again.

Brewster shook his head. "You were there. It would be like sailing into a whirlpool to save someone already at the bottom."

"But the point is, he's leaving them," Cassidy said, searching the sky along with his friend.

Brewster didn't say anything. He kept peering into the grey sky as if hoping to see a bird, or some other form of life.

Cassidy pulled his cap down over his head. Perhaps he was being unfair to the captain. He'd seen the look in Banner's eyes as they cleared the nightmare. It was the only thing that had ever visibly shaken the man, other than the strange ghost from the party in the borealis. The clouds changed to cottony masses, reducing their visibility by hundreds of yards. "So where is he taking us now?"

"Don't know, but he's set on it like nothing I've ever seen. Once, I remember—" Brewster cut off as the distant clouds crackled with green electricity. "This isn't just a stop. He's after something. And we're close to something."

"Another gate?"

"Gate of all gates," Brewster said. "Open the windows."

Cassidy's brow furrowed, but he opened the two windows in the boxy canopy Karl had constructed atop the gun platform to shield them from the wind. The smell of ozone hit him full in the face as wind gusted in. It brought his senses to full as the *Nubigena* struck the web of light. The aluminium structure shuddered as it pushed through. Other gates had been without turbulence, but this one rattled the struts and girders as if the Zeppelin were skimming the rift's shockwave.

As the *Nubigena* passed through, reality brightened. It was difficult to explain, even to himself, but the dull grey of the canvas shone as if the light itself were more *real*. The ozone faded and fresh air filled the gun-box. It felt warm as his lungs filled with the new air. Cassidy's head swam as if he'd never breathed oxygen before. "This is *real*," he said, almost laughing. "It's *real*."

Brewster grinned. "It's *real*, alright. More *real* than you or I will ever be, but it's dangerous, too. If we don't find a storm soon, the ship will continue, but we won't. We need the energy or we'll fade out."

The *Nubigena* seemed to breathe the *real* air as well. It moved faster, almost joyous, like a schooner catching a quickening gale. Cassidy braced himself against the sudden acceleration. "She likes it."

Brewster nodded. "It's her world."

The airship sliced through the cumulous formations, speeding towards a patch of darkness in the distance. "Why can't the Armada follow us here?" Cassidy asked, as they neared the storm. The *Nubigena* picked up more speed as if anticipating the black clouds.

Brewster shrugged as they entered the nebulous mass. "Same reason *we* don't do well here. If it weren't for this ship—"

Thunder shattered the still air and lightning gave the clouds veins. The rumbling clouds enveloped the ship like a clutching hand. Cassidy felt the difference immediately. His skin livened. He felt solid. Strong. He felt like he could fly on his own.

"I need to head down," Brewster shouted, over the rush of howling wind that gusted through the open windows.

Cassidy stopped him from closing the windows. "I'll be there in a few," he said. The wind brought a menagerie of new sensations. His skin was on fire with a kind of warmth he'd never felt, despite the cold of the air. His mind felt alive. It was as if he'd been flying a crippled plane all this time. He laughed out loud. His thoughts were more detailed. The lines in his hands were deeper and more distinct. This is reality, Cassidy thought.

My God, I'm an alien here.

Chapter 7

The *Nubigena* broke out of the black clouds and made for land. Rain poured over the sides and drenched the windows with sheets of water. Even with the storm overhead, the energies still filled Cassidy with churning vigour.

"It's a good storm," Banner said as he levelled out a hundred feet above the ground. "This one will last."

There was nowhere to moor the ship, but Franz took the helm and dropped the Zeppelin down past fifty feet. The raging storm blotted out the sun, so Brewster, Cassidy and Ned accompanied Banner down the rope ladder in darkness as Karl turned the crank.

"Stay here." Banner trotted off into the rain.

A burst of lightning illuminated the ground, and Cassidy realized they stood in a vast cemetery. Tombstones and statues stretched to the horizon. In the distance Banner stood before one of the graves. Rain beat down on his flight coat, plastering his mat of dark hair to the sides of his head.

"What's he doing?" Cassidy asked.

Ned shrugged.

Brewster squinted into the rain. He stuffed his hands deep into his pockets and pulled his shoulders up nearly to his ears as if it might stop the rain from getting in them. "I've only seen him here once before," Brewster said with a dark grimace. "It must be the grave of his dreamer. The last time the captain came here he was in pretty bad shape."

Another bolt of lightning showed the captain kneeling before the grave. Brewster shook the last few drops from what had been full bottle of brandy.

"What do we do?" asked Cassidy.

Ned stood behind them looking as lost as Cassidy felt.

"Nothing," Brewster said. "Just keep your eyes peeled."

"I thought the Armada didn't like to come here," Cassidy said. He flicked his gaze around as lightning struck again, but the cemetery looked empty.

Brewster scanned the blackness. "There's more out there than the Armada. Twilight Bounty hunters, for instance, are made of sterner stuff. Besides, this place just gives me the goddamned creeps."

Another bolt struck. Banner stood before them looking tired. He motioned to the ladder and they ascended. Cassidy climbed with amazing ease. His muscles enjoyed the work. He liked feeling them strain and burn against the rungs. Every sensation felt so much more *real*. Even pain felt good.

When they reached the ship Banner retired to his cabin in silence. Brewster's forehead furrowed. Ned looked lost. No one wanted to speak. Cassidy knew why. It was something about the look on Banner's face. A sadness that just didn't look right on his features. Didn't belong—like a prince wearing a peasant's clothes.

All three sat staring at each other until Ned finally left, mumbling something about needing his sleep. Cassidy watched him go. Brewster sat still and stoic, watching the wall. "How did Banner find his dreamer?" Cassidy asked.

Brewster broke from his meditation and lit his pipe. He looked thoughtful. "Who the hell knows? It's just a guess."

"Then we can still live even after our dreamer dies." Cassidy said. He peeled off his rain-soaked jacket and towelled it dry as best he could.

The Englishman shrugged. "Don't think about those things. They'll drive you mad."

Cassidy couldn't stop thinking about his dream. His one damned repeated dream. Same story without an ending. "I need to find mine."

Brewster nodded. "Sure, me too." He puffed on his pipe and gave Cassidy a thoughtful look. "Meet him, shake his hand and say, 'what the devil was all this about?'"

"Do dreamers know?"

Brewster sighed. "They'd better. Someone better."

Banner was a different man the next day as if he'd entered his quarters the night before a glum caterpillar and emerged with radiant wings. "I'm hungry," he announced to the crew who gathered around his door, their eyebrows furrowed, jaws set. "Let's get supplies."

The *Nubigena* managed to jump from storm to storm as each thinned or decided to go the wrong direction. They tacked along what Brewster said was the mid-east coast of America, following the turbulent coastal weather. The ship didn't even mind hurricanes. If anything, it fed on the high winds, though Banner rode the eye for quite some time, enjoying the effect of the swirling winds radiating out from the ship in all directions.

Cassidy had expected to feel at home flying over America, but nothing looked familiar. Nothing about the coastline, or the buildings, or the squares of land or expanses of wilderness. Surely he'd flown over some of it in the past. He must have some memories from his dreamer.

"Now that looks good," Banner said, pointing down at the bright lights of a city. "Has anyone here been to New York?" Two raised their hand, but he didn't look around to notice. "The Big Apple," he said, shaking his finger at the towering buildings, "has the best nightlife in the world." He laughed his boisterous laugh and tipped the *Nubigena* towards the tallest building.

Brewster turned to face Cassidy. "What's wrong, Old Boy? You look piqued."

Cassidy grimaced. "The people down there. They're *real*." The Twilight had felt less *real*, but more natural. Looking down on this city made him feel distant. He was an invader here.

"Get him dressed," Banner said over his shoulder. "We'll find something swanky with a live band."

"A live band?" Cassidy asked.

Brewster shook his head. "What you Yanks call music. Vulgar if you ask me, but it does get the blood pumping."

"What will we do there?" Cassidy searched his memory for any type of domestic life in his past, and couldn't even find snippets. Nothing but flying planes.

"You'll dance," Banner said. He manoeuvred the *Nubigena* into mooring position and barked a series of orders into the speaking tube. "The storm will last several hours."

"How do you know?" Cassidy asked, looking out at the rolling sky.

"I know storms," said Banner. "I know storms like I know this ship."

Brewster took him back to the supply cabins and found an American dress uniform. "Women love servicemen," he said, and shook dust off the jacket. "Better leave the gun though. Mauser's don't go well with a Yank officer's suit. What's your rank anyway?"

"Major," Cassidy said. He'd never tried to remember his rank before, but somehow knew what it was.

"Oh, major, is it? Dreamer decided you were too good to be an LT," Brewster said, grinning. "Gold leaf for you then. Put one on your cap, too." He dug through a drawer for service patches and pins. "Ladies *really* love high-ranking officers."

Oh God, please no, Cassidy thought. The idea of merely walking among these people sent jolts of fear down into his stomach, let alone the thought of talking to women.

"Don't look so scared," his friend said, as if he'd read Cassidy's mind. "It's just dancing."

In twenty minutes Cassidy stood on the roof of their mooring building with Brewster, Banner, Ned and Franz. The only door had been latched from the inside. Cassidy looked around for another opening.

Brewster touched his arm. "Watch. You'll have to learn this." The Englishman passed his hand over the handle. The lock clicked and the door swung open. "There's a lot of little tricks like that."

"We can do that?" Cassidy asked.

"Dreams are as concerned with what can and can't happen as the rest of them. Lets us bend the rules a bit."

Cassidy tried to take pleasure in that thought, but knew it was because they were less *real*. What they did here didn't even matter as much to reality itself. "Looks like fun," he said and tried to smile.

When they reached the ground floor Banner passed Franz a roll of money and told him to go get supplies. Cassidy wondered where the German would find a store at his hour, and one willing to sell to Jerries, but he didn't ask. Franz left the building and vanished into the shadows as the rest of them made their way down the sidewalk. This *Big Apple* was nothing like Arcadia. It looked like a labyrinth of buildings, walkways and roadways. Crowds of people. Both vehicles and carriages filled the streets, making their way in the flickering glow of gaslight.

"We're a hazy concept here," Banner said, gesturing to the city. "Most people won't even notice you unless you want them to." They walked in silence. Several people passed without a glance. Ned whistled. No one turned to look.

A man across the street caught Cassidy's eye. The man stood watching them with a wicked grin. He wore a tweed suit, black bowler and leaned forwards on a strange umbrella. The crook appeared to have been fashioned from the head or spine of some dead reptile and the canopy was smooth leather.

"Stay away from him," Brewster said, pulling Cassidy along. "Don't look at him either. He's not a man."

The man reminded Cassidy of the one he'd met on Arcadia. The one who'd offered him the taste of a different drink. He pulled his eyes away. A small child waved at Cassidy. Cassidy waved back. "So, kids can see us?" he asked. The child's parents tugged him around the corner of a building.

"Sometimes," Brewster said. "But they don't remember. We're like—"

"Dreams," Cassidy finished. Ice formed on his insides. He felt like a ghost drifting through a city that didn't care about his existence. Life aboard the *Nubigena* had never felt more like a trap. He could never escape into this place. It would be even harder than jumping ship in the Twilight. "How do you make them notice you?" he asked as a couple pushed past without a glance.

Banner tapped a man on the shoulder. "Pardon me, sir, but do you have the time?" The man started as if the captain had appeared out of nowhere, but he collected himself and read Banner the time off a gold pocket watch. "You'll get the knack," Banner said. The man stared at his pocket watch as if trying to remember why he'd glanced at it in the first place. "Here you have to force an impression."

"You turn it off and on," added Brewster. "You have to concentrate, but it's not hard."

"Anyone thirsty?" Banner asked as he stopped outside a colourful sign that read The Lilliputian.

They tipped their caps to the doorman as they entered a lounge. The lobby reminded Cassidy of a palace: all gold trim, red velvet and mirrors. Did Banner have enough money to afford this place? One of two well-dressed men standing near the entranced narrowed his eyes as the four walked passed. The other, a fat man in a pin-striped suit walked towards them, muttering something about servicemen.

"Airmen," Banner corrected. He smiled his charming smile and shook the man's hand. "We're two weeks back from Europe," he said, "and we heard your chef was the best in town."

The fat man gripped his lapels and drew himself up several inches. "He is," the proprietor said. "And our band is second to none."

"Do they play anything new?" Ned asked.

"New?" the fat man asked.

"Don't bother the man," Banner said. "Whatever they play is fine." The four of them sat down at a corner booth and ordered entrees and wine.

Cassidy sipped the dark red liquid. It tasted sweeter than it did aboard the airship, and a barrage of separate flavours bloomed inside his mouth. He wished he could order wine himself. The steak was different, too. He could taste each spice the chef had used in preparation as a separate flavour. Food he'd eaten before tasted like paper compared to this. It was as if he'd never eaten before. Never had a drink before. He almost hated to swallow, allowing bites and sips to roll around his mouth as long as possible.

Banner and Ned hardly finished their food before they were out on the dance floor. Brewster motioned Cassidy to join them. "Go on. I'm going to let my food settle," Cassidy said.

When they'd gone, he stood, but the thought of facing the throng of people paralyzed his feet. He glanced back at Brewster. "I need the lavatory."

"Don't take too long," the Englishman said, grinning.

Cassidy nodded and found the closest exit.

"You all right?" asked one of the waitresses as he exited the adjoining bar.

He nodded. "Just looking for the..." Cassidy tried to remember what he was going to say. She was short. Red-haired. Green eyes so deep and *real*. Her delicate scent made his head light.

"Looking for a drink?" she asked.

"I'd love a drink," Cassidy said.

"Anything you like," she said. "I'm April."

He opened his mouth. It started forming the shape of a W. Anything but that. "Perhaps later."

April nodded. "My brother's a pilot. I mean, he was," she said, forcing a smile. "They said he went down in the ocean, but wouldn't tell me which one." Her shoulders lost the stiff facade of a high-class waitress. "I didn't mean to say that. I don't know why. You just remind me—"

Cassidy reached out and took her hand. He didn't know why either, but couldn't help it. Her skin felt warm. Were all *real* people so warm? "I'm sorry," he said, meeting her eyes. "I'm sure he was a great pilot."

She sniffled and levelled her gaze. "You must be shipping out soon."

"Soon," Cassidy said, nodding. He hadn't let go of her hand. Prickles of electric sparks passed into his skin. Her life energy. Her emotions. They flooded over him in waves that felt more *real* than his own.

"I've got to get back to work," she said, slipping her hand out of his. April turned to leave, but stopped and dug a large silver coin out of her vest pocket. "For luck." It rested on the tips of her fingers, staring up at him. "I don't know your name, and I'd rather not," she said, pushing it towards him, "but if you make it back, and you're ever in Darcy, Virginia..." She brought a hand to her lips to stop their trembling. "Just bring it to me so I know you made it back. I'd like to know someone made it back," she said, looked embarrassed and hurried off to the bar. "If you don't, I guess I'll never know," she said over her shoulder.

Cassidy stood staring at the coin, trying to recognize it. It looked newly minted with a woman in a flowing gown on its face, gesturing off to her right, the word LIBERTY written above her head. On the other side stood an eagle with unfurled wings. Why did the disk of silver feel so heavy? More *real* than anything else he'd ever touched. His pistol was *real*. The ship was *real*, but something of this strange girl April was still in the metal. Something of her life-force perhaps. The emotions she'd felt when she handed it over. An overwhelming sadness lingered in the milling and etched surface. Did he remind her of her brother? The thought of her brother sent a jolt of pain through him. Images of the young man bloated and dead in the sea. Her imagined memories perhaps. Grief. So much grief.

He stumbled into the lavatory, sick to his stomach. April's pain still flooded through him as he sat in one of the stalls with his face in his hands. Even her emotions felt more *real* than his own. Bitter loss. Love.

Longing he couldn't put into words. He cried. Wept for a man he'd never met who'd gone down on some ocean somewhere in a world he'd hardly touched.

Cassidy sat up slowly as the young woman's pain leaked away. He wiped the tears from his face, stood up and pushed the stall door open. The lavatory looked much like the rest of the place, far too ornate for any of its actual functions. The counters were marble and brass. A man in a red and gold uniform stood ready to hand him a towel.

Cassidy examined himself in the mirror. He splashed icy water over his face and watched the drops run off his skin without leaving it wet. It seemed his own body rejected the *real* liquid, or it rejected him.

The man in red and gold offered him the towel. Cassidy pretended to dry his already dry face and handed the man a small coin from his pocket. A nickel, perhaps a dime. He couldn't remember the difference.

Outside, a woman wearing an emerald green gown stared at the city through an arched window. She glanced over at him and smiled. "Are you in the Army?" she asked, stirring a blue cocktail with a glass swizzle stick. The stick matched the red of the cherry that bobbed in the azure liquor.

"Sort of, ma'am," he said. "I fly fighter planes."

She gave a half-smile. Her eyes matched her dress, but the green was more watered down than the waitress's eyes had been. She was pretty, but not too pretty. Her face looked almost plain with a small chin and a too-large nose, but he decided it was her poise that made her almost beautiful. "Is that what they do in the Army now?" she asked, teasing with her eyes. "Fly?"

"Yes. I mean—" Cassidy stammered. He couldn't think of anything to say, so he managed, "I fly against the Germans."

"How unfortunate for them," she said, approaching with an exaggerated sway of her hips. "Kill many?"

"Well, I—" Cassidy wasn't sure. His memories of killing the two Armada fighters and the Twilight pirates were crystal clear, but past that…had he shot down any in the dream?

"It's okay." She ran a finger down the sleeve of his uniform. "I'm not squeamish. Are you one of those aces we hear so much about?"

"Probably," Cassidy said, nodding. "It only counts if it's over our own lines and there have to be witnesses. You could shoot several down, but if no one's around to see it, I mean, there has to be proof that it was you who shot them down, and even then—" Cassidy realized he was babbling.

"My, you servicemen do go on." She pulled the cherry from her drink by the stem, sucked the liquor off and popped it the rest of the way between her lips.

For a moment, Cassidy thought she'd swallowed the cherry whole. Her eyes widened. Something bone white emerged from the middle of her torso, sticking through her dress. Blood blossomed over the emerald green. She crumpled to the floor, revealing the man with the bowler hat from outside standing behind her. His strange umbrella stuck straight out of her back like a flag marking its territory.

Chapter 8

Cassidy reached for his gun. Remembered he didn't have one. Realized he didn't have anything but his fists. He charged.

The bowler man pulled the umbrella from the woman's back and planted the tip on the floor beside him as if holding a cane and smiled.

Cassidy aimed his shoulder for the black bow tie. He made contact and the world changed. His blood froze. His body numbed and the world became a mass of swirling colours. He shook the dizziness out of his head and found himself lying on the floor against the far wall. A sheet of maroon wallpaper took up his entire field of vision.

"Whatever were you thinking?" the bowler man said. His accent sounded British, high society. He leaned up against the wall beside Cassidy cleaning his spectacles with a silk handkerchief. "You're a dream," the man said, flashing white feral teeth. "Might as well throw air at me."

Cassidy groaned as he tried to sit up. "Why did you kill that woman?"

The man sighed. "Because I liked her. My wife would never approve."

"You murdered her. For nothing," Cassidy seethed through gritted teeth. The woman's dead eyes stared at him as if pleading for him to act. Avenge her.

"She's only meat," the man said, and slipped his spectacles back on.

This couldn't really be happening. Cassidy shook his head. One moment the blood was all over her gown. The next it was gone as the umbrella soaked it up.

"You," the bowler man said, shaking his gloved finger, "shouldn't even be here. I'd eat you, but you'd taste like cardboard."

Banner lurched out of nowhere and stood between them.

The man's face darkened. "You're not a dream. But you look like a dream. How strange," he said, putting his finger to the edge of his mouth. "Oh, well. Cheerio." He extended his umbrella upward and opened the canopy. "Enjoy New York." The umbrella lifted him into the air and he vanished through the ceiling.

Voices sounded down the hall. "Best not let them see you," Banner said.

Cassidy willed himself invisible. It was so easy. Just a thought. Several men rushed around the corner and sped past him. They bent over the woman, checking her pulse. "She's dead," one of the men said. "Thought she must have fainted, but she's dead." The other men looked ashen.

"Can't they see the blood?" Cassidy whispered, uncertain whether or not they could be heard.

"What blood?" Banner asked.

"It was there. I swear," Cassidy said.

Banner shook his head and answered at full volume. "That creature was something dark from the Underworlds. The vicious things they do here translate as other things. They'll probably find she died of a heart attack or something."

Cassidy's stomach churned. "It was a cherry pit. She must have choked on a cherry pit." His eyes watered as he looked down at her collapsed body. "I could have saved her. She was only choking."

Banner nudged him to go. "Not likely," he said, as he pushed Cassidy around the corner towards the lounge. "The creature wouldn't have let you." Men brushed past on their way to the growing crowd. They didn't appear to actually *see* Cassidy or Banner, but avoided them unconsciously as if they were furniture. "Creatures like that," Banner continued, "can do unspeakable things to us. But at least *we* can see them."

Cassidy nodded. He still felt sick. Couldn't forget the woman's eyes, the way they'd bulged when the umbrella pushed through. The way she'd pleaded with him silently as she died, probably believing he was in on the murder. "It's like I'm seeing behind the world," Cassidy said. He faltered and leaned against the wall. "My God, I'm seeing the secret way men die, and there's nothing I…"

Banner stopped and grabbed Cassidy by the lapels. He drew his eyes in tight on Cassidy's face. "Don't think about it, man. You're only seeing part of it. There's a lot more you'll see, and there's nothing we can do." He released Cassidy and pulled away. "Like it or not, it's not our fight. It's not our world at all. We're just shadows here." His features softened. "I wish the *real* world was all daisies for you, but in the end we're not really welcome."

Cassidy nodded, but couldn't stop thinking about the woman in green even as they made their way back to the *Nubigena*. It was as if, for a moment, life had made sense. As if he'd recognized something in her. Recognized something about himself that he couldn't touch except through her. Something he would never be able to touch now that she was dead. Or was he thinking of April? He'd met them so close together and the experiences were already melding in his head.

He pulled the coin from his pocket and gripped it hard, trying to find April's pain deep in the niches. Drops of sorrow leaked into his skin. He would always have this. This was more *real* than anything else he possessed.

"Women'll do that," Brewster said, as they sat in the galley, back on the ship after dinner. The Englishman sipped tea and smoked a new blend of pipe tobacco from the supplies Franz had picked up. "You fall in love with a single look, a wink, a touch of their hand and bam, the world makes sense. Then it's gone. You get over it." He leaned back and blew a cloud of warm smoke into the air. "And you'll meet many more."

Cassidy stared out the window at the torrential rain and bursts of electric fire that blinked in and out of existence across the rolling clouds. "I don't know that I was in love with them. Either of them. I just felt..." Cassidy wasn't sure *what* he felt. But they'd been so *real*. And that had made *him* feel *real*. Like he could touch her and not feel like a ghost. He pulled out the coin and showed it to Brewster.

"That's called a Walking Liberty," Brewster said. "Minted recently. Worth half a dollar. Nice piece."

Cassidy slid the coin into a deep inside pocket of his jacket. Didn't want to use it up. April's pain was a currency more dear to him than blood.

"The storms are thinning," Brewster said. He stood and stretched. "That means we'll head back to the Twilight soon."

"I was enjoying the *real* world," Cassidy said, without looking up, his eyes still fixed on the dark clouds beyond the window.

"We always come back," Brewster said. "We just can't ever stay. I'm turning in, though. Gun watch tomorrow, you know."

Cassidy listened to the Englishman's footsteps fade. Wondered if the dream actually needed sleep, or if it wasn't just habit.

The ship felt asleep now. Empty. He smoked a cigarette and listened to the thunder. It thrummed in his chest as if it were the long-delayed heartbeat of the storm itself. Had he ever smoked before coming to this ship? The movements felt natural, but he couldn't picture another time he'd ever done this.

Something red flashed in the corner of his eye. One of the starboard engines shed a large sheet of its outer covering and flames exploded out the side. It was one of the main engines, the ones attached to the Zeppelin's rear hull. Cassidy bolted from the galley and made for the back stairwell.

Karl slept near the engine room and Cassidy found the door to his quarters without trouble. After several loud raps he pushed it open. Karl's cot lay empty.

Cassidy made for the engine. The flames had already burned a hole in the canvas shell. They threw fiery shadows across the mammoth interior of the ship's main cell forcing freakish shadows to lurch across the looming ribs. The gas bladders still swelled with helium. The fire couldn't ignite it, but could burn through.

A shadow flickered across the curved wall and a scream rang out. "Karl?" Cassidy shouted as he approached the licking flames.

A creature emerged from behind a girder that ran down to the engine. The thing looked very loosely like a man, and stood taller than Cassidy, but pencil thin. Instead of skin or clothing it wore a glistening shell like a black insect. Its head was elongated and its feet looked more like claws. The creature opened its mouth and let out a high pitched squeal that reminded Cassidy of the sound a stuck pig would make.

Cassidy reached for his Mauser. Again, he didn't have it. An image of the pistol in its case flashed through his mind, lying on his bed.

Loaded.

Ready.

Useless.

A coarse German accent rasped from behind the creature. "Cassidy. Get help." He could just make out Karl's jagged features beyond the creature's left foot. Blood ran down his cheek. His right arm extended out at a wrong angle.

The creature squealed again and charged. Cassidy moved. His mind went blank and focused. Instinct took over. The spindly black arm swung in a cutting arc, but Cassidy had already leapt back and was around the side of Karl's tool shed before the creature could pounce again.

Cassidy grabbed a four-foot crowbar leaning against the wall and wielded it like a two-handed sword. The creature sprang around the corner and landed on all fours, crouched like an attacking spider. Cassidy swung the crowbar but met empty air. The insect-like creature leapt over his head and landed behind him with the sound of chittering claws.

Jumping aside as the razor-like shin of the creature passed beneath Cassidy, he landed, swinging the crowbar downward at the chitinous head. The hardened steel made contact. There was a sound like a cracking egg.

The creature stumbled. Cassidy drew back for another blow. It spidered sideways on all fours and sprang again. The crowbar clattered to the deck as Cassidy lay pinned beneath the black body.

He scrambled to slide out from beneath the creature's wiry frame, but it held his arms and legs to the deck. The claw-like hands felt like steel around his wrists. The crack in its cone-shaped head oozed a thick yellow liquid. It squealed again, high and victorious. Its beak mouth opened and descended towards Cassidy's face.

The sound of metal thunder cracked and resounded twice through the cavernous insides of the *Nubigena*. The cracked head exploded sending a shower of yellow goo across the floor and girders. The creature convulsed several times and collapsed with a sound like falling paper clips.

"Cassidy? Are you good?" Karl wheezed hard.

Cassidy struggled from beneath the corpse. He nodded as he tried to catch his breath.

The old engineer leaned against a support girder, bleeding onto the dull metal. His right arm hung twisted by his side. A .45 revolver dropped from his left fingers. It landed on the deck with a heavy clunk. "Is gremlin," he rasped, and slid down to the ground. "We pick them up in the air."

Cassidy pulled himself up to his elbow and examined the thing from a distance. So that's a gremlin, he thought. He'd heard of them. They'd plagued large aerocraft since the beginning of aviation, but he'd always imagined them as small goblin-like creatures.

Boots thundered up the stairs. Banner, Brewster, Ned and Franz levelled their weapons.

"Dammit, Banner," Karl spat from his slouched position at the girder. "You are too late. Drop the engine or it will take us down."

The hole in the canvas was widening, and through it, flames licked up into the Zeppelin's belly. Banner and Ned rushed to the support jacks.

"Jammed," Ned yelled.

Banner levelled his Luger and emptied six shells into the supports. "Careful," Karl yelled. Ned joined in, dispensing his revolver's payload until the metal snapped and the fiery engine plummeted away.

"Blasted vermin," Banner said, as he helped Cassidy up. "I hate gremlins. Damnable aerial spirits get pissed off just because they get caught in the metal."

Cassidy rubbed the back of his head. Ned and Franz attended Karl, who groaned with every move. His arm had been broken in two places and a gout of blood stood out against the side of his head. While the two of them held him down, Banner set his arm. Only Franz and Cassidy understood half the words Karl used, but Cassidy doubted anyone missed his meaning.

Cassidy returned to Karl's quarters after the excitement died down. He paused at the door and grimaced. He's a German, Cassidy kept thinking to himself, but knocked.

"What?" Karl's voice rang from inside, harsh and impatient.

Cassidy opened the door. The old engineer lay on his bed, a bandage around his head and a mass of gauze around his right arm. He smoked a cigarette with his good hand.

"Just wanted to check on you," Cassidy said. "That thing tore you up pretty bad."

The old man stared. His blue eyes bored into Cassidy's. "You," he said, pointing at Cassidy with the glowing ember of his cigarette. "The magnetos on that Fokker will always work. Always. I promise." He blew a cloud of smoke. "You are new." He paused. "You are young, to us."

Cassidy nodded, assuming the man meant that he was the most recent member of the crew. Karl's German sounded much thicker and more broken than Franz, who seemed almost fluent.

"Come," Karl said, standing. "I want opinion." He led Cassidy to a section of the vast inner cell he'd never seen. Behind a hanging tarp stood an array of various machines. Two stood taller than him by several feet. "This," Karl said, pointing to a semi-circular unit with thousands of yards of thin wire wrapped around the central stem, "is dynamo. Light materials. Very expensive. Generate a lot of electricity. This," he said pointing to a large ten by ten foot box covered in glass tubes and wires, "I don't know. Look."

Cassidy stepped forwards and peered into the box through a wide gap in the front. Inside thousands of tiny gears and wheels sat motionless. "I've never seen anything like it."

Karl sighed. "Of course not. But I hoped."

"Do you know if it works?" Cassidy asked.

"Cannot even turn it on."

Banner's ability to jump from storm to storm with very little time in between astonished Cassidy. The captain seemed able to predict everything about the weather just by gazing over the horizon and tasting the breeze.

As Brewster predicted though, the storms thinned, and talk continued about returning to the Twilight. The loss of a single engine didn't slow them much since the *Nubigena* had six, but they'd have to get a new one eventually. For now, Karl rigged an old plane engine in its place.

"This might sound like a crazy question," Cassidy said to Brewster, as they gazed out one of the aft windows of the gondola, "but what all do we do? I mean, do we have some kind of mission or purpose?"

Brewster looked thoughtful as he watched the grey clouds vanish behind the ship and form a purple line. "Survive," he said, at last. "The Armada will hunt us until we're dead, or whatever it is they do with captured dreams."

Cassidy nursed a whisky. "Why are we so much of a threat?"

Brewster shrugged. "Hell, I don't even know who they are. Police of the Everdream, yes, but beyond that..." He trailed off. "I just know they've been chasing Banner long before I hooked up with this outfit, and he's the only one who's held out this long. I've talked with a lot of people in the Twilight."

Cassidy took another sip. Energy cracked in the distance. Reflections of the strange light bounced off the rolling clouds. The *Nubigena* trembled.

Brewster gave a sardonic grin. "Say goodbye to reality."

Chapter 9

Cassidy's chest tightened as the ship broke through to the Twilight. The drabness hit him with full force now as the *real* world contrasted so sharply with the muted colours of this in-between one. The clouds were green this time, but a sickly shade like overcooked peas. The sky looked as if someone had come along with a straw and sucked just enough vibrancy out to leave a hazy memory of what *real* colour had been.

He thought of the woman in the green dress. The fabric had reminded him of what a forest canopy would look like if it were gathered up, squeezed into one long bolt of fabric and sewn into a single evening gown. And her eyes. If Cassidy never remembered another thing about her, it was the green of her eyes. He'd just let her die. He'd almost let Karl die. Cassidy slammed a fist against the metal frame around the circular window in his quarters. Pain forked through to his bones. The Mauser would never be off his side again.

He lay on his cot and stared at the ceiling, feeling the Twilight air creep into the ship. In a few minutes he would be breathing it again instead of the ozone-thick smell of the storms. The richness of the air in the lounge. April's scent as she'd handed him the Walking Liberty. Have I ever loved anyone, he wondered again, as he drifted off to sleep.

Cassidy stood in a sepia briefing room, receiving orders from a commander too blurry to recognize. Several airmen stood next to him, snapped salutes and then made for their fighters. The Sopwith he always flew stood on the runway, looking as if it had come right out of the shop.

The interior of the plane looked like a Fokker though, with controls similar to the one he flew now. He turned dials and flipped switches without thinking. He pumped up the gas tank as the flight crew armstronged the prop. The fighter thrummed as if it couldn't wait to take to the sky. Everything happened on automatic. No thoughts. No options, just pre-recorded action.

He taxied the Sopwith to line up with the others and in moments he was in the air. Time jumped ahead in spurts. They were engaging the Germans now. He didn't know where, but a castle loomed below, surrounded by acres of brown and red fields. A dot appeared in the distance and he was drawn to it as if nothing else existed in the world, his hatred raging out of control. A single fighter—

Cassidy's eyes flew open as red light streamed through the glass portal of his quarters, igniting the walls with a shifting watery effect. He leapt to his feet and peered out at the sky beyond the starboard hull. A shimmering galleon rode the air beside them, matching their speed. Its fluttering sails shone with their own light, along with the vessel itself. Pirates? Cassidy thought. In the air? He grabbed his Mauser and headed for the bridge.

Cassidy burst through the door. "There's a ship out there." Half the crew already stood at the helm.

Banner glanced over, then turned back to the red ship, still flying starboard. The captain's expression had been grim, but he muttered just loud enough for everyone to hear, "It's all right, boys. She's just saying hello."

Brewster nodded to Cassidy from across the bridge. He wasn't smiling either. Franz adjusted his gun belt.

"Get up to the crow's nest," Banner said to the young German, using the term Brewster had recently given to the gun platform up top. "Make sure Ned doesn't do anything stupid." Franz snapped a quick salute and was gone.

"Who are they?" Cassidy asked, trying to sound nonchalant, but the red glow sent tremors into his voice. Brewster and Banner exchanged furtive glances. "Are they ambushing us?"

Brewster shook his head. "Twilight's a big place. We're bound to see them from time to time. They travel mostly in the *real* world."

The red ship glided closer, to within feet of the *Nubigena's* hull and a light coloured flag stood out on the main mast. The pirate crew began throwing lines. The black grappling hooks stuck straight to the main hull and gondola as if magnetized, instead of hooking on. The lines became rigid making the Zeppelin and the glowing vessel one.

"Shouldn't we do something?" asked Cassidy.

"We're going to do something," Banner said, setting the controls to remain on course and speed. "We're going to go say hello."

Everyone except Karl stood by the main door as Banner looked out the hatch window. "Okay," he said, twisting the handle and swinging the hatch open. A gangplank extended from the galleon. Men stood in two rows facing each other at the other end. "They've signalled a greeting first, so we're going over there. Be civil and courteous, and watch yourselves," Banner said as he started across.

"They look like pirates," Cassidy said.

"Of course they're pirates," Banner snapped.

Cassidy brought up the rear as they made their way over the thin bridge. He couldn't feel any wind, as if the plank had invisible walls keeping the gusts at bay. They crossed as easily as they would have on the ground.

Sailors stood out on the decks wearing the uniforms of a 17th century European navy, but time had aged them to resemble more the tattered garments of military vagrants. Banner and his men filed onto the half deck and inspected the crew. A man stood in the centre. White hair flowed down his shoulders and over the grey naval uniform. His yellow eyes twitched between the members of the *Nubigena's* crew, like a feral animal taking in its surroundings. A scar ran from his forehead to his ear as if he'd narrowly missed a lunging strike in a sword duel.

Beside him stood a shorter man in similar uniform. Probably his first mate.

Banner gave a crisp salute. "Captain Falkenberg," he said in a military tone, "permission to come aboard."

The grey captain remained silent for long seconds as he continued studying the men before giving a grim nod. "Where's your crew?" Captain Falkenberg asked. His voice came out tired and gravelly. "You had at least twenty last we met."

Banner glanced back at his men and returned his attention to the captain. "I see the ship still sails."

Cassidy tightened his grip on his belt, wishing he could wrap his fist around the Mauser. All eyes fixed on the two captains as they regarded each other across the deck. Captain Falkenberg gave a slow nod. "You still flying that bloated contraption?"

Banner nodded. "Nothing ever catches her."

Falkenberg put up his hand and brought it down in a waving gesture.

"At ease," the man beside him shouted. The ship came to life as the lines of sailors broke formation and returned to their stations around the ship. They spoke a language Cassidy didn't know, though it sounded close to German.

"Parley," Falkenberg said.

Banner nodded his approval and turned back to his men. "Cassidy. Ned." He motioned them to follow, leaving Brewster and Franz to watch the gang plank to the *Nubigena*.

The captain led them to his cabin beneath the quarter deck. Cassidy couldn't help involuntarily brushing the Mauser's grip with his arm as they passed the gaunt sailors. The second mate pushed the door open.

Falkenberg sat down at the end of his private galley table and regarded them with his yellow stare. He motioned for them to sit. They did, but in a formation so that no one stood behind them, and Cassidy noticed Banner positioned himself in view of both the captain and the door.

"I'd been hoping we'd cross paths," Falkenberg said. He continued glancing between Cassidy and Ned as if daring them to make some kind of move.

Banner sat back in his chair and folded his hands behind his head. "No wine?"

The captain grunted and a sailor brought them each a goblet of foul grog.

Banner eyed the murky liquid. "You used to serve wine."

Falkenberg growled. "You used to have manners." He rapped his pale knuckles on the table and motioned to Cassidy and Franz. "They know?"

Banner shrugged. "Know what, Captain?"

Falkenberg bit his lip. His breathing got heavier. "Your captain used to serve under me."

"First mate," Banner said.

"First mate," the captain added. "Sailed with us for several years before running off to fly in airships."

Banner sighed. He leaned towards Falkenberg and rested his elbows on the table top. "You said parley, Captain. What about?"

The captain contemplated silence for almost half a minute. "A favour."

"We've delivered your letters before, brought you supplies," Banner said with a shrug. "I've never minded doing that."

Falkenberg shook his head. "Bigger favour." He folded his hands and leaned closer so his and Banner's heads were only inches apart. "The boys prefer the air in the *real* world, but I get tired of being trapped on the sea, so I've been dipping into the Twilight more than I used to.

"A few months ago we ventured in farther than before. Our ship was intercepted by some kind of airship, like yours, but more like a big balloon." The captain made shapes in the air as if trying to outline the craft, but gave up. "Anyway, this ship wanted to trade. We had nothing they wanted, and I don't suppose we could have used anything they carried, but we did exchange stories." He glanced over at Cassidy and Ned. "I guess your captain here hasn't told you, but I'm a cursed man."

Cassidy squinted.

"The good captain here lost a few games with the devil," Banner said, cutting in. "He's not the best poker player."

Captain Falkenberg brought his fist down on the table. "It wasn't a game. That demon tricked me into—" He cut himself off. "My men and I are cursed. We'll be sailing about till Judgment Day and there's nothing to break us loose."

Cassidy glanced at Ned and over at Banner to see if they actually believed the story. Their expressions looked neutral. "The captain on the ship," Falkenberg continued, "told me about something called Celestial Pardons." He held up a hand before anyone could speak. "I know you modern folk put little faith in the Almighty, but whatever these scrolls actually are, they can let us die, and we can move up to the Heavenly Realms."

Banner shrugged. "I'm happy to hear it."

"There's one in the Everdream," Falkenberg said.

Banner began to rise. The captain placed a pleading grip on his sleeve. "It's on the edge, Banner. The Armada hardly patrols it. You could get it in a few minutes. There wouldn't be any risk. I'd go there myself, but the ship can't get that far into the Twilight. You fly into the Everdream all the time."

"Only for men," Banner said. "Never for anything else."

"You owe me mercy," Falkenberg said.

Banner shook his head.

"You *owe*."

Banner's face tightened. "I served you."

"For a few years," the captain said, his voice rising to a shout. "My men have sailed endlessly for over two hundred." He grabbed Banner by the shirt and pulled him close.

Before Banner had even reached the captain's face, Cassidy had the muzzle of his pistol at Falkenberg's temple, but Banner waved Cassidy back.

"You owe me," the captain shouted. His teeth showed, full and bright. "Who found you in the sea floating on a wooden plank, about to fade out of existence as the storms moved on? Who pulled you up out of the brack? You would have been the ghost of a memory if it hadn't been for the energies in this ship, *Captain*. You're alive because of me." Falkenberg remembered himself and released his grip. "Just do this one thing."

Banner was visibly shaken. He eyed Cassidy and shifted his gaze to Ned "I'll have to talk to my men. They have a say."

Falkenberg opened his mouth, but closed it again. He gave a heavy sigh and retreated back in his chair.

Cassidy remained standing. He holstered his weapon. Was Banner serious? Ned didn't speak, but kept his steely gaze level on the grey captain.

"We'll talk it over," Banner said and moved towards the door.

The first mate handed Banner an envelope, which Banner stuffed into his jacket. Falkenberg ran a hand through his mane of grey hair. "When can I know?"

Banner stopped. He didn't turn around. "You'll know if I bring you a scroll."

Chapter 10

"Is it really all that dangerous?" Cassidy asked. He and Ned stood around the billiard table in the recreation room. Ned and Cassidy played well, but Brewster's brain lacked the ability tell the red from the white balls, causing nothing but confusion every time the Englishman played. Instead, he sat watching, sipping gingerly at a cup of jasmine tea.

"You can't even imagine," Brewster said. He placed the cup on the saucer balanced on his right knee. "Banner picks us up in random dreams people are having. I've never quite figured out how he knows where to look, but the point is we can only fly in and out without being detected because people in the real world sleep and wake up by the millions. Moment the bubble breaks, they know we're there."

Ned tapped the cue ball. It struck a red one and bounced it off three sides before it came to rest beside the other red ball. No one knew the precise name of this billiard game, but it mattered little because no one could remember how to win either. "But, Falkenberg says it isn't in someone's dream."

Brewster took another sip of tea, his forehead furrowed into deep waves. "That's the problem. It's in a weird little offshoot of the Everdream proper. Imagine the whole thing as a big mass of..." he looked at his cup as if searching the bottom for a good description, "stuff," he finally settled on. "It's a big ball off which people's dreams sort of sprout as they fall asleep. Dreams aren't made of nothing. They blister off the main mass each time a person starts dreaming, and are reabsorbed when they wake." He made a fist and cupped his other hand around it. "So, you've got an outer membrane and then an inner barrier around the Everdream itself. Dream bubbles grow between the two," he said around the pipe somehow still clenched in his teeth. "The peninsula extends into the bubble section and almost touches the outer membrane."

Cassidy cued up and tapped the white ball. It knocked Ned's red ball off two walls and put it in one of the pockets. "That's a good thing, right?"

"Billiards," Ned said, as if that meant he'd won. "Another game?"

Cassidy set the stick aside and picked up his whisky on the rocks. "I mean, this scroll is on the edge where it's not heavily patrolled?"

Brewster snorted. "Breathe on any inch of the Everdream and they'll have ships there faster than you can inhale again. It's like a giant bug landing on your bare skin. That Falkenberg imbecile has no idea what he's talking about."

Cassidy took a seat across from Brewster and stirred the whisky with his finger. "Will the captain really do this?"

Ned shook his head. "That crazy pirate must have something big on him," he said, setting his own stick aside.

"That *crazy pirate* is The Flying Dutchman," Brewster said. He finished off his tea with one final gulp. "Their history goes back further than me. Further than Karl."

"Did he really save Banner's life?" Cassidy asked.

Brewster shrugged. "Bloody hell if I know."

Franz opened the door. The young German looked flushed. He wrung his hands as if trying to wipe something off his skin.

"What is it?" Brewster asked, getting up. His saucer crashed to the floor. Ned and Cassidy stood, too, and gathered around the nervous German.

"He's going to do it. He's all happy and confident about the plan. You know how he gets. Says we can be in and out in a matter of minutes, the Armada be damned."

"You're serious?" Brewster said. His thick moustache flared.

"Ya," said Franz. "But he says he'll put anyone off in the Twilight that doesn't want to come and he'll nab them on the way out. Says we'll stir up the Armada like wasps, and we'll have to stay in the *real* world for a few months, but it can be done."

"Is this Dutchman really worth that kind of risk?" Brewster shouted.

"Says it'll be a hoot, whatever that means," said Franz. "Says, it'll be a good exercise."

Brewster's body went rigid and he sat down. "Man's gone mad," he muttered. "Stark, raving mad."

"So, what's *your* story?" Cassidy asked, trying to break Brewster from his distant reverie. The Englishman sat stirring milk into his tea. Tea he'd been stirring for ten minutes.

The older man sighed, took a long sip and sat down. "Not much to tell, quite frankly." He pulled out a bulldog briar pipe and an English blend of tobacco Franz had grabbed for him on their trip to the Big Apple. "First thing I remember is being shot down in the biggest aerial battle I've ever seen. Fifty fighters, at least; Jerrys, Frenchies, our own boys. Perhaps a Yank or two flying RAF planes."

Cassidy observed how meticulously Brewster packed his pipe; stuffing the bottom of the bowl loose and increasing the tamp as he made his way to the rim. "I mostly remember the nose dive," the Englishman continued, "and trying to push away from the Sop before I went for the silk." Brewster lit the bowl with a match, moving the flame in a circle to make the tobacco burn evenly. "I floated down as guns tore the sky to ribbons and smoking fighters made their way to the grave."

Brewster gave the pipe small quick puffs until the tobacco glowed red. He wasn't looking at Cassidy anymore. Wasn't talking *to* him, but staring instead at a spot somewhere beyond. "It's strange. That's still the most vivid thing I remember. Remember it better than I recall yesterday, but it took me months to pick it out of my head." He paused, then woke from his reverie again and coughed out a thin cloud of smoke. "Anyway, I landed safe enough. No one else had, and war was still raging up in the sky. And this ship came out of nowhere. Broke out of the clouds and picked me up. I'm sure it's a lot like your story," he said, and clicked the stem against his teeth.

"How about your dreamer?" Cassidy asked, interweaved his fingers and leaned forward. "Do you think you'll ever meet him?"

Brewster shook his head. "Never met anyone who's met their dreamer. The dream just fades and poof, that's it. You're in or out."

Cassidy leaned back. He had hoped his friend would remember things better. "I still don't understand how Banner finds us."

The Englishman laughed. "Queue up at the ever growing club, Old Boy. From what I understand, it took a lot of trial and error. He's better at finding those of us that are *well-formed*, so to speak. See, it all depends on how vivid we are in the dreamer's mind. Some poor boys he picked up were no better than walking lumps of clay. They barely held themselves together long enough to get out of their own dream, and then melted to puddles of grey on the deck." Brewster shook his head. "Saw one once. Lived only few hours. Not a pretty sight. Bled into the deck and faded away. Seems once you lose your mind...or consciousness perhaps, you're a goner."

"I'm worried about this mission," Cassidy said, trying to nudge Brewster out of memories that obviously pained him.

The Englishman fidgeted with his pipe. Took a puff or two. "This Dutchman fellow's not the sort Banner would usually take up with."

Cassidy shrugged. "Says he saved his life."

"That's what worries me. I never knew anyone to save the captain's life. He's not the kind to owe a man something."

"I take it he's never told you how he got his start?"

"Not really," Brewster said. "We've all heard how a god of a man dreamed him, and dreamed him so strong that Captain Banner sailed out of the dream and into the Twilight on a galleon he wrestled from a fellow dream. That's why everyone stays no matter how crazy he gets. They believe in him." He shrugged. "Me too, I guess."

Cassidy tried to read Brewster's expression, but couldn't penetrate the indecipherable British facade. "Do you actually believe all that? I mean, the god of a man dreaming him and all?"

Brewster gestured with his pipe. "Who knows? Captain doesn't tell the story himself, you see. Others tell it. He's always mum about his past."

Cassidy tried to imagine what Banner had looked like back then. How long ago that must have been. A hundred years? Two hundred? "I want to meet my dreamer," he said. A lump swelled in Cassidy's throat as he said it. Didn't know why he said it, but the words just slipped out. "I need to know who made me."

Brewster gave a knowing nod, but looked sad as the tobacco went out in his pipe. "Don't know if that's for us to know, Old Boy."

They were silent as they stared out at the ever twilight sky.

Banner's eyes twinkled as he surveyed his crew across the map table in the battle room, which was really the galley covered in what looked like half-finished maps. "I've been over it a thousand times in the last few days," he said, "and it *can* be done. Done without losing a man." He cracked a long wooden pointer down against the centre map, a cloudy mass which Cassidy took to be the Everdream.

The crew exchanged glances as Banner smiled.

"Cassidy's our man!" Banner said.

Cassidy's attention snapped back to the captain.

"Don't look so frightened, Major," Banner said, pointing the wooden stick at Cassidy's chest. Calling him by rank only occurred when the captain was trying to be military-like. "You're the best damned pilot I've ever seen, and this'll be a walk in the park for you." He circled an area on the map that looked like an outcropping of black clouds.

"According to Falkenberg's notes, the Scroll's in a church right here on the border," Banner continued. "Apparently, it's an old church on an island that drifted out of the bulb and into the main territory of the Everdream before the dreamer woke, and it's been permanent there ever since. Armada's got no use for it, so they leave it empty. Nothing else around for miles."

"They'll still know the moment we cross the border," said Franz, glancing over at Cassidy with obvious concern. "He'll be caught in an instant."

Banner grinned. His smiled widened as if this was the question he'd been waiting to address. "If we flew the *Nubigena* in, yes. But that's not our plan. See, what they actually detect so damned fast isn't dreams. Hell, they're dreams themselves, right? It's the *real* stuff that tweaks their antennae. This ship lights up like a Roman candle, especially with the engines turning."

He pointed to the black blob where the church was supposed to be located. "See how it sticks out. Now, what we're going to do is fly past it without touching the outer border." He moved a Zeppelin model into position just short of the target point.

"When we get just about here, we let that Fokker go and slingshot it into the Everdream."

The crew blanched in unison. "Why in God's name would we do that?" asked Brewster.

Banner's fingers cracked as he gave them a sharp snap. "Glad you asked." He pulled out a tiny model of Cassidy's Fokker and positioned it beneath the *Nubigena*. "Karl's outfitted it with an extra seat, just big enough for one passenger. You'll be cramped, Ned."

Ned paled. He gripped the table to steady himself.

"Cassidy may need help, and you're the lightest," Banner said, without breaking speed. "Anyway, we slingshot you two without your engines on."

"Impossible," Brewster said. Ned looked like he was going to throw up.

Banner pretended not to notice. "Karl's got those magnetos working like liquid lightning. Says it'll start in a downpour. No armstronging involved." He aimed the pointer at Cassidy. "Major, you'll coast as far as the momentum will carry you. There's little wind resistance in the Everdream and the gravity isn't as severe, but that also means less lift for the wings. Start the prop at the last second. Fly it in. Grab the Scroll and get back in the air. We'll pick you up on the other side." He snapped the pointer on the map again and left it there. "We'll be at full speed by the time they rally their ships and we'll gate into the real world. Hell," he said, clapping Cassidy on the back as he made his way around the room, "it'll be good practice for us all. Keep us sharp."

He's serious, Cassidy thought. Banner's actually serious.

Ned threw up.

Chapter 11

Cassidy ran his hand over the fuselage of the Fokker. It had been moved into the rear bay to make the necessary modifications for the mission. Karl's work was impressive. If Cassidy hadn't known better, he'd never have guessed the craft hadn't been built with an extended tail and small passenger seat right out of the factory. The plane looked new. The paint gleamed and Karl had written *Valkyrie* down both sides in electric blue.

Cassidy climbed in and tested the resistance of the stick and pedals. Turned to watch the rudder and elevator flap move as he imagined pitching and rolling.

"It will swoop like eagle," Karl said. His voice came from the fighter's starboard side. Cassidy looked up to see the engineer watching from the shadow of his tool shed.

"Can't believe it's the same plane," Cassidy said, running his hand over the Spandau guns.

"Is not the same plane," Karl said. "Is only yours now. Valkyrie. In our mythology, they are war goddesses who bear fallen warriors to Valhalla."

"Not sure that's a good thing, but it's beautiful," Cassidy said as he climbed down from the cockpit.

Banner approached from the stairwell. "Ready to be the first dream in and out of the Armada stronghold?"

Cassidy tried to grin. "No, I'm not, but I guess I'm earning my keep."

Banner blinked. After an awkward pause, he grinned and shook Cassidy by the arm. "Best damn flying I've ever seen. Knew you would be."

"How?" Cassidy asked.

"What?" Banner's smile faded a hair.

"How did you know who I was and where to come for me?" Cassidy met Banner's steel grey eyes. "And why don't I just go back. The Everdream wants me. It's always wanted me."

Banner's smile vanished.

"It was home," Cassidy continued before he lost his nerve. "I'm not complaining, Captain, but I didn't exactly ask to be rescued."

The skin around Banner's eyes turned red, along with his cheeks. "I gave you a life, Airman."

"Then who's my dreamer? I know you know, and I think I deserve something for this."

Banner put his hands on his hips and took a deep breath. "Make it back with that Scroll and we'll talk. Believe me though, you'll wish I'd never told you."

Fifteen minutes later, Cassidy sat in his cockpit, waiting. It seemed like an hour since they attached *Valkyrie* to the *Nubigena's* belly and headed for the Everdream. Cassidy's heart quickened as a black dot came into view in the distance. The Fokker trembled as the Everdream came closer. He tried not to show fear, if for no other reason than because Ned's face was turning green in the rear seat. Cassidy hoped the young man wouldn't throw up again. If he did, hopefully it would be over the side. The fighter jolted as Ned adjusted himself in the seat. "You okay back there?" Cassidy asked.

Ned slapped Cassidy's shoulder and gripped hard.

Cassidy patted the quivering fingers. "It's gonna be alright, kiddo," he said, keeping a tremor from his voice. He'd either get answers for doing this or a one way trip back to the Everdream. Banner wasn't as sure about this as he pretended. That winning grin and overconfident attitude might work with the rest of the men, but Cassidy saw deeper. Knew the man was regretting his debt to the damned pirate. How many others would live to regret that debt remained to be seen, but he supposed that was the price of being crew under a man like Banner.

"In and out," the captain shouted from above. "We'll pick you boys up in twenty minutes." The wide smile flashing down at them, and Karl's trademark frown, were the last things Cassidy saw as the hatch closed.

The *Nubigena* accelerated through the mists. Long thin strands of solid fog twisted past and around the ship. It was beautiful, Cassidy thought, but was it part of the Twilight, or gasses given off by their destination?

"You hanging in there?" Cassidy asked as he glanced at Ned over his shoulder again. The young pilot had already donned his flight-cap and brought the huge goggles down over his eyes.

"How do we know when to let go?" Ned asked through chattering teeth.

"He said I'd know," Cassidy hollered, trying to overcome the scream of the wind. The ship accelerated. Five engines hummed. The Jerry-rigged plane propeller buzzed as it tried to keep up with the others. A dark cloud morphed out of the streaming mist and grew fast.

"Is that it?" Ned shouted. His voice sounded far off as rushing air tore most of the volume away.

Cassidy didn't have to answer. It was the Everdream if anything was. The mass of black contrasted with the Twilight as complete darkness, sucking in light so that a stringy haze surrounded the inner darkness. This had been the great purple shape he'd seen filtered through the atmosphere of the dream he'd first escaped. This was the tugging presence that wanted him back. Wanted them all back. Would it speak to him again?

The *Nubigena* headed for the mass as if on its way to puncture a lesion in the Twilight sky. Cassidy put his hand on the release. Ned squirmed in his seat. The Zeppelin accelerated until it almost tipped the outer layer, then banked hard in the kind of impossible manoeuvre only Banner was capable of coaxing from his ship.

Cassidy's stomach lurched as the belly of the *Nubigena* grazed the black nimbus surrounding the outer membrane. Banner said Cassidy would know. He did. He felt the apex of the climb. The very point where the momentum reached its perfect arc. A gentle tug and the plane fell away, his stomach still back on the ship.

Valkyrie glided towards the cloud. The wind stopped when they touched the outer rim. Sight and sound dampened as the fighter slipped through the membrane with an audible pop which sealed behind them. Below, an island rose up to meet them. Not really a peninsula, per se. Instead, it seemed cut off from the rest of the mass, though thin lines of shadow connected them. Bridges or tethers, he couldn't be sure.

Without the momentum gained from the airship the *Valkyrie* would have plunged into an instant dive, but Cassidy glided the fighter in the direction of the only structure in sight. It rose from the landscape like an arch growing from shadows. Not just a church. A cathedral, Cassidy thought.

Ned screamed. They were losing altitude fast as the gentle gravity of the Everdream increased. Cassidy wound the magneto hard and hit the switch. The props spun. The engine roared to life. He pulled back on the stick and levelled the fighter just in time to skim the bumpy ground. It landed hard but the landing gear absorbed the shock without shattering and he rolled the *Valkyrie* to a stop twenty feet from the cathedral door.

Cassidy cut the engine and leapt to the ground.

"Let's hope like hell *that* didn't alert them," Ned said with a tremble in his voice as he landed with a harsh thump beside Cassidy.

"Let's just assume it did," Cassidy said, sprinting for the edifice.

Ned agreed with a nervous nod, his heavy boots thudding the ground at top speed. "We're going to die, aren't we?"

A few fast strides took them to the mammoth entrance. The huge doors opened to a dusty sanctuary. Thin light streamed through the dull stained glass as they made their way down the main aisle to the altar. "I thought this was supposed to be empty," Cassidy whispered as they passed the silent pews. "Why are people here?"

A few parishioners sat scattered through the otherwise empty pews. A group of nuns prayed near the altar. A priest stood silent in the shadows. "Perhaps they were left over from the dream. Got stuck with the church," Ned said as they reached the altar where the Scroll had been said to lay in a box in plain sight.

Cassidy grabbed the young pilot's shoulder and drew him back. "Why wouldn't they carry dreams off that drifted into their borders? Or absorb them? A church I can understand. Perhaps it got stuck because it was a structure, but why leave the people?"

Ned flicked his eyes around the room. "I don't know. Perhaps some dream people don't have much consciousness," he said, opening the box and plunging his hand in, "but let's just get this and fly." He withdrew a rolled up piece of shining paper.

"Leave it," Cassidy said, glancing from one kneeling penitent to the other.

Ned paused. Looked from Cassidy back to the box and shoved the Scroll into his jacket. Everyone in the cathedral looked up at the same moment.

"Run," Cassidy yelled and bolted for the front door. He reached the far edge of the pews, but Ned screamed behind him. Cassidy turned to see two nuns tackle the young airman, each holding a leg as Ned fought to crawl away. Both nun's eyes glowed a harsh hue of red.

Cassidy drew his Mauser and fired off four rounds. The Everdream atmosphere dampened the sound, but the sharp cracks still resonated like thunder in the enclosed space.

The first two shots took one nun in the face, jerking her back. The second two rounds vanished into the other nun's habit. She froze for a moment, then fell to the side.

Ned was on his feet and running before the second nun's head struck the pew beside him. Cassidy dropped to one knee and spent no more than one shell on each as the others dove for their prey. Nuns and parishioners crumpled as bullets split open their skulls and tore through their chests, exposing colourless facsimiles of *real* organs. The bullets were doing far more damage than they should, as if the people were made of soft fruit. Did his own insides look like that?

Ned rushed by in a mad dash and slammed the door open. Cassidy finished off the Mauser's payload and ran. He leapt and was in the cockpit, pumping up the tank and revving the magnetos before the first Armada agent, a priest this time, cleared the doorway and started towards them.

Ned fired off all six shots from his revolver. The bullets tore gaping holes in stony ground, but missed the priest by several feet. The magneto fired. The props spun as the engine turned over and Cassidy throttled forwards. Karl's modifications had certainly changed the way the Fokker flew. The extra length made the action on the stick sluggish, slowing the pitch. He wouldn't be able to manoeuvre as fast, but he would compensate by...by doing everything quicker.

"He set us up. That old bastard set us up," Ned shouted as the fighter caught air and began its ascent. "Can we get back to the ship before the Armada brings in the cavalry?"

"Before?" Cassidy shouted back. "They'll already be there." As they broke through the clouds, the *Nubigena* floated motionless, surrounded on all sides by hundreds of airships. It hadn't even reached the rendezvous point, probably stopped minutes after he and Ned entered the Everdream.

Cassidy cut the throttle, rolled to the side and pitched until they'd turned a full 180. He levelled out and gunned the engine again. "Dump that Scroll."

"Why?" Ned asked as they slipped over the far edge of the cloud of Everdream. "It's still got to be worth something."

"It's probably made of some sort of dreamstuff they can track. Why else wait until you picked it up."

"How do you know," Ned asked. His voice came out high and panicked.

Cassidy growled. "Because they're not following us," he shouted glancing over his shoulder at the empty space between them and the shrinking *Nubigena*. "Probably think we'll lead them to anyone we might have dropped off. Now dump the damned thing."

Ned tore the Scroll from his jacket and let it blow away. "We don't have a chance now."

"Just tell me where we can go."

Ned was silent for a minute. "I don't know this area."

Cassidy aimed the *Valkyrie* at the farthest point from the nebulous Everdream and throttled down to conserve fuel. The mists thinned and the Twilight returned to its usual clear skies of purple clouds and dim light. Floating islands pocketed the empty space and Cassidy looked for one that might provide rest and fuel.

"I could sure use the hotel on Arcadia right about now," Ned said. His speech had returned to its normal pitch, but Cassidy still heard a tinge of panic in his voice.

"I'm shooting for something more low-key," Cassidy said as he steered towards a medium-sized island with only a few buildings. "We'll have to hide this plane."

Ned groaned. "Just make sure we find a shower and someone who does laundry."

"Why?" asked Cassidy.

"I think I wet myself coming out of that church."

Cassidy nodded. The tiny island grew as he neared. He tilted his fighter towards a good landing spot when two bi-plane fighters banked from behind the far edge, their wingtips marked purple and blue.

Chapter 12

The fighters looked like the Armada Albatrosses he'd fought after his rescue. There was no time to manoeuvre away. He would have to take them out of the sky before they could report him, assuming the Everdream didn't already know.

Cassidy checked his guns and moved to engage. Another Albatross breached the mountain's peak, followed by a tri-wing Fokker. The Fokker rolled, burst between the other two and curved, cutting one off from firing.

Cassidy throttled back. He knew that Fokker. It was burned into his broken dream memory the same way it was probably burned into every pilot on both sides in the Great War. The entire fighter was painted a shiny blood red with white trim and a black iron cross on each wing. Heat rose in his chest as the Fokker banked and dove, slipping between the other fighters again and again as it manoeuvred for a good shot. The goddamned Baron. He forced his thoughts through the anger. Is the enemy of my enemy my friend today? The same unnamed hatred for the German pilot flared like a flame across spilled gasoline. But, if the Armada ships downed Richthofen, they'd be on him and Ned in seconds.

"Oh, for God's sake, just help him," Ned hollered from the rear seat. "They'll kill us."

Cassidy seethed. He sped up and locked onto the closest Albatross. The fighter turned to make another go at the red Fokker. No time to play fair. Cassidy nosed down and opened fire, catching one Albatross's tail rudder with a shower of rounds. It rolled out of control and fell out of the fight.

The Baron's tactics were amazing, Cassidy marvelled in spite of himself. Not quite the pilot he might have expected though. Instead, the German made no overly intricate manoeuvres to outwit his opponents. Nothing spectacular or fancy. He stuck to smooth calculated moves that put him into position for firing where he couldn't be hit. The Baron's Spandaus let loose and a second Albatross fell into a nose dive.

Despite the flawless execution of Richthofen's flying, the Baron looked hesitant. Seemed to be taking several extra seconds to shoot. Cassidy throttled back, dove and fired on the third Albatross. The red fighter let loose both Spandaus again and their combined guns shredded it to bits of metal and canvas.

Cassidy trained his guns on the Baron. The tri-wing flew in a slow steady arc and made for the island. The Spandau levers felt cold as the red Fokker crossed Cassidy's sights and continued past down to the flat surface.

Cassidy put down and pulled his older modified Fokker up beside the newer tri-wing. He watched the German climb down. Richthofen looked older. Slower. Cassidy hopped to the ground. "Come on," he said to Ned and slapped the fuselage with his gloved hand. The younger pilot pried himself from the back seat. His head had been down, his entire body packed into the seat. He'd probably spent most of the battle with his nose between his knees.

"Cassidy," the Baron said. He'd already removed his leather gauntlet and extended his pale fingers.

"Baron," Cassidy said in a cool tone. He didn't extend his hand.

"Manfred, please," the German said, withdrawing the handshake. "There are no Barons in Germany."

"What happened to your head?" Cassidy asked.

Richthofen touched the white bandage that wrapped around his crown and extended below the flight cap. "I was wounded a few days ago. Is nothing." The German brought a fist to his chest. "You and I fought as one. Let me buy you both a drink."

"I'll buy myself a drink," Cassidy said, pushing past.

Richthofen shrugged.

The two buildings on the small island turned out to be a very small hotel and a pub. Cassidy and Ned headed for a drink with the Baron close on their heels. The pub looked like it had come straight out of New England, but like everything else in the Twilight, it was a patchwork of various decades crossed with truly foreign accents. Oil lamps stood beside arc lamps. The doors and windows opened automatically with exposed gears and pistons that made the decor both futuristic and archaic at the same time. Cassidy pulled up to the green coppered counter and ordered whisky on the rocks. Ned took a golden lager.

Richthofen sat on a stool beside Cassidy and ordered dark cognac. He still moved slower and seemed more distant than Cassidy remembered. "So," the Baron said after a long sip, "how is the captain enjoying his new pilot?"

Cassidy held his temper. He sipped the cold whisky and looked at himself in the bar mirror noting how different *he* looked from the last time he'd stared at his visage. Not his image, per se, but the way he saw himself. The world wasn't new and unknown anymore. This time he and Richthofen looked like comrades in arms after a great battle. Cassidy glanced away. "Banner's gone," he said, snarling. "They're all gone."

Richthofen narrowed his eyes. "They've left the Twilight?"

Cassidy bit back several colourful adjectives and downed the rest of his drink. "Another," he said as the barkeep took his glass. "Falkenberg--. They're in the Everdream. Maybe dead. I don't know."

The German set down his cognac. "They've got the Zeppelin? The *Nubigena?*" He leaned back and ran a hand over his bandages.

Cassidy started his second drink. "Why do I always drink whisky on the rocks?" Cassidy mumbled. "I mean, I think of ordering something else, but the words always come out the same."

"I thought it's what all Americans drink," Richthofen said. He leaned forward onto the bar.

Cassidy watched himself and the German in the mirror together. Both staring at themselves. "So who finally shot the Red Baron?"

Richthofen shrugged again. "British, French, one of you Yanks? I don't know."

"You're not flying right," Cassidy snapped. He hadn't meant for it to come out as hateful as it did.

The German took a deep breath and closed his eyes. "I know," he said. "I won't ever fly the way I used to. But I can still drink."

Cassidy downed another whisky, and then another. Ned sucked down lagers faster than the barkeep could pour. Six empty glasses sat before the Baron, who had to have been knocking them back while no one was looking.

"What will you do?" Richthofen asked after a long pause. His speech slurred, accent stronger. "Vhat vill you do 'bout Banner."

Cassidy laughed. "I don't know. I have no damn idea what to do."

The Baron clapped him on the back. "Don't worry, American. I have an idea or two."

Cassidy remembered very little of the rest of the evening. He knew he drank a lot. Knew Ned passed out first. He knew that he and Richthofen told off-colour jokes and, or perhaps not, had gotten into a fight with some of the Twilight locals.

One way or the other, it was morning. Cassidy lay in a hotel room, head pounding like a Prussian regiment had decided to perform their marching drills in the middle of his skull.

Ned stirred on the floor. Richthofen hung over a chair, head back, snoring like a wounded animal. Cassidy was somewhat sprawled across the bed, but only the top half of his body actually lay on the bed proper. Seeing the German's face still made him want to spit, but despite himself, he needed the pilot. Something about a plan Richthofen had come up with the night before.

When everyone regained consciousness and their heads cleared enough to fly, Richthofen paid for their stay and they dragged themselves to their planes. The fighters had already been refuelled. Cassidy checked the guns to make sure the belts still held enough shells for a surprise dogfight. "How far are we going?" Cassidy asked as he climbed into the cockpit. He vaguely remembered the German saying they could get help somewhere and Cassidy's head throbbed too much to let him argue about it. Ned thudded into the rear seat, groaning as he slumped over.

"Not far," Richthofen said, revving his own magnetos. His voice sounded pained, the hangover probably aggravating his head wound. The props spun and the engine hummed. "You can fly behind me in case I betray you."

Cassidy growled under his breath. He'd been thinking the same thing.

Chapter 13

Richthofen guided them to a small island that looked like an industrial wasteland set in the middle of a lush rainforest. Cassidy set his fighter down near a canopy of thick foliage. He and Ned covered the Fokker with vines and leafy branches and helped Richthofen do the same. The bold red of the Baron's Fokker required them to double the thickness.

Cassidy dug around in his cockpit. He wished he'd thought to pick up more supplies at the hotel since Karl had only loaded the craft with provisions for a short sortie. First aid kit. Rations for two days. A flashlight. Enough bullets to reload his Mauser, plus the strip his holster carried. And .45 shells for Ned's revolver. The Baron carried nothing but his sidearm.

Cassidy shook his head. "This isn't much," he said, stuffing everything into a mailbag and throwing the strap over his shoulder. "I hope someone here has food."

"They'll have provisions," Richthofen said, leading them into the thick jungle.

It made an imposing obstacle. Their service knives did little good against the tree-thick vines and masses of bramble. Large gelatinous insects crawled between the trunks and roots. Snakes with wings like coloured rice paper made their way from treetop to treetop. They lit on the large membranous fruits that grew there like plump sacks of purple liquid. Perhaps the serpents were pollinating them. Like bees?

Ned kept his sidearm in hand, pointing it at loud noises, including a flock of green cranes. Cassidy worried a shot might wake up the entire jungle, but holding it seemed to make Ned feel better. "How far to whoever we're meeting?" Ned asked as the leafy canopy far overhead filtered out more and more light.

Richthofen said nothing but pushed deeper into the foliage.

"Can't be too far," Cassidy said to Ned as the young pilot stepped over a rotting tree trunk. "When we landed, I judged us at about a mile from whatever that complex is."

Ned kicked at the next rotting log. It shattered into a colourful myriad of various species. A blob of fibrillating pudding, which had been lying dormant at its centre, lashed out at Ned's boots with tendrils that looked like kelp. Ned leapt back and stumbled over a jutting root. Cassidy reached back and caught him in a firm grip. "Watch those surprises," he said. "Rather not lose you before we even get there."

Ned gave a weak grin. "I don't know what to do now," he said. "I've never been anywhere but the ship."

The Baron continued up ahead, pressing on as if following an invisible path apparently only he could see.

Cassidy nodded. "We'll find the ship again."

Ned stopped. His lips trembled. "Cassidy…I don't think I can. I mean, I can't go back to that place. We won't have a chance."

Cassidy grimaced. He turned to the young pilot and locked eyes. "I don't know how we're going to do it, but we owe the boys this."

"Why?" Ned snapped. "The captain sent us out on a suicide mission."

"That's a point," Cassidy said. "But we can't let everyone down just because he made a bad decision."

"But we'll die."

"No," Cassidy said, shaking his head. "Worst case scenario, we go home."

"That's not my home."

"Then what is?" Cassidy asked. "The ship? If the *Nubigena* is your home, then you're saving it, so let's do this."

"Don't stop," Richthofen said from up ahead without turning around. "The creatures here are dangerous."

Ned glanced at the ground where hundreds of the colourful insects had gathered around his boots.

"Just go," Cassidy said, pushing Ned along. The young man remained silent as they made their way through the jungle until they reached the rusty pipes and spires of what Cassidy could only classify as a wreck. The city, or complex, appeared to stretch for half a mile or so. What he had taken for an industrial structure looked more like what might happen if a cluster of factories threw out all their junk and it happened to collect into the general shape of buildings. Hundreds of feet of rusty piping snaked up, down and around the giant metal drums and boxes that made up the bulk of the structure.

Smokestacks and steam pipes dotted what he could see of the roof. "People must still be living here," Ned said, indicating the occasional bursts from the pipes.

The Baron led them around the wall of metal refuse until he found an opening between two of the metal boxes which formed a narrow alleyway. Cassidy entered the tight squeeze with Ned close in tow. Light vanished until the alleyway opened into a small courtyard.

Several people started as they entered the enclosure. Two men and a child drew back. They were dressed in leather boots, knickers and green waistcoats. The two men wore battered metal goggles on their head, and their long dirty lab coats hung down to the tops of their boots. The young boy wore brown knickers, a vest, tan shirt and flattop hat, brim backwards.

Cassidy motioned for Ned to put the weapon away. "You know these people?" Cassidy asked Richthofen as he looked from one man to the other. They looked similar but one appeared much older than the other. Their ears were slightly pointed and their skin held the soft glow he'd come to know as clear signs of Twilight people. Neither man moved.

The German shrugged. "I know *of* these people. I visited this island once, a long time ago."

Cassidy decided on a slight gamble. "We're crew of the Zeppelin *Nubigena*. We're Banner's men."

The two men looked at each other. The younger one spoke. "That giant airship from the real world?" he asked, taking several steps forwards.

"Yes," said Cassidy. "We're not Armada, if that's what you're worried about."

"It's always a fear," the man said, looking them over as if trying to find some tell-tale characteristics in their faces. "Them don't have much business with us, but they do come through from time to time looking for dreams."

Cassidy nodded. "Tell me about it. This is Ned," he said, motioning. "And this," he said, pointing to the Baron, "is—"

"Manfred Albrecht Freiherr von Richthofen," the Baron said. "I'm from what you refer to as *the real world*."

Their scowls shifted into sudden smiles. "Name's Tuck," the younger man said. "That's Birch, my father, and Ress, my son."

Cassidy tipped his officers' cap. "This *man*," he said, indicating Richthofen, "said you people might know something about the Everdream." He was going to say friend, but held back.

"We know a thing or two," Birch said. He stepped closer. "Probably more than most. I seen that ship of yours once in port. Never got to see a *real* aerocraft before. No one in the Twilight ever seen the likes of that Zeppelin. Banner and his men. You boys are a legend."

Cassidy grimaced. "Hopefully not."

The inside looked much like the outside, except that the people there had developed some fascinating technology he'd only seen glimpses of elsewhere. The walls crawled with cogs and wheels that took up much of the space, all rotating with each other like a giant clock organism moving down the corridors.

"We study the Armada," Tuck explained as he led them to their rooms. "See, none of us ever fully understood what they are. We don't understand much about the Everdream either, for all that matters, but we've been working on it for thirty years."

Cassidy stopped as one of the Twilight women walked around the corner. Her round face and green eyes glowed in perfect sync with her elven features. She wore an emerald evening gown and her hair cascaded over the sides of her head in a fountain of curls and braids. Her beauty unnerved him. Something about the curve of her lips looked both inviting and feral. "You're the dreams," she said, as if he and Ned might be some cute animals brought from out of the jungle. Her friend, a slightly shorter version of her, gave a small curtsy.

Cassidy and Ned tipped their caps. Richthofen gave a ceremonious bow. "Fräulein," he said.

The two women walked on, glancing over their shoulders. Ned gulped.

"Yes, we were a scientific observatory," Tuck continued, as if he hadn't noticed the women. "I mean we still are, but we sort of decided to stay after the official project was over. We've done a lot of research." The three pilots continued staring after the two women for several seconds before catching up to Tuck, who rattled on without a break. "My father has been here since the beginning. I joined later. It's an intriguing study, to say the least."

Cassidy gave him a half-smile as they entered their new rooms. "That'll all come in handy, I'm sure."

Tuck stepped forwards to follow them in the room. Cassidy reached out to shake his hand. "It's been a pleasure, but we're very tired."

"Of course," Tuck said with a weak smile. "Perhaps in the morning."

"I need a bath," said Ned as the door shut. "And a stiff drink."

Richthofen seconded the call for a drink, but opted to go to his own adjoining room first and make himself more comfortable.

Ned started into the lavatory, but turned back. "Do you think they have any...you know...*other* kinds of women here?"

"You mean prostitutes?" Cassidy asked prying the boots off his swollen feet. "You ask, and I'll kill you."

Ned grinned. "It's just been a while, okay?"

The lavatory door closed and Cassidy lay back on his small bed. It made him think of the luxuriant hotel in Arcadia. The memory of silk dangling from the ceiling and Shea across his bed felt like it had been years ago. Shea. All legs, beautiful curves, soft skin…and her eyes. Cassidy put his arm over his face and pictured her just as she'd been that night. Naked. Comely. Crawling with vines painted into her skin. Spread out for no other reason than to please him for an hour. Why hadn't he touched her?

Cassidy stood up and tried to shake the images out of his head. The ghost of something still nagged at the edge of his mind. Had he ever loved anyone before, or just wanted to? If he'd only been born minutes before Banner found him, why did he feel so old? There was a lifetime hiding somewhere. One he'd lived, but was now blocked up in the recesses of his head. That or he was a baby born walking.

He peeked through the doorway to the German's room to see if he was already asleep. Instead, he found Richthofen sitting at a small table changing the cloth wrapping on his head. "I'm sorry," Cassidy said, turning away.

"You've seen worse," the German said.

"I suppose," Cassidy said, stepping through the door. "But not since my dream."

Richthofen tried to nod, but winced as he did so. "How much do you remember?"

"Not much," Cassidy said. "Bits and pieces." The cloth wrapping lay on the table now, exposing a deep gash and dried blood. "Why do you want to help Banner?" he asked with more anger again than he really felt.

The German shrugged. "Banner is a friend. And besides," he said, pulling a clean strip of cloth from his mailbag, "there is little left for me back home."

Cassidy couldn't resist a small scoff. "Why? You're the biggest killer the Germans have. You must be a hero to them."

Richthofen put the cloth down on the table and dabbed at his head with a wet towel. "Heroes are only good when they are being heroic, or when they are dead. I am neither right now."

Cassidy leaned against the wall and folded his arms. "What, you haven't killed anyone lately?"

"It's a war, Mr. Cassidy. I don't want it any more than anyone else." He gestured in the air as if regarding something far off. "Someone made someone angry. So they assassinate Ferdinand and now everyone is having us kill each other. We fight for whatever country we happen to be born in. I fly. I shoot down fighters. I am a hero. But I will never fly like that again," he said, motioning to the wound on his head. "I am slow now. I will eventually be shot down." He looked at the floor, took in a great breath of air and let it out in a deep sigh. "I want to be shot down. I'm tired."

"Don't they notice you're gone when you come here?" Cassidy asked.

"Not really," Richthofen said, shrugging.

"Don't you tell them about it?"

Richthofen snorted. "Would you? They'd say my wound has made me mad. I'd rather die now than face that."

The German's eyes made Cassidy uncomfortable. They pleaded, as if he wanted Cassidy to pull the trigger. "I don't know if they'd give you a medal for dying in the Everdream," Cassidy said.

Richthofen gingerly wrapped the clean cloth around his head and fastened it with a clip. "How many Iron Crosses do you think it would take to drown me?"

Cassidy scowled, turned on his heel and returned to his room. He still couldn't place why he felt so much anger for a man who had killed pilots from a country he hardly recognized. The rage felt like more than it should be. He wasn't a citizen of anywhere.

The bed looked good. Fresh. Clean. He lay down and wondered if he'd dream.

A knock sounded at the door. Cassidy groaned and pulled himself off the bed. It was Tuck. "Sorry to bother you," the Twilight said, smoothing the sides down on his handlebar moustache. "I know you're resting, but—" He broke off as if uncertain how to finish the sentence.

"It's okay," Cassidy said. "What's happening?"

"Just curious," Tuck said, averting his gaze. "I mean, I have lot of questions to ask."

Cassidy nodded. "Show me this *observatory* you told me about, and I'll tell you all I can."

Tuck smiled. Cassidy decided Ned would be all right for a while, so he started down the hallway with his new host. "You fly with Banner in the big ship?" Tuck asked. "They say he travels to the *real* world. And that other pilot with you. He is *from* the real world? And you, you are a living dream. We meet your kind occasionally, but they never elude the Armada for long."

Cassidy gave a slight laugh. It was strange to have someone from the Twilight consider *him* interesting. He gave Tuck a brief rundown on his experiences since his rescue.

"That's not surprising," said Tuck. "You must be a strongly recurring dream. Whoever dreamed you, dreamed about you a lot."

"That's comforting," Cassidy grimaced. "If only I knew who it was."

"Real world's probably a big place," the young Twilight said. "And the Everdream…" He trailed off as he turned towards a gear-covered wall and pulled a lever. Steam hissed from the edges of a door that slowly appeared as bolts and screws receded. It opened like a hatch, spilling a thin layer of white mist over the corridor tiles. "The Observatory," Tuck announced as the mist cleared.

Cassidy had imagined some sort of large telescope, but, instead, found a brass wheel three times his height floating in the middle of a vast room. Every inch of the observatory lay covered in instruments, lights and various shapes of coloured glass that throbbed with light.

The brass wheel turned in the air and electric arcs crackled across the smooth surface within. "We can see the Everdream from here," he said as he twisted knobs on one of the many consoles in the room.

Pictures flashed across the surface. One to the next, arbitrary and maddening. Creatures. People. Landscapes that defied physics or even his ability to remember them. "Can we see Banner? Can we see the crew?" Cassidy asked.

"It's random," Tuck said, shaking his head. "We've never been able to make any sense of the Everdream. The geography changes moment to moment as people sleep and wake, and we rarely see past the dream bubbles. Of course," he added, cocking his head to the side. "If we did see the interior, we wouldn't recognize it because we don't know what it looks like."

Cassidy chewed his lip. "What do you know then?"

Tuck continued fiddling with the controls. "Reams of information." He pointed at stacks of parchment piled in a corner. They appeared to be a continuous sheet of thick accordion paper, covered in tiny holes instead of letters. Cassidy didn't pretend to understand the technology. "It's mostly technical data, but ask me anything and I'll tell you all I can."

Cassidy rubbed his chin. "Is there any way to get in without them showing up a moment later?"

Tuck gave a flippant gesture. "Of course. Just don't go in flying anything from the *real* world. You light up like a candle at night. Use a Twilight ship, perhaps." He narrowed his eyes and looked worried. "Something else you might want to think about. When *real* people sleep, part of their minds shift over to the Everdream and shape their dreams out of the material already there. That's why it forms the bubbles. We still haven't figured exactly how the process works. But, if an actual dreamer, a person from the real world stepped in, it would probably alert them like a match in a powder keg."

Something cold and hot at the same time rolled over in Cassidy's stomach. He hadn't wanted the Baron along in the first place, but at the thought of *not* having him along, he realized how much he'd come to depend on the German's presence in his planning. Ned wasn't going to be much use. Cassidy felt alone staring at the great circle where images of the Everdream's vast bulbs pulsed and changed. "Do you even know why the Armada makes dreams for people?"

Tuck looked perplexed. "The Armada? No, you misunderstand, Mr. Cassidy. The Armada are only the police. They're like fingers to a huge body. The forces that work inside the Everdream are something completely different. We're not even sure if what we've seen of them in the observatory is actually them, or just some kind of facsimile they use to speak with their police force."

Cassidy took a deep sigh. "Do you have a Twilight ship I can use?"

"Come to think of it, I have better than that," Tuck said, the same excited sparkle returning to his eyes. "We have a small airship from the Everdream itself. We can't say for certain whether or not it's Armada, but it is a native vessel from inside the mass. They shouldn't notice it at all. They probably won't notice *you* either, since you're made of the same stuff. It's small, but it can seat the two of you."

Cassidy grimaced. "It only needs one seat."

Chapter 14

Cassidy couldn't sleep. Richthofen's snoring from the adjoining room reminded him of a clogged fighter engine. Ned had gone out and hadn't come back. Probably got lost trying to find prostitutes.

Cassidy slipped out into the hallway, trying not to wake Richthofen. Enemy or friend, he needed the German well-rested.

Twilight people still roamed the corridors. They stared at him as he passed as if trying to decide what he was made of. Did these people ever sleep?

The lights were dim now, but green and red pieces of coloured glass illuminated the walls. He noticed a number of casually dressed engineers stepping in and out of a large door. Poking his head in, the room looked like a lounge. It was dimly lit, like the halls, but here it seemed to be for the sake of atmosphere. The exaggerated gears on the wall cast moving shadows across the floor. They looked more decorative than functional and he wondered how much of the machine work in the rest of the compound was just for show.

Cassidy found an empty stool and leaned against the steel rail that ran the length of the counter. The bar looked similar to the New English one from the previous island, but the gear-and-cog motif gave him a headache with the constant movement. A mechanical device moved up, down and across the many bottles of various liquors, ales and lagers, plucking them one by one from the shelves and delivering them into the barkeep's hands.

"What'll it be?" The barkeep asked without turning around.

Scotch and soda, Cassidy thought. Gin and tonic. A light ale. Schnapps. Dammit, he'd even take schnapps. "Whisky on the rocks," Cassidy said and bit his tongue. "No barkeep, make that a…" he concentrated hard, "a whisky on the rocks."

"Okay," said the barkeep, tapping a key on the wall that looked like an elaborate typewriter controlling an alchemy lab, "two whiskies on the rocks."

"Thanks," Cassidy said as the two drinks plunked down in front of him. The green-eyed woman from earlier sat in the shadows at the end of the bar. "On second thought," he said, "I'll have what she's having." The barkeep grunted and set another whisky on the rocks beside the other two. Why did all the women he met have green eyes?

"It's my favourite drink," she said and slid to the stool beside him. "Twilights on the bigger islands get to meet dreams from time to time. But here we only see them through the Observatory."

Cassidy sipped at his whisky and examined himself in the bar mirror. Why did all bars have mirrors? Was it some intrinsic rule of reality? "I'm sorry," he said without glancing over, "I wasn't trying to…" She caressed his arm.

"Of course you were," she said. "It's okay. I've been wanting to talk."

Cassidy rubbed the back of his neck. He polished off the first of his three drinks without glancing over. "I guess you're one of the scientists here?"

"No," she said, leaning sideways over the bar, trying to get her head around to look at him. "I'm just here to be a woman. The men get very bored."

Cassidy sighed. "You mean, you get paid to…"

The woman threw her head back and laughed. "Of course I'm a scientist. Why? Were you wanting to buy some fun?"

"N-no," Cassidy stammered. "I just wanted a drink. I'm—" He cut himself off before he said anything *more* stupid.

She laughed again. "Relax. My name is Elena. I'm sorry. I didn't know dreams were so awkward around women."

Cassidy gave a long exhale and went for his second drink. "I'm just a little on edge. Big day tomorrow." His ears burned. His heart beat five times too fast. He started to get up to leave.

Elena gripped his arm. "It's okay, Flyboy. Finish your drink. I just wanted to talk, not scare you back to your room."

Cassidy gulped down his second drink. His skin itched. He'd wanted to run into this woman again, but only now admitted it to himself. He felt bad about it. No, guilty. No, fearful for her. She still wore the emerald green gown, and at any moment he half expected an umbrella to come stabbing through her mid-section. Red on green. The blossom pattern of blood on a leaf flashed through his mind. The third drink lay empty between his hands.

"Two more, Briss," Elena said to the barkeep.

"I need my wits for tomorrow," Cassidy said. He twisted. Realized his penis was rock hard and hung up on his inner thigh. "I need to go."

Elena stroked his hand. "Have you ever been with a woman?"

Cassidy leapt from the barstool. His head spun. He reached out to grab the rail and the world streaked.

Cassidy awoke on an examination table. Elena smiled from overhead. "I'm sorry, Mr. Cassidy," she said. Her eyes weren't green anymore. Hazel? No, yellow. But they sparkled with playful fascination. Had they only been green because he wanted them to be green? "I just needed to test a few theories."

Cassidy closed his eyes as tears welled. A sick lump pushed up in his throat. He tried to roll off the table.

Elena held him with a restraining arm. "Don't move yet. You've just overloaded your inner boundaries. It's always been my theory that only so much is transferred from dreamer to dream. Physically you seem perfect, but I know there are holes. For instance, your emotional stability. It only goes so far."

Cassidy kept his eyes closed. The lump in his throat verged on gagging him. "I could have told you that," he said, clutching at his stomach.

"I just needed to see," she said, her voice cold and clinical. "There must be a certain amount of moral core that transfers. Something that wrestles with the base instincts you also seem to possess. Now, have you ever actually been with a woman, Mr. Cassidy? I can tell your equipment works."

Cassidy groaned. "I don't know. I can't remember."

"I mean *since* you escaped the Everdream."

He breathed hard, trying to keep the nausea down. "No."

"Have you had the opportunity?"

Cassidy couldn't keep Shea out of his mind. The vine tattoos. "Why do you care?"

"I study behaviour, Mr. Cassidy. I want to know why you didn't do anything when you had the opportunity. I know I gave you an erection earlier."

Cassidy grunted and twisted off the table, breaking her grip. "That's none of your damn business, ma'am," he said, but refrained from adding anything worse than *damn*.

"Please, Mr. Cassidy," she said as he ran to the door. "I still have questions. Your friend Ned was far more receptive."

Cassidy stopped and glanced back. "Receptive? Did you sleep with him?"

Elena gave a thin smile. "No, but my associate, Phiielselly says his sexual functions are quite active. She's been studying him for several hours."

Cassidy threw the door open and stumbled into the corridors beyond. He had no idea how to return to his room from wherever he'd been taken, but didn't particularly care. His head was swimming too hard. He couldn't tell the difference between arousal and the sickness in his stomach. At the moment they were the same thing and it was something she'd done. Her phrasing. She'd hit on some internal limit he didn't know he had.

Cassidy found a dark corner, curled up and wept. He couldn't remember ever crying before, but as the hot tears burned down his face he longed for the coming day. Death would be better than this.

One of the techs found Cassidy hours later and helped him to his room. Ned still hadn't returned. He would probably be gone all night, caught up in the raptures of being *studied*. The Baron still snored in the next room. Cassidy listened to the sawing sound grating through the wall as he drifted off to sleep. In a strange way it reassured him.

The dream came in bits and pieces. The briefing room. The flight. Parts of the battle. The castle rising against the sky. He still couldn't see the dot that appeared in the distance. It was a fighter though. It wasn't coming for *him*. Cassidy was going for the fighter. The dream vanished as he awoke.

Cassidy sat up. He peeled the sheets off his sweaty skin. It was dawn, or rather the slightly more purple blue that passed for dawn in the Twilight. Lights inside the complex varied to mimic the daily cycles of their world. Ned still hadn't returned, but the German was already standing at the end of Cassidy's room, dressed and tightening his leather gauntlets.

"Ready to fly?" Richthofen asked, glancing around. "Where is your friend?"

Cassidy shook his head to wring out the last hazes of his dream. "Studying, I'm sure."

"Ya," said Richthofen, "they woke me while you were gone." He cracked an amused smile. "They wanted to study me, too."

"And?"

"These Twilights are odd people. Not my game. You dream of the castle?" Richthofen asked. "The one with many spires, each taller than the next. It reaches for the sky as you engage in battle with a thousand other fighters."

Cassidy's pulse quickened. "How do you know that?"

"All airmen dream of battle," he said. "We love the fight." He waved a hand in the air as if exalting the very idea of air combat. "I always despised my enemy. Enjoyed killing him. In a way, I hated you most of all."

Cassidy narrowed his eyes.

"For the same reason you hate me."

Cassidy clenched and unclenched his fists.

"It doesn't matter. You are a dream. I tire of hate and blood."

Cassidy couldn't place the look on Richthofen's face. A kind of resigned regret, but mixed with a tired sadness. "It's war, right?"

"War," Richthofen said. "And why do you fight in it?"

"Because you fly better than anyone else, I guess. It's what you do."

The German shook his head. "No. My brother, Lothar. *He* is a great pilot. He has always flown better than me. *I* see the Fokker as a gun platform. My purpose is merely to position it to fire. I am not a great pilot. I am a great shot. And I am tired of shooting."

"Why are you telling me?" Cassidy asked. "Why now?"

The Baron sighed. "You do have a first name. Banner should tell you."

Cassidy rose from his bed. "I have a full name and Banner won't tell me? Why?"

Richthofen poked at the wound on his head. "We need to go."

Cassidy gritted his teeth and nodded. He explained the situation, outlining everything Tuck had told him the day before. And everything about the plan he'd had to devise since Richthofen couldn't come with him.

The Baron nodded. "Then for now you will just fly in. This is the plan?"

"Best I can come up with."

Richthofen clapped him on the shoulder. "You are a brave man, Major Cassidy," the Baron said. "Perhaps we can both die as heroes."

"Perhaps," Cassidy said. *Heroes.* He left the room and made for the bay where Tuck said he had stored the small airship.

The young scientist met him along the way. "You want the craft? You're really going to do it?" Tuck asked. "I knew you would. I've had it prepped."

Huge doors opened into an immense hanger. Single and double-winged planes littered the bay floor and hung from the ceiling. They resembled the types of planes he knew, but all were covered in the same strange copper instruments he'd come to expect from Twilight technology. Several large balloons stood in one corner near a number of land vehicles, but what most caught his eye was the airship that stood in the middle. It looked like a cross between a Zeppelin and a balloon.

The bulbous portion resembled a distorted purple football, tethered to the dangling basket with an elaborate rigging of black net. The gondola was largely wood, reinforced with brass ribbing, like the *Nubigena's* gondola, but more boxy.

Tuck beamed. "It's our finest dreamship. Nothing compared to that amazing vessel of your captain's, but the *Nimbus* is fast for a semi-rigid and it's quite dirigible. If you don't mind," he said, pointing to a ball-shaped instrument mounted to the front, "the measuring equipment is still attached. We only dare skim the outside boundaries, but you'll be headed straight into the heart. When you get back it'll provide all kinds of new data."

"Fine by me," Cassidy said, examining the craft. He unlatched the hatch and peered inside. The controls were similar to the *Nubigena* right down to the helm and foot pedals. He wondered if Karl might have gotten some of his ideas for modifications from Twilight engineers or from the Everdream.

"You also might want to take this," Tuck said, handing him a pocket watch. The timepiece whirred as Cassidy opened it, exposing an instrument far more complex than any he'd seen before. "It's synchronized with our own time here. We can track you with the Observatory."

Cassidy closed the lid and placed it in his pocket. "You wouldn't have another one laying around, would you?"

"Of course," Tuck said. "I'll get you one."

Cassidy spent several hours familiarizing himself with the controls and various instruments. With any luck, he wouldn't get into any aerial combat, as the vessel had no offensive capabilities to speak of. He would bring a rifle, however. If it came down to it he could always shoot out the port window.

"Cassidy?"

Cassidy stuck his head out to find Ned standing a few feet away, shifting his weight from foot to foot. "Sorry I've been gone so long."

Cassidy shrugged. "Just getting ready."

Ned bit his lip. "I need to tell you something."

"Yeah?" Cassidy said, not looking up, but examining several instructional diagrams.

"I don't know if I can do this." Ned wrung his hands. "I can't go with you. I've decided to stay here."

Cassidy nodded, but still didn't look up. "I know. I haven't been planning on you going."

"I thought you needed a co-pilot."

Cassidy put down the papers and looked up. "You're a good kid, Ned. I like you. When all is said and done, you're not a bad guy. But you're a coward. If I took you with me, I might as well kiss myself goodbye, along with any chance of getting anyone out of there alive. I suggest you go back to playing doctor with the Twilights."

Ned stepped forwards. "I'm not a coward, but you know good and well they've already been killed, or absorbed, or whatever it is they do. If *we* go, the Everdream will have everyone."

"We wouldn't even be here without Banner," Cassidy countered.

"But what good are we dead?" Ned broke off and looked at the ground.

"Get on," Cassidy said, returning to the diagrams. "I have a lot to get ready for."

Ned remained for several seconds, turned, and left without another word.

Cassidy took a deep sigh. For a moment he'd hoped that calling the boy a coward might awaken something in him. Ah, he's young, Cassidy thought. He's young. I'm old.

Chapter 15

Cassidy had already checked every aspect of the ship a hundred times. He was stalling now. For all his own talk of honour and bravery, perhaps he'd been too hard on Ned. Richthofen was probably immune to the Everdream. He was a *real* person. A dreamer. Cassidy had as much chance as a drop of water attacking the ocean, and Ned surely thought he was on his way to death.

Cassidy sighed, fieldstripped and reassembled his Mauser. Loaded it cartridge by cartridge instead of using the metal strip. He opened the breech, chambered a round and uncocked the hammer.

Ned hadn't returned to see him off. Cassidy couldn't blame him, but the gesture might have been nice. The pocket watch ticked and whirred as he opened it. Soft lights pulsed inside, showing his time and location. Would it have any idea how to read anything but the time while in the Everdream, or would the locator dial just spin? He hoped it would still be able to communicate with its mate Tuck had given him.

Cassidy entered the gondola and wheeled the hatch shut. He sat in the pilot seat and ran his hands over the wood and metal wheel. Captain of his own ship, even if for just one mission.

The bay doors at the end of the hanger slid open on giant toothed gears. "This is it, Old Boy," he said out loud. He imagined Brewster in the seat beside him. Banner, perhaps, sending him off. The cabin felt vacant, like an emotional vacuum.

He flipped switches, bringing the instrument panel to life. Coloured pieces of glass lit up one by one. Internal cogs and wheels turned. The rear prop rotated and moorings unlatched, allowing the small craft to ascend just above the deck. Cassidy adjusted the buoyancy and glided the dirigible out of the hanger and into the purple skies.

The ship felt strong and stable as he moved away from the island. He was warm. Comfortable. No wind in his face. No pump to keep the pressure up in the fuel tank. The gondola enclosed him completely. The sensation wasn't altogether appealing.

He couldn't remember feeling more unsafe going into battle. How could you engage an enemy without the elements around you? His instincts. Senses. They all relied on touching the air. Tasting it. This would be like fighting in a diving helmet.

The dark cloud of the Everdream loomed before him. It looked bigger than he'd remembered. Was it coming for him, or was he moving towards it? The cloud surrounding the massive planet-like structure was too big and too close for him to tell the difference.

He considered where in the vast blackness to enter, but doubted it made much difference. The crew could be held anywhere. Even the *Nubigena* would be an infinitely small dot in the planet-sized vastness.

Cassidy kept the throttle to medium as the *Nimbus* slipped through the hazy outer boundary exposing a distant membrane beyond. The dream bubbles pocketed the area between the outer boundary of dense gasses and the opaque membrane like shadowy pods growing off the dark centre. His memory of being here had been a blur, as Banner had gated through with such speed. Passing closer to the pod-like bubbles he saw entire worlds inside. They looked like dark snow globes with smoky gasses obscuring a complete view of the vast landscapes, but he could make out vague interiors. Cities. Cloud buildings. Some entire bulbs were nothing but giant houses that must have gone on forever to the dreamers that roamed their halls at night. Ocean bulbs. Bulbs that looked like chessboards with coloured shapes moving across the surfaces.

It's my world, Cassidy thought. One of them, or one like them, had been his home for the brief time it existed. Did the one dream he dreamed every night show up here? Was it the same bulb as his dreamer's bulb, or did the Everdream grow one just for him. And why couldn't they just pluck him out of it while he slept?

As he gazed at the dark membrane from which the bulbs grew, the image of the purple mass arose in his memory. The Everdream itself, filtered through the atmosphere of one of these worlds, calling out to him. Begging him to return. He grimaced. This was really him returning, not a first visit.

Cassidy moved towards the membrane as several bubbles shrivelled to nothing, while more sprouted in other places. They grew and collapsed in constant rhythm, the Everdream a fertile undulating organism. These were the spines of an enormous living creature and somewhere in the centre must lay the heart and mind. Did it have either, or was it a dead machine whose only purpose was the creation of men's dreams?

He tried to imagine the sleeping humans in the *real* world, slipping silently into their little dream worlds and waking without any knowledge that somewhere beside their own reality, this thing/world pulsed and thrived, and they were only its nightly guests.

Cassidy pushed the airship past the dream bulbs to the membrane itself. The *Nimbus* ripped through as the thin layer gave way to a sight Cassidy couldn't take in all at once. The bulk of the Everdream, which at this range appeared to stretch on endlessly, was made up of millions, perhaps billions, or trillions or more of floating rock platforms of various sizes, connected by bridges and columns of the same grey matter. It looked as if a rock the size of a small planet had been worn through by millions of years of wind and erosion, until what remained looked like the skeletal structure of a vast unfinished building.

The airship moved into the immense empty spaces with no trouble. If the structure had not been so open it might have had a cave-like feel, but, instead, the vast gaps opened through to blackness beyond. Bursts of vaporous red and purple gasses filled pockets with a thin haze. At first glance, he would have thought the entire world was dead, abandoned untold aeons ago, but as he neared he noticed movement across the platform surfaces. He couldn't make out what they were, but shadows bounced and slithered over the slabs.

Endlessly open, Cassidy thought. You could hide a billion Zeppelins here and no one would ever find them. He manoeuvred towards the centre, hoping at the very least to make it to the heart of the Everdream and get either his bearings or at least some answers. Then he saw the airships.

Vessels with purple and red stripes moved through the infinite spaces. None flew towards him, but made their way from platform to platform. Were these Armada ships, or vehicles of whatever native race *commanded* the Armada?

A burst of coloured light shot through one of the spaces, followed by more. They bounced off the platforms, bridges and the root-like columns connecting them until they dispersed into the outer membrane. The bursts became more frequent as he made his way closer to the centre.

Other ships avoided the blasts of slow-moving light, so Cassidy did as well. But he steered towards the source of the lights assuming it had to be something important. The mind of the Everdream perhaps.

The bursts increased until they showered like exploding rain. He cut the engines to quarter power as the gap he followed opened into a wide clearing.

Cassidy almost steered into a wall as the source of the illumination came into view, resembling a god-like cloud-shaped creature spewing light. He knew it well. Sandwiched between two narrow slabs floated the *Nubigena* in all her glory. The coloured light radiated where tethers connecting the ship to the stone burst and fizzled, only to be replaced moments later by more anchors. The Everdream was trying to keep her from touching anything solid, but she fought the lines like an untamed elephant.

A blue aura emanated from the Zeppelin's hull. An explosion burst out as the rudder drifted too close and ate into the stone slab. The rock gave off the bursts of colour, released by whatever corrosive effect the ship had on the Everdream.

It's *real*, Cassidy thought. The ship's too *real* for this place, and they don't know what to do with it. Tethers kept snapping and now he could see the machines on the surrounding platforms shooting more lines down from harpoon guns.

Cassidy gritted his teeth and edged the *Nimbus* into the corrosive blue aura. The tiny craft shook as he manoeuvred atop the *Nubigena*, the blue energy tearing at its metal and fabric. Here the dreamship was different than outside the Everdream. Softer. He steered over the gun platform as the *Nimbus* began disintegrating. He fell through the floor and landed on the *Nubigena's* cold metal turret, clinging to the handle, his leg dangling down over the rough canvas.

Above, the *Nimbus'* gas bladder sprung a leak and deflated above him. He pulled himself to the platform as the rest of the small airship melted onto the *Nubigena* and became a puddle of coloured goo. Cassidy's chest ached watching it die.

Cassidy turned away, opened the hatch and made his way into the *Nubigena's* cavernous interior. He slid down the ladder and gazed up at the inflated gas bladders. "Karl," he yelled. The engineer's quarters were empty. He stepped down into the gondola and ran yelling, "Banner, Franz, anyone!"

He'd hoped the Everdream would keep the crew captive on the ship, but no such luck. Cassidy now wondered as he walked between the very solid *real* walls of the Zeppelin why he and the others didn't disintegrate touching the ship. The Everdream had to be made of different stuff than what they used to create dreams. Or perhaps...

It's my will, Cassidy thought as he touched the cool metal of a door latch with his bare skin. My will is keeping me solid. His head swirled as he thought about that. Something Banner had once said. He wasn't sure what it meant, but it meant *something*. About him. About what he was.

Cassidy shook the feeling away and continued exploring the ship. Plenty of time later for pondering his existence, if and when he got out alive.

His quarters lay untouched. Nothing missing except the crew. He searched the empty spaces of the ship, the nooks and crannies where no one ever went. There had to be something. Some clue as to where they'd taken everyone.

Cassidy crawled into a repair shaft beneath the floor, aided by a flashlight he found in Brewster's room. Perhaps Banner had left something for him. A message. A weapon. Cassidy swept his light over the dark interior. A pale shadow twitched in a far corner of the shaft. It lay prone in a space barely bigger than the wraithlike body. The skin and clothing was translucent, aluminium girders showing through like phantom ribs. Was it dead?

The dark head turned. Vacant eyes opened and looked at Cassidy, or rather through him as if blind. Cassidy peered closer. The face was shaggy with a bushy beard. The hair looked as though it had grown wild for months, and the ghostly grey eyes had dilated to pools of black.

Cassidy recognized something familiar about the figure. He'd met this ghost, only it hadn't been a ghost. It reached out as if trying to touch clutch Cassidy's arm from twenty feet away. Cassidy crawled towards it, inching forwards on elbows and knees. Staring deep into the face, he bit back a scream. "Jayce!" he shouted. "Jayce, my God man, is that you?"

The poor creature trembled at the mention of his name. He croaked through dry lips. "Darkness," he said, his voice distant and strained. "Darkness. I am nothing. The void is…"

The void. Nietzsche's void. The horror of what must have happened struck Cassidy like a round of Spandau shells. The desperate lad must have crawled into this space trying to escape the void they'd flown through. How long had that been? The poor devil must have lost his mind in the darkness of the little crawlspace believing he was still in the void all this time. My God. "Jayce," he said again. "Jayce, it's Cassidy. I'm here. You're here. Come back."

Jayce looked right at him, but couldn't seem to focus. "Cassidy?" he murmured. "Cassidy. You're Cassidy. We just picked you up."

Cassidy nodded emphatically as he pulled himself over to the ghostly shape and laid the flashlight on the floor so it lit them both. "Yes, yes. But that was a long time ago. Come back now. Come back." He grabbed Jayce's hand. It was hard to hold onto. Soft and airy. He had to concentrate to keep his hand from slipping through like ghostly flesh. Will. He had to use pure will. "You're here Jayce. You're on the *Nubigena*. You're Banner's man. You remember Banner?"

"Banner," Jayce said. His eyes closed as if trying to lock onto something. "Banner. The ship. Brewster. Franz. Karl. Charlie," he said. As he spoke, his body became more substantial. He clasped Cassidy's hand in a death grip, then lunged to hug him. They held each other in a tight embrace as Jayce solidified. "I'm Jayce," he said as he pulled away, his gaze locking onto Cassidy. "I'm Jayce."

"You are," Cassidy said. "You're Jayce, and I hate to tell you this, but we're in the deepest trouble you've ever seen."

"Just trouble," Jayce said. "Thank God. I thought I was in hell."

They crawled back into the main gondola, though the young airman had to grab Cassidy's belt to keep going. Cassidy dragged Jayce to his feet and filled him in on everything that had happened, repeating himself several times as the young pilot's head bobbed in slow rhythm. He took it well considering the recent trauma. Jayce sighed when Cassidy had finished. "What do we do now?"

"No idea," Cassidy said. "I've been playing it by ear so far. Can you fly this thing?"

Jayce shook his head. "The *Nubigena*? Not a chance. I'm ok with a bi-plane, but..."

Cassidy grimaced. "I watched Banner a lot."

"You can fly anything," Jayce said. "Banner went on and on about it before he picked you up. That's why we came to get you."

Cassidy ran hand through his hair. "How did he pick us? Where did he find out about me, or even where I'd be?"

Jayce shook his head. "Wish I could tell you. He never told us how he picked any of us either. The captain always seemed to know which bulb to go to."

"Alright," said Cassidy as he stood and started for the control room. "We've just got to figure out where everyone is being kept."

Jayce grinned as he caught up. "That we can do. Banner's got a strong aura we can feel. Taught some of us how to find him if we ever got separated."

Cassidy nodded and opened the door to the helm. "Wish he'd gotten around to teaching *me* that trick. Think you can handle being first mate?" he asked. Cassidy flipped switches at the navigation console then moved to the helm. The engines engaged and the *Nubigena* tugged at its moorings.

"Can you handle being captain, Major?" Jayce asked.

Cassidy grimaced. Felt the *Nubigena* come alive as he gripped the helm and placed his feet against the firm pedals. She was accepting him. He hoped she'd fly the way she did for Banner.

Chapter 16

Cassidy throttled the *Nubigena* forwards. A series of loud popping sounds came from the hull as the eroding tethers tore lose. Jayce sat at the navigation console, trying to make sense of controls he'd only watched others use.

"Do you feel Banner anywhere?" Cassidy asked. Though it had been simple to manoeuvre the smaller *Nimbus* between the slabs, he found the structure of the Everdream far more confining to the massive *Nubigena*, a vessel which exaggerated each tilt of the pedal and each spoke of the helm a hundred-fold.

Jayce looked up from the controls. "I'm trying to find him. We always used the trick on land in the Twilight and the *real* world. It's more faint here. This place is dampening everything."

Cassidy scanned the latticework of stone that stretched in all directions. Vast. Silent. Empty except for airships that seemed to keep their distance from the Zeppelin. The craft was apparently dangerous to anything it touched, but they gathered in mounting swarms. "Can you at least give me a direction?"

Jayce gripped the sides of his head, his eyes closed tight. "I'm sorry. There's so many directions."

The *Nubigena* moved as slow as Cassidy could set the engines, but avoided the platforms and columns by mere yards. Cassidy narrowed his eyes. "Get to the side window and tell me what you see."

Jayce moved from the console and pinned his face to the glass to glance different angles. "We're melting things. I think you've already hit a wall or two, we just can't feel it."

"What? Damn." He was a terrible pilot. What had made him think he could fly this ship? On the other hand... "Jayce, sit down," Cassidy snapped. He brought the ship around and aimed at the heart of the skeletal planet where a cluster of slabs formed a hexagon. "Can you at least tell me where he's not?"

Jayce shrugged. "He could be just about anywhere behind us, but I don't feel him in front of us."

Cassidy nodded. "Thought you'd say that. Makes more sense to keep everyone away from where they were keeping the ship." Thousands of Armada fighters peeled out from around the purple and red airships. The *Nubigena* throttled forwards and slammed into the hexagon. The Zeppelin was a mere needle stabbed into an orange, but at full speed, the soft resistance felt like they were moving through mud. Streaks of black liquid slid down the windows as the Zeppelin cut through the stone masses.

Cassidy reversed the engines, sliding back out of the hexagon to make another stab. Armada fighters dove, slamming into the gondola as they exited the structure, but splattered like insects against the craft.

As the black liquid slid away, thousands of Armada ships gathered surrounding the *Nubigena* on all sides. Cassidy pulled a large broadcasting cone from the corner and opened one of the windows. "I'm crew of this ship," he hollered out at the fleet. "I don't know what you want from us, or this vessel, and I don't care. But if you don't guide me to the rest of its crew and my captain, I'll spend the next few hours turning the heart of the Everdream into sludge."

The Armada ships remained motionless for several minutes before an inhuman voice grated back. It sounded as if whatever creature was speaking was not only a non-native to the English language, but to spoken languages of any kind. "Come. Speak. Not harm," the voice croaked.

"That's not the Armada," Jayce said. "I've heard them speak. It's got to be the Everdream itself."

Cassidy nodded. "Got to be."

"Take you. Crew," the voice grated.

Jayce glanced from the ships back to Cassidy. "Why don't they just destroy us? They have thousands."

"They can't," Cassidy said. "Not here. I think I know why they fear us so much." He turned the cone back out the window. "I have a pilot who will stay at the helm. If you attempt to board, or if I'm not back in an hour, he'll start flying." Cassidy turned back to Jayce. "I don't think they can step aboard here in the Everdream, but if they do, use *real* bullets. Nothing from the Twilight."

Jayce nodded. "Makes sense. That's what we've always used, but I guess here they're even softer."

Cassidy nodded. "We're made of different stuff. Imagine tiny animals running around in your brain. That's what we're in. A brain. They may be like bones and tissue out there, but here there's nothing but clay." He left the bridge, moved to the main door and opened it up to the vast fleet. One of the smaller airships pulled alongside. An Armada pilot stood with the side door open and a bridge extended. The pilot looked squat and purple. Cassidy could only compare it to a withered dwarf with pale soft-looking skin. It motioned to Cassidy's sidearm.

"I'm keeping this," Cassidy said, clapping a hand to the wooden holster.

The creature motioned him to continue. Cassidy leapt past the melting end of the gangplank and climbed aboard, glad for the time being that he was a dream and wouldn't slip through the deck into the abyss below.

The Armada ship looked different from the ones he'd seen outside of the Everdream. Whatever material made up this gondola appeared to flow, as if a coloured molten liquid rolled across the surface. When he touched it he realized why. The ship was only mimicking a solid object. In reality, it *was* liquid. Liquid and organic.

The Everdream really was an organism. He stood inside some kind of mind, and these ships were like cells. Outside the mind, it could solidify into dream structures, but within the Everdream's inner boundaries, anything substantial was dangerous. The Armada pilots inside weren't even as solid as dreams. Cassidy wondered how much power the Everdream was having to exert in order to hold Banner and crew.

The disembodied voice came again. "Is acceptable."

Cassidy couldn't tell if this was a statement or a question, but the ship moved away and back towards the fringes. He remained standing as it made its way through the many gaps towards one of the platforms near the outer membrane and landed. Both the ship and pilot melted away, and he was left standing on a surface about the size of a large room that looked like rock, but felt smooth as glass.

Brewster, Karl and Franz stood staring at him like they were seeing a ghost. The Englishman stepped forwards. "Is it really you, Old Boy? Are you *real?*"

Cassidy couldn't help breaking out in a hearty laugh. "*Real?* Are any of us?"

Brewster grinned and gave him a bear hug, which Cassidy returned with a strong squeeze. "Had to ask," Brewster said, releasing him. "How did they get you? We thought for sure you'd gotten away."

"I did," Cassidy said. He gave Karl and Franz a quick salute, which they returned with claps on the back. "Ned and I got out clean."

"Then why?" Brewster said, taking a step back. "My God, you didn't come back on purpose, did you?"

Cassidy turned and surveyed the situation. The platform they stood on had sheer edges. No holes. No roots leading to other platforms. Nowhere to escape *to*. The Everdream didn't have to exert much energy at all, just threaten them with a fall into nothingness. "Any idea why they haven't killed you?"

"Absorbed us, is more like it," Franz said. "I think they—*it*, wants to know something before that happens."

"Where's...Banner?" Cassidy asked.

"No idea," Brewster said, shaking his head. "They've got him somewhere else. They seem rather upset about something with him."

"Where's Ned?" Franz asked.

Cassidy kept his jaw set. "He's gone."

"I thought you said he got away," Karl said.

Cassidy nodded. "We got separated. I've no clue where he is now."

Brewster shook his head. "Sorry to hear that. He was a good man. Perhaps we'll find him back in Arcadia."

"Perhaps," Cassidy nodded. "Good news is, I've got Jayce back on the ship."

"What ship?" Karl asked. "Jayce is dead."

"He was never dead," Cassidy said. He related to them how he'd gotten to the *Nubigena* and found the young man still reliving the nightmare of Nietzsche's void.

"All that time," Brewster said. He stared at the ground. "Poor bloke. Must have been torture."

Cassidy reached into the belt beneath his flight jacket and pulled out two Webleys and a Luger. He handed Brewster and Karl the revolvers and Franz the automatic.

"I'm afraid we won't be able to use them," Brewster said, turning the weapon over in his hand and checking the cylinder. "They'll never let us off this rock."

"I'm not giving them any choice," Cassidy said. He turned away and looked back in the direction of the *Nubigena* where it floated somewhere beyond the slabs aimed at the heart of the Everdream. "I want to see Banner now," he yelled.

The Everdream remained silent for several minutes before speaking. "Yes," the disembodied voice croaked. "Banner."

"I'm not sure I'm following you," said Brewster as they waited for something to happen. "You're as trapped as the rest of us."

Cassidy shook his head. "If you're right, the worst they can do is reabsorb us. Either they can't, or they're afraid to."

Karl raised an eyebrow. "Afraid? Why?"

Cassidy pursed his lips. "These Armada agents aren't solid enough to kill us."

Franz shook his head. "Perhaps, but they can do anything to us so long as we're touching the Everdream. They immobilized us before we got here. The ropes snapped not long after they dropped us off, but we're paralysed if they touch us."

Cassidy moved that around in his mind. "Maybe, but they're scared of the *Nubigena*. It's *real*. It hurts them. Jayce'll tear them up if they don't let us out."

"It still doesn't make sense," Brewster said, rubbing a finger over his moustache. "Why haven't they just killed us? They've had nothing but chances before you got here."

"It's Banner," Franz said. "They want something from him, and hope they can use us to get it. He's different. We all know it."

A similar airship to the one that dropped Cassidy off drifted towards them. It landed and melted away into nothing, leaving a limp shape that lay motionless on the platform. Cassidy rushed towards the captain, the others close on his heels. He knelt and turned Banner over. A shudder ran through Cassidy as blank eyes stared past him.

"My God," Brewster said.

"He's white as a ghost," Karl said.

They knelt around their captain. Cassidy cradled Banner's head in his arms. "Banner," he said, trying to draw recognition from the distant eyes. "Banner! You're here, Captain. It's Cassidy. All of us."

Banner moaned and flicked his eyes around, but didn't lock onto anyone.

Cassidy took a deep breath. "My name is Cassidy."

Banner twisted up his features. He shivered, rolled off Cassidy's lap and wailed.

"I know you know me, Captain."

"I'm sorry," Banner spat. "I should have let you all stay in the Everdream. I was wrong."

Cassidy rolled him back over and shook him by the shoulders. "Maybe, but it's done. We're free men whether we like it or not and I'm not melting back in. We're *your* men now."

Banner's eyes cleared a little and seemed to focus. "They'll never let you go, boys. I've doomed you all. They'll suck you in and do who knows what before that. I should have left you."

Cassidy shook his head. "I don't know what to believe anymore, but I'm sure as hell going to die on my own terms. Now we're getting out." He lifted his head and shouted out at the Everdream. "Take us to the *Nubigena.*"

"No," Banner said. His voice dribbled out like a feeble child. Unlike Jayce, Banner still appeared solid, but his skin was beyond white. Sucked dry of all colour. "This is what they want."

An airship formed around them, growing up from the platform. Before Cassidy could stand, they were in the air and headed towards where he'd left the *Nubigena.* The small craft manoeuvred back through the myriad of gaps and pulled alongside the Zeppelin. A plank extended to the main door, but stopped a foot away, the far edge melting as it came too close to the *Nubigena's* hatch.

"Trap," Banner rasped. "All of it."

The airship jolted and began to fade as if forcing them to the plank.

"No doubt, but at least we'll have the ship," Brewster said. He helped Cassidy drag their captain, each taking a shoulder. Karl and Franz took Banner's feet, and together they heaved him aboard.

Jayce met them in the bay hatch. "What's wrong with him?" he asked when he saw Banner's white form.

"Tortured, I suspect," Brewster said. "Don't wish to imagine how."

A harsh gale struck the ship. The crew carried Banner to his quarters as Cassidy and Jayce rushed to the bridge and engaged the engines. The savage wind was blowing them away from the heart, out towards the membrane. "Reverse the engines," Cassidy shouted as he took the wheel.

"Why?" Jayce yelled.

"Just do it."

Jayce grabbed the throttle and thrust it into full reverse. The engines moaned. The *Nubigena* bucked. "What are they doing?" he yelled over the roar of the wind.

"Blowing us back to where we aren't a danger," Cassidy said as the ship lurched forwards. The engines screamed against the powerful gale. "Stop the engines," he bellowed. "They'll burn up."

Jayce cut the throttle. The *Nubigena* flew forwards at an uncontrolled velocity.

"Dammit," Cassidy snapped. "All their *physical* power is on the edges. Once they get us past the membrane, we'll be in their creation zone, where they make the dreams."

The *Nubigena* tore back through the membrane and sped between the dream bulbs in mere moments.

"My God," Jayce said as they neared the vaporous outer boundary. "You mean—"

The Zeppelin struck the border like a solid wall. Jayce flew over his console and crashed into the far wall below the windows. Cassidy slammed into the wheel and sank to the floor. Blood ran into his eyes and the world blurred.

Chapter 17

Cassidy woke with his face in a small pool of blood. He touched his head. Felt a deep gash. A splotch of red showed where he'd struck part of the helm's support frame. Jayce groaned nearby.

"What the hell was that?" Jayce asked. His voice sounded far off as if dampened through thick air.

"They've got us," Cassidy said. He pulled himself to a seated position. His head hammered. "Since this is the area where they make dreams, we're probably in some kind of dream-bubble they've created just to hold us."

Jayce shuffled, trying to sit up, but couldn't seem to get his legs under him. "Dammit," he yelled, and struck the floor with his fist. "They wanted to get us all in one place. Just waited for you to show up."

Ripping a piece of his scarf, Cassidy tied it around his head. "Can't believe I didn't think of that. Just stumbled in like a damned idiot trying to save everyone."

Jayce let out a short harsh laugh. "I'm still liking this better than the void."

Cassidy tried to nod but his head hurt too much. "We're not completely sunk, I still—"

"You all right, Old Boy?" Brewster said from the doorway. "Blimey, what happened to your head?"

Cassidy winced. "Tried to hammer a bolt in with my skull."

"Use a spanner next time," Brewster said. "Karl should teach you these things."

Cassidy grinned. "Everyone make it?"

Brewster grimaced. "Karl's hurt his back. Franz and I got lucky because we were already braced. Banner rolled across the floor and hit a wall, but he's in such bad shape I don't think he could be any worse."

Cassidy closed his eyes for a few moments and ran through his limited options. "I need to see Banner," he said, gripping Tuck's location watch through the fabric of his pocket. He squeezed a switch and felt the tiny machine thrum against his skin. Time for Plan B.

Brewster nodded and helped him to his feet. They hobbled down the corridor to the bay where Banner still lay motionless. Cassidy sighed. Franz and Karl hadn't even gotten the captain to his quarters before hitting the holding dream. Banner lay propped up with a pillow in the middle of the aisle. His glazed eyes stared at the ceiling.

"I'll check the rest of the ship," Brewster said over his shoulder as he sprinted away, leaving Cassidy alone with the fallen captain.

"Banner." Cassidy kneeled beside the pale man. "I need to know what they want."

Banner glanced over, then back at the ceiling and closed his eyes. "They want to know why they can't absorb me."

"Why can't they?" Cassidy asked. He put hand on Banner's shoulder. "Dammit, I need to know."

Banner pried his eyelids open. A tear ran down his cheek. "I'm not really a dream. More than just animated Everdream stuff. They can't get past my consciousness." His breathing became shallower. His lips parted again, but he could only whisper. "Drained everything they could. But I'm...still...here." He closed his eyes and his head fell sideways.

Cassidy's heart shuddered. He gripped Banner by the shoulder and gave it another shake. "What makes you different?"

Banner coughed out what might have been a laugh. "Doesn't matter," he rasped. "Never mattered. I exist because I *say* I exist. That's the only truth there is. It's about will. Remember that. You can do it too."

"Why don't you tell the others?" Cassidy spat.

The lines in Banner's forehead creased with pain. "Won't listen. Do what they're dreamed to do. Good pilots. Soldiers."

"Then why me?" Cassidy asked. "Why tell me now?"

Banner rolled sideways, eyes wild. Grabbed Cassidy by the lapels and drew him close. "You're the only one who ever asked," he said and thumped back to the cot. His eyes shut and he was unconscious.

A solid knocking hammered at the outer hatch as Brewster returned to the bay with Franz. It stopped for a few seconds and started again.

Cassidy glanced between them. Brewster shrugged. "Little point. We let the bastards in or they'll tear the ship apart."

Cassidy released the hatch. An Armada agent stood outside, floating in mid-air. He was taller than the other one Cassidy had seen and more solid. No soft features or liquid skin. This one could kill.

"You are Cassidy?" The agent said, stepping inside. His voice was more natural than the voice in the Everdream. It must have had difficulty communicating within its own mind, but here it seemed to have no trouble through this Armada emissary.

"Why are you doing this?" Cassidy asked.

"You belong here," it said without emotion. "We made you. We made all of you. You're a part of us."

Cassidy took a deep breath. He'd half wanted this a few days ago. Considered breaking free of the crew and returning to whatever he'd been. He couldn't remember why he'd ever wanted that now. "I don't want to go," said Cassidy. "I'm free. I have my own mind."

"It's against the order of things," the agent said. "Understand. We mean none of you harm. But you must return."

"Then why haven't you just done it?" Jayce shouted from behind. "Why torture us like this?"

The agent stepped forwards and looked down at Banner's emaciated body. "This dream is an abomination. We must know what he really is."

Franz's blue eyes flared as he drew the Webley from his belt and fired in one swift snap of his wrist. The bullet tore into the emissary and it fell backwards out the hatch.

A moment later, the weapon wrested itself from the young German's hand and flew out the hatch as well. Another emissary moved through the door at blinding speed and slammed Franz against the wall, knocking him unconscious. "If you use your weapons again, we will be forced to restrain you all," it said with the same emotionless voice as the first.

The crew glanced at each other. Cassidy wanted to fire as well. At this point, what did it matter? At least it would feel good hurt one of them. But it didn't matter, did it? The Armada were all just blobs of dream matter that would return over and over. "It's not that easy," Cassidy said, digging into his fragmented memory. "Banner's not something you can understand. He's a god from the lower worlds."

Brewster glanced at him with narrowed eyes.

Jayce blinked hard.

Karl nodded. "He is ancient. Woden One-Eye of the gallows tree. If anything should happen to him, his family will make war on you."

The emissary was silent. Somewhere, deep in the nebulous cloud, the Everdream considered the possibility. "This seems doubtful," the emissary said at last. "Woden visited us once. If this creature were a god, he would have spoken by now."

Cassidy couldn't believe the Everdream had even considered the possibility. Was this Woden Karl spoke of *real*? A clicking came from Cassidy's pocket. He pulled out his watch and flipped open the lid. A red light flared. The emissary regarded him with what might or might not have been a strange look. Cassidy turned towards the bridge. "Jayce," he said over his shoulder, "shoot him and keep shooting." He bolted for the helm.

A shot rang out. A loud thud sounded from behind followed by more shots, shouts and more thuds. Cassidy had his Mauser out as he made it through the bridge door and slammed the hatch shut. He pushed the throttle all the way down and leapt to the wheel. The engines screamed as the dream field held them fast, but he levelled his eyes on the horizon of the holding dream, trying to find the outer boundary beyond the atmosphere. The watch continued its clicking as the red light blinked. Behind him the steel hatch buckled and tore away.

Cassidy whirled and emptied his gun into the line of agents who rammed into the room. At least the damnable things were bottle-necked. The Mauser bullets tore down the corridor, slicing through several agents at once, creating a growing pile at the entrance. He fired off his eighth round as agents from the back staggered over the bodies.

Two shots left.

One.

Another agent scrambled over the pile and fell through into the bridge. Cassidy glanced out the window as the red Fokker tri-wing barrelled through the dark boundary. Its twin guns spewed their steel-jacketed payloads as the very *real* fighter penetrated the dream world with its very *real* pilot. A dreamer in Everdream, Cassidy thought, and glanced back to see a second agent climb in and freeze in place.

The *Nubigena* shuddered forwards, accelerating from nothing to full speed in a matter of seconds as the holding field broke. The weird physics of the Everdream took over and slingshot them past the border and into the pink free-space of the Twilight.

Cassidy picked himself up off the floor and steered in the direction of anywhere. If he'd known anything about how to find Banner's gates, he would have taken one immediately for the *real* world and hoped like hell for a storm on the close horizon. But, without the captain's knowledge, or whatever it was that allowed the man to instantly find proverbial needles in their haystacks, Cassidy made for the most remote spot he knew.

Brewster stumbled in through the sludge of dissolving Armada agents. "Damned if these things don't fade properly," he said shaking gobs of dreamstuff off his boots.

Cassidy glanced behind and returned his gaze to the deep pink of the clouds that began gradiating to yellow. "Is everyone alright?" he asked.

Brewster coughed. His voice came out hoarse as if he'd been choked, or his windpipe struck. "Alive, I think. Unconscious. Hit us hard."

Cassidy nodded. "I'm sorry. It was the only way."

Brewster coughed again and spat. "Only way, bloody hell. What happened?"

"It was my B plan," Cassidy said without looking. "Richthofen is tearing into the Everdream with everything he's got. His fighter's *real*. He's *real*."

"Don't follow," Brewster choked out as he moved over to the navigation controls, obviously trying to correct whatever mistakes Cassidy and Jayce had made. "Thought you hated him."

"Didn't have much choice." Cassidy searched the side windows for signs of pursuing Armada but didn't see any. Too bad he could only see out the front and sides of the windows. "Point is, Richthofen's a dreamer. The Everdream won't know what to do with his presence inside it. His influence. Think about it, *real* people are the clients. They have the power to shape dreams and he's in the middle of the place they're made."

"You're over my head," Brewster said. He cleared his throat hard and his voice came out more normal. "Head twenty-six degrees starboard. There's a good place to hide that way until Banner gets his legs on straight."

Cassidy adjusted their bearing. "Can you find gates?"

Brewster snorted. "Couldn't find a barn door on a farm. We're stuck if the captain doesn't come around."

Cassidy was silent. The wiry yellow clouds darkened to deep magenta and navy blue. Stars showed through in places. This had to be the edge of Twilight. Something different than he'd seen so far. The furthest from Dusk and Dawn if such concepts truly existed in whatever strange metaphor this world followed.

Jayce made his way to the helm, leaning on the wall and holding a hand to his head. He dropped into a chair and sank down. "Karl and Franz are with Banner. We got him into bed. Where we going?"

"Gunyin," Brewster said.

Jayce gave a loud sigh. "I don't like Gunyin."

"I know," said Brewster. "But neither does the Armada."

As they spoke, the red Fokker flew past the forward windows and Richthofen gave a thumbs-up. Cassidy waved back, though he doubted the German could see. The crimson fighter rolled and banked, and was gone. Cassidy couldn't have imagined a stranger ally, but as Richthofen vanished, his chest felt tight. Something deep inside still hated the Baron, but a part of him also hoped he hadn't been wounded taking on the entire Everdream like that.

Perhaps it would even be a while before the Armada would be able to pursue now. It didn't matter though. When they did, they would pursue with the dogged ferocity, not of hungry wolves, but angry, vengeful ones. He hoped to God Banner would know what to do. "Will we be safe in Gunyin?" Cassidy asked.

Brewster cracked a sardonic smile. "No one is safe in Gunyin."

Chapter 18

"What really happened to Ned?" Brewster asked as he flipped switches and checked headings.

Cassidy didn't speak for several minutes. "I told you, we got separated."

Brewster let out an audible sigh. "Chickened out, did he? Don't know why Banner got him in the first place. He's not a bad pilot, but we always had to nurse him through dogfights, back when we had more fighters."

"He probably just wasn't cut out for battle," Cassidy said. "Some men—"

"He was a pilot," Brewster snapped.

"So what's this place we're headed?" Cassidy asked, changing the subject. He didn't want to talk about the observatory. He particularly didn't want to talk about Elena or the *tests* they were probably putting Ned through.

"Gunyin? It's what they like to call an outpost, but it's more like the place Twilights go who don't do well with other Twilights."

"Sounds lovely," Cassidy mused.

"Always."

After about an hour Franz joined them, leaving Karl and Jayce behind to watch over the captain. Cassidy felt relieved to see the young German since operating the ship was ten times more complicated without Banner at the helm. The engines had probably endured all manner of strain in their fight against the Everdream's forces of nature, though the *Nubigena* still flew like a well-fletched arrow.

A dark chunk of rock loomed on the cloud horizon and grew to the size of a large egg-shaped mountain with the narrow end dipping down. On closer inspection the island looked like a dead world. The surface was pocketed with holes and shadows. Derelict wooden structures covered some of the holes. Rustic hangers, perhaps, or extendable ports.

"I say we find one of the darker places near the top and bury ourselves," Franz said, staring at the oncoming rock. His jaw tensed as they neared the looming mass.

"No point," Brewster said, shaking his head. "They'll already have seen us." He looked up at Cassidy. "Guide her over to the big one with the metal awning. It's one of the few she'll fit through."

Cassidy spun the wheel, trying to mimic Banner's deft movements, but it took him twenty minutes just to line up with the hole. Brewster cut the engines to just above zero and Cassidy inched her into the narrow tunnel. He could scarcely see in the scant lighting of the few torches pocketing the porous walls. He kept the gondola just above the ground, which probably meant ten or fifty feet and hoped like hell he wouldn't scrape the top.

Brewster and Franz helped as best as they could, maintaining a close watch on the curved walls beyond the window and shouting out the distance. Cassidy found manoeuvring a Zeppelin inside a narrow shaft much like threading a needle with his eyes shut, with a thread the size of a steamship.

The Zeppelin shuddered as it scraped the wall on its port side. Cassidy nudged the wheel starboard. Sweat poured beneath his arms and down his ribs. A thin sweat that evaporated not long after it dripped down his forehead and stung his eyes. He gritted his teeth. Banner would kill him for damaging the *Nubigena*, assuming Karl didn't get to him first.

"Can't we go any slower?" he asked.

"We're only running one engine and it will choke out if we go any slower," Brewster said from the starboard window. "We're almost there, just keep her steady."

The tunnel opened into a hollow space that vanished into vast darkness. He could just make out the dim shapes of other airships anchored to ports along the immense cavern walls.

"Over there," Brewster said, pointing to a dock jutting out from the wall on their starboard side.

Cassidy had to fly into the centre and turn around just to bring himself in line with the dock. Brewster cut the engines. A man on the dock looked aggravated, climbed a steel ladder fastened to the rock and ascended to the upper mooring plate. He fished at the *Nubigena* with a long rod, hooked and towed it in with a line he put through a ring in the plate.

"How dangerous will this place really be?" Cassidy asked as they made their way to Banner's quarters.

Brewster snorted. "Remember how bad Arcadia was at the docks?"

Cassidy nodded.

"This isn't nearly that civilized."

Banner looked no better than before. His eyes were closed, his breathing still shallow.

"Captain," Cassidy said, looking down at the gaunt shape on the bed.

Banner raised his eyelids like a man trying to lift bags of sand. "Cassidy," he said through pale lips. "You scratched my ship."

"I'm sorry, Captain."

Banner tried to smile, but winced. "How did we...the Armada..."

"Rest up," Cassidy said. He gave Jayce and Karl a worried glance, which they mirrored back. "I'll tell you everything when you're on your feet."

Brewster ushered everyone but Karl into the hall and took them out of Banner's hearing range. "We can't stay in the ship. They'll think something's wrong and come aboard to take over. Franz," he said, motioning to the young German, "stay with Karl. Wheel the hatch shut and if anything walks, crawls, or *swims* in, for that matter, shoot it in the head. Don't talk to it first. Don't give any warnings."

Franz nodded.

"We've already been too long," Brewster said. He checked his Webley and grabbed a mailbag with his basics and extra ammunition. "Follow my lead."

They exited the bay, stepping directly onto the dock where a series of mooring lines kept the ship from drifting into the wall. Cassidy looked around at the myriad of other docks that spotted the ovular walls of the inner core, lit by more sporadic torches. Everything else was complete darkness except the open top of the mountain, through which he saw faint stars and clouds gliding above.

A grungy elderly dockhand approached like a hungry man coming to smell a dead fish. Brewster pulled several coins from his mailbag and handed them over.

"Not enough," the dockhand said, eyeing the change in his gnarled hand. "Price's gone up."

Brewster gave him a contemptuous glare. "It's plenty," he said, and gave the old man a harsh punch in the gut. The man doubled over, clutching the money in an iron grip. The Englishman pushed past and led them down the ramp to a set of wooden stairs.

"Was that really necessary?" Cassidy whispered.

"I wouldn't rough up an old man if it wasn't," Brewster said. "They're all watching us for weakness and that old bastard was just the canary in our coalmine. Now hush, keep your eyes sharp and a hand on your sidearm."

The stairs ran down to a landing and from there the crew took a tunnel into the rock. The sounds of pounding rowdy music from an out of tune piano and talking and laughing hit them as they rounded a corner and died again to distant noise. The door opening and closing, Cassidy thought.

A short man with ratty brown hair, a scarred face and lager-smelling clothes shoved past them without glancing back. Moments later they found the door, a large wooden slab that opened only with a great heave from Brewster.

Cassidy had never seen a bar like this. The proper word was probably tavern, and even *that* seemed too sophisticated a term. Mead hall perhaps. At least a hundred men, and an assortment of what he might have called women, but certainly not ladies, partied on the edge of madness. Men sang out loud and off-key while chugging beer from steins bigger than their heads. Several engaged in drunken brawls in the middle of the floor, where other men stepped over or kicked them in the head.

In one of the corners, a man pinned a woman against a support beam, lifted her skirt and proceeded to have his way with her from behind. A group of onlookers screamed obscenities and laughed as the man thrust into her as if his actual target was the support beam itself.

"Banner's Boys," one man shouted as the room finally noticed their entrance. The man looked like a pirate rejected by slightly classier pirates. His shaggy half-grown beard was caked with foam and a musket-style pistol hung wedged in his oversized belt. He swaggered up to them chanting, "Banner's fucking boys. Banner's fucking boys," he sang, speech slurred. "Banner's fucking, Banner's fuck, Banner's fucking his boys."

Brewster pulled out his Webley and shot the man in the head. He reholstered his gun, stepped over the corpse and approached the bar.

Cassidy tried to take in the reaction of the crowd without appearing to look. They seemed unphased. Almost amused.

"Where's Banner?" the barkeep asked. "Never seen you boy—er, men without him."

Brewster shrugged. "Picked a girl up near Arcadia. Haven't seen him out of his quarters since."

The barkeep laughed. "'Bout time. Finally found something he fancied, eh? Never liked anything *I* tried to sell him."

"I never liked anything you tried to sell either," Brewster said.

The barkeep must be more than just a barkeep, Cassidy thought. The owner perhaps. He tried to place what Brewster sounded like as he snapped out his words. His manners seemed so exaggerated. Even through the thick accent he was different. Cassidy grinned. Brewster was trying to sound like Banner. Trying to *be* Banner.

Cassidy's eyes flicked about the room. While most were caught up in beer and any number of other activities he didn't wish to guess at, several other men stood here and there, their stares pinned on Brewster and the other airmen. The watchers all carried guns. Some wore muskets like the man Brewster had killed. Others carried more modern weapons.

"So, the Armada gettin' heavy?" the barkeep asked.

"No," said Brewster, "we came here for the fantastic food and sterling atmosphere."

The barkeep laughed. "How long you need'a stay?"

"Week or two," Brewster said with a shrug. "Like always."

"Pissed 'em off good this time, I hear," the barkeep said, lowering his tone. "Heard they's swarmin' like you shoved your whole arm in a hornets nest an' scooped out its guts."

Brewster kept his eyes level. "When aren't they?"

"'Tis true," the barkeep said. "Stay long as you like."

Brewster gave an affirmative nod. Cassidy and Jayce tried to look natural as they guarded the Englishman's back. They flanked him, each scanning their side of the room. Cassidy imagined in the past the crew had appeared much more formidable with Banner leading a six- or seven-pilot entourage. He wondered how many of these *intriguing gentlemen* they had managed to piss off in previous years. Knowing Banner, he'd probably revelled in angering the locals purely for the sake of principle.

Brewster turned and they followed him back towards the door. The crowd was thicker now and they pushed their way closer. Cassidy found himself touching his holster with the side of his hand in case someone tried to grab at it. It was important not to look scared, so he barrelled through on the Englishman's heels.

The door opened as they reached it and a large man wearing a full cloak and carrying a pump-action shot gun came through. He scowled, but let them pass. Cassidy breathed a sigh of relief as they returned to the dark tunnel without incident.

"So, how did you and our Bloody Baron get so chummy," Brewster asked as they walked. He was hiding the tension well, but the question was an attempt to break the pensive mood and Cassidy heard the crack in his voice.

Cassidy snorted. "Wouldn't say we were friends, but Richthofen was the only one willing to help and he was there when it counted."

Brewster gave an understanding nod. "Arrogant Prussian bastard, that one, but Banner always thought the world of him."

They passed several lit touches and entered an area of relative darkness. An odd coldness blew over him. "He's not like before," Cassidy said without breaking the tone of the conversation. He slipped the Mauser out of its home. "Got wounded. It's affected him. I think part of the reason he flew with me was in hopes of getting killed."

"Never a good sign." Brewster's voice went up a notch, though Cassidy couldn't tell if it was in response or if he'd noticed something.

A man came out of the shadows laughing. He sounded like he'd just been in conversation, but Cassidy couldn't see who he'd been talking to. "You boys are from the Stormship, aren't you?" the man said, turning his attention to them. He reminded Cassidy of many of the others in the bar, a kind of grungy Twilight pirate. His teeth were white and straight, but his face and hands were stained with grease and soot and his clothes probably hadn't been cleaned since they'd been bought.

Brewster nodded and quipped, "Bar's back there."

"Oh, I know my way to the bar, Friend," the man said. "I'm at the bar every night, *Friend*. But that's not why I'm asking, Friend, though I do appreciate the advice, I do."

Brewster pushed past him.

"Hold, Friend," the man said, touching Brewster's shoulder. "I happen to have acquired a map, that is to say it is presently in my possession, but I'm bereft of transportation."

"Not interested," Brewster said without looking back. "We've got our own places to go."

"Oh, Friends, I'm sure you do," he said, walking backwards to keep up with us, "but it's a mutual business venture I'm thinking of. A venture of adventure, as it were."

Brewster still hadn't looked back. Without telegraphing his intentions he stepped back and knocked the man over with a harsh slam of his shoulder. At the same time he drew his Webley and fired into the shadows. Another shot resounded at the same moment and a savage groan came from the darkness.

Cassidy glanced down at the man Brewster had toppled, who now tugged at the pistol in his belt. Cassidy fired once. The man lay still.

Jayce was already on one knee, searching the darkness ahead, his Luger cocked and pointed into the distant uncertainty.

Pinning himself to the wall, Cassidy aimed at the alcove of shadows to their left. "Come out," he said, levelling the muzzle chest-high in the hope of making whoever was there think he could actually see them.

The large cloaked man they'd seen earlier stepped out of the alcove, his shotgun trained on them with one hand, its stock trapped beneath his arm and a revolver in his other tight grip. Cassidy tried to imagine how the man had doubled back already, but there was no telling how many passages the caves held. "Coulda' shot you boys up good," he said. The hood of his cloak was pulled back and Cassidy could see his mass of grey hair spilling out around it. "Armada says there's more for us with you in one piece though."

Chapter 19

Cassidy stepped forwards until the shotgun barrel rested against his chest and touched the muzzle of his Mauser to the man's head. Jayce and Brewster kept their vigil on the darkness ahead. "How bad do you need that money?" Cassidy asked.

"Nothin' personal," the big man said. "You can't blame a man for takin' a good opportunity."

"I'm not going to blame you," Cassidy said, adjusting his finger on the trigger. "I'm going to kill you."

"Point well made," the big man said. "But if it's not me, it'll be someone else. Bounty just went up a thousand percent on all of you. Ship, too. Your captain the most. At least I'd be good to you, 'til I turned you over."

"You're too kind," Cassidy said. He fired. The big man's head exploded. Cassidy twisted to the side in the same moment as the shotgun went off, sending a shower of lead into the wall behind him. One ricocheted and ripped through his sleeve. He turned to Brewster, who still stared into the darkness. "I thought you said this place was dangerous."

Brewster snorted without looking away, but started moving.

Cassidy and Jayce slid along the wall, pistols still levelled, while Brewster crept down the centre. Cassidy tripped over something. It dissolved when he kicked it. "Think I found the other one you shot. Must have taken a while to die."

Brewster nodded. "There could be a fourth. Maybe twenty. It's becoming a bloodbath. If they didn't need us alive, we'd probably all be corpses by now." He gave them both an apologetic glance. "Sorry blokes, this wasn't one of my better ideas."

"Hell, you say," Jayce said, taking quick glances over his shoulder. "I don't understand how the news got so far ahead of us though."

"Me neither," Brewster said as they reached the central core. "Must have communication we don't know about."

The *Nubigena* loomed above them.

Cassidy started up the ramp to the dock. As they reached the top, bullets shattered the wall in front of them, sending a scatter of fragments across their path. They dropped to their stomachs and returned fire. "I thought they didn't want to kill us," Cassidy said. Brewster squeezed off several rounds. Two bodies grabbed their chests and faded away.

"They aren't," Brewster shouted. "They're trying to pin us in." There appeared to be at least two more shooters. "They're out-ranging us with those rifles."

Cassidy attached the wooden holster to the butt of his Mauser. He rolled into the open, rose to his knee, took aim and shot one of the two as the untrained marksmen fired wildly. Jayce and Brewster rose up with him and sank several rounds in the other man with a barrage of combined projectiles.

"Don't you think that was bit of a risk?" Brewster said as they ran for the hatch.

"Well," Cassidy said between pants, "They're not supposed to kill us, right?"

Brewster cracked a grin and shook his head. "You're crazy," he said as the hatch opened and Franz ushered them through, rifle in hand.

The young German looked exhausted and shaken. "Had to kill about ten," he said as he slammed the hatch behind them. "The Lewis gun has gone through four chains."

Brewster gave an audible exhalation. He pulled a knife from his boot, reopened the hatch and dashed outside. The others clambered to the windows and the open door to cover him as he slashed at the four lines tethering the gondola. The *Nubigena* drifted away and Brewster leapt several feet to make it back inside. "Jayce." The young man wheeled the hatch shut. "I want you up on the gun platform. Franz, starboard gun. Use the Maxim. I'll use a Lewis on the port. Cassidy, I want you ready to take us out of here. I think they're about to forget about handing us in, no matter how much the Armada is paying. They may decide they can't afford to leave us alive."

"*Nubigena's* nose is still moored," Cassidy said as everyone ran for their stations.

"I know," Brewster said over his shoulder. "We'll have to shoot the line."

"Cassidy, Brewster." Karl poked his head in the door from the rear corridor and shouted, "Banner is on his feet."

Brewster nodded to Cassidy. "Go see him. I've got to get to the gun." As the Englishman turned to go Banner staggered out from behind Karl. He was still pale. His hair stuck out on the right side of his head and he leaned against the wall, but still he forced a smile.

"Trying to kill us, are they boys?" Banner asked. He put his head down and took several deep breaths. "Take me to the helm."

Karl and Cassidy each took an arm as Brewster cleared the way. They helped Banner to the helm and propped him up in front of the wheel. "Why are we still moored?" he snapped, wrapping his fingers around the spokes. He seemed to draw some energy from the *Nubigena* herself. It was as if just standing there, being captain, made him taller and straightened his shoulders. He turned. Although his skin was still damp and it didn't look like he could stand without the wheel, his eyes brightened. "I said, why the hell are we still moored?"

Brewster saluted and vanished. Less than a minute later, the top gun turret fired off a volley of shots and the Zeppelin drifted out towards the centre.

"Engage the engines," Banner said. Cassidy pushed the throttle down and felt the ship pull away.

The darkness erupted with gunfire. Bursts lit up the core as muskets and small cannon blasted away. They had few machine guns, but the two Lewises up top and the *Nubigena's* side guns responded with bursts of rounds.

Cassidy's hands flew over the controls as he did his best to compensate for his scant knowledge with instinct and luck. "They'll block off the way we came in."

"Of course," Banner said. "Now get everyone somewhere stable and belt yourselves down."

"What about the gunners?" Cassidy asked.

"Forget shooting. Belt them down too." Banner turned. He still looked like a half-animated corpse, but he smiled that singular smile the captain seemed to have patented. "Just let me fly."

"But the throttle," Cassidy said.

"Forget the damn throttle. Just get back there."

Cassidy released the handle and ran. It took him all of two minutes to make his way up into the Zeppelin's main cell, but the hardest thing was getting Jayce down off the platform. He pounded a steel bar against the girders until the young man poked his head down and Cassidy shouted for him to get down. As Jayce slid down the ladder, the *Nubigena* began to climb. The crew huddled into a cabin made for such emergencies and belted themselves to chairs fixed to the floor.

"Shouldn't one of us be up there?" Cassidy asked.

"Nein," Franz said as the craft lurched upwards. "Leave him alone with his woman."

They exchanged glances as the Zeppelin climbed, rocking them back to a ninety degree angle.

"How is he accelerating and steering at the same time?" Cassidy asked.

Brewster laughed. "Sets the wheel, moves to the throttle and moves back. I've watched him do it."

"But we're climbing," Cassidy yelled. "What the hell is he doing?"

Gunfire cracked the air, but trailed off as the ship tilted back all the way, putting the crew on their backs. "He can't do this," Jayce shouted. "Zeppelins can't do this!"

Karl shrugged. "Not that I've ever seen, but…"

The *Nubigena* accelerated faster, pushing them into their seats as it rocketed upwards. Out the window the inside of the hollow mountain flew by. The ship stood straight now, gaining altitude at breakneck speed. The light of torches rushed by in streaks. In a final burst of speed they were in the stars, the Zeppelin slowly levelling off.

Cassidy tried to imagine what it must have looked like to anyone from outside; the great stormship emerging from the mountain top like a giant bullet fired from the base of a volcano. It couldn't be done. How could Banner have remained upright enough to steer? And Zeppelins couldn't do that. They just weren't made to fly that way. But it had happened, and they watched the dark mountain slide into the nothing below.

"He really is mad," Brewster mused. "Thank God, the man's insane."

They unstrapped and made their way up to the helm. The unconscious body of Banner hung from the wheel, his arms dangling, head and upper torso arched back. Cassidy and Brewster reached him in a single stride.

"My word," Brewster said. "He's tied himself on."

Banner had looped his leather belt through the spokes of the wheel. Cassidy held him up as Brewster unfastened the buckle and Jayce cranked the throttle back to zero.

Whatever action-induced adrenaline had pushed Banner to stand and fly, had left as quickly as it had come. The gaunt captain sagged in Cassidy's arms. Only the light breath on Brewster's silver cigarette case confirmed he was still alive.

It took ten minutes to hoist him gingerly back to his cabin where Karl tended to him with the compassion and fear of a young mother. "He has killed himself," the old German moaned. He looked like he might cry, but instead pulled the sheets up to Banner's white chin and said a quiet prayer.

"Didn't know you prayed," Brewster said.

"I learned," Karl said. "I even think I know what it means now."

Cassidy felt a lump well in his throat. *Learned?* Could dreams learn? "Don't let him get up again," he admonished Karl, as if the old German needed to be told. He stumbled to his quarters under the excuse of exhaustion, but when he got there he laid down and put an arm over his eyes without sleeping.

Elena had hurt him worse than he'd realised. She probably ordered whisky on the rocks because she saw it was his drink and wanted to dig in the fact that he was helpless to change his own mind.

What were the Twilights anyway? After death they faded like dreams, but weren't dreams. Weren't human either. Some hybrid? Or simply an in-between race as their name implied? Where did Twilights, or dreams, go after death? Did they simply fade into oblivion?

Cassidy wondered if he could ever pray. How did Karl do it? What about God? The Everdream existed. The demon with the umbrella existed. There was nothing in his memory but vague concepts he couldn't put words to, as if these were things he used to know, or maybe things he believed before but couldn't remember.

Why did it disturb him so much for Banner to be catatonic? The rest of the crew acted the same way. Brewster had acted so relieved during his few minutes of not having to command anymore. Cassidy had seen it on his face the moment Karl told them Banner was on his feet. Now...

Someone knocked at the door. Cassidy took his arm away from his eyes.

Brewster poked his head in. "Sorry, Old Boy," he said, pushing himself in farther. "Jayce is keeping the ship on keel, so I thought I'd pop back and see how you were doing."

Cassidy motioned him in. The Englishman took a seat and broke out his pipe. He went through the meticulous ceremony of packing, lighting and puffing, before he leaned back and relaxed. "You still haven't said what happened to the Fokker. Karl's on pins and needles."

"Gone," Cassidy said, staring at the ceiling.

"I see," said Brewster. He clicked the pipe stem against his teeth. "Did Ned take it?"

Cassidy sighed. A part of him wanted to tell Brewster about the fickle scientists. About the strange technology there. About the witch of a mind doctor, Elena. Instead, he gave a noncommittal grunt.

"I'm not trying to put my stick in where it doesn't belong," Brewster said. He sent several clouds of bitter smoke into the air. The peat in the English blend gave off a pungent stench that was pleasant only because Cassidy associated it with his friend. "But it just seems that something's eating your guts out."

"Still trying to work the day through my head," Cassidy half-lied. "Keep expecting the world to explode."

Brewster gave a grave nod, sucked in on his pipe and exhaled more smoke. "If it's any consolation, I'm still not through it myself. 'Til you showed up I'd hardly ever shot anyone up close. Downed fighters, but that's different."

"I'm a bad penny," Cassidy said, putting his arm back over his head. "A Jonah."

"Come on, Old Boy, you landed heads up. World's just gone a little mad."

"Since I showed up," Cassidy reminded him.

Brewster shrugged. "World was always a little mad."

"So what's the new plan?" Cassidy asked, still trying to steer things away before they landed on his original rescue from the dream.

"Run like hell," Brewster said without the crack of a smile. "No strategies until the captain wakes up again. We're just going to take the long way around the Twilight. Keep away from any type of civilization and shoot at anything that flies, even if it's a bird."

Cassidy nodded. He sat up and rubbed his face. "Are we ever any more than bad echoes of a dreamer somewhere who dreams of us every night, wakes up and forgets they ever knew we existed?"

Brewster stood and pulled Cassidy from the bed. "That's got you worried again, eh. Philosophy's no good. Trust me. Sometimes just existing brings its own meaning."

"How can you be sure you exist?"

Brewster sighed. He blew more smoke, looking thoughtful, as if he might draw some meaning from the pipe itself. He slapped Cassidy on the back and opened the door. "I know I exist because I'm the one about to have a drink."

Chapter 20

Cassidy slept little as the next few weeks became an uncalculated game of cat and mouse. The Armada dogged them. Bounty ships followed just out of gun range. The *Nubigena* ran through boxes of ammunition, mostly spilled from the Maxims and Lewis guns. They ran low on food as well, and even Karl complained of all the boiled cabbage they endured because he'd insisted on bringing so much aboard on their last *real* world visit. None of them required food to remain living, but not eating took its toll on their minds. Minds which couldn't forget needing it.

At the beginning of the third week, Banner stirred for the first time since Gunyin. Cassidy reached his room along with Brewster. Jayce, Karl and Franz were already there. They exchanged glances as the captain blinked his eyes open. "How long?" he asked.

"Weeks," Cassidy said. "Perhaps a month."

"Damn," Banner said, trying to sit up. "How's our supplies? What's our status with the Armada?"

They gave him their best guess.

"We've got to gate," he said, forcing himself to a seated position and then to his feet with the aid of the end table. They tried to help but Banner brushed them away. He staggered in place, eyes wandering and unfocused.

Franz handed him a cane. Banner glared at the young German, but snatched it anyway and hobbled into the main corridor. "I'm hungry," he said, heading for the bridge. "I need a drink." He took a bowl of cabbage soup and a neat glass of scotch at the helm. He stood at the bow window and rested his hand against the aluminium mullion between the panes of glass. "You've done well, boys," he said, eyes fixed on the drifting clouds and the nothingness between them. "It's time for a holiday. What do you say?" He turned his head but his body remained rigid and braced against the steel. "Paris? Budapest? London?"

Cassidy spoke for the rest of the crew. "Anywhere with food and no Armada."

Banner motioned Cassidy over. The others retreated to the back of the control room. He put one hand on Cassidy's shoulder and locked him with a stern gaze. "You broke us out," he said, his voice low but firm. "Whether you stay with us or go your own way, I'm not forgetting that." He released Cassidy's shoulder and turned back to the helm. "Get back over here," he yelled at the rest of the crew.

Cassidy took up position leaning against his favoured support girder as Franz, Brewster, Jayce and Karl took their positions. Stay or go? It was hard to imagine going now. Even if death meant oblivion, the Everdream was the enemy in every way now. He had come to hate it. The whole damned hive-mind made him sick.

Banner smiled his Banner smile, pushing his thin moustache into a straight line. "Berlin," he said. "I haven't seen Berlin since the war started."

Franz and Karl perked up. Cassidy and Brewster exchanged anxious glances. "Where's your Fokker?" Banner asked Cassidy.

"Gone," Cassidy said.

Banner nodded. "We better get a new plane. Berlin's a perfect place."

Cassidy had already forgotten how good it felt to gate into the *real* world, but as the lightning crackled around the ship and the smell of ozone hit him, so did the fresh air. He could smell everything in it. A thousand different odours that ranged from flowers to the exhaust fumes of the engines. The more time he spent in the Twilight, the more he forgot about smells. About bold colours. *Real* tastes.

He had little time to smell the roses, however, as Banner brought them within range of a raging storm. The grey Zeppelin turned into it and Cassidy watched Banner's visage strengthen as lightning spread across the clouds and the *Nubigena* slipped in like prodigal child returning home. Colour returned to the captain's cheeks. His eyes lit up with the electric cloud veins, his grey irises almost blue, looking wild and restless. Banner stood straighter. Spun the wheel in sharp, clipped movements, his feet playing at the pedals like those of a grand piano, quickening and sustaining the notes of a Beethoven concerto.

Any other ship would have been torn to pieces by the torrent of wind and beating rain, but Banner *sailed* the storm like riding a tsunami. This was his place of power, and, in it, he was a god. No less a true deity than Karl's Woden or Poseidon in the raging sea, or Hel in the darkness of the black Underworld. *It's my storm*, Banner seemed to say with the branching lightning, *and the Nubigena is my lover.*

"God, Cassidy, can you feel it?" Banner said, glancing over.

Cassidy pushed himself away from the girder and stood near him. "I do," Cassidy said, and almost laughed, because he *could* feel it. It was rocking a lump into his throat that made him want to laugh and cry at the same time. The storm showered him with feral energies that bounced through his body and set his mind aflame. "I feel alive," Cassidy said just loud enough for Banner to hear.

The captain nodded. "Damn right, you're alive. Wait 'til you smell the food in Berlin. And the smell German girls get when they sweat between their breasts. Milk maids. They have the smoothest skin."

Cassidy laughed. He'd begun to suspect his dreamer had left love out of the blueprint altogether, but at that moment Cassidy felt something stir. Hope? Or was he just aroused by the thought of meeting *real* women again?

The *Nubigena* broke through the clouds and a rain-soaked Berlin came into view. Franz got up from his console and peered down at the landscape.

"Franz," Cassidy said, looking over his shoulder. "Can you really remember Berlin?"

"No," said Franz, though his smile hadn't gone away, "but it's *like* I remember it. It still feels like home." He turned to Cassidy. "I guess because I want it to be."

The closer they got, the more it didn't feel like home to Cassidy, though something about the landscape tugged at his chest. Something so familiar, but foreign, it irritated him just to look at the skyline. "Won't they notice us?" Cassidy asked.

Banner shrugged. "Yes and no. Even though the ship is *real*, they'll just register it as something that belongs. They just won't know why, or who we are. That's the advantage of *real* objects that spend too much time in the Twilight."

They landed, mooring themselves with an anchor this time and tied off to stakes they hammered into the hard ground. "Brewster," Banner said, "stay with the ship. I want Franz and Karl to see Berlin."

Brewster answered with a salute and got back on board. He hadn't seemed keen on exploring the streets of the German capitol anyway.

"Cassidy," Banner yelled over the roar of the rain. "There's an airbase about half a mile east. Grab whatever looks best to you and fly it out without them seeing you. You can do that with a machine the same way you make yourself unseen." He tossed Cassidy a roll of marks. "Leave this in someone's office who looks important enough to take it."

Cassidy nodded, stuffed the money in his jacket and started walking. He hadn't noticed it before, but the rain didn't soak him as it did the few people he passed huddled in oversized coats and hoods. The water ran down his uniform but didn't penetrate, or didn't care to penetrate, as if it were headed for the ground and felt no need to bother with him. So even to the weather he was a shadow, Cassidy grimaced.

He trotted across wet grass. At least the storm energies still flowed through him. Even with all the apprehension built up from walking in *enemy* territory, his spirits remained high. He was looking for a new fighter. Banner hadn't cared to ask what had happened and, God willing, he never would.

The airfield proved to be a large one. Probably the main testing ground for new aerocraft. Cassidy strode past the guards and through the checkpoint without even a raised eyebrow. He concentrated on not being seen. Remaining intangible. I'm a ghost, he thought and couldn't help the panic the thought brought with it. His heart quickened. He knew he wasn't really a Yank. These Germans weren't really his enemies, and for all that mattered, he'd never been in a single battle of The Great War. Still, it lay in shattered pieces throughout his consciousness, the memory of the carnage, the fires, the sky full of blasting fighters. He couldn't help the dark sense that he was creeping into the demon's mouth, and while making it through the entrance meant he had passed the teeth, it might close at any moment.

The grounds crawled with airmen, though most non-pilot officers seemed to prefer the inner warmth of their offices over the cold Berlin rain.

A group clustered around someone a hundred yards off. Cassidy approached and noticed a single pilot in their midst. He seemed to be trying to wave them off as they pushed pieces of paper in his face. Papers that wilted as the rain soaked through, all but disintegrating in their hands.

The airman shouted at them. His German sounded savage but pained, and Cassidy understood every word. It disturbed him every time he heard German spoken. He must have been the dream of a spy. Perhaps his dreamer had walked this very airfield, stealing information on aerocraft and the highly prized secrets of German technology. Field agent? Pilot? French dreamer? British? American would be nice, though he knew they'd only recently entered the war.

The group dissipated with a final shout from the pilot, though they continued to yell praises of adoration even as the group bled away into the rain and mud.

When they cleared, Cassidy saw the tired, strained look of the man's features, though they were all but eclipsed in shadow. His face was drawn. His arms hung limp. Shoulders drooped. A scarlet stain showed through the white bandage around his head.

"You," Richthofen said, as Cassidy approached. No one had regarded Cassidy as anything more than a strange breeze. Why could the Baron see him no matter how invisible Cassidy made himself? "Am I dreaming, or what in God's name are you doing in my sweet Berlin?"

Cassidy dug his hands into his pockets. He hunched over as if huddling from the cold, although he didn't actually feel it much. "You look tired."

Richthofen turned and trudged down the airfield. Pilots and ground crew moved away as he scowled ahead. "They think I'm a damned god," he spat. "They think I can…" He sighed. "I'm only here now in Berlin, instead of where I'm supposed to be, because they want to pin another ridiculous medal on my chest. I used to have a silver cup made for each pilot I downed. How mad is that?" He stopped and crushed a spent cartridge into the damp ground with his heel. "I'm broken, Cassidy. My mind," he said, pointing to his skull. "It doesn't work right anymore. They think I can fight for weeks without sleep and shoot without bullets and fly without fuel. They're insane, and I'm spent."

He stopped and took heavy breaths as if he were going to cry, or scream, or shoot people. Instead, Richthofen turned down to a dark section between two buildings where the overhanging roof cut off some of the rain. He leaned against the wall and slammed a fist into the grey brick. "I'm not their knight anymore. I'm a pawn and I want to stop."

"You saved our asses," Cassidy said, not knowing what else to say at the moment. "Banner's fine. He's weak, but he's flying again."

Richthofen gave a slow nod. "Ya. I meant to ask. That's good." He raised his head and a slight smile peeked through his hard features. "That was a good fight, no? I enjoyed it."

"How do you do spend so much time away?" Cassidy asked. "They must miss you."

Richthofen broke out a cigarette. He offered Cassidy one, and they both lit up. "Time is different. I spend days drinking in the Twilight. I return, and a few hours have gone by. Banner says it's because of the particular fixed gate I come through. Others don't work that way. Arcadia is my only peace now." He took a long drag and blew out smoke. "They are writing a book about me. They say I wrote it, but I don't write. I don't have time." He glared at Cassidy as if he were the German government. "It's complete scheisse. I'm not that man. No one is that man. He is a myth. An arrogant, egotistical myth."

Cassidy leaned against the building opposite Richthofen, so that only a few feet separated them. He drew in on his cigarette and breathed out a cloud through his nose. "I'm a half-drawn picture," he said, half to himself, half to The Red Baron. "I keep waiting for someone to come and tell me something. To look at me and say, *this is who you are. You're so and so. You live here or there and this has all just been a bad*—" He covered a tremble of his lips with another a drag from the cigarette.

"What are you here for?" Richthofen asked.

"I'm trying to find a new plane."

Richthofen nodded as if he understood. Not why Cassidy didn't have a plane, but why he couldn't go back for the old Fokker. Knew he didn't want to face Ned and that woman again. "Did he send you with money?"

Cassidy tossed Richthofen the roll of marks.

"Take one," Richthofen said. "One of the new Fokker prototypes. They're fast. They turn well. Good guns. I helped design them."

Cassidy nodded. He turned to go.

"John Cassidy," Richthofen said.

Cassidy turned back.

"You dream of a great dogfight. Fighters clutter the sky. Then you see a dot in the distance. Among all the planes you pick it out as if a cord connects you both and it draws you in." He paused and ashed his cigarette. "You are there for *him*. There to kill him. His fighter is red."

Cassidy stumbled sideways. He fell against the wall. Pictures flooded his mind. He couldn't breathe.

"I have dreamed about you almost since we started the war," Richthofen continued. His eyes looked distant. The lines around them crinkled and straightened.

In Cassidy's mind, the guns of his Sopwith Camel rattled as the holes in his memory filled in. He dove and spun and banked. He manoeuvred between Fokkers, Albatrosses, Sopwiths and Nieuports. His guns rattled again as his target darted beyond his sights. The Sopwith stalled, began to smoke and dove. The red Fokker exploded into the ground in front of the many-spired castle.

"I always knew the Americans would enter the war. They were a myth with teeth. We didn't know what to expect, but we knew they would come. And I dreamed of you. No," Richthofen said, shaking his head, "not a dream. A nightmare. The pilot who would someday down me. Fly me to the edge, and over, and into the ground."

Richthofen dropped the butt of his cigarette and crushed it into the damp grass. "Perhaps not a nightmare," he said. "Perhaps a wish."

Cassidy looked up. It was hard to make eye contact. "You told Banner. Told him about your dreams."

The Baron shrugged. "He said the nightmare would go away. It did. I dreamed my dreams without dying. Next thing you know, he walks into the Arcadian lounge with my nightmare beside him. I thought I would die." He paused. "I don't have any answers for you, John Cassidy. I'm not a god." The Baron turned and trudged away. The tips of his soggy grey coat vanished into the pouring rain as he left the dry space between the buildings.

Cassidy shook. He stumbled out into the rain. The dream was full in his mind. Every damned minute of it, right down to the point where three German fighters had combined their guns to bring him down, shredding his fighter. He'd brought his Sopwith down and bailed out just before the plane crashed. Hit the ground with a rolling thud. Survived by a hair.

The Baron's Fokker had burned in front of him. The pilot had still been alive. On fire and alive. Screaming. Cursing. Cassidy remembered *all* the dreams. All the variations. All the nightmares in which he'd starred. The planes had changed. The battle. The ultimate fight. But the castle had been there each time. The castle and Richthofen's burning plane. Tongues of fire leaping up around the crimson red paint and black iron crosses.

Not a dream, Cassidy thought. He'd been a bogeyman to the red pilot the Allies called Death.

Chapter 21

Cassidy found a bi-wing Fokker VII that looked like it had just come out of the shop. He ran his hand over the smooth rounded fuselage, the tail rudder and elevator flap. The dual Spandaus looked pristine and fully loaded with chains of 7.8mm shells. He lifted the leather cover over the cockpit, exposing an immaculate interior, complete with leather trimming and chrome accents. The wings were as straight as a captain's bars and water beaded against the sealed and stretched canvas that covered the wing frame.

The engine appeared to be at least a Mercedes D.III and he could probably push the fighter to no less than 110 mph. Probably more. The prop was longer than Cassidy was tall. It had been carved from a deep rich alder, rubbed and sanded smooth. The German adornments could be repainted, though in a strange way, the twin Iron Crosses felt familiar even as they revolted him other ways.

Cassidy climbed into the cockpit, pumped up the fuel tank pressure and switched the motor on. The fuel gauge read full. There were probably magnetos, but using them didn't feel right. Not on the craft's first flight. Instead, he hopped down, grabbed the prop in both hands and gave it a sharp downward yank. The engine engaged immediately. Cassidy climbed back aboard, strapped in and taxied out to the runway.

If anyone heard the engine over the pounding rain, they didn't seem to care. Probably assumed some pilot was taking one of the planes up for a test flight, and it wasn't worth getting wet to check.

As Cassidy throttled forwards, several pilots glanced towards the fighter but didn't react or seem alarmed. He could have been any German pilot. When the Fokker reached flying speed and he felt the wings dancing with the rushing wind, he pulled back the stick and took to the air.

It handled better than anything he'd ever flown. The stick was so responsive. The pedals required no more than the slightest pressure to roll the fighter over. A thrill took over that could never have been described in words, but it cascaded over him in waves of intense heat. Something about having his own fighter. Not the government's, like in his dream. Not the *Nubigena's* that just anyone flew. Banner meant this to be *his*. John Cassidy's.

John Cassidy. The name sounded both foreign and beautiful in his mind. The complete memory of the dream he'd come from made it even more solid. "John Cassidy," he said out loud. The name was *his*, like the new Fokker was his. Richthofen had given him both in a way. True, the name was that of a nightmare and Banner had paid money for the plane, but the Baron himself had told him which kind to choose and had even helped design it.

Cassidy banked and dove and rolled, not caring that the rain covered his *real* goggles. The storm energies streamed through him. He felt the storm itself like some people felt sunshine. Perhaps the same way Banner did. Perhaps the feeling came from owning something *real*.

He took the Fokker into the clouds to see if he could do what Banner did. The fighter shook hard with turbulence, but Cassidy eased it into phase with the roll of the storm, which he felt in his blood now. The savage bolts of lightning. The pound of thunder in his chest as he slipped between the warring fronts. He'd caught the pulse of the storm and matched his heartbeat to it.

Cassidy moved through the harsh wind like a salmon twisting upstream, finning through the tremulous eddies and furious currents. His heart leapt and he laughed out loud. This was what it was like to be kin to the storm. To be natural to it. To be as much a part of it as air and accumulated moisture, and the raw blue energy and cracks of thunder.

Born of the storm.

Nubigena.

He didn't know how he knew. Perhaps Richthofen's classical schooling, or some grey knowledge he'd picked up from Banner, but *Nubigena* meant "born of the storm", and this was why. Strangely, it didn't explain how he understood perfect English. Richthofen spoke it well enough, but with a thick accent and Cassidy had more than once run into words the Baron didn't know.

There had to be more to him than just his dreamer's knowledge and memories. The Everdream must add some things in to fill dreams out. It must draw on it vast repository of...of what? How much did it know? He'd have to talk about that one day with Brewster.

Cassidy nosed the fighter down below the clouds so he could see where the great Zeppelin moored. It rested against the ground like a half-bridled cloud, bucking at its moorings. And on the ground, standing with his feet apart, hands planted on his hips and his mouth open in raucous laughter, stood Banner, watching him. His white scarf whipped in the wind and he looked like a god scrutinizing his son as he rode a chariot of fire for the first time. Apollo? Prometheus? Where had he heard those names?

Cassidy landed. Jayce and Franz ran up, checking the fighter out like a rider would a new filly.

"Ah, they have gotten better, I see," Karl said as he examined the engine. "BMW. I have never heard of that. Configuration looks brilliant, but I have to take a good look. Is beautiful."

"Can you still work on her?" Cassidy asked the old German.

He looked indignant. "Of course I can work on her. I'll make her even better. I still know things they don't. I'll always know things they don't."

Given his recent realization about the Everdream knowledge, Cassidy believed that. No telling how much had been pumped into Karl to make him the dream engineer of Graf Zeppelin.

"Those guns look like they can really spit out the lead," Jayce said, running his hand along the barrel of one of the new Spandaus.

Banner regarded the fighter with distant fascination. His love was the *Nubigena*, but Cassidy could tell the captain was impressed with the Fokker by way he kept cocking his head as he eyed the smooth fuselage. "I guess Karl better put a new mooring on her," Banner said.

Cassidy shook his head. "With your permission, Captain, I'd like to try landing and taking off up top."

Banner narrowed his eyes. "*Land* on my baby?" He ran his eyes over the Zeppelin from stem to stern as if trying to imagine what that would do.

"I've heard they launch off large ships now. Why not the *Nubigena*?" Cassidy asked.

Banner gave him a sceptical look and glanced at Karl.

Karl shrugged. "Landing would be very hard, but perhaps. I'll get materials here, but it'll have to be done in the Twilight."

Banner nodded. "Do it. Later we can put two or three more down below again, like we used to."

"What will you call her," Jayce asked as he examined the German decorations. "Can't stick with the old crosses."

Cassidy shrugged. "I don't know yet." He turned back to Banner. "Did we already get supplies?"

"Ha," Banner said. "Franz and Karl saw the sights. Jayce and I got wine, liquor, game, sausage and a bunch of other things I can't pronounce. We also appropriated more munitions than we can ever use." Banner gave a dismissive gesture. "For the next few weeks anyway. See you in the air," he said with a quick salute and everyone boarded except Cassidy, who mounted his new Fokker.

The magnetos brought it to life with a single crank. He lifted off ahead of the Zeppelin, eager to touch the storm clouds, which edged towards the brink of moving on. He banked into a steep climb.

The storm accepted him again. He slipped into it like an electric mantle and felt where the denser mass of energy had moved to. On instinct, he flew towards it, skimming once again the violent currents.

He felt something else, too. A soft place. A field in the rolling clouds where they created a rippling vortex.

He neared the place and felt it throb and pulse. Green light exploded from its centre and radiated out in crackling waves. The smell of ozone increased.

Behind him, the *Nubigena* tore through the outer shell of a dark cumulous cloud. The ship appeared as if it had been a part of the cloud, but shed its skin and left it behind to dissolve into the rest of the storm matter.

Cassidy banked and slowed so that he flew above the Zeppelin now. He knew where it was heading. He'd found the gate first. The round nose struck the wall of green light and branches of electric current ran along the length of ship and up to him so that it forked and arced over the controls and wings and down the tail.

Together the *Nubigena* and the Fokker VII gated into the Twilight. The clouds shifted from black to light purple. Cassidy half expected to find the Armada on the other side, but Banner continued to elude them with whatever sense or luck he possessed. Cassidy thought of The Flying Dutchman. Banner hadn't mentioned him yet, but surely knew he'd been betrayed. Was he just going to let the affront slide?

Cassidy scanned the skies for signs of fighters or airships. Perhaps he should do this more often. Fly scout when they gated and while they flew through uncertain territory. Cassidy took it upon himself to make his way out in front of the ship, then back and to the sides in an escort pattern.

A line floated above the horizon of clouds. He throttled forwards and flew over it. The line turned out to be a disc at least a few miles in diameter. It was solid water, a floating ocean with no earth mass to support it. He flew beneath, and, as he'd suspected, the water hovered without trench or basin. Reverse waves licked downward, rolling down and then up.

Cassidy flew back above the surface and came in close enough to see a platform floating on the water. A giant sheet of rusted metal with a variety of small buildings dotting its surface.

The *Nubigena* landed. There was no ground crew there to tether the ship, so Jayce and Franz leapt to the ground and tied it off.

Cassidy landed beside the Zeppelin. "Where's this?" he asked as Banner exited the gondola.

"The Water," Banner said, holding his arms apart as if referring to the entire expanse of drifting ocean. "What else would they call it?"

"It's safe?" Cassidy asked.

Banner shrugged. "Safe to the extent that no one is here. As far as I know, it's been abandoned for years, but it's great for repairs."

Brewster hadn't seen the new Fokker yet, so came down for a look. He examined it for several minutes, then nodded. "It's a hell of a fighter."

"Doesn't anyone else get upset that I'm the only one who flies anymore?"

Brewster grinned. "We all had our turn," the Englishman said. "They'd all rather be in the ship with Banner than out going one on one with the Armada."

"I can't imagine not wanting to fly," said Cassidy. "Ever."

Brewster shrugged. "Guess it depends on how we're dreamed."

"I met him," Cassidy said. He folded his arms and stared at the fighter. "I know who he is now."

Brewster cocked his head. "Met *him*, Old Boy?"

Cassidy took a deep breath. He laid a hand against the Fokker's body and leaned against the frame. "I ran into Richthofen at the airbase. I finally know why he looked at me the way he did the first time we met." He gave Brewster a short version of the meeting.

Brewster sucked in on the tepid Twilight air. He leaned against the Fokker as well and seemed to lose himself in the paint design. "My God," he finally said. "No wonder you can fly the way you do. Probably based you on everything he thought a Yank could do and everything his brother *could* do, and everything *he* can do. Also explains why you can shoot like that."

Cassidy gave a slow nod. "I feel like I should have known. Every time I looked at him, I should have guessed."

"Does it make you feel any different? I don't even have inkling about mine. Is it like meeting…God?"

Cassidy turned around, leaned back against his new plane and looked out at the soft lavender clouds hovering over the gentle waves. "For a minute. I mean, I felt connected to something. Almost *real.*" He sighed. "Don't know. It all just made sense, there in the storm. Now I'm back to thinking, *what was I really?* I mean, Richthofen must have had a thousand dreams in his life and I'm just a terror that haunted him since the war began. In the end, I'm just a random splinter of someone I barely know."

Brewster wet his lips. "You could drive a bloke mad with all that thinking, you know?" He shook his head, turned around and stared out at the same clouds. "I mean, you've got to stop asking. Live life. If I got caught up thinking through all that, they'd have to scrape me off the floor of the asylum."

"I guess I just wanted to be the result of someone's purposeful creation. Instead, I'm a collection of random thoughts and fears."

Brewster laughed and slapped Cassidy on the arm. "Come on, mate," he said. "You've got to be your own man. Bring out your own personal meaning. Besides, for all you know, people from the *real* world are just the dreams of some distant creatures they can't even conceive of."

Cassidy grinned. "I thought you weren't into philosophy?"

Brewster smirked. "I think about it. I just don't dwell on it."

"Well, I also know things Richthofen can't know," Cassidy added. "The Everdream must have put more in."

"Next, you'll be rattling off things about the Akashic Library."

"What's that?"

Brewster shrugged. "Haven't the foggiest, but the term is in my head somewhere."

Cassidy tried to smile, but couldn't. He pulled away from his plane and walked to the edge of the metal platform. Brewster stayed back at the fighter. On land, this might have been a beach, but here, the water lapped over the sharp edge and slipped back off, into the *ocean*, if one could call it that.

Cassidy wondered if he could swim. What would happen if he dove in? Would he drown? Would he come out the bottom and keep falling forever? Was there anything below the Twilight? Or was it nothing but endless clouds?

He knelt down. Was there any life in the water, or was the little floating ocean completely dead and abandoned?

Chapter 22

Cassidy retired to his quarters while Karl worked on the *Nubigena* and the new Fokker. Apparently a dangling arm would be fixed to the bottom of the plane, which would lay flat against the fuselage, but he could release it when landing. Karl's theory went that the arm would grab a cable stretched across the landing surface he was building atop the Zeppelin. Now if only he could learn to land and take off with so little distance. But if Banner could do the impossible with the Zeppelin, perhaps he could do the same with a plane.

Cassidy's quarters looked the same way he'd left them, but a sensation rushed over him that he hadn't felt before. Something akin to familiarity, but not. Cassidy closed the door and lay down on his bed. He felt the rush of sensation again as he looked around the room. The dress uniform Brewster had given him hung in the corner. He'd already put his holster on the chair beside his bed and his jacket rested next to it. These things had been done without thinking. Home, Cassidy thought. Was he forming new habits?

He stretched his legs, then decided to pry his boots off and enjoy the first moment he'd spent of true relaxation since...since whenever the last time had been. He had trouble remembering that. Cassidy drifted into sleep.

The clouds parted as he flew with his squadron. The Jagdstaffel, Richthofen's elite squadron, engaged them in a fury. They exchanged rounds, rolled and banked. Fighters exploded and dove for the ground.

Out of the distance a red fighter appeared and he flew towards it. Cassidy gripped the gun levers tight and sighted for the Baron's tri-plane as it approached. The scene was so specific now. Practiced. Cassidy knew every moment of it and it felt like déjà vu cascading over him as he engaged Richthofen.

The Baron dove. He banked. The Baron rolled. Cassidy dove. The red tri-plane flew through his sight, but the guns didn't fire. He looked down and realised he hadn't triggered them.

Richthofen looked at him from his plane and knew. Knew he should be dead. Knew something was different. And then the other fighters were gone and only their two planes were left.

Cassidy's Sopwith.

The Baron's Fokker.

They held their fire and matched speeds. The fighters descended like falcons coming to perch and landed at the base of the many-spired castle. Richthofen edged out of his fighter and cocked his head as Cassidy leapt down from his. "Do I know you?" the Baron asked.

Cassidy nodded. "You know me."

"You are here to kill me," the Baron said. He looked lost. Confused. Glanced around as if he stood in an alien world. "I feel I've dreamed this before."

Cassidy nodded. "I know. And I've always wanted to ask," he said, motioning up at the medieval structure, "is this your family castle?"

Richthofen stared up at the structure as if trying to take it in. This must be how most dreamers were in their own dreams. Strange how, for once, Cassidy was the natural entity, not the alien. Could one wake in their own dream? Was this still Richthofen's dream, or his own dream now? Did they share this dream? Was this just the version of his dreamer that Cassidy's mind created?

The Baron shook his head. "Family castle? I don't think so. I'm not sure. When I was a child, perhaps…" They walked to the front gate, which raised, and they entered.

"Did you used to visit here?" Cassidy asked as the gothic interior stretched above them.

"Perhaps," Richthofen said. "My family—" He fell to his knees and gripped his head. Screamed as the blood gushed from a wound that opened the side of his skull. "I can't," he howled as much to himself as to Cassidy. "I can't do it anymore. Something's wrong."

The dream faded. Cassidy groaned and sat up. His skull throbbed. He made his way down to the head and splashed water on his face. A bottle of aspirin stood near. The top was screwed on too tight. His vision blurred. He shattered the bottle. Shovelled pills into his mouth and swallowed hard.

"Cassidy?"

Cassidy looked up. Banner stood outside the door. Cassidy slumped back against the wall and buried his face in his hands. "Why the hell didn't you tell me?"

"Tell you what?" Banner asked, stooping down. "Your name's John. I was going to tell you. I didn't have a chance yet."

Cassidy took his hand away from his face. "Richthofen. Why didn't you tell me about Richthofen?"

Banner's brow furrowed. "What does he have to do with any of this?"

Cassidy laughed. His head hurt so bad, he couldn't help it. "Why couldn't you just tell me the truth?"

Banner sat beside him and stared at the floor. "Have you told anyone?"

"Does it matter?" Cassidy asked. He was crying now. His head felt as if it were being ripped to pieces.

Banner's eyes narrowed. He folded his hands and leaned his head back against the wall. "I used to tell everyone. They always left the ship to go on some foolish pilgrimage to find their dreamer." He gave a deep sigh. "And they'd get caught or killed. Many just dissolved because their dreamer was in the *real* world, somewhere outside a storm. They didn't care, just ran out into the wasteland and faded to nothing."

Cassidy tore at his hair as if trying to rip the pain out. He pulled himself to his feet, stepped over Banner and stumbled down the hallway.

"Cassidy," Banner called. "It wouldn't have helped. It would have just confused you."

The ship quaked. Banner leapt to Cassidy's side, trying to prop him up. "We're under attack," Banner said. "Dammit, I can't believe they found us this soon."

Through the windows, Cassidy saw Armada airships cresting the ocean's horizon. His head cleared as adrenaline pushed the pain away further than aspirin ever could. He turned to the captain. "Drag the plate over the edge and cut the line," he said and ran for the hatch.

Banner blinked several times. "What the devil for?"

"Just do it."

The captain nodded and sprinted for the helm.

Cassidy made his way outside as bullets rattled off the metal platform. The Fokker still rested where he'd left it, though it appeared Karl had already done something to the underbelly. A quick run and a leap and he was in the cockpit, revving the magneto. He noticed an extra lever Karl must have installed, but he'd have to play with it later.

The engine engaged and he throttled forwards. Two airships were in sight, but dark shadows beneath the ocean brought a sick dread to his stomach. A gentle pull on the stick and the Fokker VII caught air, dodging rounds as it picked up speed. Airships instead of fighters seemed odd. Perhaps this was a change in tactic, or they were out of *real* planes. Good, Cassidy thought. He might have an advantage against dreamships.

The *Nubigena* lifted into the air as Cassidy pushed his Fokker above the Armada crafts. The Zeppelin's mooring lines remained attached to the platform, dragging it across the ocean.

Both airships ignored Cassidy and made for the *Nubigena* instead. They probably assumed he was running, but Cassidy throttled down, pulled a hairpin turn and dove at the first airship, Spandaus blazing. The two levers worked as one on this Fokker, allowing him to fire both guns and still control the plane without pinning the stick between his knees.

Cassidy emptied enough bursts into the football shaped air bladder of one ship to rupture the cell. The gondola splashed into the water, covered by the mass of purple fabric. The other airship had noticed him and broke off its attack on the *Nubigena*. Cassidy smiled. Instead of engaging, he continued his descent below the rim of the ocean disc.

As he feared, another airship and two *real* fighters lay beneath, out of view. They headed towards him, bringing a grin to his face. The second airship from above the ocean made its way below as well and all four opened fire.

Cassidy continued his plunge until the enemies above were forced to angle down for attack, then pulled the Fokker out of its dive. His new fighter responded better than anything he'd ever flown. The two fighters dealt with the manoeuvre easily, but the airships couldn't compensate. By the time he'd reached them again, the fighters were on his tail, blazing away, with the two airships only just making their way behind him.

The dark shadow of the square platform made its way across the transparent ocean above. The *Nubigena* would soon clear the edge. Cassidy made for where the Zeppelin would emerge. He adjusted his speed. Rolled and pitched to keep the Armada bullets out of his hide.

He glanced behind. They were all there, firing away in perfect, predictable formation. The grey nose of the *Nubigena* slipped over the edge of the blue disc of water above. It looked like a cloud coming out from behind the moon. Cassidy rolled to bring himself beneath the ship and nudged the stick forwards a hair. Full throttle. The Fokker cleared the water first, ahead of the *Nubigena*. He pulled hard on the stick and doubled back to the ship.

As he flew back along the Zeppelin's tail, the metal platform crested the water and tipped downward. The *Nubigena* released the line. Both Armada airships struck the plate, full on as it slid over the edge. The lead fighter slammed into it a moment later, ringing the solid metal like a bell. The second fighter rolled at the last moment and peeled out on the far side. Cassidy flew after him as the *Nubigena* cleared the ocean. He couldn't believe three pilots had fallen for the ploy. He'd only hoped for two.

Behind Cassidy the purple sky crackled with green light as he opened fire on the last fighter. The Albatross dove and he followed. He glanced over his shoulder to see the *Nubigena* nosing into the gate. Almost to the gondola. He needed to leave now, or he'd miss his window. But the fighter was so close. Cassidy fired again, clipping the tailfin. This pilot was better than most. Perhaps they'd taken to sending the dreams of *real* people instead of their own constructs.

A fluttering began in Cassidy's chest. It felt good. So good to have an opponent who really knew how to fly. The Albatross turned and engaged. The flash of his guns blasted between the blurring props and Cassidy rolled to avoid the burst of screaming bullets. His new Fokker responded with gentle ease, rolling and diving in one smooth motion.

Cassidy dove and spun. The Albatross flew above the water island, using the ocean as a shield. Cassidy tried to fire through, but the bullets wouldn't penetrate. He cut his throttle and turned the Fokker over to fly inverted to the water, making himself a mirror image of the fighter above. His landing gear skimmed the bottom of the ocean. The edge of the water neared and he pushed the throttle all the way forwards.

As the Fokker's nose passed the ocean's edge, Cassidy dipped the landing gear into the water. The plane shuddered as the dense ocean yanked on the rear wheel. He gritted his teeth as the manoeuvre flipped the Fokker end over end, flipping him into a straight line with the Albatross.

The other pilot panicked and tried to nose himself under the Fokker. Cassidy fired as the Albatross's own landing gear caught the water and flipped its tail in the air. The Fokker rolled around it with a gentle touch on the right pedal.

That Albatross spun out of control. Cassidy made his way back around and emptied another barrage of gunfire into the plane. It burst into flames and shattered into a shower of sparks across the blue water.

Cassidy turned back to the *Nubigena*. It was gone. So was the gate.

Chapter 23

Cassidy flew through the space where the gate had been. A spike or two of residual energy arced over his instruments, but the air was empty. In the *real* world, in the storm, he'd felt the gate, but how Banner managed to find them in nothingness, he couldn't imagine.

Whatever the case, it did Cassidy no good now. He couldn't tap, or notice anything except how empty the world could feel when there was no planet below, no islands on the horizon and he was flying a fighter with limited fuel.

Cassidy throttled back to conserve as much fuel as possible and aimed at a random spot in the sky. If not for gravity, he wouldn't have known up or down in the blue soup of the Twilight. Was there a planet somewhere out of sight below, or did the Twilight simply possess its own inner physics?

It mattered little as the silky clumps of condensation blew by. Brewster had told him islands appeared at all levels. The very concept of horizon meant nothing either, as the clouds appeared at various heights as well. The fuel gauge read just over half, though he'd found it difficult to judge gasoline consumption in this variant reality. Even time seemed to stretch and bend a little, though there was no way to tell whether or not the effect was only in his mind.

After what felt like several hours of straight flight, dots appeared in the distance. One by one they got bigger, but proved to be no more than large rocks floating through space. Towards the far edge of the cluster, a larger one came into view. As he flew farther, it kept growing. A huge one, Cassidy thought. It looked like an upside down mountain, with smaller mountains jutting from its centre.

On the near side he saw structures and a host of airships circling, docking and leaving. The point of no return edged closer as the docks themselves came into view. Run or land? He checked his fuel. The Fokker still had a quarter tank, but the next island could be a few miles away, or a thousand. He considered flying an eighth tank out and using the rest to return, but he didn't like the thought of relying on the Twilight's idea of consistency.

Cassidy grimaced and nosed down towards the docks. He recognized the main structure on the edge. He recognized the docks. Arcadia.

His chest tightened at the thought of flying in without Banner and whatever luck or protection came with being crew of the *Nubigena*. The only advantage was that perhaps he'd be less sought after, even flying his *real* fighter, which probably stuck out to Twilights the same as if he'd been riding a flying horse. He hoped he could fuel and take off before anyone gathered enough force to bother him.

The Arcadian runway ran along the edge of the island and ended just short of the docks. He brought the Fokker in easy and taxied into one of the free spaces. "I need fuel," he yelled to a young Twilight in overalls and a greasy red cap.

"Damn, Mister," the young man said as he came up the ramp and approached the fighter, "this thing's *real*."

"I know," said Cassidy. "Can I get fuel for her?"

The young man nodded. "Sure you can. We keep some special, but we'll have to bring it from the tunnel. That'll take some time." He motioned to the stairs. "Might as well go in and have a drink while you wait."

Cassidy took a deep breath. The last thing he wanted to do was walk into the hotel. The *other* last thing he wanted to do was look suspicious. He couldn't begin to imagine how many bounty hunters might lurk in a port this big, and Armada agents could be just about anyone. He stuffed a wad of Arcadian bank notes into the young man's hand. "I'll do that," he said and tried to give a confident smile. "That would hit the spot right about now."

The stairs looked more like a ladder. Each step had been cut no more than four inches into the mountain and he found himself using both hands *and* feet to climb. His glance darted in all directions as he breached the top and crossed the docks. He'd almost been killed once less than six yards away, and Banner had been with him. So had Richthofen.

Pilots, dock crew and a variety of other sundry people crowded the vast wooden planking. Some looked like mercenaries or soldiers of some other kind. Twilight police? He didn't know if Arcadia had any kind of authorities or not.

The lounge and bar looked exactly as he remembered. He'd already paid the young Twilight most of the little money he had in his pockets, and what remained would be lucky to bring him a drink.

He sat down and waited for the exotic barkeep to approach. Just one beer, he thought, as the same, almost effeminate blonde Twilight with spiky hair walked over and set an empty tumbler to the side. Beer, he thought. I want a beer. "Whisky, on the rocks," Cassidy said, through gritted teeth.

The barkeep looked taken aback for a moment, but recovered his pristine composure. "Shall I put this on Captain Banner's tab?"

Cassidy flicked his glance around again. Did everyone here know him? He gave a begrudging nod.

The barkeep gave a knowing wink and reached for the whisky. "Will you need a room tonight, sir? And will you require company?"

Cassidy shook his head. "No thanks," he said, "and no. I don't have long."

The barkeep dropped several cubes of ice into a cut crystal glass with a pair of silver tongs and poured four fingers of amber whisky over it. "Too bad. Shea still talks about you." He set the glass down in front of Cassidy with an elegant flair and leaned in. He gave a flirtatious, conspiratorial smile. "I think she'd like to see you again."

"Maybe next time," Cassidy said. He lifted the rich liquid to his lips and took a long sip. It was good whisky. Very good whisky. Single malt. He'd forgotten what a difference a nice bar made. How superior whisky could be. Still, he would have given the world to order anything else.

"It's you again," came a voice from behind. No other voice could have made those words sound the way they did. They didn't say, "It's you again," as if it were a question. They didn't say it as if the words even meant what they stated. Instead, they curled into his ears like smoke and drew him back towards the mouth that made them. The syllables even arched like a woman's smooth spine. They rubbed into him and hooked him and stroked their way down his chest.

Cassidy turned just enough to glimpse Shea as she moved to the bar and leaned against it. The wood seemed to mould around her body and tremble at her touch.

The green leaf markings snaked down her neck, over her chest and down the soft valley between her breasts where curves peeked past the V cut of her green gown. The leaves continued to the sharp angle of the reverse V, just above her navel, and continued down to the shaved crevice between her legs, down her inner thighs and ended in the tapered vines around her delicate ankles and…Cassidy tried to bring himself back.

For a moment he did, but then something soft, an almost transparent smell wafted in. The green odour of young saplings, dew in the morning, cut grass after the rain. Her green eyes. Her red hair.

Cassidy moved a shaking hand back to his drink. She was different this time. Trying harder. Prepared for some reason. Why? Had she been paid to torture him? He pulled the glass to his lips and knocked back the rest of the drink. The cold ice hit his lips and the burning amber tore down his throat and up into his head, flared across his skin in a sudden rush of alcoholic heat. "Sorry, I don't have long," he said, and set the glass back down. The cubes rattled as the glass struck the counter.

Shea slipped onto the barstool beside him. Her eyes looked moist, her lips drawn. She stared at her hands and a tear ran down her cheek. "Why?" she asked and looked up at him. She was no less beautiful, but her allure faded as if a mask had slipped off and shattered to the floor. "Tell me it's because you're a dream. Tell me it's because you just weren't dreamed with that part of you."

Cassidy gave a single slow nod and stared back at his empty drink. "I thought that for a while," he said and flicked the glass with his index finger. "But the truth is I'm still waiting for someone." He met her shining emerald eyes as if for the first time. They weren't calling him to bed, or trying to wrestle him into it. They were just pleading for an answer. It was a look he, if anyone, could understand.

"How do you know it's not me?" she asked. All seductive nuance was gone. It was a real question. A quivering, almost childish question, one he doubted she'd ever asked before. "Is it just because I'm...a professional?"

"No," Cassidy said, shaking his head. "And I guess I don't know. I don't *know* anything at all. But I am waiting 'til I recognise it."

Shea nodded. She attempted a smile which turned to something eminently more sad. "Perhaps next time, Cassidy," she said, and pulled coy playfulness back into her voice as if recovering her nature, or at least the nature she'd adopted. Her soft footsteps padded away.

Cassidy turned back to his empty drink. It was strangely appropriate: a hollow glass with slowly melting ice. He missed Shea. Wanted her back just for the conversation.

"Another drink?" The barkeep asked as he passed by.

"I could use a smoke," Cassidy said. He held the empty glass in his hand and rolled it between his fingers.

The barkeep opened a wide cigarette case and offered it to Cassidy. "How about that drink?"

Cassidy slid out a single cigarette and put it between his teeth. He lit it with a glass-encased lighter from the bar. A thin stream of smoke blew out his lips. "Sure," he said. "It's a day for drinking."

The barkeep filled another glass with ice and four more fingers of whisky. "In Arcadia," he said, as if reciting an age old mantra, "we only water it down if you ask us to."

Cassidy nodded and sipped the second drink.

"You can put that one on *my* tab," a man several stools down said, and toasted Cassidy with a shot of red scotch. The man hadn't been there a moment before. He wore a black snap-brim Fedora and a three-piece banker's suit. The pocket watch fob glittered against his pin-striped waistcoat and his boots looked military shined. Cassidy recognized him as the same man he'd met his first night in Arcadia. "On second thought," the man said, "throw that out. Get him a single malt Scotch, no ice. Real stuff. None of that Twilight shit."

The barkeep gave a quick nod and reached beneath the counter. "This costs more than twenty of any other drink in the bar," he said, and drew out a crystal cut bottle with a burgundy label. It looked old. More importantly, it looked real. The dark crusty label shone brighter than anything around it, to say nothing of the liquid inside. Cassidy grimaced at how subdued the colours of the Twilight were in comparison. As the Scotch poured, the glass filled with a deep, vivid liquid. The barkeep put the bottle away as if ashamed of the contrast.

Cassidy stared at the liquid. It looked as if it might burst out of the dingy prison of a glass and escape across the counter.

"Never had anything but whisky, have you?" the man said. It was hard to place his accent. It could have been American. It could have been English. It could just as easily have been Polish or Czech.

Cassidy shook his head. "Not often."

"That's a shame," said the man. "Try it."

Cassidy lifted the glass to his lips and took a light sip. The warmth and flavour erupted in his mouth. It burned like fire through gas-soaked paper. He'd tasted real liquor, but the reaction was much more severe in the Twilight where his senses reacted less to the dull environment.

The man rolled the remains of his own Scotch around in his glass and put it down. "My name is Barnabas," he said, and put out his gloved hand.

Cassidy shook it with a hesitant grip. "Cassidy."

"I know," Barnabas said. "That man you fly with isn't all he seems."

Cassidy took another mouse sip of Scotch and rolled it around in his mouth. "Tell me something I don't know."

Barnabas broke out in a smile. "I will."

Cassidy lifted a single eyebrow.

Barnabas nodded. "I'll tell you what he really is. I'll tell you where he comes from. I'll tell you how to walk around in the real world, outside of storms. And I'll teach you how to order something other than whisky on ice."

Cassidy returned to his cigarette, which had burned half-way down and left a tube of ash on the table while he was lost in the taste of Scotch. "Can you teach me about love?"

Barnabas drew his lips into a sour pucker. "Women," he said. "I can teach you all you want to know about the flesh, but what you're wanting to know is outside my realm of..." he paused as if trying to find the right words. "Outside my realm of expertise."

Cassidy took another sip. "I have no reason to trust you."

Barnabas shook his head. "In this place, I could be anything. Hunter. Police."

"No," Cassidy said, blowing out more smoke. "You don't look Twilight. And you don't look Armada." He was about to say, *you do remind me of a lunatic with an umbrella*, but decided not to. Something about the white of his teeth. Too white. He took another sip to cover it. "What do you want?"

"*Your* expertise," Barnabas said, flashing those self-same bone-white teeth. "I need a dream to do things I can't."

"Hard to imagine something I could do that you couldn't do yourself."

Barnabas smiled again. "Perceptive of you. But there are limits."

"Do I need my fighter?" Cassidy asked.

Barnabas smiled. "Won't even need a ship."

"Then I'm bringing my sidearm."

"As you wish," Barnabas said, extending his hand towards the staircase.

Cassidy finished off his last sip of Scotch and followed the well-dressed man. The drink made his head spin. *Real* Scotch must also have a stronger effect here, he thought. Much stronger. He fought hard to concentrate on not stumbling. He scanned the room for dangers as they crossed the lounge and ascended the stairwell. Barnabas didn't even look over his shoulder to see if Cassidy was following. The man seemed so sure of himself, Cassidy thought. Too sure.

He touched the wooden holster with his left arm.

Barnabas twisted the handle of his hotel room door and walked through. Cassidy edged in behind him, checking left and right for a possible ambush. "It's just my room," Barnabas said.

It wasn't *just* his room. Though Cassidy got a good look at it as he entered, it changed the moment he passed the threshold. The light dimmed to almost nothing. The walls were closer now. No carpet. No bed. Rows of shelving lined the walls, stacked with thin corked phials.

"Where are we?" Cassidy asked. His gun was already in his hand and levelled at Barnabas' head. The *man* looked odd, thin and pushed together as if seen through curved glass.

Cassidy realized he was standing in a transparent cylinder and he was moving upwards. Above him, a hole just bigger around than himself filled with a brown plug. A giant hand pushed the plug in firm. A large eye stared in at him.

"I'd appreciate you not firing that thing in there. It'll bounce around and tear your little body up before I get a chance to use it." The voice of Barnabas boomed in on him and the giant hand set him up on a shelf between two other phials. "Keep tight. I'll be needing you soon." Barnabas moved out of Cassidy's line of vision and was gone.

Chapter 24

Around Cassidy gaunt figures slumped against the inside curves of their own glass prisons. The dream to his left appeared asleep. He wore a blue gown and royal headdress. To Cassidy's right, a naked white body lay on its back, mouth open as if gasping for air. Cassidy couldn't tell if the body was alive or dead. Man or woman.

Cassidy fired several rounds into the stopper above. A cloud of shredded cork rained down. He slammed his shoulder against the glass in the hopes of knocking his phial from the shelf, but it didn't budge. Slumping down against the smooth wall he tried to imagine what purpose the creature had for dreams in jars.

Cassidy sighed, holstered his weapon and sat down. He deserved this. Not half an hour in Arcadia and he'd already met something far worse than anything he'd planned on. Worse how, he couldn't say, but this *creature* in the fancy suit was nothing native to the Twilight. He should have pressed Banner further for more information when he'd had the chance, but doubted it would have made much difference. Barnabas had lured him with the things he truly craved: answers, freedom. *Freedom?* Now there stood irony like a dark angel waiting to cleave him in two.

Barnabas hadn't come back for…was it days? Weeks? Cassidy had whiled away most of his time cleaning and field stripping his Mauser and thinking about how stupid he'd been. He was nowhere near

Arcadia anymore. At least he doubted it. Nowhere near his fighter. Perhaps nowhere near the Twilight. The door to the creature's room could have taken him just about anywhere.

"Ah, a knight. How long, dear Sir, have you come to this unfortunate oubliette?"

Cassidy glanced in the direction of the voice. The man in the blue gown to his left had finally come around. The silence had kept things from feeling *real*, but hearing someone speaking to him brought reality back with full force. He stood and walked to the edge of his bottle. "A while," he said. "'Fraid I've no way to know."

"Ah," said the man in the blue gown. "My name is Delaine, and you'll pardon me if I don't stand. I've been here quite a while longer than *quite a while* and I don't seem to have much left in me."

Cassidy gave a quick nod. "Any idea what this place is?"

Delaine shrugged a weak shoulder. "I would think it an apothecary, but of what kind, I cannot say."

"What does he use us for?" Cassidy asked.

"Ah, Sir Knight, even Merlin himself might not guess at the wiles and ways of such demons."

"Demon?" Cassidy asked. He stuffed his hands deep in his pockets.

"What else?" Delaine said. "What but a demon could conjure such evil?" He tried to raise his hand in some gesture, but let his fingers slip back to the glass wall. "I was a conjurer in whatever distant kingdom I lived. I can no longer recall the name. But these arts are beyond me." He stared upwards as though trying to search his memories. "I escaped my dream by chance. Tripped and fell and…and wound up here after but a few days of freedom." He tilted his head to the side and cast his tired eyes on Cassidy. "It was a pleasant dream, I came from. Probably a child's fancy. An innocent dream." His look seemed to say, *and you?*

Cassidy folded his arms. "I'm a fool."

Delaine tried to shrug again, but managed only a slight lift of one shoulder. "We are all fools. The fool behind you was here when I arrived. He could stand then. He could speak. He had been a star, or so he said. He had been a star, snatched from a dream of living worlds. They dream too, you know."

Living worlds, Cassidy mouthed. He was about to ask Delaine more, but the man in the blue gown had fallen back to sleep. Cassidy hoped the poor dream was dreaming.

The next few days, or weeks, brought nothing. Barnabas hadn't entered the room again. Delaine stirred a few times, but didn't wake.

It was difficult not to consider shooting the glass itself, but the demon, or whatever he was, had probably told the truth about the dangers in that. Cassidy considered cleaning his Mauser again, but the thought of it made him sick.

The door finally opened and Barnabas walked in. He turned, eyed the many phials and ran his finger down the row, stopping on Cassidy. "Yes, my little airman," he said, plucking Cassidy from the shelf, "it's time."

Barnabas popped the cork and dumped him out onto the floor. The world rushed by and Cassidy found himself full-sized and on his back, spine aching. He moved towards his pistol.

"Now, now," Barnabas said, holding up a restraining hand. "I need you, and I'd rather not have to shatter your arms right now."

Cassidy scrambled to his feet, but let his arms hang down at his sides. "Whatever it is you want me to do, I don't think I'll feel like it."

"Oh, don't let that bother you," Barnabas said with a dismissive wave. "Most of what I need you to do, I've already done. All you must do now is—" A loud rapping sounded at the door. His head jerked to the side. "What in...?"

Cassidy shrugged. "Someone you know?"

Barnabas narrowed his eyes. "They can't be knocking at the door. It isn't really a door. It doesn't go anywhere unless I want it to be there."

The harsh rapping came again and Barnabas took a step back.

"Should I answer it?" Cassidy asked. "Could be important. Room service?"

Barnabas didn't answer. He didn't have to, as the door flung wide of its own accord and the Englishman with the umbrella stepped in. "Barnabas," he said in a jovial tone. "Why didn't you answer?"

It was hard to tell exactly what the look on Barnabas's face meant. Anger? Fear? Astonishment? Reproach?

"I did knock," the Englishman said, in mock apology.

Barnabas remained silent and rigid as the man with the umbrella made his way around the room as if browsing an antique shop. He peered at the collection of phials on the shelves. "It's quite a collection," he said after several minutes.

"It's also outside your jurisdiction," Barnabas said through gritted teeth.

The Englishman touched the crook of the umbrella to his forehead as if thinking. "Jurisdiction?" he mused as if trying to recall the proper definition of the word. "Jurisdiction?" He tapped his head again with the bony crook. "Ah yes. Jurisdiction. I don't think I really need it."

Barnabas's expression tightened. He slipped his hands into his pockets in a casual gesture, though Cassidy guessed he was grabbing for a weapon. "You can't take me back, Tamelicus," he said, as if trying to extend the conversation. Stalling perhaps.

Tamelicus, Cassidy thought. The demon had a name.

"Take you back?" Tamelicus said. "Why?"

Barnabas narrowed his eyes and froze, his hands still deep in his pockets. They stared at each other for several seconds, neither twitching while Cassidy took it as a hint to step back.

Something silver glinted as Barnabas' hand cleared his pocket. Tamelicus moved across the room in a blur of motion as the Englishman impaled Barnabas through the stomach with the umbrella in a single movement. The jaws of the skull at the tip of the handle came alive and sank its fangs into flesh as Tamelicus buried the umbrella to the hilt.

Barnabas' face contorted in a soundless scream. The eyes of the lizard's empty sockets glowed red and the body to which it had attached itself shrivelled and dried into a grey husk. Tamelicus withdrew his weapon and the pin-striped banker's suit fell to the floor, covered by a shower of dead skin. A silver pistol clattered to the floor.

The Englishman gave a deep sigh and hooked the umbrella over his arm. "Don't I know you?" he said, regarding Cassidy for the first time. He rubbed his chin with his gloved hand. "Of course," he said and broke into a wide smile. "The little paper shadow from New York."

"Why did you do that?" Cassidy asked, looking down at the pile of clothes.

"My Sygnet was hungry," Tamelicus said and petted the umbrella's crook with his hand. "It rarely gets to feed so well." He smiled again. "When *he* is happy, *I* am happy." He turned back to the door. "Cheers," he said and poised to step out.

"Why don't you kill me?" Cassidy asked. "Why do you just kill people in front of me?"

Tamelicus turned and squinted. "I can't *kill* you. You're not alive. It would be more like blowing out the flame on a candle. Flames are fascinating, temporal creatures, but hardly worth extinguishing." He moved closer. "Though you *are* interesting to watch. Like observing an ant try to heft a leaf three times its size into a hole half as small. I can't help but stare in rapt fascination."

He looked into Cassidy's face as if trying to read his thoughts. Tamelicus' eyes were hard to concentrate on, swirling colours that turned in on themselves as they moved across the irises. "Besides, he wasn't a *people*. He was…like me."

"A demon?" Cassidy asked.

Tamelicus grimaced. "I've always thought that word inappropriate, or at the very least inadequate." He gave a flippant gesture. "Whatever the case, your friend here," he said, regarding the pile of clothes again, "was one of my Gentleman. An officer in my employment who decided to get greedy."

Cassidy gave his own quizzical look.

"Hell," Tamelicus said. "Dreams are unsubstantial, but in a world of a billion or so damned, they can easily stand in for an escaped soul unnoticed." He gestured to the phials on the shelves. "Souls carry a hefty price on the Underworld market, and trafficking is rampant. Now you," he said, pushing a finger into Cassidy's chest, burning where it touched his shirt, "I think he had different ideas for. You've become a bit more solid than most. Probably wanted to use you as a shell for something dangerous. Wish I'd asked him about it first, but it felt so good to suck the juices from his corpse."

Tamelicus shrugged. "Must be off." He turned on his heel and made for the door. "I'd leave right behind me," he said over his shoulder. "This room isn't anywhere you'd understand, and it'll incinerate moments after I leave."

"Then why bother mentioning it? Why help me?" Cassidy asked.

Tamelicus stopped and let out a gentle laugh. "Help you? My dear, dear paper shadow. No one can help you. Your captain did you no favours stealing you away." He turned again, his face etched with a cynical pallor. "You have no soul. When you die you will fade to smoke. You won't even return to the dreamstuff from whence you were taken."

"Can I take them, too?" Cassidy asked, pointing to the shelves.

Tamelicus said nothing but continued for the door. His left foot crossed the threshold. Cassidy ran to the shelf and scooped up as many phials as his two hands could pincer between them. The demon's right boot cleared the threshold as Cassidy leapt through. Light exploded around him.

The demon was gone and so was the door. Cassidy lay on the floor of the Arcadia hallway. Behind him was an open door, through which he saw a normal hotel room. He picked himself up and stowed the phials in the large pockets of his flight jacket. He examined the man in the blue gown before adding him to the others. The medieval phantasy still lay asleep.

Cassidy found Shea working the lobby. "I need to talk," he said, imploring her with a touch to her arm.

"I hope you want to do more than talk," Shea said, striking a pose both sultry and natural at the same time. Most women of her profession would have paid half their wages to learn the pose; the way she flared her breasts, arched her back and leaned against a pillar as if she were taking a quick rest without looking forced. "I didn't even know you were here. You vanished months ago. We heard old Barnabas had gotten you."

"Please," Cassidy said. "It's important. I'll pay."

Shea smiled. "Your room or mine?"

"I don't have a room," Cassidy said.

Shea showed him to her boudoir. "I hoped you'd come around," she said as the crystal beads leading to her bed chamber parted without her touching them.

The room smelled like her. Not incense or perfume. It smelled like her skin. Like her hair. She sank into the bed, letting the thick comforter and satin sheets half enclose her. Shea wasn't really trying to seduce him now. It was just her nature. The sexual side of her that seemed not so much to have taken over, but had been held in such controlled check that it shone through when she opened her eyes, or her arms, or legs. It was like a warm but blinding light, set behind a shutter that had no choice but to flex open and shut.

Cassidy felt himself moving towards her as if he were falling forwards. The bed rose to meet him. He was cold and she was warm.

He pulled himself away and leaned back against the wall. "I don't know who else to ask," he said.

Shea blinked. "You pay more visiting me here."

"That's fine. Put it on my tab," Cassidy said, wondering if this had been another mistake. "I have a number of dreams."

"I wouldn't know," she said, leaning back against a vast assortment of elegant pillows, "I don't dream."

Cassidy shook his head. "They're escaped, or rather, stolen. I need to know what to do with them."

"In phials?" she said narrowing her eyes. "My God, you *have* seen Barnabas!" Shea recovered from her shock and flicked slender fingers through the air. "Sell them. There're five or six fences here in Arcadia that would be glad to pass them on to the Everdream for a good price. Or sell them to...other entities. I'll set you up and take a small percentage."

Cassidy started to turn back to the door. "I shouldn't have come. I'm sorry."

Shea came to her feet in a flowing motion and laid a hand on his arm. "No. Please," she said. Her eyes had changed and so had her voice. For the second time he felt he was actually speaking to her and not the mask she wore for clients. "There are places they can go. Places inside Twilight islands." She sat him down on the edge of her bed. "Ones like *you* would never want to go there because it's not safe to leave. They're permanent communities."

"How do you know about them?" Cassidy asked.

Shea pulled her dress around herself as if she were cold, or as if she suddenly felt modest. "I used to help with the underground, many years ago. I still send dreams there from time to time."

"Why?"

Her gaze fell for a moment and she looked back up at him. "I hate seeing anything in pain. And I know what some buyers do with dreams. How many do you have?"

Cassidy reached in his pockets and brought out two handfuls of glass phials.

Shea's eyes widened. "There must be—"

"Thirty-two," Cassidy said. "I didn't want to let them out until I had somewhere to put them."

She sifted through the bottles and lifted the gaunt naked dream of a star up to her face. He still gasped for silent air. A look of genuine horror crossed her face. "What have they done to them? Who did this?"

Cassidy ran his eyes over the rest of the phials, their charges mostly sleeping or gently stirring. "Someone who won't ever come looking for them. At least a hundred others were probably destroyed."

A green tear ran down Shea's face. "I'm so sorry. Is this where you've been? Did you kill that creature?"

"Not me," Cassidy said shaking his head.

"Then who?"

Cassidy inhaled a sharply. He looked down at the man in the blue gown. "Can you take them somewhere safe?"

Shea nodded. "I promise. It won't be the freedom you and Banner have, but it will be better than this."

"Not sure how much to say for the freedom *we* have." Cassidy nodded and stood.

"Your hour isn't up," she said, trying to return to the sultry tones of her comely persona.

"Keep the change," Cassidy said. "I need to find my plane."

The man down at the runway told Cassidy his fighter had disappeared over a month before.

"Exactly how did my plane manage to vanish?" Cassidy asked. It was the same young man he'd met when he landed. "I tipped you to keep a good eye on her."

The young man stammered. "You were gone so long. I mean, I didn't even know if you'd come back."

Cassidy rested his left hand on the Mauser holster and leaned forwards, locking eyes. "I don't care who took it," he said, seething out the words. "I don't care why. I don't care how much they paid you." He leaned in closer, forcing the young man to bend backwards. "I just want to know who has it."

Chapter 25

Cassidy felt a tinge of guilt over pushing the man so hard, but, first, the dock man had accepted some sort of bribe. Second, it had become obvious that while Arcadia might be civilized by Twilight standards, the law still rested on those with the biggest weapon and the strongest arm. Barbaric, but true. Now he just had to hope the man had been telling the truth.

Besides, Cassidy thought as he finished his several mile walk and neared a group of airships moored to the backside of the island, this will probably get me killed. He stopped for a moment to look the ships over from afar, then stuffed both hands in his pockets and continued.

The airships didn't have the fantastic colourful beauty of the ones moored at the hotel. These looked like makeshift battleships, bristling with guns and plate armour. They looked too heavy to be supported even by the large balloons holding them aloft, but he chalked it up to Twilight physics. Unlike the *Nubigena*, they didn't have to fly in the *real* world.

This side of the island didn't look like the hotel side either. The structures appeared to have been fashioned from triangular pieces of a dark material he could only assume had been pilfered from some other construction project. If this place wasn't the abode of pirates, he couldn't imagine what might be.

Cassidy shuffled through a number of plans in his mind. Several clever ploys and complicated schemes seemed almost plausible.

Perhaps he could knock one of the guards out and take his clothes, or show up under the guise of wanting to join their ranks. Surely he could sell himself as a mercenary pilot. Banner had told him they hired dreams on local ships.

His mind went blank when a man stepped out in front of him from behind a large boulder. The pirate, for lack of a better term, wore a dirty naval uniform of the late seventeenth century. His beard hadn't been trimmed and he carried what looked like a musket with a magazine sticking out just ahead of the trigger. Cassidy tried to imagine how such a device could even function. The bayonet that topped it off had been serrated and appeared to be made of something that looked like glass.

"Sorry, mate," the man said with a thick and hard to define accent. "This may not be quite the place you're looking for."

Cassidy kept his hands in his pockets. "That all depends," he said, ignoring the guard's weapon. He turned to the side and stared out at the tethered airships.

The guard glanced over to see what he was looking at and turned back. "Depends on what?"

Cassidy whipped his hand out of his pocket as if withdrawing a gun, but instead gripped his chin between thumb and forefinger. The guard took a jerky leap backwards and levelled his bayonet. Cassidy ignored him. "It all depends," he said, rubbing his chin, "on whether or not there happens to be a Fokker VII fighter over there." He motioned to the structures.

The guard narrowed his eyes.

"A Fokker VII," Cassidy said in slow, enunciated words. "It's a German fighter plane. Green with black iron crosses on the wings. Very new-looking. Very nice. Very mine," he said, turning his head and boring into the man's eyes on the last two words.

The guard wet his lips. "You'll have to talk with the Commodore about that."

"You have a commodore?" Cassidy said, still speaking slowly in the most patronising tone he could muster. "You mean *you* don't run this outfit?"

The guard straightened up and returned his rifle to attention position. "No, Sir, I don't. But I can take you to him."

Cassidy nodded as if praising a child. "Good, good. Well go." He brushed past the guard and made his way down a small hill. At the foot he came to an abrupt stop. "Which building?" he asked.

"Commodore's on the ledge right now," the guard said, indicating an area just the other side of the first structure. "Hope he don't mind seeing you right now."

Cassidy crossed the distance at a fast enough gait the guard had to run to keep up. Cassidy rounded the corner of the bizarre structure, which consisted of triangular panels jutting out at irregular angles instead of fitting together to form flat surfaces.

Across from it a chunk of rock extended out over the edge of the island and a man stood at the tip, apparently holding court with six other men also dressed in seventeenth century European naval officer uniforms.

The Commodore, which Cassidy took to be an assumed moniker more than an actual rank, was distinguished by a slightly less dirty suit and a feather-plumed hat. Cassidy approached with the guard in tow and reached a mere ten feet from the group before they noticed him.

"Oi," the Commodore yelled. "Who the hell are you?" The other six turned to face Cassidy.

A cacophony of fears ran through Cassidy. After facing two of Hell's own infernal agents he'd felt nigh immortal, but as the soldier/pirates faced him, hands on pistols and swords, the realisation struck home of just how in over his head he was. He adjusted his officer's cap, brought his right foot to the top of a small piece of rock and folded his arms over his knee. "I'm looking for a plane," he said and flashed a grin as if he were asking about the weather.

The Commodore stared at him for several seconds in stunned silence. "A plane?" He finally said. "What sort of plane?"

"A German Fokker VII," Cassidy said, still forcing a smile. "It's a fighter," he added when no one said anything. "It's from the *real* world. Hard to miss."

The Commodore adjusted his stance. His men shuffled their feet and glanced back and forth between their commander and Cassidy. "Aren't you one of Banner's men?" he asked.

Cassidy gave a curt nod.

"Didn't know he was in port," the commodore said. He shifted his balance again and looked over Cassidy's shoulder as if he might see the port through the mountains of Arcadia.

Cassidy continued his smile, trying to channel Banner's countenance.

"So," the Commodore said, picking up the tone of his voice, "Banner's in the market for a new fighter?"

Cassidy shook his head. "Just want ours back. I assume that means you've got it."

A scowl crossed the Commodore's face. He glanced around, looking for Cassidy's backup. "Why'd he send you alone?"

Cassidy spread his hands, palms up and shrugged. "Only takes one to fly a plane."

The commodore rested a hand on his sabre. Flexed his fingers. He seemed to be considering a number of things at once. These probably included whether or not he was being eyed at a distance by scoped rifles, an attempt to surmise just how dangerous Cassidy really was by himself and, last but probably not least, how much face he would lose if he simply gave in without a fight.

For the first time, Cassidy rested a hand on the holster of his Mauser. "If it helps any," he said, still jovial and smiling, "I just need the plane. Banner didn't say I *had* to kill anyone."

The Commodore glared. "I think you're either a madman," he said, gripping the handle of his sword, "or you're completely full of shit."

Cassidy had gone too far. He'd forced the man's hand. Pushed him into a corner. Cassidy winced inside, but tried not to change the expression on his face. The Commodore and his men appeared to all be carrying flintlocks, but the magazine in the guard's musket gave him pause. The technology here couldn't be counted on to follow *real*-world standards. Cassidy also wasn't a shootist, per se, and the Mauser's holster hadn't been made for quick-draw access. Still, he visually counted out the men on his fingers and gave an exaggerated shrug. "I have enough bullets."

"I've met Banner," the Commodore said. He hooked his thumbs into his belt and looked off as if remembering. "I don't think he's here." He looked back at Cassidy. "I don't think he has your back."

Cassidy had already sized up the group. The Commodore himself seemed like a close-range sort and was probably most formidable with his sabre. The officers to his right and left looked like the duelling kind, though one's pistol looked shiny and new, probably well-cleaned, every day. The other's flintlock was clean, too, but looked old and well-used. He would be the first to draw. The other four were mere footmen. They'd prefer range fire and didn't have bayonets. The guard behind him would probably just run away when the shooting started.

Cassidy numbered the men in his mind and allocated a shot for each with two shells to spare. He would step to the left as soon as the one officer drew, blocking them off and using the first footman as a shield, who Cassidy would shove as he went for his own Mauser. They were close together and a .103 shell could easily pass through two or three men with a lucky shot. He might get even more lucky and take out the duellists.

All this ran through his head in less than a second. A part of him realised he had to figure a lot of it out on the spot. Richthofen was an amazing shot and a hell of a pilot, but he doubted he'd passed down much knowledge of close combat. This was Cassidy thinking. Cassidy learning. He listened to the guard behind him shift his weight. Move back. The officer with the well-worn pistol moved his hand closer to the gold-trimmed butt of his flintlock. Time slowed. This was going to happen fast.

"Boys!" The voice came from behind Cassidy, breaking him from the battle trance. All eyes moved to a spot over his right shoulder. He knew the voice. How the hell had *she* gotten here?

"Shea?" the Commodore said, easing his hand off the handle of his sabre.

She pushed past Cassidy as if she'd never seen him before and made her way between the other men. Her glance fell on each as she went by, touching them with the tips of her manicured fingers. They melted an inch or two. Their mouths gaped. Shea was in full form, flashing her green eyes, her scent wafting around them. She wore a travel cloak but it gaped open in the front, exposing a dress, which as usual, covered very little.

"Commodore," she said as she reached him. "You haven't come to see me in weeks." Her mouth formed a pout. "I finally had to come see you," she said and slowly ran a finger down the side of his face. "What are you boys doing?"

No one spoke. If Cassidy thought she'd had a significant effect on him, it was nothing compared to what she did to a group like this. Among sex-starved pirates this woman was in her element and all-powerful. They glanced between themselves. Wanted to kill each other over her. Probably only the Commodore had enough money to afford an hour with her. The object of their eternal phantasies, standing closer than they'd probably ever been allowed before.

She caressed the Commodore's chest and slid her hand into his shirt. Even here, in front of his men, he seemed to be having trouble controlling himself. Cassidy could see he wanted to send them all away and have her right then and there, despite the business at hand.

Shea's hand slid into the Commodore's pants. The soldiers appeared stuck between leaning closer and retreating. She breathed on the Commodore's neck. His left arm came up around her back and he turned into her full mouth. She broke the kiss and cocked her head to the side where they couldn't tell whether Shea was kissing his neck or whispering in his ear. Her hand worked the contents of his pants. His face changed. Eyes widened.

"I'm going to my quarters," the Commodore announced and started towards the first structure. Shea walked with him, her hand still down the front of his pants, still massaging.

The soldiers stood, mouths agape. Cassidy couldn't blame them. He didn't know what to do any more than they did.

The Commodore turned his head and spoke over his shoulder to Cassidy. "Come, Airman. You can examine the craft while I have my way."

Cassidy glanced at the stunned soldiers and back at the couple as they made their way inside. He followed at an awkward distance. There seemed little else to do. He was still alive, which was more than he'd expected at this point. The idea of a ship's captain, even a roguish pirate one, behaving like this in front of his men still baffled Cassidy, but who was he to judge the Twilight and Shea's effect on men.

The three entered the building, which appeared to be half airship hanger and half pigsty. He assumed the Commodore's quarters must lie farther back and hopefully looked better than the wreck outside.

Cassidy shut the outer door and Shea took her hand out of the Commodore's pants. A two-inch hook knife glittered at the tips of her fingers.

"You fucking bitch," the Commodore said, reaching for his sabre. "You could've snagged one of my bollocks."

Cassidy had his pistol out before the blade cleared its sheath.

Shea gave Cassidy a soft smile and slipped the hook-knife up her sleeve. "You should tell me before you wander around the island," she said, unbuckling the Commodore's weapon belt. It fell to the ground along with his sabre and pistol.

Cassidy shrugged. "Seemed simple enough."

Shea winked and turned back to the pirate captain. "The Commodore and I have history." She walked around behind him, took a chunk of his hair in hand and yanked his head back. "Stiffed me for two nights' pay. I *was* giving him a couple weeks before I showed up, but…" The commodore gave a low growl, but didn't move.

"You shouldn't have come," Cassidy said. He searched the hanger with his eyes for anything resembling his Fokker. "You could have been killed."

Shea laughed. "What, with you here to protect me?" She gave a flippant gesture with her wrist. "Actually, I brought three body guards, and they had rifles on us the whole time." She licked the commodore's ear and smiled as he flinched away. "Commodore knows I'm not bluffing. Don't you, Baby?" She gave him a savage elbow to the ribs which must have struck a nerve cluster because he doubled over and gagged.

Cassidy spotted a large shape beneath a canvas tarp. He walked over and dragged the heavy fabric away, revealing his Fokker VII in pristine condition. They'd probably been afraid to actually fly it. Either because they couldn't, or for fear of becoming Armada targets.

"See you later, Mr. Cassidy," Shea said, the Commodore's hair still wrapped in her fingers.

"I'm not leaving you with him," Cassidy said.

"You'll have to," Shea said and pinched the Commodore behind the neck. "We have business still."

Cassidy looked at the pirate captain, still doubled over in pain. "Are you going to kill him?" he asked Shea.

"Kill him? No," Shea said, pulling the struggling captain towards the back of the hanger. "He just likes it rough. Pays extra." She bent close and the Commodore whispered something. She touched a panel on the wall and the hanger swung open.

Cassidy nodded to her and climbed into the cockpit.

"By the way," Shea called before he started the engine. "If you're looking for your ship, someone saw a Zeppelin in The Starling."

"Where's that?" he hollered back.

"A ways from here, straight out," she said, pointing beyond the open hanger. Cassidy nodded and started the engine. The Starling? he thought. Tell me that's not a bird with teeth.

Chapter 26

It felt good to be back in the sky again. Part of him wanted to return and lay waste to the Commodore's small fleet of airships with a belt or two of *real* world solid Spandau rounds. The bastard had lost him time. On the other hand, he hadn't known which way to find Banner until a few minutes before. Why hadn't Shea just told him in the first place?

He tried to imagine what *a good ways* actually meant. Something in miles or metres would have been nice, but he assumed her units of measurement would be different from what the plane's instruments read and without the sun, moon, stars or recognisable land masses, he had no way of figuring distance any other way. Cassidy hoped The Starling, whatever it was, would be easy to identify.

Flying cleared his mind. He had hardly attempted to process the last few months, and now it rushed in on him as the Twilight clouds flew by. Why did he feel almost *real* one moment, for instance in the heat of action, then like a ghost afterwards? How much of his thinking was Richthofen and how much was his own? Was any of it his own thinking or was everything in his head a combination of the Baron and the Everdream? Did John Cassidy really exist? Or was he just a drifting concept with no concrete past or future, and nothing but a transient present? Was only the moment *real*?

He thought about Banner. How *real* the captain seemed. How solid. And Brewster. The man was capable of living life just to live it. Didn't care about the future or the past. Didn't dwell on constant questions of who and what he was. Cassidy wondered if the Twilights had philosophers and theologians. The demon with the umbrella had told him dreams didn't have souls. What *was* a soul?

And Barnabas. The creature had given nothing but more questions, not the least of which being, *had anything he said been true?*

Cassidy checked his gauges. Checked the sky for signs of anything but clouds. Checked his tail for anyone following. Nothing. Empty. Cobalt and pink wisps.

Time stretched and shrank in his head. He tried to calculate how long it had been since Banner had rescued him from the dream. How long he had flown with the *Nubigena* crew? How long had he spent in the glass prison? How long since he'd eaten? He was starving, but starvation hadn't killed him. Did he just *think* he was starving?

A small group of airships appeared in the distance like a cluster of stray balloons, standing out against the purple clouds in various primary colours. Despite being so dangerous, the Twilight was also beautiful. Cassidy kept his eye on them as he continued past, but instead of approaching, they drifted another direction.

The fuel gauge told him he'd only burned a quarter tank, but it vexed him that there was no assurance he could find another place to refuel. The Fokker was a fine plane, but it was meant for short-range sorties. Its engine was made for speed, not fuel economy.

Cassidy sat back and tried to relax as the soft vibrations of the control stick thrummed up his hand and into his body. He worried too much. He knew that.

The Starling was unmistakable. A large array of scaffolding, girders and beams had been shaped into the loose form of a bird, its wings outstretched. Cassidy guessed that at one time it had been some kind of artificial island, built perhaps as a half-way port between more natural islands. Now it looked like a twisted skeleton. Whatever covering or platforms that existed once had long since fallen away, or been scavenged.

Cassidy flew among the juts and joints of naked metal, searching for any sign of the *Nubigena* or its crew. Up close, he never would have known the structure resembled anything like a bird, but calculated he must be somewhere around the left wing. At the very tip a grey mass stood out against the steel. He throttled towards it. As he neared, he made out the unmistakable shape of the *Nubigena*, drifting, moored only at the nose by a cable so long he didn't even see it at first.

She looked derelict. Cassidy couldn't help thinking of an expired animal floating in a stream. The landing platform on top had been finished. At least they hadn't forgotten about him. Banner, with all his optimism, had probably just assumed they would meet again.

Cassidy had never landed on anything adrift before, but lined up, reduced speed as much as he could without stalling and pushed the button Karl had built into the console. A catch released on the bottom of the fuselage with an audible click. He hoped it would do whatever it was supposed to do.

He guided the Fokker down over the *Nubigena's* tail and cut the throttle completely. Cassidy glided down, touched the platform and felt the cable snag. It felt like slamming into a wall as the fighter lurched to a shuddering stop a few feet from the edge of the runway, which ended just short of the gun platform.

Cassidy hopped down and found mooring collars that easily attached to the landing gear. Karl was never anything but thorough when it came to design.

He entered the gun platform from the outside door and made his way down the ladder to the floor of the main cell. The silence disturbed him. He'd never noted how much noise the engines made. The ballasts. The gas bladders as they adjusted their buoyancy. It was as if the *Nubigena's* voice, perhaps even her heart, had been crushed, and he was invading her derelict corpse.

Karl's quarters stood empty. Cassidy made his way down into the gondola. His heart sank notch by notch as room after room proved empty. Brewster's. Jayce's. Banner's. Everyone's. His own looked the same as it always had and he moved on through the galley and main corridor to the bridge. The door stood open. The helm moved left and right between several spokes as the gentle wind moved the responsive rudder back and forth. The elevator flap was moving, too, because the pedals worked up and down as if a phantom was flying the dead ship.

Banner never left the helm without the safeties engaged. What in God's name? Endless scenarios played out in this mind. Pirates. Bounty hunters. The Armada.

Cassidy wandered back through the ship. Food sat on the galley table, uneaten. Wine and coffee still undrunk. Cigarettes burned to grey cylinders of ash. He found Brewster's pipe beside the chair in his quarters, packed, but unlit.

Silence closed in on him as the vacant ship drifted. It had become an abyss. An empty eggshell, unchipped, but having spilt its egg and yolk somewhere along the way. Cassidy clutched at his neck. He loosened his scarf which had been tied like a cravat and stuffed into his shirt. It didn't help. His throat still constricted.

Cassidy stumbled to Banner's quarters, pulled a thick vinyl disc of Beethoven from the bookshelf and wound the Edison talking machine. With trembling hands, he fit the disc over the pin in the turntable and placed the stylus on the edge. A flick of the switch and he adjusted the speed until "Ode to Joy" eked from the brass funnel as he fell to his knees and cried. He was asleep on the floor by the end of the second movement.

Cassidy woke to a silence even more barren than the one he'd fallen asleep to. The talking machine lay still, its spring unwound and spent hours before. He'd needed to see the *Nubigena* again so badly and hadn't realised how much until now. Needed to see Banner and Brewster. Hear their voices. What little existence he had in this world was so tied up with them. Tied up with this ship itself, but even *she* refused to speak. He remembered looking up at her the first night in Arcadia. The beautiful goddess of the storm, a half-tamed cloud that now lay dead around him.

He'd find them somehow. Cassidy stuffed thousands of Twilight and *real* banknotes from Banner's desk into a canvas bag. No telling how far he'd have to go this time. How much information he'd have to buy. He climbed back up to his plane and shoved the bag behind the seat. After a deep sigh, he climbed back down to the gondola and took one last look around the ship.

Cassidy screamed down the row of cabins one last time. Something crashed at the end of the corridor. The sound had come from the aft section. He dashed for the stairs and up into the vast emptiness of the main cell. A shadow moved. He ran to it, grabbed its shoulders and turned it around.

Karl's ancient features faced him, but the crazed eyes couldn't focus. The old German pulled away, grabbed a spanner and began twisting nuts inside one of the strange machines he'd once showed Cassidy. Karl muttered to himself in German, but Cassidy couldn't make out the words.

"Karl," Cassidy said. "Karl. It's Cassidy. Karl, it's me."

Karl looked up at him again, but went back to fiddling with anything he could get his hands on, though he didn't seem to be actually *doing* anything. It was as if he were mimicking work without knowing what to do. Cassidy grabbed him by the shoulders again and locked eyes. "Karl," he shouted. "Where's Banner? Where is everyone?"

The old man shrugged. "They are here," he said and tried to return to work.

"Where?" Cassidy asked, refusing to let him go. "Where are they?"

Karl flailed his arms as if pointing everywhere at once. "They are all over the place. I need to work. Fix everything," he said and pulled away. "So much work."

Cassidy grabbed him again and pinned his back to one of the aluminium supports. "Karl. What happened here?" he said, trying to keep his voice calm and slow, but he knew he was still shouting. "What happened?"

Karl stopped struggling. He stared off as if watching something in the distance. "The Borealis. The colours. They come through like a storm," he said. His face contorted as if he were re-experiencing the horror. "Not good storm. The colours," he said again. "The colours."

Cassidy let him go. Karl sat down on the deck, his features slack. The last time Aurora Borealis had come through it had brought the ghosts. What had this one brought?

He considered restarting the engines and getting the *Nubigena* back in motion, but something inside told him that might be a bad idea. After all, where had Karl been all this time? He'd searched everywhere, including the hidden crawlspace where he'd once found Jayce.

Cassidy ran down the corridors, calling everyone's name again. A gaunt shape stumbled out of a cabin he'd just checked. "Franz?" Cassidy said as the young German fell into his arms.

"Is Hell," Franz said, trying to stand up. His wild eyes fluttered, then closed. He went limp for several seconds and he sat bolt upright. "They're all in Hell."

Jayce showed up on the bridge. Cassidy found him sitting at the navigation desk flipping switches on a dead console. Brewster sat smoking his pipe without lighting it.

Cassidy continued his back and forth search of the ship for hours. Exhausted, he sat down where Jayce had appeared. The young man was now fast asleep in his quarters. All of them were either asleep now or continuing pointless chores. None of them speaking much other than gibberish.

The helm still twisted back and forth, the pedals going up and down like a see-saw. A hazy shadow materialized at the large wheel. It faded in and out of existence for several minutes before Cassidy could make out the concrete form of Banner, who clung to the spokes to keep himself upright.

Banner turned. Cassidy flinched. The captain's face looked like nothing he'd ever seen. His normally cool grey eyes all but bulged out of their sockets and red veins stood out against the white around his irises. "Banner," Cassidy said as the darting eyes tried to focus. "Banner! Dammit man, what happened?"

Banner blinked and shook his head. "How long?" he asked.

"I don't know," Cassidy said. "I just found the ship."

The captain nodded, as if half-remembering that Cassidy had been absent all this time. "The Borealis," he said, and stopped, trying to find words. "There were others. Thousands. Dreams. Souls. I don't know."

He flexed his fingers around the spokes of the helm as if trying to milk reassurance from the solid wood. "It pulled us out to the fringes. Dragged us through...when it moved beyond, I guess we snapped back." Banner shook his head. His eyes still appeared to be seeing other things. Other places. He seemed half on the *Nubigena* and half back in the Borealis. "Is anyone else—"

"You're the last to show up," Cassidy said and gave Banner a squeeze on his shoulder. "They're not well."

Banner nodded. "It'll happen again," he said, and bit his lip as if trying to hold back what he was saying, even from himself. "We've got to get everyone off the ship."

Chapter 27

"How?" Cassidy asked. He glanced out the windows. "I thought the Auroras didn't hurt us."

Banner shook his head. He paced the small control room, wringing his hands. "We've been sold out. The Everdream must know all our hideouts now. Must not want us back anymore and they're just trying to kill us now." He returned to the wheel and gripped it until his knuckles turned white. "Was it you, Cassidy? Just tell me. You're the only one that hasn't been with us, both times."

"Me?" Cassidy asked, more shocked than hurt.

Banner shook his head and gave deep sigh. "No, of course it wasn't you. Even if it was, I guess you'd have the right, considering you came back and saved us all." He bent over the wheel and shook.

"Captain," Cassidy put a hand on his shoulder. "We're all going to die if you don't get your head on straight."

Banner spun on him. "How dare you—" he stopped. "I'm sorry," he said, shaking his head in anguish. "The Borealis field took us somewhere. I can't explain what it did. I feel like we were tortured for years, and the Everdream threw it at us somehow..." He trailed off.

"Everyone else is babbling," Cassidy said. "I'm not sure they even recognize me."

Banner nodded. "It was worse than the void in some ways. They could be like that for a while. God!" He slammed a fist against the helm. "I never thought—Cassidy, crank us up. We'll worry about everyone later."

Cassidy gave a nod and leapt into the navigation chair. The engines turned over and Banner straightened his shoulders a little. "Where are we going?"

Banner exhaled a large breath. "I don't know how I can bear to lose her. She's all I've got."

Cassidy remained silent as the *Nubigena* skirted the Twilight borders. He was never certain what *border* meant in the case of the Twilight, but every time the crackle of green energy began, Banner turned the ship, only scraping the surfaces instead of heading straight into them like before.

He seemed to be doing it on purpose, as if testing the boundaries, either to find a certain gate, or as a bizarre form of navigation. Banner usually steered them starboard, but not always, and Cassidy gave up trying to understand whatever labyrinthine maze they were trying to make their way through.

"Check on them," Banner said, breaking the silence for the first time in hours. "Get them all together."

Cassidy glanced over the controls and gauges one more time. He only understood about half of them, but it made him feel better to check.

Going aft he found the crew continuing menial tasks as if re-enacting the last things they'd done on the ship before their minds had slipped away. Brewster packed his pipe, smoked it and packed it again, each time standing up for a moment before sitting back down. Franz played billiards, over and over, while Jayce lay in his bed and stared at the ceiling.

Karl fixed and refixed the same engine over and over again. He still babbled. They all babbled, but didn't talk directly to anyone, and their eyes still seemed to be seeing other places. Cassidy tried to herd them together, but they kept returning to their tasks the moment he let their arms go. Eventually, he locked all but Karl in the galley, hoping to keep them there long enough to get wherever the *Nubigena* was going. Karl refused to leave the engine room, insisting so much still had to be done even though he wasn't even working on the engines anymore, but tampering again with the strange machine that wouldn't turn on.

Cassidy reported back to Banner, who returned a grave nod and continued his journey through the borderlands that only he understood. After hours of what seemed like pointless manoeuvring, they approached a black pyramid standing motionless on the dark edge of the Twilight.

Banner stopped the ship and regarded the structure.

"What is it?" Cassidy asked.

"A prison," Banner said. "An asylum."

"Is it one of the safe houses for dreams?"

Banner shrugged. "Call it what you will. I'll never step inside again." He breathed deep, exhaled and ordered Cassidy to throttle forwards. They moored to the tip of the pyramid and waited while a black slab of triangular slate rose from the surface and made its way to the main hatch.

Banner and Cassidy stood waiting as the slab connected and the *Nubigena's* hatch swung open. A small man, almost a dwarf, stepped inside and gave a low bow. He wore grey robes and the creased lines of his face almost melded with the deep wrinkles of the fabric. His bald head and pointed Twilight ears gave him the look of an ancient Germanic creature said to have lived before the coming of man. A goblin, Cassidy thought. A gnome.

"I'm honoured," the creature said. "My name is Lolem. I was told this ship would never grace our borders again."

Banner nodded. "It's an evil day," he said, and opened the door to the galley. The zombie-like crew ambled out. "I need you to take care of them until I return. *If* I can return."

Lolem furrowed his already wrinkled brow. "That is not usually our policy," he said. "These places must remain a secret."

"I know," Banner said. "This is for me. It's a favour."

Lolem considered it for a few moments and nodded. "You've done us many boons in the past," he said. "Can you get them onto my platform?"

Banner and Cassidy corralled the crew onto Lolem's craft. Brewster was the last to go. Cassidy wanted to say goodbye. He tried to get the airman to look him in the face, but Brewster stared past as if looking for something back on the ship. Cassidy pushed a pipe into his hands along with a pouch of tobacco and a box of matches. "We will be back," Cassidy promised as the skiff pulled away. He thought of Karl still in the engine room, refusing to leave.

"You could stay, too," Banner said as Cassidy wheeled the hatch shut.

"Like hell," Cassidy said. "Every time I let you out of my sight, something bad happens."

Banner gave a weak smile, but his eyes twinkled. "Best Jonah I've ever had on my ship," he said and made for the helm.

Cassidy followed close behind. The muscles in his chest tightened as the silence set in again. It was only he and Banner now. He, Banner and a crazed engineer roaming the *Nubigena's* nerve centre.

"I had a dark premonition of this," Banner said as he stood at the wheel once more and guided them away from the pyramid. "The first time I saw you, I feared that one day you'd be the only man left with me." He turned and locked Cassidy with his grey eyes. "And if you're my last man, I've done alright."

Banner turned back to the helm. Cassidy took a deep sigh. This could really be it. The ship's final flight and the captain's last stand. A strange emotion that felt a mixture of pride and fear rose in his chest at the sight of Banner's silhouette against the windows. God, what he wouldn't have given for a storm. A *real* storm.

As the *Nubigena* turned starboard, Cassidy noticed a soft nimbus of crackling green light encircling the pyramid. This place was some pocket of the Twilight border. A tear in its fabric that had grown into a sanctuary. The green became brighter as they left, illuminating the walls of the slim channel they'd come through. Now he could see that the corridor had been almost as narrow as the ship herself. Any vessel coming here would be in constant danger of gating into who knew what if they flew deep enough into the sides. No wonder it was so well protected.

"They were my men," Banner said, more to himself than Cassidy. "I picked them all myself and rescued them one by one. My ship. *My ship*. You might not think I care about them, but those boys were like—" He didn't finish his sentence.

"Where to now?" Cassidy asked, trying to break Banner from his dark mood.

"I need to go back," was all Banner said.

Cassidy feared he knew where that meant.

The captain manoeuvred between several more gates and took a hard starboard turn into one. The crackling light exploded around the ship and they were in a *real* world storm. The *Nubigena* had come out dead in the eye of another hurricane. The turning wheel of black cumulous twisted around them, the endless forks of blue lightning blistered a bright circle across the eye like an electric cornea.

They nosed down and landed, protected by the calm of the massive eye. Strange how the hurricane seemed to stop and wait for them as if protecting Banner's unearthly stormship. Cassidy knew they must be near the coast for the hurricane to remain intact, but had never known what coast this was. They were in America, however. He was fairly certain of that because he'd seen this cemetery before.

Banner landed in the same clearing of gravestones. The nose and tail stretched well beyond the clearing, shading hundreds of statues and markers from the storm. Rain poured down the rounded sides and the buffeting winds dragged at the Zeppelin. The eye was still above, but seemed unstable as if it were breaking apart and coming back together, waiting for Banner, but uncertain. "Why is there always a hurricane when we come here?" Cassidy asked.

Banner glanced up. He looked confused. "Hurricane?" He looked about as if noticing the insane winds for the first time. "I don't know," he said and started off for whatever grave he always haunted.

Cassidy wouldn't stand back as the rest always had. He gave Banner several minutes head start, then trotted after him. He stopped as the captain knelt before one of the graves. He talked to it, though Cassidy couldn't make out any words. It looked almost as if he were *praying* to it.

Banner cried. He prostrated himself and dug his fingers into the grass and wet earth. A shattered bottle lay inches away. He grabbed both sides of the tombstone as if he were shaking a man and shouted at the grey surface. "They're gone," was all Cassidy could make out at first, and then something that could have been, "I'm going to lose her."

He means the ship, Cassidy thought. He actually means the ship. Cassidy stepped closer and shouted into the blistering wind. "So you *can* outlive your dreamer."

Banner broke from his weeping to laugh. "My dreamer? I wish to God," he said, turning. It looked as if the rain had dug grooves in his face. He looked old. Beaten.

"Who are you?" Cassidy asked, shouting louder than was necessary, even in the sounding wind. "What the hell are you?"

Banner glanced up at the gravestone and Cassidy read the engraved words in the blue flash of lightning: William Charles Banner, May He Find His Peace.

Cassidy fell to one knee beside his captain. "Your dreamer's father?" he asked.

Banner laughed. "Ha. Never. This man's father was an officer. A great military man with little patience for a son born lame. A son who spent his life in a wheelchair. Beat him for not being able to run from him." Banner stood and kicked the curved stone hard. He kicked it again, harder, near the top. The stone cracked through the centre and another sharp blow from his heel left a jagged edge aimed at the sky.

William, and the bottom of the C, was all Cassidy could read of the name now. "I don't understand," Cassidy said, shouting over a roll of thunder. "*What* are you?"

"A failure," Banner yelled. "And a damned lousy captain. A damned lousy man." He stood and made for the ship.

Cassidy caught up in a few long strides. "You were dreamed by a god of a man," Cassidy said. "You rode a galleon out of your dream and into another and out into the *real* world."

A bolt of lightning split the sky in the distance, striking the *Nubigena* dead centre. Cassidy waited for flames to spread across the canvas, but, instead, the surface glowed the same electric blue as the lightning. "But the ship is *real*," Cassidy said as the light glowed brighter. "How?"

"Hell, yes, she's *real*," Banner said without breaking gait. He said it like a man speaking of his lover. Another bolt of lightning struck the ship, arcing across the vast main cell. "She was a German experiment to harness electricity and control the storm. *I* didn't name her *Nubigena*. Karl was a brilliant engineer Graff von Zeppelin used to dream about before I got to him. Knew more about this ship than the people who put her together. Told me there was copper wiring wound around the main supports of the frame. Beyond me. Something about Tesla's inventions. Problem is, Karl couldn't use any of it because the damned thing never worked. Government gave up on it."

The hatch arced blue light as they opened it and the static heat ignited a madness in Banner's eyes. "That mad German's gone and done it. Karl's made it work somehow. I could fly around the world ten times without a storm after that burst of electricity. And perhaps *make* a storm myself."

"We can fly without storms?" Cassidy asked. He closed the hatch, shutting out the rain, but the sounds of it and the wind and the thunder continued.

"I think so," said Banner, his eyes flashing, "now that Karl's got it working. God, if only…" His voice drifted off and he seemed to remember the oncoming Aurora Borealis.

Karl came rushing down the corridor. "Did you see, Captain? Did you see?"

"I saw," Banner said. "It's beautiful."

"I had repairs to do," Karl said. "I had repairs and I repair." He turned and ran back to the engine room. "Better," he yelled over his shoulder. "I make better."

Banner dashed for the helm with Cassidy close behind. They lifted into the hurricane. Banner's influence somehow kept the ship from shredding in the torrential winds, though Cassidy suspected something about the Zeppelin's experimental nature might be part of the reason, as well. What had it been designed to withstand in its quest for energy?

Cassidy remembered the way the eye of the storm had stuttered. It had been unstable because the ship had taken over. He imagined what it must look like to anyone who glimpsed the *Nubigena* now, the glowing blue light of an airship bigger than most buildings. They'll think we're from Mars, he mused.

Banner gated at the edge of the hurricane and slipped out into the Twilight. "We're going to have to scuttle her," Banner said. Tears welled at his eyes again, but he held them back. "Karl's just got it all working and we're going to have to scuttle her and run like bandits now that the Borealis has our scent." He ordered Cassidy to throttle the ship all the way forwards and glanced left and right for an island to crash into.

"Won't we all die?" Cassidy asked, though he already suspected the answer. He'd known the answer since he decided not to stay with the rest of the crew in the asylum.

"Might have a chance," Banner said. "Wouldn't count on it though." He spun the wheel, searching for a better heading. "No," he said, as he glanced out the bow windows. "Not already."

Cassidy stood. Banner's face was white and something like a swatch of rainbow ripped out of the drifting clouds in the distance. "Can't we run?" Cassidy asked.

Banner shook his head. "It's too big. I'm sorry, Major," he said, turning back to the windows. "I can't get us out of this one."

Cassidy considered cutting the throttle and saving them what time he could, but it felt wrong. This was death best faced head on and at full speed. Death, or whatever madness the Borealis would bring.

Chapter 28

The *Nubigena* slammed into the wall of colour at full speed, knocking Cassidy against his seat. Shaking his head, Cassidy saw a shadow appear at the bridge door. Sweat poured down Banner's face as the shape entered the helm. A man. Cassidy had seen him before. The ghost from the first Borealis. The one who'd remained after the others left. He wore the same brown coat and his face looked just as gaunt and sunken.

"You," Banner said, his voice distant with terror.

"Who is he?" Cassidy asked, pointing to the ghost who stood unmoving, his dead gaze locked on the captain.

"The dream of a god of a man," Banner said in a far off tone. He turned to Cassidy. "It was a good story, wasn't it? Kept the men going."

Cassidy was silent. He looked from Banner to the ghost. Dead on, Cassidy could see the strained features better. The phantom looked like Banner. Like a shell of him. Aged a thousand years, but definitely Banner.

"Dreamed my whole life of being an officer like my father instead of a cripple," Banner said. "Dreamed it every night." Tears streamed down his face again, but he made no sound of sobbing. "Then one night, I don't know, I was twenty or so, I woke up in one of my dreams. I mean, I realised I was dreaming. I looked around at a world my own mind had created for me. I was strong. I was standing tall in the uniform of sea captain." Banner's eyes remained locked on the ghost. Cassidy wasn't sure whom Banner was speaking to, him or the wraith. "I did take control of a galleon. That part was true."

Banner turned to Cassidy. "I decided to leave. What did I have in the *real* world; a broken, lame body? A father who loathed the sight of me? So I left. I sailed out of my own dream and into another and another. I didn't know where I was going. I didn't have any idea where or how to get anywhere, but I sailed. I struck the black void for the first time. It almost swallowed me. But I believed. I believed so strongly. I wanted my dream to be *real*."

The wraith moved closer as if fighting its way through sand. The closer it came, the more it looked like Banner, but still ancient and haggard. "I made it through," Banner continued. "I sailed through the Nietzschian void on nothing but raw hope, sinking my mind into my own reality, and then I hit a gate. I don't know how, but I called it to me somehow. It's something I can do because my mind is *real* but my body is a dream. Born of both worlds in a way. A dreamer in the body of a dream." He said it as if it were a mantra he'd said to himself before. Perhaps over and over in the mirror. Cassidy tried to imagine what the captain had had to do to his mind to keep himself sane. What had it been like to straddle both worlds for so long?

"I wound up in an ocean in the *real* world," Banner continued as the ghost pushed itself nearer, "and my ship of dreams faded around me. Reality was dissolving my body as well, but my *real* mind anchored me. Kept me from losing myself. If it hadn't been for the part of me that was a dreamer, I would have evaporated in moments. Rotted to dream clay."

"And the Dutchman?" Cassidy asked. "Was that true?"

Banner nodded. The ghost had stopped. It seemed to be listening. It wanted to know this story. "Falkenberg found me clinging to a piece of wood. The energy in his cursed ship kept my body from becoming mush. Then, somehow I learned to travel outside the storms. Willed myself to remain solid. Kept me together."

The ghostly man pushed closer again, clawing through whatever invisible barrier stood between him and his goal. "I visited myself," Banner said. He couldn't seem to take his eyes off the ghost, or move from where he braced himself against the helm. "I slipped into my house and found my body in a coma." The ghost stopped again, listening more intently. "I watched it for days. Without me inside, it withered away and eventually died. I guess my spirit moved on. I'm sorry," he said as the ghost pushed closer again. "I had to leave. I couldn't live my life in that bed."

"Could I have walked the *real* world without a storm?" Cassidy asked.

Banner crushed himself against the helm as the ghost, his spirit, came within a few feet. "Yes. You very well could," Banner said. "I've never met anyone as solid as you. Richthofen dreamed of you so often. Nightmares are always the most solid." He put up a hand as if trying to hold the ghost at bay. "Get in your plane, John Cassidy. You've done your duty. Any debt you've ever had to me is repaid a hundred times." The ghost touched Banner and they began to meld together. The captain screamed. "Karl and I have to go down with the *Nubigena*. She's our love, but you—" he broke off screaming as the ghost and he melted together, twisting his features like clay. He fought to speak. "Fly against the Borealis. My spirit has something do with this field. I'll hold it back as long as I can."

There was a burst of light as Banner and his soul became a solid being. It still looked like a young Banner, but so much more him. His eyes shone and he looked taller than before. "Now," he said, his voice echoing. "I can't control the Borealis, but I can influence it a little."

Cassidy paused, but Banner snapped a gesture towards the door. Cassidy ran, tearing his way through to a hatch that took him into the main cell and up the ladder to the gun platform. Colours filled the cell, thickening as he forced himself up to the turret. He fought to keep his mind from dissolving as the rushing colours tore at him, trying to drag him into a kaleidoscopic vortex. This must be what the others had faced. Liquid madness in the air. His mind tried to leak out as he crawled along the makeshift runway on top of the *Nubigena*. The colours swarmed, thicker than down in the main cell. Karl had re-moored his plane near the tail, and it took him precious minutes to unlatch the landing gear.

Cassidy felt himself floating away, off the deck and into the rainbow vastness. He gripped the Fokker, letting its reality anchor him as he pulled himself into the cockpit. Closing his eyes, he tried to shut out the colours and the maddening scrape inside his head.

The magnetos started the props without trouble. He throttled forwards into the Borealis and pulled the stick back. The Fokker lifted off, clearing the gun platform by inches. Feet? Yards? He couldn't feel the distance. Cassidy kept his eyes shut, blinking them open only for moments to try getting his bearings, but the world was nothing but gaseous reds and liquid purples. The Fokker's dials and gauges twitched and whirled. Useless. He felt as if he were fighting through water.

Cassidy pushed the throttle all the way forwards, finding he could only concentrate on one control at a time, stick, throttle or pedals. Blinking, he saw a crackling gate open up a hundred yards ahead. Banner must have opened it, or sent it. How? Cassidy fought his way forwards, but the force of the Borealis increased as he came closer.

To hell with this, Cassidy thought. He opened his eyes and let the colours flood over his senses. This wasn't about the Fokker's engines. It was about his will to fight. If there was nothing else Banner had taught him, it was that belief and hope counted for more than all the mechanical power and luck in the world.

Cassidy's awareness snapped into focus. He realized he hadn't throttled forwards at all, but back. The props barely spun and the engine was close to choking out. The Fokker floated more than flew. He willed his hand forwards and the throttle moved, fraction of an inch by fraction of an inch. The engine roared as the fighter fought the colour soup and made for the crackling green square.

Roaring his rage into the Borealis, Cassidy felt the gate break over him, setting the Fokker aflame with arcing energies. Cassidy looked back as the *Nubigena* shimmered, awash with colours that imbued themselves to the grey exterior. Green energy rose up the ship's belly, fought for dominance and overcame the rainbow sheen for a moment before the ship vanished again into the sea of gasses.

The gate faded behind Cassidy as the raging reds and purples washed out of his vision. The sky was cobalt clouds again. He sighed. Banner was whole now. A dream that had never really been a dream. No wonder the worlds had both bent to his will and yet never accepted him at the same time. Could the ship, a hybrid of *real* and electric dream just like its captain, survive?

Perhaps. Perhaps there might even be some form of natural existence there for them.

Cassidy fought back tears. The man was gone, along with the great ship. The only place he had ever called home.

Silence closed in. He reached out to the Fokker. Sent his awareness down the stick and through the pedals, to the engine, prop and down the tail of the plane. This is what Banner had done with his own craft. Connected to it like another soul to stay the loneliness of traipsing through a world never quite your own.

The fighter purred back in response. The dull hum of the engine shuddered through him and Cassidy saw the gates. They were everywhere, like ghosts. No, not gates. Potential gates. It must have been Banner's bond to the ship all along. A *real* object of travel melded to his dreamself that made this possible. This was what had happened that first time Cassidy had flown this plane in the storm. It had enabled him to see...to see...

Cassidy fought to understand what it was he saw. The hazy windows between worlds looked back at him like the distant eyes of time. What made a potential gate an open gate?

He thought of Arcadia, one of the few places he could picture perfectly in his mind. A square of crackling green solidified as the rest receded into the background. Cassidy turned and slipped the Fokker through.

Arcadia floated in the distance, its snow-capped mountains set against a lavender backdrop. It was beautiful. Almost shining now. The familiar place looked like an oasis in a desert.

Cassidy landed and came to a stop a few feet from the same grease-covered mechanic from before. The props spun to a stop and he leapt down. The young man cowered. Cassidy ignored him. There was no point in a threat. If anything happened to his plane this time—he ran his hand over the Mauser on his side so the man could see. Reaching back into the cockpit for his provisions pack, he found a large canvas bag instead. Banner's money. More money than he could spend in a lifetime. At least he'd be able to get a room.

A shape caught his eye just off the runway as he climbed back down. Another fighter stood covered in a canvas tarp. He stepped over, peeked beneath a corner and bit back a curse.

The lounge looked more inviting than before. The barkeep nodded to him as he took a stool and leaned on his elbows. "Still on Banner's tab?" the elven man asked.

"No," Cassidy said and exhaled sharply. "Start one up for me." He slid a large Twilight banknote across the bar, then returned it to his jacket. The barkeep nodded.

Despite the memory of Barnabas, the thought of another *real* glass of single malt Scotch warmed him. "Whisky on the rocks," he said and clenched his hand into a tight fist.

"Back to the old favourite, eh?" the barkeep said.

Cassidy gritted his teeth and gave a defeated nod.

The blended whisky did taste good, despite not being Scotch, or *real*. He nursed it with grim resolve.

Only a few other customers dotted the lounge, but the barkeep leaned in close. "Heard you got your fighter back from the Commodore."

Cassidy nodded.

"They say he still wants to dangle you off the edge of the island and let his men use you for musket practice."

Cassidy scoffed.

"Word is, he won't come near you because of Shea's bodyguards, but I heard from someone else he's actually scared of *you*."

"You hear a lot," Cassidy said and finished his drink. He sucked a piece of ice into his mouth and chewed the slightly-alcoholic coldness.

The barkeep grinned and put his hands up in surrender. He slid a brothel token over the bar. "Shea told me to give you this next time you were in. Good for her or anyone else you please."

Cassidy let the shiny disk sit next to his glass. He dug April's silver dollar from his pocket and set it next to the token. They were both about the same size, though the dull shine of the tarnished silver still looked brighter than the polished token. He picked up the dollar and gripped it hard, letting a few drops of April's pain eke into him. Where was she now? Had April even thought of him since, or was he no more than a ghostly memory to her now?

In the mirror Cassidy watched a young man and woman come down the stairway arm in arm.

"You're coming back tomorrow night, aren't you?" the woman said, dragging the young man towards the bar. She was obviously one of the many brothel girls trying hard to turn a return trick.

"Of course." The young man leaned in, kissed her deeply, then laughed. His laugh cut off in mid-guffaw as he looked in the direction of the mirror.

"How's the plane handling?" Cassidy asked without turning around.

The young man stammered. "Cassidy," Ned said after three half started sentences, "am I glad to see you. I thought you were dead." He slipped away from the woman and bellied up several stools down. "I brought the Valkyrie in." He paused and studied Cassidy in the mirror, his eyes darting towards the back exit. "I hope you don't mind," he continued. "I couldn't leave it at the observatory."

Cassidy glanced over at Ned and went back to sucking whisky off his last piece of ice.

"Is Banner okay?" Ned continued. "I mean, did you get them out alright?"

Cassidy pushed his glass away and turned to look at Ned. "I'm going to ask you one question. If you lie, I'm going to kill you."

Ned paled. He opened his mouth to speak, but just nodded.

Cassidy bore into him with his gaze. "I need to know if you sold them out."

"What?" Ned asked, his eyes on Cassidy's pistol.

"Someone sent one hell of a lot of trouble the captain's way and they must have known the places we liked to hide." Cassidy leaned closer. "Was it you?"

Ned's chin jutted out. "I'm not a good fighter," he rasped, as if his mouth were dry. "My stomach turns over when I get scared and I start passing out, but I'm not a traitor." He shook his head. "I just wouldn't do that."

Cassidy turned back to the barkeep. "I'm thirsty," he said. "One more."

"I'm sorry," Ned repeated. "I wanted to help. If there's ever anything else..."

Cassidy accepted his second drink and took a sip. "Good. I have some dangerous flying coming up and I could use someone with a plane."

Ned gulped. "I'd love to, Major, but I've been hired to run a shipment over to another island tomorrow morning. It'll take a couple weeks."

Cassidy let the whisky burn fill him. "That's why you told that girl you'd see her tomorrow night?" He took the brothel token that still lay on the bar and slid it over without glancing at Ned. "This is more your speed."

Ned took the token. He sat silent for several moments before standing up and walking off.

A dark cold made its way past the warmth of the whisky. Seeing Ned reminded Cassidy of everyone he'd lost. He'd been racking his brain for a way to find the black pyramid again, but only Banner had known the way. He tried to imagine weaving the Fokker down the corridor of gates and realised he didn't even know where the captain had started into the secret labyrinth that led the way.

"Ladies and gentlemen," a voice boomed across the lounge. Hotel acoustics made it difficult to determine direction, but seconds later a bright spotlight shone a large circle against the back wall. Cassidy had never been at the hotel on a night they had a floor show.

"We have a special treat for all of you tonight," the voice continued. "This week's performer hails from lands far away, but he's truly a magician of renown, even here in the Twilight. He's returned to Arcadia for only two nights before moving on to Lilliput. We hope you all enjoy this night of magic and mystery."

The small crowd had increased by the moment. A fine mist of magenta smoke drifted across the dance floor Cassidy assumed would serve as a stage. It grew thicker as the orchestra kicked in with dramatic music. Cassidy couldn't identify the composer for certain, but it might well have been Wagner.

A black line split the mist from top to bottom and a man stepped through. He wore classic evening dress: tails, white waistcoat and bowtie. His jet black hair lay slicked back and his pencil moustache was shaved to rest only on the crest of his upper lip. He was also, most definitely, not a Twilight.

Cassidy smiled. He'd never met a magician, but felt like he'd seen this man a hundred times before. It was as if this *human* filled some primal archetype in his subconscious. Cassidy wondered why he had just thought that and further wondered if he, in fact, *had* a subconscious. If so, was his subconscious the Everdream itself?

The magician gave a gracious bow, removed his white gloves and tossed them into the air. At the top of the crest they fused, sprouted legs and long wings, becoming a misshapen crane that cawed in agony. The crane fell and became gloves once more as they landed in the magician's hand.

The audience gave polite applause. Cassidy shifted on his stool.

The magician gave a broad smile and tucked the gloves into his pocket. He tugged on the chain of his pocket watch, but it slid out of his waistcoat without a watch on its end. He stroked his chin, returned the chain and reached beneath his jacket. When he withdrew his hand, it held a foot-tall hourglass with sparkling sand in the upper globe. He set the hourglass on a small table to his right that hadn't been there a moment ago. The sand didn't fall into the lower bulb, but remained suspended in the upper portion.

Gesturing to the audience, the magician indicated that he wanted a volunteer. After several seconds of chatter, a pretty young woman in a blue gown was pushed up to the front, as if offered by the audience as a sacrifice.

The magician bowed and kissed the young woman's hand. She blushed and he returned a gallant smile. He reached behind her head and plucked an eight-inch dagger from empty air. The knife was double edged with a silver blade and wire wrapped handle. Its pommel ended in a quartz crystal that glinted as he turned it over in his hands. The magician indicated her midriff with a wave of his hand. The blue silken fabric of her gown stretched almost taut across her stomach.

The magician turned the woman sideways so that she now stood to his left. He gestured as if to say, *are you ready?* The woman smiled and gave a playful shrug, as if to say, *okay, what are we doing?* The magician raised his eyebrows and lowered them again, signalling the orchestra which began a loud drum roll. He turned the sandglass over and the sparkling material within the lower portion floated upwards, grain by grain into the upper bulb.

With another grand gesture, he placed his hand on her shoulder, brandished the dagger and plunged it into her stomach. She shrieked, doubled over and fell to the floor. Blood spread out in a thin, dark pool.

Chapter 29

The audience waited in a combination of stunned silence and expectation. Cassidy leaned forwards as the magician brought several Twilights up to feel her pulse and report that she was, in fact, dead. Her eyes looked like those of the woman from New York, her features frozen in shock and pain. She was dead. Truly dead.

The magician motioned to the orchestra, and it gave him another build of dramatic bass drums and low celli. High violins filled in, coming over the top like thin air spirits darting between heavier, more substantial mythic creatures. He turned the sandglass over once again. The upper bulb, now the lower one, had filled only a quarter of the way, but now the grains reversed, returning to the mass in the upper globe.

The woman rose up from the floor as if falling in reverse. The magician's movements reversed as well. The blood spilled up from the floor and seeped back into her body. He leaned forwards, gripped the dagger's handle and withdrew it. Her expression went from pain, to horror, to fear and back to simple curiosity as he tossed the knife into the air. It vanished in a tiny cloud of metallic sparkle.

The woman looked dazed. She swooned. The magician caught her, handed her a small phial of blue liquid and whispered something in her ear. She walked back to her seat with a confused smile.

The conjuror bowed low, receiving thunderous applause. Cassidy joined in, but watched as the woman returned to her seat and collapsed. He hoped it was merely out of exhaustion. She had not been Twilight.

"I would appreciate it if everyone cleared their mind," the magician said as the applause died down. "Tonight I would like to demonstrate an ability or two I've picked up over the years, and the less you are all consciously thinking, the easier it will be for me." He smiled and gestured to a man sitting at one of the lounge booths. The candle on the table cast a flicker of shadows across his chiselled features.

"Ah, sir," the magician said, "I see you're a man of mystery. You prefer the edges of the room, and I would venture to say that you're much the same with the world. A traveller, am I right?"

The man in shadows gave a slow nod.

"As I thought," the magician said. "But that's not a difficult guess in a crowd such as this one. Allow me to add that you're a dangerous man. In fact, you're a hunter of men, both dreams and Twilights and…others," he added with a dismissive gesture. "You're searching even now. I fear the room is hardly safe," he said with a slight laugh.

The man at the booth flexed his fingers and scowled.

The magician gave another dismissive wave. "You're afraid, dear sir. My apologies if you don't want to answer. Very well, *you* dear lady," he said, motioning to a woman who sat at one of the tables that skirted the dance floor closer to him.

The woman looked up impassively. She wore a sequinned evening dress and silver gloves. The man with her leaned forwards and whispered something in her ear that made her laugh. He sported a thin goatee with a grey streak that ran through his shock of black hair.

"Twice," the magician said, "but the first time she exaggerated and the second she was faking. She's also sleeping with your brother, and for some reason, you don't seem to mind, though it's probably because you don't realise that she actually prefers his company and not just his money."

The woman looked up at the goateed man, her eyes wide and frightened. The man stood and stormed out, trying not to make eye contact with anyone. The woman followed him moments later, face flushed, eyes bright with tears.

"And you, sir," the magician said, pointing to the bar and right at Cassidy who drew his own features into blank stare. "You truly are a strange one," he said and laid his chin against his fist. "A pilot, I see, but your clothing tells me that. You also travel a great deal. You're never in one place long. An easy assumption to be sure, I know. But a dear friend has recently died—my mistake, he's not exactly dead, but— I'm sorry, I can't read beyond that." The magician closed his eyes and massaged his temples. "You have an important task ahead of you, but then a longer road after that. Your mind is fogged with endless loops of constant questions." He furrowed his brow and squinted. "I would suggest being careful for…" he trailed off as he concentrated harder. "I'd beware of nearly half the people in this room and at least two people *not* in this room. It must be nice to be so wanted."

A nervous laugh rose from the audience. Cassidy shifted his gaze from patron to patron.

"Anyway, folks," the magician said, inclining his head and clasping his hands together in front of him, "I'm afraid my mind is taxed beyond its normal endurance. Please remember, I will be here again tomorrow night." He bowed low, dropping his hands behind him. The magician straightened with both arms extended and showered the audience with a spray of flaming roses. The flames extinguished as they reached the patrons and each guest received a single red rose in their laps. No one could help looking down at their deep crimson flower and he was gone when they glanced back to the dance floor.

Cassidy turned *his* rose over in his hands. It was blue instead of red. Deep blue. The petals almost looked like glass and refracted the light into odd patterns as he rolled the stem between his fingers.

"For me?" a familiar voice asked from his left. Shea's flame-red hair came into view as Cassidy turned his head. She smelled like cinnamon tonight and her green eyes stood out in particular contrast to her hair and crème-white skin.

Cassidy passed the rose to her.

"You're too kind," she said.

"I owe you."

"Yes, you do. How about you cash in my token tonight."

Cassidy smiled. "Still not my poison, but thanks."

Shea sighed. "Is she beautiful?"

Cassidy raised an eyebrow.

"Whoever you keep breaking my heart for," Shea said.

"If I ever meet her," Cassidy said, rapping his fingers on the bar, "I'll give you a full description."

Shea gave him a pout she must have practiced for hours in a mirror. The pout had probably made her even more money than her sultry, come-hither expression. "Watch your back, John," she said and slid the rose into her cleavage so that the bud rested at the hollow of her throat. "I've tried like hell to protect you, but you make the worst enemies."

Cassidy showed his teeth. "Men are known by the enemies they keep."

Shea smiled and vanished into the shadows of the lounge where he was sure she'd claim a purse full of tokens.

The magician sat down next to Cassidy and gave a tired smile. He still wore evening wear, but his bowtie lay untied around his collar. "I need a drink," he said and motioned for the barkeep. "You look like a man who usually orders whisky with ice," he said to Cassidy.

Cassidy clicked his glass against the bar as if to say, *of course you know, you're looking at what I drink.*

"But," said the magician, "you also look like a man who's sick of drinking them." He gave a knowing smile and ordered two martinis. "My name is Leon," he offered as the drinks arrived.

"John," Cassidy said, enjoying the opportunity to use his first name. He sipped his drink. It wasn't whisky, and anything but whisky tasted like heaven. "Is the crane real?" he asked.

Leon shrugged. "A better question would be, 'are the gloves real?'" he said. "Magic is a wonderful thing, but there's always a sacrifice. For instance," he said, removing the gloves from his dinner jacket, "I'll never be able to wear them again." He pried open one of the gloves to reveal the sticky blood staining the insides. "Go through a pair each time I perform."

"Why carry them around?"

"To remind me," Leon said.

"Then the crane *is* real," Cassidy said. He suddenly realised how much he wanted it to be real. How much he hoped for impossible things to be made possible.

The magician gave a strained smile. "Real? I don't know. I just bend things a little. The Twilight allows a greater amount of bending than the *real* world, but the rules are similar. I bleed for the art a little more." He opened a button in the middle of his shirt to show a red-stained bandage beneath. "Here, I can only perform once a night without bleeding to death, but the shows are more interesting. They have to be to please these people."

"These *people?*" Cassidy mused. He felt a strange camaraderie with this man whom he could only assume to be from the *real* world, a dreamer like Richthofen. "What exactly are these people?"

"I'm still not sure," Leon said. "I've been visiting this place for several years now. Beautiful scenery. My pilot and my assistant love it."

"Assistant?" Cassidy asked.

"Assistant," Leon said. "The lovely young woman I stabbed in the stomach. We don't do that trick very often."

"Then it *is* fake," Cassidy said.

Leon snorted. "Tell her that. Never eats before or after." He sipped at his drink and gave a wide smile. "Look me up if you're ever in New York," Leon said. "I'll get you a *real* drink." He produced a calling card from thin air, passed it to Cassidy and stood up. "By the way, if you really want to find your friends, I'd look in the direction of greatest danger."

"What exactly does that mean?" Cassidy asked.

"Fortunes are a lot like advice," Leon said. "Worth about what you pay for them." He winked and was gone.

***

The evening, or what passed for an evening in the Twilight, felt good. He still couldn't get over how it never got completely dark, but only hinted at it. Teased you with it. He looked up and watched the familiar airships drift in the breeze. A lump welled in his throat at the *Nubigena*-shaped space that seemed to remain between them.

The wharf lay empty as Cassidy walked the docks. Wooden crates. Mooring lines. A handful of dock workers milling about the scattering of random sheds and vacant merchant booths.

A shadow peeked out from the edge of one of the small buildings and vanished again. Cassidy continued as if nothing had happened, but decided to skirt the wooden shack-buildings, moving around the edge of the wharf. He glanced over his shoulder in time to see the dark shape meld into the angled shadows of corrugated roof-tops.

Cassidy took the opportunity to duck into the maze of small buildings as well. He gripped the handle of his Mauser, keeping it against his side to avoid catching it on any of the sundry junk that lay everywhere as he navigated through the narrow alleys.

Hopefully the dark figure would think he'd moved on much farther and run to catch up. He waited until a flurry of footsteps rushed past and he slipped out behind the shadow. He trailed the dark figure for another few buildings before it stopped again. Cassidy moved forwards on silent feet and extended the barrel level with the shadow's head.

"I know you're back there," the shadow said.

Cassidy winced inside, but kept the pistol level. "Then you also know I'm in line to take your head off."

"Naturally," said the shadow in a gruff male voice. "May I turn around if I keep my hands in the air?"

"Sure," Cassidy said, but dropped to one knee, the Mauser still trained on the large head.

The man began to turn, hands raised. The left arm looked thinner than the other. It wore a glove over the spindly hand, and in the moment it took for Cassidy to realise the arm was mechanical, a pistol flashed from beneath the dark coat and fired. The bullet passed over Cassidy's head, where his chest would have been if he'd been standing.

He squeezed off two rounds. The first caught the man in his left shoulder. It struck something metal and drove the man back as the second round caught him lower down.

Arms flailed in the contrasting light. The mechanical arm clattered somewhere out of Cassidy's sight along with the heavy clicking of a skittering pistol. He leapt on the man, pinning him to the ground with his knee and shoved the muzzle of his pistol into the man's right eye. Cassidy glanced around in case of backup, but there didn't appear to be any.

The man tried to bring his head up, laughed and let it rest on the deck. "They told me not to underestimate you, Mr. Cassidy. I thought they meant only in the air."

His accent sounded strange. Czech perhaps, or Russian. Cassidy looked closer and realised it was the man from the lounge. The one the magician had picked on first. "So you're the dangerous one?" Cassidy said. "The bounty hunter." He pulled his pistol out of the man's eye.

The man turned his head and spat. "Nyet. Bounty hunters are nasty. I'm a soldier."

"Mercenary?" Cassidy asked.

The man shrugged his good shoulder. "Who isn't?"

"Me," Cassidy said. "Now what exactly were you hired to do, other than piss me off?"

"I was just told to find you," the Russian mercenary said. "You pulled a gun. I have no interest in dying."

"Then who hired you?" Cassidy asked.

The Russian took a deep sigh. "An Englishman named Brewster."

Cassidy showed his teeth and pushed the muzzle back into the man's eye. "That's the name of a good friend of mine. Not a good one to throw around."

The Russian didn't move. "That is possible. He didn't say why he wanted to find you. I have no reason to lie."

Cassidy squatted and checked the man for more weapons. He found three pistols, two knives and a choking wire. He threw them in the water. "You're an assassin," Cassidy said as he holstered his Mauser and sat down on a packing crate.

The Russian winced and pulled himself to a seated position. He dabbed at his wounded shoulder with a dirty handkerchief. "My name is Anton, and I do a lot of things. Govno," he said, poking at the wound. "You're using real bullets."

"You're not Twilight."

"Neither are you."

Cassidy nodded. "Yes, but you're *real*. 'Til today, I've only met one real person, that I know of, in this place and suddenly your kind are everywhere."

"Perhaps you just never noticed."

Cassidy grimaced. "Where is he?"

Anton's expression remained bleak and impassive. "He's still my employer."

"I could kill you."

Anton snorted. "You may anyway."

"I may," Cassidy admitted. "But if you tell me now, you won't have to use that mechanical arm for more than just a decoy."

Chapter 30

Cassidy left without even stopping by the hotel for a drink. His Fokker stood waiting next to the runway, fuelled and ready. The older Fokker, Ned's plane now, was gone already. The Valkyrie had somehow been demoted from fighter to mere transportation.

The almost-night still hung around the fringes of Arcadia as if trying to hold onto a few more hours of darkness before the almost-day took over. The Russian had given Cassidy good enough directions. It wasn't *"second star to the right and straight on 'til morning,"* but close enough.

He was to fly forty degrees off the hotel side of the island and fly ninety degrees downwards until he came to a patch of fireflies.

Cassidy feared missing them, but the strange description turned out to be a mass of flowing orbs that danced and darted within the confines of an egg-shaped mass, approximately the same height and width of Arcadia. He skirted the border, uncertain of what effect they might have on his plane. It was hard to leave the lights. As he tried to veer away, they tugged at him. There was no sound or physical force, but their movement hypnotized his senses. The dancing lights wanted to play. Wanted company. Wanted...

Cassidy forced himself away and veered twenty degrees to port. He didn't know what they wanted, but throttled forwards and pulled away. They faded behind him, and he couldn't help thinking he'd just escaped some kind of fairy circle. His head still wanted to think in terms of East and West, but without a well-defined sun, the Twilight still lacked any useful term for directions, except those relative to the islands themselves. At least, none they'd chosen to share with him.

Images of the dancing lights wouldn't leave. Did he remember fairies from Richthofen, or had he gotten it from stories Brewster had told him? What was Brewster doing? How had he gotten away from the black pyramid?

None of that mattered as Cassidy approached something Anton had called the Vizier's Outpost. It looked much the way the Russian had described it, a small shanty town with several diminutive buildings strung together from the remnants of dead airships into a sort of accidental island.

Cassidy put down on what appeared to serve as a runway, though he suspected it was usually only a landing site for vertical take-offs of dirigible airships. That explained the short length and lack of markings. He taxied to a vacant spot between two bleak-looking airships. The first appeared to be a large wooden box strapped between two large balloons of mismatched colours.

The second looked like a small clipper that hadn't seen its original maker in over forty years, though Cassidy wouldn't have been surprised if a number of half-competent carpenters had laboured to make their marks on the wretched vessel. Its drooping gas bladder had been patched from the remains of at least six various balloons and it now resembled a lumpy sausage with one end much larger than the other.

Cassidy continued to the main building, which probably served as hotel, bar and town meeting room. It appeared to have been fashioned from the dead carcass of a large cargo ship. Its mast and whatever balloons or gas bladders had once lifted it were long since gone, and a large hole had been cut in its side to act as an entrance, though the doors across the opening seemed to have come from some sort of barn.

Cassidy pushed the swinging doors open. A counter with room key pegs lay to his right and a bar stood against the far wall. "I'm looking for a friend in 16," Cassidy said to the man behind the counter.

"Are you?" the man said. "Is he expecting you?"

"Apparently," Cassidy said. "Otherwise he wouldn't have three men in here waiting on me." He motioned to some bruisers who sat at one of the tables. All three were built large and dangerous with Russian features. They probably expected Anton to come in dragging a pilot by the scruff of his neck.

The hotel clerk grimaced, but gestured in the direction of the stairs. Number 16 lay at the end of a short hallway. Cassidy knocked.

"What is it?" hollered a voice from inside. Cassidy knew the English accent well.

"Cassidy," he yelled through the door.

"Come in, Old Boy," the Englishman said.

Cassidy turned the knob and pushed the door open. Brewster sat eyeing him from a skeletal wooden chair across the room. He cocked his Webley revolver and trained it on Cassidy's head. "Brewster," Cassidy said, his hands in the air. "It's me."

"Shut the door," Brewster said. His eyes were still wild with madness, the rainbow sheen of the Borealis tinting his irises.

Cassidy nudged the door shut. "You need to listen," he said with earnest intensity. "The Borealis is still affecting your mind." He tried to meet Brewster's gaze, but the swirling colours threw off his concentration. "You've got to—"

"Where's Banner?" Brewster snapped, cutting across his words.

Cassidy chewed his lip. "Banner..." he started, but didn't know how to finish.

"Betrayed us all," Brewster said. He stood up and paced across the small room, his pistol still levelled. "And you helped him," he snarled. "You bloody well helped him."

Cassidy's heart pounded. The Englishman was worse than he'd imagined. "Brewster. I'm your friend."

Brewster seethed. "Friend? You're not a friend. A Judas, maybe. Worse than a Jonah. A bastard."

"Brewster," Cassidy said, trying to keep his tone calm and steady, "where are Franz and Jayce?"

Brewster kicked the bed frame, cracking the wood. "Traitors. Stayed in safety. Didn't want to leave. Well, I came back. Came back to find out why the lot of you left us."

"I was trying to—"

"You never came back," Brewster shouted. His face reddened as he shook the muzzle of the pistol at Cassidy's face. "You left us to rot."

Cassidy raked a hand through his hair as Brewster paced back and forth, ranting. He moved towards the crazed Englishman. "Look," he said, stepping close enough for the muzzle to touch his forehead. "I'm here."

The Webley shook harder in Brewster's hand until he doubled over in an epileptic fit. The Webley tumbled to the floor and he clutched Cassidy to him, sobbing into his shoulder. "It's mad, Old Boy. It's mad. All mad." He let go and staggered back. "You betrayed me." He collapsed into his chair again. "Colours, Old Boy," he said, staring off over Cassidy's head. "Can't get them out of my head. Colours."

"I'm here," Cassidy said. "I'll make the colours go away."

Brewster looked up at him through tear-stained eyes. "What's happened to Banner?"

Cassidy explained as best he could, but Brewster only cared about the sound of his voice. Nothing Cassidy said seemed to sink in, and Brewster periodically flew into sudden, violent rages. Sometimes he convulsed, then became catatonic for long periods before returning to what passed for lucidity.

"Banner's gone," Cassidy said for what must have been the thousandth time. "He's gone. The Borealis took him." Brewster's eyes widened at the word and he trembled again, but not as badly. Cassidy had worked him down from the spasmodic convulsions he'd *been* having at the mention of the Borealis. He held Brewster's head between his hands and forced their eyes to lock. Cassidy bored past the rainbow irises and concentrated on the black pupils. "I need you," he said, nodding. "I need you back. You're all I've got left."

The ordeal continued for days. Sometimes Brewster verged on the edge of complete cognisance, only to degrade into madness the next minute. The Russians had come asking about their orders. Cassidy slid money under the door and told them to go away.

He forced food and drink on Brewster, but the only thing the Englishman was capable of doing by himself on a regular basis was smoking his pipe. He did so over and over. The colours faded several shades during the almost meditative ceremony only to return moments later.

In time, Cassidy spliced bits and pieces together of the random information Brewster spit out in tirades until it formed a mosaic image of what had happened. Apparently the caretakers at the pyramid had done all they could to remove the effects of the Borealis, but sanity only lasted for hours at first and then a few days at a time. Jayce and Franz had both fallen in love with the same female caretaker and all but fought an insane duel over her.

Brewster had finally tired of the whole ordeal and decided to leave. He'd been told he couldn't, but in one of his saner moments, he'd stolen an airship and escaped. He couldn't remember or refused to recall what had happened to Jayce and Franz.

Unfortunately, Brewster's sanity had deteriorated again since he'd been alone. After becoming convinced that Banner and Cassidy had betrayed him, he'd hired Anton to track both of them down and bring them before him. In his saner moments, Brewster was highly apologetic for hiring a mercenary to track down his best friend, but Cassidy unloaded the Webley for fear of the erratic fits.

"It's all right," Cassidy said, trying to force dark bourbon down his friend's throat, followed by a chunk of rye bread. "We're going to be okay now."

Brewster nodded and knocked back the drink, but Cassidy could tell he was holding the pain behind the well-known British stiff upper lip. The Borealis had cut deep and severed parts of him Cassidy wasn't sure could be repaired. "What will we do?" the Englishman asked, shaking, but controlled.

Cassidy let out a long breath. "We're going to the real world. I don't know how it works yet, but I know there are ways we can live like *real* people, outside the storm."

Brewster shook his head. "Not a chance. We'd fade to nothing, or melt."

"Banner used to do it," Cassidy said. "It's how he met a lot of our dreamers."

"How?" Brewster asked.

Cassidy had no idea. "Force of will," he said with all the assurance he could pull across his face. "Pure force of will."

Brewster nodded. "Force of will."

It took almost a month before Cassidy decided Brewster might be fit enough to leave again. Not that he had a great deal of choice. Each minute spent anywhere in the Twilight was dangerous. Truth be told, Cassidy couldn't believe the bounty hunters hadn't found them yet. Perhaps the mere presence of the Russian mercenaries made the hotel seem like an unlikely place for hunted dreams to hide.

"Only a matter of time, Old Boy," Brewster said as they devoured supper. "They'll never stop." His hand shook, but he clamped it with his other hand and pinned it to the table.

Cassidy nodded. "We start island hopping soon. Then we work on becoming more solid."

"What makes you so sure we can really do that?"

"Like I said, Banner did it," Cassidy insisted.

"I thought you said he wasn't really a dream," Brewster said as he spooned something that looked like grey custard into his mouth.

"We are what we believe ourselves to be. Isn't that what you told me a long time ago?"

Brewster nodded. "A bit paraphrased, but I don't know that I believe that anymore."

"What choice have you got?" Cassidy asked.

Brewster shrugged. "Can't argue with that logic."

Cassidy grinned. "Sure you can, but what's the point." He picked up his whisky on the rocks. "We're all that's left of Banner's boys."

Brewster took a deep sigh and met Cassidy's gaze. "To Banner's boys," he said.

"To Banner's boys," Cassidy agreed. They downed their shots in quick gulps. "I miss the ship."

Brewster was silent for several seconds. "I miss a lot of things."

Chapter 31

The airship with the patched sausage bladder turned out to be Brewster's stolen ship. They had a good laugh as they looked up at the dilapidated vessel.

"How the hell did you get that here?" Cassidy asked as it shifted in the breeze.

"Not nearly as bad as she looks," Brewster said. "I outran a variety of ships in this."

"I'll take your word on that," Cassidy said as he walked around the vessel and peered inside the boxlike gondola. "I can't believe she gets off the ground."

"Don't listen to him," Brewster said, petting the figurehead on what passed for a prow on the gondola's bow. It looked like a deformed statue of a mermaid, brandishing what once must have been a triton, but now resembled a broken stick. The interior looked just big enough to fit three crew members, though in a spot, it probably could have transported six.

Cassidy wondered if the gas bladder could actually lift six, but the point was moot. At most, it might have to carry two, and Cassidy doubted he would spend much time flying anything but his Fokker. He stepped back and wondered at what an odd pair the two aerocrafts made. "What's her name?" Cassidy asked.

"The *Intrepid*," Brewster said. "She's earned the name on several occasions. No real guns though. I'll either need to get some, or just keep shooting out the windows like I've been doing."

Cassidy nodded. The *Nubigena* it was not, but nothing else ever could be. They would have to fly in tandem as this airship could never support his Fokker and it would need his fighter's air protection. He considered another problem. "She'll never make it in the *real* world. Wish my plane was a two-seater."

Brewster shrugged. "We'll find one. Let's grab a drink."

Cassidy gave a mock salute and they started off. "I notice you're wearing the Webley in your belt now," he said, gesturing to Brewster's pistol.

Brewster tapped the wooden butt where it protruded above his trousers. "You might want to do the same," he said. "Flap holsters are too slow and I've had two groups try to rob me here so far. Gotten to be a bit like your Old West this far out."

"So you want me to be a gunfighter?"

"Why not," Brewster said as they slid one of the doors aside. "But we'll have to get different hats."

Cassidy stifled a guffaw. It disturbed him to remember that everything he knew about being American was based on Richthofen's idea of the United States, and he had no way to know how much of it was accurate. It drove the point home when Brewster ordered a dark lager and Cassidy was forced once again to stare down at three fingers of iced whisky. He often thought of telling Brewster about his problem so that Brewster could order him something else, but any time he tried, his mind wandered on to other things. It was as if his head purposely avoided any kind of change.

Cassidy didn't mind at the moment, though. Sitting there having a drink with Brewster reminded him of old times. He imagined them back on the *Nubigena*, Franz and Jayce playing billiards only feet away, and Banner at the helm, steering them through lands unknown.

"So, who do you think really betrayed us?" Brewster asked, "I mean with the whole Borealis thing."

Cassidy shook his head. "I've been thinking about that. I don't think anyone did."

Brewster narrowed his eyes. "Don't see how."

Cassidy drew a small sip. "Banner's soul. I think it could feel him. It had probably been guiding that same Borealis to us the whole time. The angrier his soul got, the more dangerous the Borealis became. We were just collateral damage."

Brewster let out a sharp exhale. "Believe it or not, we used to have a brilliant time in those wonder-clouds. Used to take us to all kinds of strange places."

Cassidy nodded. "Part of me thought one might take me home someday."

"Home?" Brewster said and squinted over his lager.

"I guess I mean my dream. It's not the same when I'm asleep. Feels like a world I'll never see again. Closest thing I can call mine. Don't you wonder?"

Brewster shook his head and wiped foam out of his moustache. "I don't think about it."

One of the frontiersmen in town had given them a lead on a pirate named Resta, who often dealt in *real* world aerocraft. Their rarity allowed him to charge a heavy price, but Cassidy felt certain they could work a deal. Word was that Resta had recently procured a new *real* world aerocraft and would be auctioning it off to the highest bidder in a week. Cassidy hoped that he and Brewster could find the pirate first.

Cassidy watched Brewster's craft glide beneath him as he scouted the area for Resta's airship. It was said to have been seen near Arcadia a month before and the Starling a week before. The Settled Mount appeared to be the closest inhabited island, so they followed the vague coordinates they'd been given.

Cassidy scouted ahead, keeping the *Intrepid* just in sight. A small island came into view about a mile off the starboard side. Even at a distance he saw buildings dotting the mostly flat surface, so he doubled back to Brewster and led the limp airship towards it.

As they flew closer it reminded Cassidy of Arcadia, but smaller and less populated. It was about half the size, with only one mountain and no snow on it. At least thirty airships already stood moored, with several leaving and one coming. He searched the standards on their flags for the black Fleur-de-lis Resta was known to fly when outside Arcadian borders. Cassidy found the ship moored to one of the larger docks and he spat a curse beneath his breath as he recognized the battleship-like gondola. Commodore.

Cassidy found the runway near the edge of the island at the bottom of the docks, much like the Arcadian layout. He landed and immediately had the dock men cover the Fokker with a large tarp.

Brewster met him at the dock where he'd moored the *Intrepid*. He nodded towards the ship flying the black Fleur-de-lis. "That her?"

"That's her," Cassidy said. He pulled the Mauser out of its holster. He slid the cumbersome chunk of wood that was its home into his mail bag and shoved the pistol into his belt.

"Becoming a gunfighter?" Brewster asked.

"How about a pirate?" Cassidy asked.

"Always a first time. But I thought we were going to pay."

Cassidy shook his head and entered Brewster's airship. "I think diplomacy might break down the moment they see me," he said as he rummaged through a foot locker that sat against the back wall. He found a brown greatcoat and a black cloak. "In fact, it might be best that no one here see our uniforms," he said, tossing the cloak to Brewster. He dropped his cap in the footlocker and had Brewster do the same.

"Not my idea of fashion," the Englishman said as he brushed lint and dust from the cloak's folds.

Cassidy cracked a smile. "You make a smashing pirate."

Brewster grimaced.

They kept to the shadows as they ascended the stepped tiers of the harbour. Few dock men stood outdoors at that hour and the same seemed true of sailors and airmen.

An empty shed on one of the upper levels offered an excellent view of Resta's heavily-armed airship. A number of sailors stood on the exposed decks.

"They'll go whoring soon," Cassidy said. "And these kinds of men drink a lot."

Brewster nodded. "So, what will we do in the *real* world?" he asked, changing the subject as he puffed on his pipe.

Cassidy shrugged. "Haven't given it a whole lot of thought. Fly planes, maybe." He leaned against the wall beside Brewster. "But the colours. The smells. The lack of Armada breathing down our necks. I'm not sure I care what we do."

Brewster blew smoke rings. "I just want to know what England looks like on a sunny day. We were always in a storm."

"Are there any sunny days in England?" Cassidy asked.

"Good question. They must have them on occasion."

Cassidy looked out the window at the battle-ready airship. "What the hell would you need a ship like that for, anyway?"

Brewster took a glance and shrugged. "Fight something really big, I suppose. You should see some of the pleasure cruisers."

Twenty men or so shuffled down the ramp and into the hotel. Cassidy decided to give them a couple hours to get drunk and laid before he and Brewster made their way down to the ship's dock. They milled about in their disguises for a while, then continued across to another set of sheds and empty booths.

"There's only two guards," Cassidy said as they slipped into a darkened space between buildings.

"Guess we can just kill them," Brewster said, running a hand across the butt of his Webley.

"Not out of the question," said Cassidy, "but I'd like to get through this without wasting ammunition."

"I know," said Brewster, letting his greatcoat fall over his pistol. "I've watched more people die in the last few months than...can't remember, can you? I can't remember much about time either." He motioned to where part of the gondola floated near a second dock. "Let's see if there's a back door."

The airship drifted back and forth, coming within feet of the dock every few minutes. They examined the hull, looking for an opening. "What about that?" Cassidy asked, pointing to a pair of small double doors.

"Gun hatch," Brewster said. "Cannon probably. Bet it fires a full grape."

On the next in-swing, Cassidy slipped his knife into the crack between the two doors and slid it upwards until metal clicked against metal. The latch gave and the doors fell open, revealing an iron bore six inches in diameter. "Seems a bit too easy," said Cassidy as he peered in through the opening.

"Easy?" Brewster said. "Says you without the gut. Have fun slipping around that barrel."

"Can't we just push it out of the way?"

Brewster shook his head. "Airship's free floating, Old Boy. Shove something that heavy and the whole ship will go with it."

Cassidy sighed and kicked his right foot through the small window as the gondola swung towards him again. He flattened his body against the cannon and slid his head and shoulders in around the gaping mouth. The airship drifted away again. For a moment Cassidy dangled from the gondola, one leg and half his body inside while the other leg and his hind quarters hung along the outside. The cast iron of the cannon crushed in on his ribs as he squeezed through and rolled the giant gun away from the opening.

On the next pass Brewster reached for the window and attempted a similar manoeuvre to Cassidy's, but required a good deal more help to make it through the threshold. "Guess I've been eating too well," Brewster whispered as he fell through.

Cassidy relatched the hatch and pushed the gun back into place. "We've been eating the same crap," he said in hushed tones. He stopped a moment to catch his breath. "We're just getting old."

"Speak for yourself, I can't be more than five or six."

"Or a hundred," Cassidy said. "Can you really say for sure how long ago Banner broke you out? I saw his tombstone. It said 1806."

Brewster grimaced. "Don't talk to me about that stuff. There's a reason I never went near that damned grave."

Cassidy turned and pretended to examine the door out of the gunroom. He kept trying to talk about Banner in a casual way, but it tore him up to think of the grave. To think of Banner melding with that other part of himself. That other part Cassidy didn't have. Would never have.

"Resta'll be here somewhere," Cassidy said. "He's a responsible type. Doubt he's whoring." He turned back to Brewster. "Probably takes decent care of his men."

Brewster gave a quiet snort. "This is the Commodore fellow we're talking about, right?" he said as they crept out of the gun room and into the galley. "The pirate that almost killed you?"

Cassidy shrugged. "I'm not fond of the man, but he seems like a decent leader. Does what's necessary, if you know what I mean."

Brewster stopped and turned Cassidy around by the shoulder. "He's the Captain, Old Boy. I know you miss him. I'd fly through Hell to hear his voice again, but don't go seeing his face in every other captain you meet."

Cassidy took a deep breath and exhaled. The Englishman was right and it stung. "I do want to try and buy this plane. He may be a pirate, but I'm no thief."

"Nor I," said Brewster, "but we need it now. We may have lost the luxury of being gentlemen."

Cassidy looked his friend in the eyes. "Then what's the point?"

Brewster sighed. "Let's take a look at this plane. May be a pile of junk, and we'll want to go back the way we came."

Cassidy smirked. "Not the way we came, *Old Boy*. You wouldn't make it through a second time."

Brewster grinned back and they continued to the rear of the galley and into the cargo bay. It was the only place that appeared vast enough to carry any kind of aerocraft.

Wedged between packing crates full of loot a fighter poked out of the mess. The single wing Fokker stood, tired, but waiting. Its tail had been stretched and modified to accommodate a second seat, and they could see a blue letter V through the shadows. Brewster and Cassidy exchanged glances.

"I can't believe Ned would sell it," Cassidy said.

"Ned—" Brewster began, but a voice cut across his from out of the darkness.

"He did take some persuading," Commodore Resta said as he stepped out from between some crates. "Not the bravest of men, but it should warm your heart that he wouldn't even tell us where he saw you last. Shoved my sabre through his skull until he became rotten air."

Chapter 32

Brewster drew his Webley with a speed that surprised even Cassidy, but the Commodore's sabre flashed a fraction faster and Brewster's arm lay on the ground, the pistol still unfired. The Englishman fell back against a wall of crates, clutching at the space where his arm had been.

Cassidy moved for his Mauser, but the gleaming sabre was already at his throat. He backed off as the Commodore removed the pistol with his empty hand and stepped backwards. "I saw you boys fly in. It's not as if I'd ever forget that plane of yours." He gestured to them with the tip of his sword. "I finally had to send everyone off the ship to get you cowards to show up."

"We would have bought it," Cassidy said.

The commodore gave a mock gentle bow. "Of course. That's why you presented yourself from the very beginning. Best intentions, I'm sure," he said and fired several shots with Cassidy's Mauser. Brewster slid to the floor, clutching his stomach.

Cassidy tried to grab for him, but the commodore's sabre edged him back up.

"He won't last long," the commodore said. "At least Twilights have *some* substance. But you...you're just an idea. You don't last."

Cassidy lunged. The sabre flashed again. A sting flared in his ribs. He slumped beside Brewster, holding his chest. Blood spilled from his shirt, a thin line of scarlet.

The Commodore stooped to meet Cassidy's eyes. "You're a brave son of a bitch," he said and slid the sabre into its scabbard. "I admire the way you tried to take us all on back in Arcadia, but bringing in that woman..." He shook his head. "In front of my men, no less." He stood up and backed away.

Cassidy couldn't feel his limbs. His chest should have been stinging, but it was no more than a dull ache.

"I thought I'd have to string you up and torture you in front of my boys, but your fighter is down at the runway." He transferred the pistol to his right hand and examined the unique weapon. "And, I have your sidearm. Everyone will remember. It's *real*," he said, flexing his fingers around the brown handle, "you're just a concept." He squeezed the trigger three times.

Cassidy saw only muzzle flashes. Knew they'd passed through his chest and stomach, perhaps one through his head and into the crates behind him. But he felt nothing except the distant throb of prickling needles in his skin, as if his body had become a pile of clay. Brewster lay wounded beside him. Dying. A tear trickled down Cassidy's cheek. It splatted against the floor looking bright and vibrant. Too vibrant. Too *real*. "If I'm just an idea," said Cassidy, as blood bubbled out of his mouth, "then whose head am I in?"

The Commodore narrowed his eyes and looked annoyed. He squeezed off two more rounds into Cassidy's chest.

"I'm not in the Everdream, so the concept must be in *my* head." Cassidy forced himself to a higher sitting position, trying to concentrate on something *real*. If only...he dug his hand into his pocket and gripped the silver dollar. The last few drops of April's pain seeped out, filling his veins with a kind of electric heat. "If I'm just a shadow," Cassidy said, rage building in his chest, "then how are you killing me?" Banner's face rose up from his memory. Brewster's dying eyes beside him. April. Her *green* eyes. Those eyes that recognized something in him from a simple momentary glance. Connected with him in a preternatural way. "Maybe I don't want to die."

The Commodore took another step back and emptied the pistol. The last spent shell hit the floor at his feet and bounced several times before rolling to a stop against the Commodore's boot.

Cassidy worked his way to his feet. He touched his stomach where the sword had cut. The blood was gone. "Maybe I exist," he said, staggering towards the Commodore, "because I *want* to exist."

The Commodore swung his sabre, but it bounced off Cassidy's side as if striking a stone column. He swung again and pulled the trigger on the empty Mauser. Cassidy yanked the sabre away and shoved the Commodore to the floor. Tears stung his eyes as he stood over the downed pirate. *Real* tears. He smelled salt in them. "Call for your men, Commodore," Cassidy said. He raised the sabre in both hands and plunged it down, impaling its owner through the stomach and into the floor. "Tell them to man the guns. All the guns. And fly like the Devil himself is out to get them."

He dropped to the floor beside Brewster. "Just believe," he said, holding his friend by the shoulders. "You don't have to die."

Brewster gave a weak smile. "That may be the difference between you and me," he said. "You *want* it so bad. I just wasn't made like that. I'm in the moment. I want to accept this." His eyes glazed and he stopped moving. Cassidy shook him by the shoulders, but seconds later he was gripping empty air.

Cassidy stood. He took back his empty Mauser and picked up Brewster's Webley. He fired twice, blasting the Commodore's knee caps out. Resta screamed in pain.

"Dammit, you bastard," the Commodore managed, though his voice came out in thin rasps. "It was nothing personal. You're still just air, dammit."

Cassidy shoved the Webley in his belt and left the Commodore pinned to the floor, screaming as best he could with a sword through his middle. Cassidy re-loaded as he walked, pushing one shell at a time into the internal magazine. The gangplank extended off the main deck and down to the docks where the two guards stood facing the hotel. Cassidy shot them both in the back of the head. Several of the other crew ran down the steps of the hotel as he made his way to the runway. They were too far away to notice him.

Far above he heard engines engaging. He slapped a pile of bank notes into the dockworker's hand, taxied out to the runway and was in the air before the airship had even lifted off.

Cassidy flew out several hundred feet and climbed high before looping back and aiming down on the rising airship. The Fokker dove like a plummeting falcon. As the pirate dirigible rose to meet him, Cassidy opened up both Spandaus, shredding the gas bladder, his *real* world bullets punching through to the gondola below.

The ship fell back towards the dock. Its bow caught one of the island's steps and the stern continued to fall, flipping as Cassidy climbed again. By the time he'd made his ascent, the ship's prow was aimed at the sky, standing on its stern against a layer of rock, its deflated gas bladder dangling off the edge of the small island.

Cassidy fired again. The chains rattled. Shell casings pelted his face and goggles as the downward thrust of the fighter blew them back at him. He continued his barrage down the length of the upturned ship, strafing through the decks until he struck powder kegs in one of the gunrooms.

The Fokker continued its dive down past the edge of the island as a series of loud popping sounds came from behind. Cassidy pulled out of his dive and banked to see billows of fire blossom from the sides of the armoured airship. He depressed the levers to let loose another burst of hellfire as the vessel toppled from the island. The chains ran dry as the port side of the ship exploded away.

Cassidy watched it fall. The ship tangled in its own airbladder as it fell end over end, down into the abyss. Cassidy waited for the fire inside him to cease. The rage to cool. It didn't. He wanted to chase the Commodore's burning body down into the abyss and empty another set of shell chains into the flaming hulk of the ship. No, ten chains. A hundred. A thousand.

Somewhere inside the airship's wreckage lay the other *real* world Fokker, the *Valkyrie*, twisted and mangled now with whatever other *real* world objects had been stolen. They would probably continue to exist as the Twilight airship and crew burned off and faded away. They would probably fall forever. And where was Brewster now? Oblivion? Had any part of him returned to the Everdream?

Cassidy realized he was still diving. Still following the fireball of a ship as if Brewster was still on it. As if waiting for the Englishman to be released. Cassidy pulled out of the dive. Tears streamed down his face. Everyone was gone. All gone. Jayce and Franz in their far away pyramid. Ned, a man he'd undeservedly called a coward, sliced to ribbons. Banner and Karl still riding the elusive Aurora Borealis, forever imprisoned with the *Nubigena* providing their own personal stormcloud. And Brewster wasn't coming back.

Cassidy pointed his fighter in the general direction of nothing and flew. The buzz and thrum of the engine sounded in his ears. The air rushed over his face. This plane was all that was left of his world now.

Potential windows opened around him as he imagined the *real* world. Giant squares of green energy, faded and ghost-like, stood out against the dark purple of the Twilight night. He focused on the thought of a *real* world storm. One of the potential frames solidified and crackled. It loomed before him as he steered towards it and on the other side he glimpsed raging clouds and blue forks of electricity through the green haze. It would be a good storm, he thought, and throttled forwards.

The green energy lit up his instruments as the tendrils reached out for the fighter. He felt Brewster's Webley dig into his side where it lay nestled in his belt.

Cassidy cut the throttle, rolled and pulled back on the stick. For a moment, the Fokker skimmed the surface of the gate. The rolling currents of grey clouds juxtaposed in his vision over the Twilight purple. And he was back in the Twilight again. The gate faded behind him and he let go of the transient vision of the potential ones as well. Dammit!

Cassidy stared down at his instruments. He searched himself for the reason he hadn't gone through and felt only shame. Brewster was dead and Cassidy didn't deserve to enter the *real* world alone. He hadn't protected his friend. Hadn't protected anyone. They'd all fallen. What right did he have to carry on when he couldn't bring anyone with him?

He had failed even Banner. What had his life, such as it was, been worth if he hadn't actually done anything with it? His memories were still peppered with gaps and hazy pools of rippled clarity. Did he really exist, or was he just kidding himself with his thoughts of pure, solid *will?*

Cassidy couldn't feel himself. He turned to the direction of Arcadia. It was the only place he knew to go. Shea would be there. She would always be there. He could depend on her to...to what? What did he even feel for her? But he needed to be held. He was so cold. The blood in his veins had turned to ice and the wind had blown even the hot tears from his face.

He flew. The engine hummed. The props buzzed. His hand was glued to the control stick and Arcadia would soon be in sight. Miles? Feet? Time? Was there any time?

The upside-down mountain appeared and grew larger. It wasn't home, but it was a place to go.

He landed on automatic. Skipped the bar and was in a room before he even noticed. His room, though. They always gave him the same one. The same vast cold openness. His bed in the centre with veils hanging down around it that vanished into the darkness of the ceiling.

He stripped off his shirt and jacket. Ran a hand over his flesh. Why did it feel different? He was still a dream, but his skin felt a little firmer. A little more elastic. The place the sabre had cut him felt soft and smooth.

Cassidy walked through the flowing curtains of the arched window and out onto the balcony. Moored airships drifted in the night breeze. He closed his eyes and for a moment it was his first night. It was one of the few memories that remained solid in his mind from those first days. His soft flesh goose pimpled in the breeze and his eyes watered again.

He opened them and turned back to the thin drapes that flowed towards him from his room. They parted as he stepped back in and saw Shea lay on his bed watching him. She was naked, though she didn't look naked, but seemed instead a part of the bed. Her green leaf markings flowed down her spine and legs and melded into the emerald sheets. She propped her chin on her hands.

Cassidy walked to her. She drew herself to her knees and pressed herself to him. He wrapped his arms around her and her body formed to his. He gripped her closer and cried into her hair.

She kissed his chest. He stiffened and his nerves flared. Her lips tingled like blue static against his skin. Her smell licked at his senses and he could all but taste it. Cassidy gripped Shea by the back of the neck and brought her lips to his. He kissed her deep and long, as if drinking her into him and then released her.

Shea's closed eyes opened and he stared down into bottomless pools of green. He laid down with his back to her and she snuggled up behind him, her arm wrapped around his side where he held her fingers clenched in his.

Cassidy closed his eyes.

He slept.

And dreamt.

Chapter 33

There were no fighters this time. No battle. No blood. Only the castle. It rose above him, its twisting spires wrapping into the sky. Inside Richthofen stood waiting. He leaned on a cane as if standing by will alone. He wore royal robes, though the fabric looked threadbare, and Cassidy saw the flight uniform beneath it. Dirty bandages poked out from beneath a tattered crown and the Baron seemed to be pleading with him. His mouth gaped, but no sound came out.

The dream faded. Cassidy awoke to Shea's sleeping breath on his neck. She stirred as he sat up. "I'll have to get back to work soon," Shea said. "Spending the night costs money."

Cassidy gave a reluctant nod. "I'll pay," he said. "I'll pay for a few nights."

Shea gave a sardonic laugh. "You don't have that much money. And you wouldn't be getting anything for it. We didn't even..."

Cassidy stared at the green of the sheets. "I don't have anybody left."

Shea rested her chin on his shoulder and wrapped her arms around his trunk. "You don't love me, John," she said in a far-off tone. "And I wouldn't know love if it crawled in bed and bit me in the eye."

Cassidy gave a deep sigh. "I know why Banner kept going back to his grave."

"Hmmm?"

"Nothing," Cassidy said, shaking his head. "I'm scared to go to the *real* world alone, but I have to."

Shea lay back across the bed, exposing her round breasts and the spot where leaves vanished as they made it past her navel. She wasn't trying to seduce him. It was just how she moved. She was more natural nude than clothed and didn't think about it. "You'll always have a room here," she said to the ceiling, not so much to Cassidy, as if it was just something she'd realized and accepted.

"It seems so far away," he said. "The *real* world, I mean."

"You'll die outside the storm."

"Maybe not," he said. "I've learned things."

Shea sat up again. "What will you do there?"

Cassidy shrugged. "Fly."

"For who?"

"Whomever pays me," he said. "There must be things a pilot can do."

"I hear there's still a war going on. They'd pay a fortune for a fighter pilot like you."

"No," Cassidy said. "There's got to be something else."

"There's a *lot* of jobs for pilots here in the Twilight. You could have your own ship."

Cassidy kissed her again. "Thanks," he said and cupped her cheek. "But I can't."

Shea nodded. "I know. You think you owe it to the others because you're the only one who survived." She smiled. "Next time, then." Shea slipped into a robe that looked as if someone had turned clear water into fabric. It hid nothing and only accentuated her curves and the delicate tone of her skin.

Cassidy watched her go. She swayed her hips in good-bye and was gone. It wasn't just what he owed the crew. It was also the pleading in his dreamer's eyes. Richthofen.

He washed and dressed. Returned his Mauser to its wooden holster. He added Brewster's Webley to his belt, as well, sliding the naked steel behind his buckle.

The Fokker had been fuelled and tuned, and the chains in his Spandaus replaced. He didn't look back as he throttled the fighter away from Arcadia, but imagined it vanishing into a dot behind him. Perhaps Shea watched from her window. Perhaps even waved. Perhaps she hadn't.

He looked for gates, and again the potential windows appeared. His heartbeat quickened as he concentrated on finding a storm. One in Europe, hopefully near Richthofen. His dream had been clear and he had to find his dreamer soon. The only thing he knew for certain was that he would have to face this gate alone.

Green energy crackled. Cassidy gave the Fokker full throttle. Electricity hopped and skipped over the fighter and its instruments. His hair stood up as the window flashed and the world changed, and he was once again riding the storm.

The air was fresh and full of ozone. Blue lightning forked around him and the thunder followed as if welcoming him to the chaos. As if by instinct, he caught the currents and made his way into the raging clouds like an eel through tremulous water.

He did want to be here. As guilty as he felt arriving with no one but himself, Cassidy couldn't deny how good the air felt. The scents and odours. The rain. The feeling of existing in a far more solid and *real* way than he ever had in the Twilight.

The ground below looked like an open field with a barn big enough to be a hanger. He landed with little trouble and guided the Fokker to within a few yards of the wooden building.

Dropping from the cockpit, his combat boots sank into the moist earth. Rain poured. The wind gusted and he felt it running down through his clothes and across his skin. He felt the cold and the wet. Some of the water stayed on him now instead of flecking off like it had before.

As the raging storm moved overhead, the moment of truth had come. Part of him wanted to leap inside his fighter and be prepared for the worst. Be ready to re-enter the storm if he began to fade.

Part of him knew that would defeat his ability to fight the dispersal of whatever it was that kept him solid. This would be a mental fight, not a physical one. He gripped Brewster's Webley in his hand. Felt the firmness and density of its steel.

Brewster should have been there standing next to him. He'd imagined them facing the harsh dissolving conditions of the *real* world together.

The rain lightened and the air thinned as the storm moved overhead with the incredible gale of wind. The wild energy still flowed in him, rushing out his arms and legs, but it wasn't around him anymore. The energy was fading fast, spiralling through like trillions of microscopic bees flooding through his system, trying to find a way free.

There were holes for them to escape. Always holes. They slipped away. Leaked out slowly. As they did, Cassidy's skin chilled. His muscles constricted and his head became light and airy. There was little difference between him and the air around him. In fact, he was less than the air. Rice paper on water. Ash in the wind.

John Cassidy didn't really exist. Had never really existed. He was just a dream. A nightmare. The transient fear of an actual flesh and blood man. The sleeper had awoken. Awoken a very long time ago and John Cassidy had just forgotten he didn't exist anymore. Thoughts were supposed to come and go. Ideas were meant to spark and burn and die as quickly as they'd come.

The steel on the handle of Brewster's Webley was still cold from the storm. Cassidy noticed it a thousand miles away where it dangled from someone else's arm. It was clutched in someone else's fingers. Whose fingers?

Oblivion rose up out of the ether, black and huge and everywhere. He was sinking into it, a rock in an ocean of tar. He knew this blackness. This void. He'd been here before. Perhaps he'd never left. Where does a man exist anyway? In his own mind? In the mind of others? Did the universe itself remember anything of its inhabitants?

There was still the handle of a cold pistol somewhere. It had a name. It had belonged to a friend.

Brewster.

Banner.

The *Nubigena*.

John Cassidy, he thought. A man named John Cassidy. A man who had lived, and fought, and... Had he died? What happened to John Cassidy? Had the man been a story? The dream of a man? What happened at the end?

Cassidy looked down at hands and feet that wavered in and out of existence. They faded and returned, and faded again, like an elusive radio signal. The Webley felt firm, though he didn't feel the same density in the hand that held it.

"I exist, dammit. I exist!" he shouted as the air tried to sift him away and smear his body across the face of time and space. "I don't care if I can't remember how I was born. I don't care if I don't have parents." He was crying again, but at least he felt the tears as he screamed into the storm-vacant sky. "I don't care that don't know if I've ever loved anyone or not. And it doesn't matter that everyone I've ever known is gone or dead. I still exist."

The Webley was in his hand, and his hand was almost as solid as the pistol now. At least, it had a similar quality. With his other hand he reached deep into his pocket for the coin. Gripped it tight, trying to squeeze any remaining drops of April's pain into this skin. The love and thoughts and fears of a woman who had seemed more *real* to him than any other person he'd ever met in the *real* world.

And there was a little. A drip or two of residual tears that eked into his flesh and nerves.

He'd done it. Cassidy glanced around. He took in the grey sky. Streaks of light poked through as the clouds moved on. His body gave out and he collapsed. His limbs felt like rubber, but at least he *could* feel them. The struggle had sapped his energy, though, and he yearned for the electricity of the storm to return and energize him.

A young woman walked towards him from the distance. Her green dress with white apron looked damp as if she'd been caught in the storm for a few minutes before making it to cover. She had probably been sheltering in the barn and was coming out now only because she'd seen him fall.

She inched closer. He fought to toss the pistol away now, afraid of how holding a weapon made him look, but his arm wouldn't move. "Your uniform is English or American?" she asked, still twenty feet away and poised, ready to run back to the barn. "You are Allied?"

Cassidy closed his eyes for several seconds and reopened them. She was speaking German. Her accent, Austrian. He understood her perfectly and wondered if he could return the German here in the *real* world. Instead, he nodded.

The Austrian girl took a step back. "Are you here to kill me?"

Cassidy gathered what strength remained in him. "Nein," he said. "Just trying to find a friend."

The young girl hesitated. "Friend?"

"A pilot," Cassidy rasped. "A German." He paused, collecting enough energy to form another sentence. "He's—" He wasn't sure what to call Richthofen. "I just need to find him."

The young girl pried Cassidy from the ground and helped him to the barn. Cassidy collapsed again, this time onto a warm bed of hay. He lay panting and sweating.

"My name is Ilsa. You will have to get your plane inside the barn before they see you from the sky."

"Where's your family?" Cassidy asked.

"The war," she said. "Albert is a soldier. Mother and father are dead."

"I'm sorry," Cassidy said.

"I just want it to end," Ilsa said. "I don't care who wins anymore."

Cassidy gave a partial nod. "I promise, I don't care either."

"You speak Deutsch," she said. "Are you a spy?"

"Long story," he sighed, trying to remember what she'd said about the plane. In moments he was asleep.

Cassidy dreamed of the castle again, but this time it looked as if it had gone through a week of constant bombardment. The grey walls were pocked with deep gashes and several of the spires lay in shattered heaps around the wounded structure.

The giant door had been blasted open and, from inside, a muffled scream called his name. Cassidy ran inside. Richthofen lay trapped beneath a giant iron cross. "Cassidy," he pleaded. "John, please."

Cassidy woke in panic. He glanced around the barn, trying to remember how he'd gotten there. The sound of shouting men came from outside. They were soldiers, speaking German, and Ilsa's frightened voice pleaded with them. "I don't know who he is. He said he was a pilot."

Chapter 34

Panic rose in Cassidy's chest. He gripped both pistols, pinned himself against the wall and waited for the soldiers to enter.

"He's not here now," Ilsa said.

"He left without his plane?" one of the soldiers asked.

The barn door opened and the soldiers stepped in, weapons level. Cassidy tried to press himself into the wall, as if he might become part of it. As the officer shouted orders to check various sections of the barn, Cassidy trained the Mauser and the Webley in the direction the soldiers would have to come.

I'm a dream, Cassidy thought. Am I still enough of one? He concentrated on his body. Talked to the dreamstuff that had hardened enough to enable him to sustain his form in the *real* world. He tried to soften. Let up on the *realness* enough so they couldn't see him. His arms phased a little. He fell through the wall and onto the ground outside.

Ilsa turned from where she stood outside the doorway and looked up as if to see where he'd fallen from. Her eyes were wide, but she didn't speak.

The shock of falling through the wall brought his body back to being solid. He hadn't known he could do that. Wondered if he always could have, or if it was only his new control over his body that allowed him to pass through something solid.

Ilsa shooed him away with her hands.

Cassidy nodded a quick thank you and ran for the Fokker. The men sounded as if they were tearing the barn apart. One of them had left his rifle leaning against the plane. Cassidy grabbed it and leapt into the cockpit. An extra weapon never hurt and this looked like a formidable Mauser .303 rifle.

The engine started without trouble. Over his shoulder the soldiers ran from the barn, aiming and shooting. Cassidy throttled forward and pulled his fighter into the air as bullets flashed by. He hoped they wouldn't hurt Ilsa. She could say anything, including that he'd had a gun pointed at her, or that he'd threatened any number of other things. He hoped she would.

It was tempting to return and kill the men with his Spandaus, but Ilsa had been kind to him and the thought of murdering the soldiers in front of her turned his stomach. She wouldn't understand that he was only trying to protect her. And besides, the thought of killing a dreamer did something weird to his stomach. It felt wrong, like murdering a god.

Cassidy pulled back hard on the stick and banked the fighter into the clouds before levelling out. He had to do something, but didn't know what. Something to do with Richthofen. He was in trouble in some way. Needed something. Needed Cassidy, his accidental creation.

Both Allied and German planes flew the skies around him as he entered what had to be contested territory. Allied fighters tried to engage, while the Germans ignored him. He might be invisible, but his Fokker wasn't, forcing him to flee several dogfights. How had Banner kept the *Nubigena* from being noticed? Cassidy tried to escape into the clouds but several Sopwiths bearing French markings tried to sandwich him in a crossfire of streaking shells.

He rolled. He dodged. Didn't want to engage, but the French gave him little choice. They dove after him as he tried to out-manoeuvre the nimble crafts, but he was forced to bank and engage them both.

The first he hit with a volley of Spandau bursts to the tail section. The Sopwith lost stability and broke off. The second he crippled by destroying one of its bi-wings. The fighter limped away. They would both live if they didn't engage in any more fighting.

"I'm sorry," Cassidy said, though there was no one to hear him. Another two Allied fighters engaged him and he disabled them as best he could. Hopefully they'd survive a forced landing as well. He found he hardly had to think to out-fight these men. They were simple compared to the pilots in his dream and the Armada Albatrosses who had seemed to fight with a hive-mind ability.

Still, he had to get out of the air. This wasn't his fight. Wasn't his war. He had no right to kill pilots merely because they *thought* he was the enemy. Only months ago he would have turned his guns on the Germans. Used his markings to get close and shoot them out of the sky. But he'd come to terms with not being American, and as he watched them fight and kill each other, he knew for certain he was something else. Something outside. Still an alien. A visitor from another world who only looked like them. The vision of an American pilot in a German Fokker, riding the lines of war.

Cassidy's throat went dry as a red fighter broke from behind a ridge. A tri-plane with black iron crosses. Richthofen. All fighters of the Baron's Jagdstaffel flew red planes, but without even seeing the pilot, he knew this was his dreamer.

Something was wrong though. The Baron's flying. The red Fokker appeared to be in pursuit of a Sopwith Camel with Canadian markings. It wasn't like Richthofen. Cassidy knew the codes the German flew by. They were burned into his mind as sure as if they'd been his own. The Baron never chased fighters alone and across enemy lines near gunners. A barrage of ground guns tore at the air around the scarlet Fokker.

Another fighter, also bearing Canadian markings, dove from far above. As the fighter neared, Richthofen broke off for a moment to dodge the attacking plane.

Cassidy went to fire his Spandaus, but only got three rounds off before the chains ran dry. No one had noticed him yet, and it needed to stay that way. Once again, he concentrated on his body and then reached out to the plane. He'd already bonded himself to the Fokker, making it easier, but he had to move his awareness through the fighter itself. The wings, the fuselage, the engine and props. He felt them all as he did his own body and he pushed the fighter to fade a little as he drew closer.

The diving Canadian fighter missed the red Fokker and was forced to pull up hard to avoid hitting the ground. Cassidy couldn't believe how close to the ground they were flying. The gunners couldn't seem to see Cassidy's Fokker, but they were laying down a wall of fire around the Baron.

What was he doing now? Richthofen should have broken off long ago. Not only did he have a code about ground fire, but about not following another fighter once it put him in danger. *Survive to kill more enemies.* Why would he break that code now? Richthofen fired sporadically in odd bursts. Only one gun was working. The other had to be jammed or broken.

What the hell is he doing? Cassidy thought. The image of the Baron from his dream came back in blinding colour. The stricken look on his face. The wound and the bloody wrappings beneath his crown. What had he been pleading?

The gunners continued their wall of fire. The fleeing Sopwith continued at full throttle. The red Fokker was still trying to choke out a few shots with the misfiring Spandau.

Like a shot through his own head, Cassidy realized what Richthofen was trying to do. Tired, wounded and broken by war, the Baron wanted to die. Needed to die. Was pleading for it from anyone willing to give it. He didn't just want death, but a hero's death. A death of blood and honour.

Tears welled in Cassidy's eyes as he skimmed just above the gunners' heads, looking up at the bright red Fokker as it dared and begged for anyone to take it down. None of them had the right, though. These gunners. The Sopwith Richthofen pursued. None of them. And no one seemed capable.

Cassidy lifted the Mauser rifle to his shoulder and chambered a round. He aimed through the fuselage to where Richthofen sat. The red Fokker wobbled side to side. As it tilted right Cassidy squeezed the trigger. For a moment, nothing happened, then the tri-plane slowed. The nose tipped down.

Cassidy followed Richthofen as he limped his fighter to a landing. The Baron brought it to a halt with amazing grace for whatever wound he'd sustained. Cassidy landed beside him and leapt out. He ran, jumped up to the centre wing and brought himself up to the cockpit.

Richthofen didn't move. His head lay back staring up at the blue sky. Blood blossomed beneath his flight coat. The bullet had passed through the plane, through the Baron and exited his chest. The hole lay just beside the coat's lapel. "Did you do that?" Richthofen asked, still staring past Cassidy at the sky.

Cassidy nodded. He couldn't speak. His throat was too tight.

"Danke," Richthofen said. "No one here can shoot."

"I may fade away now," Cassidy finally got the words past his trembling lips. "Banner wasn't a real dream, so I don't know what will happen."

Richthofen still didn't move, as if saving all his strength to speak. "I dreamed you to kill me," he said and rolled his head to look at Cassidy. "It's what you were always meant to do. I knew it the moment I saw you standing there in Arcadia. I knew you would kill me."

"I'm sorry," Cassidy said. Men shouted in the distance. They were coming.

"It's honour. It's right," Richthofen said. He lifted his shaking hand off the control stick where it had been glued and gripped Cassidy by the arm. "I have accomplished my purpose in life. Now, so have you. What men can say that?"

Cassidy gripped him back. "Where do I go now?"

"Home," Richthofen said. "I did give you a home country."

Another man stared at the Baron now. A soldier had run up on the opposite side and propped himself up on one of the wings. Cassidy was a ghost to him. The soldier only watched the Bloody Baron staring off at nothing.

"Kaput," Richthofen said. As he finished the word, the razor tip of an umbrella popped out of his forehead and withdrew. The soldier was still oblivious.

Cassidy jumped down off the plane and ran around to the other side.

Tamelicus grinned as he wiped the umbrella tip with a white handkerchief. "My paper shadow," the dandy demon said. "Never thought we'd cross paths again, but the world is indeed an intriguing place."

Soldiers with Australian flags on their uniforms crowded around the plane. They didn't notice Cassidy, or his Fokker, as they swarmed the scarlet fighter.

Cassidy wiped his eyes. "Don't think for a moment you killed him with that damned umbrella. *I* killed him. *Me*. He wanted it that way."

The demon scoffed. "You're just a cherry seed."

"I'm no cherry seed and you're nothing. A shadow that walks around sticking his blade in things already dead."

Tamelicus tsked. "I could cut *you* up like Christmas turkey."

Cassidy drew closer so he was eye to eye with the creature. "I don't think you can. Perhaps before, but not now. I'm *real*. And you'll just have to wait around for my time to come so you can show up and pretend, shoving that piece of nothing you carry into my cold dead corpse."

"If only you could stop whining," Tamelicus sighed, cutting over his words. "You're still a shadow," he said putting the umbrella's tip to Cassidy's throat. "And this will never be your world." He tipped his bowler. "You'll need more than mental determination to make you a *real* boy. But believe what you will. They all do." The dandy demon turned and was gone.

Soldiers dragged Richthofen's body from his fighter and began stripping the tri-wing for souvenirs. Cassidy walked to where they laid the body and looked down at his dreamer. "Guess I didn't fade," he said to the still unclosed eyes. "If this was my purpose, what do I do now?" Cassidy reached down and removed the Baron's scarf. He tied it around his own neck and returned to his Fokker.

The Australian soldiers continued dismantling the red plane as Cassidy turned the engine over, taxied over the bumpy ground and lifted off. No one glanced his way. Home. Richthofen had told him to go home.

Chapter 35

Cassidy watched the war vanish behind him. He wasn't even a memory to Europe, except, perhaps, for Ilsa. He considered returning to visit her, but if she was still alive, he could be nothing but trouble for her. It seemed that everywhere he visited collapsed behind him.

Banner, the *Nubigena* and her crew had been alive and free before him. Brewster had acted as if he would live forever, smoking his pipe and drinking tea. Richthofen had been the pride of Germany. Was Cassidy a curse to everyone in his wake, or just a cursed survivor?

Potential gates appeared around the Fokker as he called them up from the fabric of reality. America, he thought, somewhere around New York. No, Darcy, Virginia, wherever that was. The home of April's pain. One of the gates glowed bright and he steered into it. The crackling energy bounced across the Fokker and faded to nothing behind him.

A mere force of thought and no one could see the fighter anymore. It must work much like his pistol and the uniform he wore. Had the world at large ever seen the *Nubigena*? He'd never gotten a chance to see if people noticed at all, or simply saw and forgot a moment later. Had the stormship been just a dream sort of memory to this world?

Cassidy was an alien creature to all of reality now. Something that didn't belong to the Everdream, the Twilight or the *real* world. Perhaps he was as alien as the strange creature he'd called Banner, that dreamer's mind in the body of his own dream.

Cassidy sat the Fokker down near Darcy and left the plane covered in branches. There was no telling how long his effect would last on the machine and he doubted the local authorities would look kindly on the sudden appearance of a German war plane.

The town looked like a painting. Like a dream he glanced in bubbles off the Everdream. It might have been nostalgia born into him by Richthofen's idea of an American's reaction to such a place, or something else Cassidy had picked up along the way. Perhaps behind the Baron's fear and hatred of enemy pilots there also had lain a certain subconscious love of another people and culture. Perhaps the feeling had leaked out of April's coin along with her pain.

The church, town hall, schoolhouse and other small buildings stood outlined against the setting sun. Cassidy felt a heat in his chest now as he surveyed the skyline that must represent some love of the Baron's own home. His love and nostalgia for some Bavarian hamlet.

Cassidy buttoned his jacket to hide his weapons, let himself become substantial enough to be seen and entered the town as a pilot returned from war. A hotel offered him a room at a discount rate and he accepted it, not knowing how long his roll of American currency would last.

His room was small, but as hotel rooms and Zeppelin cabins had been the only home he could remember, it cheered him just to see a made bed and a lit oil lamp. This town still hadn't seen its first electric light.

Sleep came easy. The foreign but familiar sheets accepted him like a prodigal son. He dreamed of the castle again. The war was gone and the shattered stones and spires were whole again. There was no Richthofen anymore, but the Baron's portrait adorned the hallway. In it he stood tall and proud in royal garb with a kingly crown and an iron cross about his neck.

Cassidy drifted from room to room finding a strange amalgamation of both Richthofen's memories and his own. This was now their home and sanctuary, and perhaps he'd even meet his dreamer once again in some random room of the castle. Or he might fly through an earthly

Borealis again. What would the Northern Lights be like in the *real* world?

Sun streamed through his window, waking him from his slumber. He washed and dressed. Several jobs presented themselves, but a position for a stunt pilot in a new air show caught his attention first. The owner wouldn't be in until the next day, so Cassidy spent the rest of the morning and afternoon exploring the surrounding fields and forests.

Here in the *real* world everything was fascinating. The colours and textures were enough to keep him busy forever. The sun began to set and he felt the pangs of hunger calling.

Cassidy returned to town and looked up and down the main street. Of the several eating establishments, a small pub called Deven's Place looked the most inviting. He stepped through the door and let the aromas of warm food and fermented hops hit him full in the face.

A few locals sat at various tables as well as a couple at the bar, but the evening crowd hadn't shown up yet. Cassidy took a stool on the far right where he could lean against the wall and take in the place.

A young woman with the red hair of Scottish highland girls approached wearing a dark green apron. "What'll you have?" she asked with a smile that made her look younger than she probably was. It was a kind of laughing smile he'd always imagined small children must have. Her green eyes widened. "I've seen you before."

Cassidy pushed the silver half-dollar across the counter. "It saved my life."

"Saved?" she began, but stopped. With a slow, quivering hand she picked up the Walking Liberty. "I never thought I'd see this again," she said, gripping the coin tight in her fist as if it might vanish if she let it go. "I don't do things like that. Just hand things out. Ever. But you looked so sad." She opened her fist to peek at the coin and closed her hand again. Her lips formed as if she was going to say something else, but stopped. Her emerald eyes glazed, as if she were looking past him to somewhere else. "Will you have a drink this time?" she said instead. "This'll buy you anything on the menu."

Cassidy gulped, forcing his mind past anything beginning with a W. His lips had already formed the awful sound. "I'll t-try cognac," he blurted and relaxed as the word came out.

"Ever have it before?" she asked.

He shook his head.

"Then why cognac?"

"It's what my fr—" He was about to say friend, but friend didn't describe Richthofen any more than *enemy*. "My father liked cognac."

"April," she said. "Do you remember?"

"Cassidy," he said. "I mean, John. Please call me John."

Thunder rolled in the distance. "There's a storm coming," April said, glancing out the window.

Cassidy nodded as a flash of distant lightning cut through the sky. "The storm dreams," he said.

"Why did you say that?" she asked, a look of sudden horror in her features.

"Nothing. Just--" He looked up into her bright eyes. They looked back at his without glancing away. Without questioning. They just stared as if expecting something. "If I buy *you* a drink, would you tell me a story?" Cassidy asked.

"About what?" she asked and a light blush came to her cheeks.

"Anything. I just want to hear you talk."

April slipped the coin into the pocket of her apron. "I do have a story for you, John Cassidy. Meet me at that table after the dinner rush," she said, pointing to one in the corner. "But you'll think I'm mad."

Cassidy nursed his cognac while April served customers. She kept glancing at him and dropping things, her movements hurried. He couldn't take his eyes off the young woman as she scurried through her duties, gripping at the pocket of her apron now and then as if checking to make sure the coin hadn't escaped.

When she finished, April shed the apron, smoothed out her skirt and sat down. "Can I—" she began, but stopped and stared down at her hands which lay folded on the table.

"I'm sorry," Cassidy said leaning forwards across the table. "I didn't mean to bother you by coming by. I just wanted you to know...I wanted you to know I wasn't dead."

April fidgeted with her hands as she continued staring at them. "Why did you mention the storm dreaming?"

"I don't know," Cassidy said. "It's just a turn of phrase, I guess." He'd disturbed her somehow. This wasn't how he'd seen this going. She was supposed to just smile and laugh and throw her arms around him or something. Or say thanks. What *had* he expected? "Storms," he mused as rain began tapping at the window panes. "They've always been a good thing for me, I guess."

April nodded as if she'd decided something and brought her eyes up to meet his. "You really will think I'm crazy, having only met me twice. But I should tell you something." She took a deep breath. "Do you ever dream, John Cassidy?"

Cassidy winced inside. Did he ever dream? Did he breathe air? Was she accusing him of something? "I dream," was all he could manage.

She pursed her lips. "I don't always remember my dreams. I mean, who does? But ever since I met you, they've gotten strange. Vivid. I dream about being someone else. Someone who's kind of me, but me from somewhere else. I'm always in a garden and you're always there. And I never remember the end, but each time I wake up weeping."

Cassidy couldn't take his eyes away from hers. This was worse than déjà vu. Every word she spoke made the soft fuzzy memory in his mind more and more crisp. A memory that had stuck in the back of his head from the moment he'd left his original dream and escaped aboard the *Nubigena*. The memory which had stopped him from being with Shea. The ache in his mind. The longing for... "We're in a garden," he said "A garden with strangely coloured grass and flowers I've never seen before."

Tears flowed down April's white skin. "Crystal petals. Purple bulbs that grow in clusters. Light shone just beneath the surface."

Cassidy nodded. "I land my plane. And there you are. Your voice sounds like singing. Like a choir." The blood in his veins pumped hot in his ears. This couldn't be happening. Was he dreaming now? No. The colours were too vivid. Her voice was too crisp. "You and I—" He stopped, realizing he almost said something inappropriate.

"I recognized something about you just before I handed you the coin," April said as her delicate fingers inched across the table. "There's always been this tugging."

"In your chest," Cassidy said. "Like you always want to burst into tears for no reason. But you remember something just beyond your memory." His hands had closed around hers. Tight. He gripped her fingers hard as if he was trying to keep her from floating away. As if the world might yank her into some gaping black mouth. "I know you," he said. "I know you like I know my own name."

She was gripping him back, her thin fingers oddly strong. The dripping tears had become a torrent down her face. "They're all staring at us."

Cassidy glanced over at the gawking customers and staff. "I've waited all this time to remember you," he said looking back at her.

April's lips trembled. "I remember you. But how?"

"I don't know," Cassidy said. "But give me a few minutes and I'll tell you a story about how the storm dreams."

That night Cassidy dreamed of a dark-skinned man wearing nothing but a cotton loincloth and a white beard that almost covered his chest. He looked thinner and wilder than any man Cassidy had ever seen. A bushman? No. An Australian aborigine.

"You're in a 'Storm Dreaming'," the man said. "The rainbow serpent just slithered by."

"I'm dreaming," Cassidy said. "Where's the castle?"

The old man shook his head. "No castle tonight. This is *your* dream. Your first dream that you've created alone."

A vast desert spread out before Cassidy. The sun was pale red. Rocks stood here and there adorned with odd pictures of men and beasts in what looked like white finger paint. "You know what I really am, don't you?" Cassidy asked.

The aborigine nodded. "You're an alien to the *real* world. You know that."

Cassidy nodded. "But, I know there used to be a garden."

"Before and after," the aborigine said nodding. "You're standing in the desert of the Dreamtime. This is where my people come from. It's where they return. You've been here too, but you must go back. Much further back."

"I don't understand," said Cassidy. "Back to what?"

"Back beyond the Storm Dreaming. You have a long way to go."

Cassidy stood silent in the dream, unable to take his eyes off the wrinkled man. "But I'm *real*," he finally said. "I'm *real* now."

The old man cracked a sardonic smile. "More *real* than you'll ever know. All dreams are fingers and toes of the Dreamtime, but you're something different. You are bound for a time when this desert becomes glass."

The aborigine's words trailed off as he faded into the air and the sand became smooth and transparent. A city of coloured glass rose to the sky, moving above him like the arms of a great mobile. "This," said a strange voice that crept into his head, "is the dream of your dream. And you must find the garden."

Back in the *real* world he knew April slept beside him. He remembered it as clear and clean as anything he'd ever known. But she was here, too. Somewhere. She meant something more than he could comprehend, but he would find her. He would know what she was.

Dear Reader

Thank you for taking the time to read Storm Dreams. I hope you enjoyed the book. If you did, would you do me the favour of rating and reviewing it on Amazon, Goodreads, and any other book-related websites you can think of? It would help me a lot and it gives other readers a better idea of how they might like the book. Thank you in advance!

If you would like to contact me or hear about my latest releases, please visit and like me on Facebook at facebook.com/JebRSherrill. You can also find me at StormDreamsBook.com.

About the Author

Jeb R. Sherrill has an oddly disjointed background. Having stumbled through everything from performing stage magic and kinetic juggling on French television and in Las Vegas casinos, to teaching martial arts and circus techniques, to competitive sabre fencing, film and stage acting, dance, songwriting, and his ongoing stint as a popular YouTube personality, he has the ADD of a 10 year old. Writing, however, has remained his greatest passion since early childhood, having also written a barrage of short stories and poetry.

Pinning down his style is difficult, however. His liquid, psychotropic images, philosophical undertones and pure unabashed strangeness have made fans across generations. A great example of this was his first published work, a Victorian science fiction piece about a man slowly melding with an alien intelligence featured in the e-zine *Would That It Were.* Best known for insane worlds, over the top characters and sometimes heady subject matter, his work may not be for the faint of heart, but reading it is always an adventure. Many of his novels exist in a loosely connected universe which will only be complete at the end of several series. Be warned, you may never look at reality the same way again.